Praise for the
Dark Tides Novels

Siren's Surrender

"Devyn Quinn writes with a sharp sense of humor, a breathtaking sensuality, and a vivid sense of style. I loved this book from the first page to the last!"
—Darynda Jones, author of *First Grave on the Right*

Siren's Call

"*Siren's Call* is a thoroughly mesmerizing ride—Quinn throws open the doors to an unbelievable world where nothing is as expected. At once terrifying and fascinating, and unbelievably entertaining, this is a book you won't forget."
—Kate Douglas, bestselling author of the Wolf Tales and the Demonslayers series

"Devyn Quinn writes her stories exactly the way I like to read them: rich, detailed, and a touch poetic. You can practically smell the wind, feel the passion, and taste the tears." —Morgan Hawke, author of *Kiss of the Wolf*

"More than a paranormal romance where the star-crossed lovers must battle huge obstacles, *Siren's Call* quickly serves up a main course of interesting characters with a side dish of archaeological and historical intrigue. The novel does not delay the inevitable, nor does it re-tread the oft-trod predictable lines of many paranormal romances. Instead, as the story develops so do intriguing questions about privacy, relationships, and what the world may have a right to know." —Fresh Fiction

"This first Dark Tides novel has a nicely inventive shape-shifting heroine. The hero is quite humanly flawed, and yet satisfyingly honorable." —*Romantic Times*

continued ...

Available from Signet Eclipse

Siren's Call

Siren's Surrender

A Dark Tides Novel

DEVYN QUINN

A SIGNET ECLIPSE BOOK

SIGNET ECLIPSE
Published by New American Library, a division of
Penguin Group (USA) Inc., 375 Hudson Street,
New York, New York 10014, USA
Penguin Group (Canada), 90 Eglinton Avenue East, Suite 700, Toronto,
Ontario M4P 2Y3, Canada (a division of Pearson Penguin Canada Inc.)
Penguin Books Ltd., 80 Strand, London WC2R 0RL, England
Penguin Ireland, 25 St. Stephen's Green, Dublin 2,
Ireland (a division of Penguin Books Ltd.)
Penguin Group (Australia), 250 Camberwell Road, Camberwell, Victoria 3124,
Australia (a division of Pearson Australia Group Pty. Ltd.)
Penguin Books India Pvt. Ltd., 11 Community Centre, Panchsheel Park,
New Delhi - 110 017, India
Penguin Group (NZ), 67 Apollo Drive, Rosedale, North Shore 0632,
New Zealand (a division of Pearson New Zealand Ltd.)
Penguin Books (South Africa) (Pty.) Ltd., 24 Sturdee Avenue,
Rosebank, Johannesburg 2196, South Africa

Penguin Books Ltd., Registered Offices:
80 Strand, London WC2R 0RL, England

First published by Signet Eclipse, an imprint of New American Library,
a division of Penguin Group (USA) Inc.

First Printing, February 2011
10 9 8 7 6 5 4 3 2 1

For Quincy

Alicia —
Enjoy !!
Dewyn Quinn

ACKNOWLEDGMENTS

It's hard to believe it's time write up another page of thank-yous for the second Dark Tides book. My, how the time flew by! You can pretty much bet that *Siren's Surrender* could not have come to be without the following people:

Jhanteigh Kupihea has actually survived a second book with her hair intact. I say that because I'm sure she would like to pull most of it out when dealing with the insanity that is Devyn and the process of writing a new book. Fortunately she has the patience of a saint. She also has a very sharp red pen, and her use of it makes me look smarter than I really am.

Roberta Brown is still my agent and still holding my hand. I am thankful she's there to listen to my concerns and sort out the messes I seem to get myself in. She's my rock in this business, and without her advice and career guidance, I would not be where I am today.

Bestselling authors Morgan Hawke and Darynda Jones generously took the time out of their own busy schedules to read the book and give me a couple of killer quotes. Thank you, ladies!

I also need to mention my beta readers, Tracey and Lea. These girls are always willing to suffer through draft after draft and haven't yet told me I really need to go flip burgers instead of write. Kate Douglas is still there, letting me bend her ear. Vanessa Hawthorne needs to slap me for forgetting to mention her in the last book as part of my posse. And, Buddy, I didn't mean to lump you in with the ladies. You stand on your own, a fabulous friend and talented writer.

A mention also has to go to reader Jackie Hussein for providing the title of *Siren's Surrender*. Thanks, Jackie, for racking your brain so we'd have something to put on the front of the book.

If there's anyone I've forgotten, I'll catch you the next time around!

Chapter 1

Turning into the hotel parking lot, Blake Whittaker guided his black sedan into the nearest available space and killed the engine. Instead of making an immediate grab for the bag in the passenger's seat, he simply sat, staring into the distance.

It was amazing how things had changed since he'd last been in Port Rock. Almost seventeen years had passed since he'd last set foot in the small Maine fishing village. And while the old familiar landmarks were still in place, a lot of things looked different. The hotel, for instance, was new. Back when he was a kid the ocean-front acreage overlooking the bay was undeveloped, offering an unobstructed view of the open water and the small island that lay about a mile offshore.

Little Mer Island, he thought. That was where he'd be heading first thing tomorrow. To get there he'd have to rent a skiff, crossing over the wide-open waters of the bay.

A flush prickled Blake's skin as his heart sped up. Despite the humidity permeating the warm summer night, he shivered. He hated deep water of any kind. Aside from a shower, he did his best to stay far away from the stuff. It didn't matter if it only filled a swimming pool, or the wide-open ocean. The less he saw of it, the better.

Mouth going bone-dry, his grip on the steering wheel tightened as a series of images flashed through his mind. For a brief second he wasn't a thirty-three-year-old man, but a four-year-old boy facing an insanely furious woman filling a deep old-fashioned claw-foot tub with ice-cold water.

Forcing himself back toward calm, Blake blew out a few quick hard puffs, filling his lungs and then quickly expelling the air. The strain of clenching his jaw made his teeth hurt. The last thing he needed was a full-blown panic attack while sitting in the parking lot. Thank God the lot was abandoned. There was no one around at such a late hour to see him melt down.

Catching hold of his fear and forcing himself to stuff it away, he slowly uncurled his fingers. A low curse slipped between his numb lips. "Damn." Just thinking about his mother made him twitch, setting his nerves on edge.

He hadn't expected that memory to come crawling out of nowhere and ambush him. He did his best to forget those petrifying moments when his mom was drunk on vodka and raging with malice.

Men. She hated them. Every last blasted one and . . .

And some things are best left alone, Blake reminded himself. Remembering his mother was like sticking his hand into a den of poisonous snakes. He was bound to get bitten, but he just couldn't stop prodding the deadly reptiles.

He'd better stop it or he was going to get bitten. Badly.

Coming back to Port Rock certainly wasn't helping matters. When he'd finally gotten old enough to leave it, he hadn't intended to come back. Not ever. At the age of seventeen he'd gotten the hell out, going as far away as he could. A one-way bus ticket and a suitcase was all he had to his name. If he hadn't just joined the army, he would've had no place to go at the end of the trip.

Blake rubbed his burning eyes. To be sane himself, to continue being sane, he had to quit tearing at the scars marking old wounds. There were a lot of ghosts lingering in his past, a lot of skeletons shoved into his family's closets.

Shut them, bolt them, and go on. That was the way he'd always gotten things done. As a kid he'd put on the stiff upper lip, taken the beatings, and gone about the business of living as best he could.

He'd survived.

Sighing again, he shifted his body in the uncomfortable seat, feeling the cramp in his legs. The three-and-a-half-hour trip through a massive thunderstorm had taken its toll on his nerves.

Palm rasping against a day's growth of whiskers, he reached for the cup balanced between his splayed legs. He took a gulp of its contents: unsweetened black coffee. It was cold and tasted like shit. As much as he didn't like coming back to Port Rock, he had a job to do. Not a hard one. Not even difficult. Just ask a few questions, poke around a little. It wasn't rocket science.

But it was top secret.

As a special agent, Blake presently worked in the A51-ASD division of the FBI. Had it not been a highly covert organization, the A51 would have been familiar enough to tip off most Americans as to its purpose. After all, Area 51 was the nickname for a military base presently located in the southern portion of Nevada in the western United States. Supposedly the base's primary purpose was the development and testing of experimental aircraft and weapons systems.

That was somewhat true. And anyone not presently situated under a rock knew about the intense secrecy surrounding the base, one that had made it a popular subject among conspiracy theorists who held a belief in the existence of alien life on Earth.

The crackpots weren't wrong, either. Blake Whittaker knew for a fact the federal government took the existence of aliens very seriously. The genesis of the current operations stemmed from an incident in 1947 in Roswell, New Mexico. At that time, the military had supposedly recovered alien craft and corpses, purportedly held under lock and key, never to be revealed to the public.

It was absolutely true in every respect.

The ASD had been created to cover not only future occurrences of possible alien activity, but also to investigate other incidents deemed alien, paranormal, or hereby inexplicable.

Curious. Strange. Bizarre. You name it, the ASD had an agent on it.

And that was why he was in Port Rock. Because

something curious had taken not only a strange turn, but a bizarre one as well.

It had all begun in the 1950s, when an intense concentration of electromagnetic energy was located in the Mediterranean Sea. There was no rhyme or reason why the energy should be at that precise spot, or what caused it. Using the latest technology in deep-sea exploration, scientists had yet to discover the source. Given the location of the disturbance, most theories ranged from a geothermal field due to volcanic activity, to some sort of alien homing signal or beacon.

For the most part, the energy seemed to be harmless, a phenomenon never to be explained. Naval ships in the area monitored it, and no changes had been reported in the last sixty years. Whatever it was simply was.

And then something happened.

From the data he had, Whittaker knew that an undersea salvage group, working under the name of Recoveries, Inc., had moved into the area. The outfit had recently filed in federal court for salvage rights for what they claimed to be the lost civilization of Ishaldi. Nothing unusual there. Treasure hunters regularly hit the Mediterranean in search of everything from ancient Egyptian barges to Spanish warships to World War II aircraft. After all, for the three quarters of the globe, the Mediterranean Sea was the uniting element and the center of world history.

What had exactly occurred was still to be explained. During the first dive, tragedy had struck, some kind of seismic activity taking place deep beneath the water. The resulting quake was strong enough to be detected by hydrophones, and was unlike anything scientists had ever heard through decades of listening.

The undersea quake had also claimed a victim. Jake Massey, the archaeologist leading the recovery efforts, had been reported missing at sea. A month had passed since that fateful day and his body had yet to be recovered.

More interesting than the quake and the regrettable loss of life was the fact that the former low-level energy field had gone haywire. The electromagnetic field had suddenly tripled in strength. Its signal—if it could be called that—had begun to interfere with radar and radio transmissions, seemingly swallowing up everything electronic in a single gulp. It was like a big black hole had suddenly opened at the bottom of the sea. No ship could get within ten miles of the location without interference. As the area was one of the most heavily sailed shipping lanes in the world, it was a pain in the ass for seacraft to detour around.

In the scheme of things, Blake's job was fairly simple. He'd been sent to question Massey's partner about the incident. The feds wanted to know if Randall's crew had seen, heard, or encountered something outside the norm during their time beneath the water. Given that the seismic activity had taken place at a depth of more than three miles beneath the water, Whittaker sincerely doubted they would have any useful information to offer.

Blake grimaced, tossing the empty cup onto the floor on the passenger's side. Flicking on an overhead light, he consulted his notes, a chicken scratch of random information on a pocket-sized pad.

According to intelligence, Kenneth Randall presently lived on Little Mer with his wife, Tessa. Since the loss of Jake Massey, the group had suspended all salvage efforts and the company had gone inactive. An investigation by the U.S. Coast Guard, which monitored recovery efforts in the Mediterranean, had ruled Massey the victim of an unfortunate accident.

Still, the A51-ASD had a job to do. His conclusions on the matter would be the deciding factor on whether a follow-up was warranted or if the matter was marked closed.

The barest trace of a smile crossed Blake's lips. Most of the incidents he looked into turned out to be bogus, of no real scientific value. He'd worked for the agency for almost five years and had yet to see anything unusual. Logic and science could usually explain away most of the reported phenomena.

Tucking his pad away, Blake ran his fingers through his hair. He caught a brief glimpse of half his face in the rearview mirror, a thatch of messy black hair and bloodshot blue-gray eyes. Lines of disgruntlement puckered his forehead. Shadows lingered behind his gaze, the ghosts of disappointment and disillusionment. One of his irises had a thin streak of amber through the lower half, as though someone had taken an eraser and begun to rub out one color before replacing it with another. People, especially the crazy ones, were frequently unsettled by that odd eye. It was something he used to good effect when employing his best "don't lie to me" agent stare.

Blake glanced at the single bag he'd packed for the

trip. Aside from a necessary change of clothes and his netbook, he carried only a wallet, his cell, and his service weapon. Spending a lot of time on the road had taught him to travel light. He didn't plan to be in Port Rock more than a day.

The sooner I can leave, the better. He didn't want to hang around his old hometown, rehashing memories that were better left alone. Some things needed to stay buried.

Opening the car door, Blake got out. The cool breeze winnowing off the bay was like a balm on his flushed skin. A day's worth of sweat clung to his flesh. He felt wet patches under his arms, trickles of perspiration making its way down his spine to his underwear. Sweat fogged his vision as he pushed a mat of sticky hair off his forehead.

He pulled in a deep breath, letting the crisp sea air clear his foggy mind. Stretching his arms wide, he rolled his shoulders, trying to relieve the ache at the base of his neck. He'd wasted enough time. Right now what he needed most was a hot shower and cool, clean sheets.

Grabbing his bag off the passenger's seat, he locked the car and headed toward the brightly lit lobby. *Wrap things up tomorrow and I'll be on my way to Boston by six.*

Gwen Lonike glanced up at the clock on the wall and sighed. At ten after one in the morning, her night was just getting started. "Shit."

She hated being up this late, but her night clerk had

called in sick an hour before the eleven-o'clock shift change. Naturally the three-to-eleven clerk didn't want to pull a double and her part-time emergency clerk wasn't answering the phone. That left Gwen, who'd already put in an endlessly long day, the only one to cover the graveyard shift.

Reaching for her mug of freshly brewed coffee, Gwen took a deep gulp. Her eyelids felt like lead weights. Despite the babble of the television playing in the lobby, she was having trouble staying awake. A single reservation had yet to be claimed. Once the last guest had checked in, she could catch a quick snooze on the sofa in the reception area.

She sighed again. "Oh, goddess," she murmured to no one in particular. "Why can't I hire reliable help?"

Gwen looked around the hotel's lobby. By The Sea was located on approximately five oceanfront acres overlooking the bay. A short walk would take visitors to the shore for a better view of the tall master schooners sailing the bay, as well as the working lobster boats coming into port with the day's catch. Perched in the distance was the famous lighthouse of Little Mer Island. Unlike larger chain hotels, hers was independent, with a smaller, more intimate appeal.

Gwen checked the clock again, disappointed to find a mere twenty minutes had passed since her mind had wandered off on a variety of paths. She'd already cleaned the lobby, run the nightly audit, and flipped through a variety of satellite channels. A night clerk's job was basically just babysitting the front desk, being available to check in late-coming guests and set wake-up calls. At five, the morning greeter would arrive to begin setting up the breakfast bar. At seven, her relief would arrive. Then she could crash and burn until noon.

Other than that, the work was mind-numbingly boring.

Yawning, she contemplated the paperback she'd picked out of the basket the local library regularly refreshed for the guests. She'd picked out some legal thriller, not exactly terrible but not really interesting enough to keep on reading.

The bell over the door tinkled, indicating the arrival of a living, breathing soul.

Bypassing the gift shop that had closed at nine, a man hurried over to the front desk. Dressed in a navy suit that looked like he'd slept in it for a week, he carried only a single small bag.

Standing up, Gwen briefly eyed her computer screen before looking at the man across the desk. Layered black hair, pale skin, face weary with fatigue. Tall and lean, he was kind of attractive in a messy, rumpled sort of way.

Not that she was looking. The rule for all hotel employees was a strict one: No fraternizing with the guests.

That included the owner.

"Mr. Whittaker, I presume?" she asked, pasting on a perky smile of welcome. Though she was tired and more than a little grumpy herself, there was no reason not to give a paying guest a proper welcome.

Setting his single bag down on the floor beside his feet, the man nodded. "Yeah, that's me." Reaching into his pocket, he drew out his driver's license and credit card. "Sorry I'm in so late."

Gwen accepted his offering, opening his folio and running his card for the single room he'd reserved. While she was waiting on the printer to do its thing, she programmed a key card that would give him access to the room. She handed it over, along with the paperwork for his signature.

"That is a nonsmoking room?"

Gwen nodded. "Yes. All the nonsmoking rooms are on the first floor. You're number twenty-eight."

Blake Whittaker nodded as he signed. "Good enough. There is a reserve on that room in case I decide to stay a second night, right?"

Gwen gave him back his card and license. "I've got the room on tentative hold until noon tomorrow. You'll have to let me know by then whether or not you're going to stay longer."

Whittaker thought a moment, then shook his head. "I'm not sure how long business is going to take. Can you give me until around six to decide?"

She shook her head. "Check-out is at noon, and check-in begins by two. That's the absolute latest I could hold the room." If he was going to let it go, she'd still have to schedule it for cleaning. Since the maids left by one, that meant she'd have to clean it herself if she wanted it active.

"Come on . . ." Blake Whittaker's gaze searched for and found her name tag. "Gwen. Surely as manager you've got a little pull around here." He flashed a smile that lit up his eyes. For a moment he was almost animated.

"Owner," Gwen corrected. "And you let me know something by at least four or I'll go ahead and charge your card whether or not you stay on."

He nodded. "Not going to miss a dime, are you?"

She widened her smile. "Not in this economy."

Whittaker turned toward the wide bay windows overlooking the distant water. "You can save me a little time tomorrow by telling me the best way to reach Little Mer Island. Do they still run a skiff for tourists to see the lighthouse?"

Gwen shook her head. The island tours had ceased a couple of years after her parents were killed, and that had been over sixteen years ago. The fact that he had some familiarity with the island pegged him as a former local. "The island is closed to visitors nowadays," she answered, keeping her answer short and simple. "The owners prefer their privacy." If Whittaker entertained any notions of seeing the famous landmark, he'd have to do it from a distance.

Shifting gears, he said, "I'm actually going there on business, not to see the sights," he countered. "I understand Kenneth Randall lives there with his wife, Tessa. She's the actual owner of the island, right?"

Gwen's heart lurched. "Yes, along with her sisters." She narrowed her eyes. "And I'm one of them."

Square jaw hardening, he nodded. "I know. That's why I'm talking to you."

Oh, yeah. He was a real funny guy. Just the kind she didn't like. "So what do you want?"

Blake Whittaker reached back into his pocket. He

flashed a badge. "FBI," he said crisply. "I'm Special Agent Whittaker, from the field office in Boston."

Gwen looked long and hard at the identification he presented. Damned if it didn't look real.

Invisible fingers clamped tightly around her throat. Her attitude vanished. This could be serious. Very serious. What could the FBI possibly want with her brand-new brother-in-law? "I—I don't understand. What's going on?" Her voice was little more than a nervous squeak.

Whittaker noted her distress. "Now, calm down," he countered. "It's a routine follow-up. I just want to talk to them about the day Jake—" He broke off, fumbling for a small notebook.

Trying to clear her mind, Gwen suddenly felt both sick and shaky. She considered her options for a few seconds, then decided it wouldn't be worth trying to pretend she knew nothing. Lying would only make things worse.

Mouth cotton-dry, she forced the single word out. "Massey."

"Jake Massey. Right. About the circumstances under which he disappeared."

The invisible fingers moved higher. Gwen's head felt as though it were being squeezed in a vise grip. "I was under the impression the coast guard had already investigated the matter and concluded it was an accident."

Whittaker tucked his badge away. "This is just a follow-up, ma'am. Nothing for you to get alarmed about. It's standard procedure."

Hearing his words of reassurance, Gwen naturally assumed the worst. "Surely you don't think they killed Jake and threw him overboard or something like that," she spluttered. The words sounded stupid the moment they left her mouth.

Brows knitting in obvious surprise, Whittaker looked at her with all the patience in the world. "I'm not saying anything of the sort, ma'am. I simply need to ask a few questions to clarify the facts." He offered a brief smile. "And if I can get some cooperation, I'm pretty sure you can have your room back by two."

Gwen looked at him suspiciously. You were never supposed to trust the men in black. "You won't need to stay longer?"

In a gesture of appeasement, Whittaker put his hand over his heart. "Believe me when I say I sincerely hope I don't have to spend more than one night in this town. In fact, I'd like to get the hell out ASAP."

Gwen swallowed hard. "Meet me in the lobby at seven," she allowed. "I'll take you across the bay to Little Mer." It wasn't like he couldn't get across himself. All he'd have to do was walk into the sheriff's office and make the request.

A frown briefly cast a shadow on Whittaker's features. "Sounds like a plan to me." To distract himself, he glanced at his watch. "But if I'm going to make it out that early, I'm going to need some sleep."

Licking her dry lips, Gwen allowed a thin smile. "Of course." She pointed left. "Just follow that corridor to the end, and take the stairs."

Agent Whittaker bent and claimed his single bag. "Thanks."

Gwen forced out an answer. "My pleasure." It wasn't. She lied.

"Be here tomorrow, right?"

Jaw tightening, Gwen took a moment to clear her throat. "That's what I said."

"Thanks again. Appreciate your time." Whittaker turned away from the desk, trekking back through the lobby.

Gwen watched him go, keeping an eye on him until he disappeared. At this point she didn't trust this dude as far as she could throw him. The fact that he was poking around the events in the Mediterranean meant the matter wasn't finished. Not by a long shot. Why waste valuable manpower running down the facts of an incident the U.S. Coast Guard had already cleared?

She fingered the folio she had yet to file. "Something's up."

And it all revolved around Jake Massey.

Although she couldn't prove it as fact, Gwen suspected the archaeologist might have been involved in some unsavory business involving the smuggling of stolen artifacts. When he'd arrived back in Port Rock with the pieces purportedly gathered from the ruins of Ishaldi, he hadn't exactly explained how he'd gotten them into the United States.

It wouldn't be the first time Jake had been caught manipulating the facts, or using those manipulations to fatten his checkbook. After getting bounced out of U

Maine and losing his sea grants, Jake had kicked around as a treasure hunter. Could be the feds weren't interested in Ishaldi as a historical rediscovery, but rather the monetary value such a find would entail.

Sitting back down, Gwen pinched the bridge of her nose and squinched her eyes shut. "I shouldn't have trusted the bastard." Eager to keep Jake's findings under some sort of control, she was the one who'd bought him back to Little Mer Island.

And, if she were brutally honest with herself, she had been more than willing to share in any of the bounty that might come to the surface. The hotel was breaking even, but barely, and Tessa was struggling under the upkeep on Little Mer. At that point in time, the money they had just wasn't going far enough.

Their circumstances had changed, fortunately for the better.

Still, the last thing any one of them needed was a G-man poking his nose into their business. He might find out more than he needed to know.

Like that mermaid thing they were trying to keep on the QT.

Oh, goddess above. What if they've found out about the sea-gate?

Having the federal government in the know would be disastrous.

Gwen pressed a hand to her forehead. The beginnings of a headache beat at her temples. "I've got to squelch this," she murmured.

The minutes ticked away. A plan began to take shape. As the one taking Whittaker to the island, she had the upper hand. Keeping the agent by her side until he left Port Rock would allow her to control what he saw and heard.

All she had to do was give her sisters a little heads-up.

Retrieving her cell phone from her purse, Gwen pecked out a quick message and hit send. She could warn Addison, and Addison, in turn, could get word to Tessa and Kenneth.

A quick smile of satisfaction crossed her lips. She hated to be deceitful, but when it came to family, the Lonike girls had to stick together.

Chapter 2

Anchored just off the coast of Port Rock, Maine, the seventy-two-foot twin diesel-powered yacht bobbed gently on the water. A miasma of sparkling colors rippled across the waters of the Atlantic as the sun rose from the east, lighting the rocky shores of the distant island.

Smiling to himself, Jake Massey lowered his binoculars. There it was. A place he'd believed he'd never see again. Little Mer Island.

Stomach doing a quick backflip, his grip on the specs tightened. Damn. Even though four weeks had passed since the catastrophic events in the Mediterranean, he still couldn't get over the fact Tessa Lonike had tried to end his life.

Jake's teeth clenched. "Goddamned bitch," he muttered. "She hasn't seen the last of me."

Not by any means.

He lifted his binoculars again, gaze searching every familiar inch of the island. The sun's light reflected off the glass tower of the lighthouse, as though winking to acknowledge a secret between the two of them.

Turnabout is fair play, baby, he thought. It was only a matter of time.

A voice from behind interrupted. "She is there?"

Glancing at the woman who'd walked up, Jake nodded. "Yes. That's the place."

Queen Magaera leaned into the rail surrounding the small observation deck. "Good. We need her as soon as possible."

Jake eyed his new partner with appreciation. Dressed in a flowing caftan in a shade of aquamarine, she'd arranged her hair in a crown of silver-blond braids. Her alabaster skin was clear, untouched by the vanity of cosmetics. Shoulders thrown back, chin thrust out as if in challenge, she looked like a woman used to getting her way.

"We're close to getting her back," he said. "Another day and we'll be on our way to Ishaldi." Thanks to an accident with her Mercraft, Tessa had unintentionally keyed the sea-gate to accept only her psychic resonance. No one could enter or leave the lost city unless Tessa led the way.

Magaera allowed a slight smile. "Good. I want the sea-gate reopened as soon as possible. I will require more than eight soldiers to retake our share of the Mediterranean waters."

Jake offered a terse nod. "I don't see why we can't accomplish that. The waters rightfully belong to the Mer people."

A thin smile of approval parted Queen Magaera's

lips. "I am pleased you have chosen to stand at my side as the Mer attempt to regain what they have lost." Her accented voice lent each word an exotic edge. English wasn't her native language, but the Mer had a telepathic ability that allowed them to pick up foreign tongues very quickly.

There was no denying their intelligence. The Mer were unquestionably the superior race when compared to mere human beings. Even their technology, which was thousands of years old, was impressive.

Jake pressed a hand over his heart. "Of course I will. I have pledged my loyalty and will serve you to the best of my ability." In the back of his mind he counted up all the advantages he'd recently gained by switching his loyalty to the queen and her minions. For one, it had saved his ass from execution.

At this point, staying alive was a victory.

Queen Magaera cocked her head. "I trust you not to betray me." Her gaze was distant, noncommittal. She was still wary of humans, those she considered to be members of the lesser species. It would take more than vague oaths to earn her confidence. He had to prove his loyalty with action.

Jake could hardly blame her. Through the last month her nerves had been frayed to the max. Making the transition from her dying world to a strange new land was difficult. A mermaid's natural instinct was to remain in the water, far beneath the surface.

Not that she'd had much choice. Though the Mer could live in the water their whole lives, a human being could not. The only way Jake could survive was by returning to land. Thank God for the Algerian trawler engaged in a little illegal deep-sea fishing.

He blew out a breath. "Of course not. I've done everything I said I would."

Queen Magaera tightened her grip on the railing. "I suppose I have no choice but to trust a *husla,* a lesser." She turned her attention back to the wide-open space of the Atlantic. "There was once a time when we Mer owned the waters of this planet."

He hurried to reassure her. "And you will again."

"It must be soon." The queen lifted her hand to the gem hanging around her neck. "I sense restlessness in those left behind."

Jake nodded resolutely. "I promise it won't be much longer." He flicked his head, missing the brush of long hair against his shoulders. Alas, he'd had to part with his long blond locks when he'd assumed his new identity. As far as the world was concerned, Jake Massey, archaeologist and explorer, had perished in the Mediterranean Sea during a diving accident.

At least that was what the newspapers had said.

Truth be told, right now he was better off as missing, presumed dead. If no search-and-rescue teams were looking for him, then they wouldn't be poking around the site where the sea-gate was located.

After Tessa had blasted the undersea temple to bits, all hell had broken lose. Jake barely remembered anything, just a rush of water followed by a cold black void. Before losing consciousness in the frigid abyss, he was sure he was a goner.

Somehow one of the guards who'd accompanied

Magaera through the sea-gate had gotten hold of him, sharing with him the Mers' ability to breathe under water.

He'd regained consciousness, floating in a vast open sea in the middle of the night. But he wasn't alone. Not by any means. Queen Magaera and her cadre were close by, keeping watch under a starry night sky at the surface of the sea. There was no way they were going to let him get out of sight. He was the only guide they had to surviving in the human world. As for what had happened to Tessa and Kenneth, he soon learned that they'd managed to make it back to the *DreamFever* just fine.

In fact, the ship was nowhere to be seen on the wide-open waters. It didn't take much brainpower to figure out they'd left him behind.

So there he was, stuck in the middle of the freaking Mediterranean Sea with one pissed-off Mer queen and eight of her servants. Though the temple was in ruin, the sea-gate was still accessible. That was if you could make a dive three miles beneath the surface of the water. The Mer could handle that one just fine.

Right now things were at a stall. Tessa had slipped through their fingers. With her went control of the sea-gate.

A plan had to be made, and quickly. Which was kind of hard to do when floating in the middle of the fucking sea. Swimming in water for a few hours was one thing. Living in it for a few days was quite another.

Enter the Algerians, who were obliging enough to illegally drop him off on the beach of Kokkinos Pirgos. He couldn't have asked for a more fortuitous place to come ashore. The beach was only fifty meters from a hotel, with taverns, a couple of cafés, and even a minimarket.

Arriving on the beach, Jake had no passport, no money, and his BlackBerry had shorted out after being submerged in the sea.

The one thing he did have was contacts.

His ex-partner in Recoveries, Inc., was a Greek man based in Crete. A simple phone call was followed by the arrival of a "friend of a friend," who put a roof over his head and provided enough euros to replace his clothes. Forty-eight hours later, he was setting step two in motion.

It was amazingly easy to do when you already had the first part taken care of.

That would be the money. He had a good amount tucked away in a secret numbered account. One he could access from anywhere in the world. No passport or ID was required, and there were no limits on deposits or withdrawals. The account even came with a totally anonymous ATM card. All it took was a simple e-mail to have a new card sent out by overnight courier.

Jake had always suspected there would be a time when he would have to disappear, though he'd imagined the circumstances under which he'd have to go on the lam would be far different. Before his former partner had bowed out of Recoveries, Inc., they'd been involved in some illegal operations—namely artifact smuggling. Research and recovery wasn't a cheap operation to enter into, and the cost of crew and equipment was astronomical.

Not all the money had gone back into the business.

He'd skimmed a bit here and there, socking it away for the proverbial rainy day. He'd continued to hide numerous dollars even after he'd bought out Niklos Sarantos and offered a partnership in the company to Kenneth Randall. Though Randall didn't know it, Jake had also managed to siphon off $250,000 by charging Kenneth for equipment Recoveries, Inc., had already bought and paid for. All in all, he had $1.9 million in his little tax-free offshore shelter.

But that wasn't the only deception Jake had tucked away for a rainy day.

The second part of any successful getaway was to know the wrong sort of people who ran the right sort of scams. A couple of years ago a nice chunk of his ill-gotten booty had gone to purchase a new—and legal—identity. Enter Jean Luc D'Marquis, a Canadian of French descent from Quebec. He'd chosen Canada because of its proximity to the United States and he could speak the language well enough to get around without arousing suspicion.

Unfortunately his looks had to change. His shoulder-length hair was banished, switched for a shorter, darker style. Nonprescription colored contacts changed the shade of his eyes to a striking gray.

But that didn't mean Jake Massey had to stay dead forever. There was always a chance a miracle could occur.

Without a doubt Tessa would know that was possible. She and Kenneth had already done all they could to put some distance between themselves and the Mediterranean Sea. After the so-called "tragic diving accident" that had supposedly claimed Jake's life, Kenneth Randall had shut down Recoveries, Inc., ceasing all operations.

Nobody was talking.

In this case, silence was golden.

And an opportunity to be taken advantage of.

Getting his old partner back hadn't been difficult either. All it took was a couple more phone calls to Niklos and the two were back on the water. But this time the men weren't seeking lost treasure or smuggling ill-gotten booty. No, the cargo they presently carried was a billion times more valuable and volatile than any other contraband they'd ever dealt in.

Mermaids.

And not just any mermaid, mind you, but a queen.

At $700,000, the yacht was a steal. Small enough not to arouse suspicion yet well-appointed enough to accommodate Magaera and the eight Mer who'd crossed through the sea-gate with her.

It had taken time to get the operation into motion. But Jake had done as he'd promised, securing a way for the Mer to get around safely without arousing suspicion. Like Magaera, his main objective was to get back to Maine.

A smirk lifted his lips. *I've still got a little score to settle with Tessa.*

Oh, yeah. He'd get even.

Tessa might think she held all the good cards, but she held a losing hand and could only bluff so long. In opening the sea-gate, she'd unleashed a race hungry for the taste of freedom. There was no going back now. Soon, very soon, people all around the globe would know about the Mer. He imagined the coverage would be massive, a media frenzy. And he, Jake Massey, would be the man at the center of the rediscovery and return of the mermaid.

Now that he had the proof, Jake savored the notion of payback. The fees he'd charge on the lecture circuit would be enormous. That is, if he had any time. A new age was about to dawn. And with a little cunning and determination, he would be able to reap the rewards of being the first human ambassador between mankind and the reemerging Mer. It was bound to be a lucrative gig, and he was determined to take every advantage.

Even if he had to lie, cheat, and steal to do so.

After all, it wasn't like he hadn't done it all before.

"I have waited long enough," Magaera warned, her voice gravelly with impatience. "Every day the girl is out of my reach is one more day my people must wait for their freedom."

Jake fingered his binoculars as he eyed the distant island. Located about a mile off the mainland, Little Mer was almost completely cut off from the outside world. The only communication system lay in the two-way radio located in the lighthouse. The isolation Tessa treasured would be her downfall.

"I don't see why we shouldn't do it right now," he decided. "Send your best soldiers."

Lips thinning, Magaera nodded. "I will send Arta Raisa and Doma Chiara. They are fierce in spirit and will not fail me."

Jake knew that for a fact. Just like mermaids of legend and lore, the Mer were a bloodthirsty race. They bore no love for humans, considering them less than animals. If they found a human inferior, they enslaved or slaughtered them. Only a very few did they find acceptable enough for breeding.

Thank heavens he'd been one of the chosen.

"Send two more, just in case," he stressed. "And remember we just want Tessa. She's the only one we need."

Queen Magaera's blue eyes sparked with interest. She easily picked up the direction the conversation was heading in. "And her mate?"

Oh, yeah. Here was the chance he couldn't miss. It was time for a little payback. In spades. He had disliked Kenneth Randall on sight. The man who'd taken his place in Tessa's bed was tall and plain, a knuckle-dragging Neanderthal. That she'd rebuffed his attempt to get back together and chosen Kenneth over him burned him up into tiny cinders.

Kenneth wasn't good enough for Tessa.

Jake's eyes narrowed. *I want her again.* And he'd have Tessa, damn it. As a slave. To serve his every desire and decadent whim.

Desire trickled through his veins, warm and liquid. He liked that idea. A lot. The things a Mer could do in bed were wondrous.

And the tail. Oh, man. The tail . . .

He couldn't suppress the chuckle bubbling up in the back of his throat. "Get rid of Kenneth." He bit through each word as though each were a deliciously tasty morsel. "I want him gone."

Chapter 3

7 a.m. sharp

Blake Whittaker stood in the lobby. At this point in the morning, sleepy-eyed people were beginning to wander through on their way to breakfast. Though small, the hotel offered a continental breakfast, complete with a smiling attendant who poured the coffee and helped patrons navigate the complexities of the waffle machine.

Considering the fact he was about to make a trip across the water, Blake had skipped eating. For one thing, he considered it an abomination to get up early and immediately begin shoveling down a meal. For the second thing, he hated boats almost as much as he did the water. During the few times he'd had the displeasure of riding in one, he'd never failed to get sick. The last thing he wanted to do was puke his guts up in front of Gwen Lonike.

It wouldn't look professional.

So even though he was dying for a cup or two of

strong hot black coffee, he'd forgo the pleasure until after he'd returned to the mainland. He planned to grab a cup at some fast-food joint.

On my way out of this hellhole, came his dark thought.

"Port Rock," he mumbled under his breath. "Born here, raised here. Won't look back when I leave here."

He checked his watch again: 7:05. His tour guide was one late lady.

Blake glanced toward the front desk. A thin woman with frizzy blond hair and splotchy red skin was busy with customers. The elusive Gwen had vanished. She hadn't been behind the desk when he'd come down from his room, ten minutes before the hour she'd agreed to meet him.

He was just about to amble over and bother the clerk when the door to the manager's office opened.

Purse slung over one shoulder, Gwen Lonike hurried out to join him. She carried a large travel-capped coffee mug. "Sorry," she said, blurting out her apology. "I needed a minute to wash my face and comb my hair." She flicked a damp strand away with a distracted hand. "I'm ready when you are."

Trying not to stare, Blake gave her a quick once-over. Though her clothes were the same as she'd worn last night, she looked fresh and crisp. A fitted white blouse hugged her breasts and narrow waist. Black slacks accentuated her long, sleekly muscled legs. Lustrous red hair cut in a modern shoulder-brushing shag framed her pert face. She wore no cosmetics. Didn't need them, either. Nature had given her thick black lashes and full red lips, along with a smattering of cute freckles across her upturned nose. All together she looked absolutely adorable. Her only accessory was a small crystal pendant, which hung from a delicate gold chain around her neck.

A two-ton anvil could have landed on his head and he wouldn't have noticed. Last night he'd been too tired and distracted to give her a second glance. Now he was looking closer, and he liked what he saw.

His inner temperature rising, Blake felt a shiver clamor up his spine. The fine hairs on the back of his neck stood up. His skin suddenly felt hot and too taut to stretch over his bones. There was a definite reaction going on, one he hadn't felt in a long time.

Wow. Just wow.

He caught a whiff of the light scent she'd recently spritzed her clothing with to freshen it. The smell of crisp fresh pears almost made his mouth water. Desire sped through his brain. Though he usually didn't get too worked up over a nice-looking female, there was something about this one that definitely set his male antennae to humming. He couldn't quite put his finger on what it was, but Gwen seemed different from other women.

Special.

It was an impression that didn't occur to him very often when a woman was concerned. But now that it had, he was finding it difficult to shake the notion.

Blake gave himself another minute to savor the attraction, then firmly put a mental foot on it and tamped it down. He wasn't here to make friends or flirt. He was a federal agent, investigating this woman's sister and brother-in-law. He'd have to forego her appeal and keep things impersonal. All he wanted were the facts.

Cold, hard, plain, simple facts.

Blake reached in his shirt pocket for his shades. "Lead the way." He slipped them on, glad for a chance to hide behind their impenetrable shield. It was too damn bad he had to be in town on business.

If there was one thing he loved, it was the chase. He generally didn't have any problem with the conquering part either. It was the aftermath that usually landed him in hot water, the part that involved walking out and shutting the door behind him. He rarely remembered a woman's name and never looked her up a second time. Forgetting was less complicated.

Except he doubted he'd be able to shove Gwen Lonike out of his mind. He normally didn't go for redheads, nor could he even put his finger on the source of his attraction. But he knew enough to recognize the warning signs when he saw them.

He gave himself a rigid mental shake. *Not going to happen.*

He had sex merely to satisfy the physical. Nothing more. He purposely kept his distance from any romantic entanglements, preferring to keep his heart under lock and key. No one, especially a woman, would ever make him feel small, weak, or afraid ever again. He might go to bed alone, but at least he'd be able to sleep at night.

Tipping her mug to show it was empty, Gwen made a quick gesture toward the breakfast room. "I hope you don't mind, but I'm starved. Mind if I pop in to grab a snack and fill up?"

Blake tried not to let his annoyance show. Not everyone could squelch the needs of the physical as well as he
could. Hunger, thirst, exhaustion. He could put it all off,
as long as necessary, to get the job done. Still, he didn't
have to be a total dickwad. He could show the lady a
bit of courtesy. What was another ten minutes to let her
grab something to eat?

He cocked his wrist, checking his watch for the tenth
time since he'd walked into the lobby. "Of course," he
allowed.

She took a few steps, then stopped and turned. A
single brow arched in question. "Aren't you coming?"

Thinking about the trip across the bay, he shook his
head. "I'm good. Thanks."

Her freshly glossed lips turned into a smile. "Not
even a cup of coffee?"

Truth be told, Blake would have been happy to main-
line a gallon. And then follow it with ten more. Though
the bed beneath his back had been comfortable enough,
he had barely managed to close his eyes for more than
a few minutes. He'd refused to let himself dwell on the
past, yet remnants of his troubled childhood never failed
to creep up from the darker corners of his mind.

So what if he came off as a hard-nosed bastard? It
fit the image of a G-man just fine. Besides that, his type
of job didn't exactly encourage close personal relationships. His ability to keep his mouth shut and his emotions tightly controlled was one of the prime reasons
why the bureau had recruited him. The only thing he
ever intended to be married to was his career. He was

the perfect agent. He might as well have been incubated in a test tube.

He cleared his throat. "I'm good to go."

Gwen shrugged. "Whatever." She disappeared into the breakfast room. A few minutes later she emerged with her cup filled and her mouth full of some sugary confection.

Meeting up with him, she rolled her eyes. "Oh, I love it when they bring them in fresh from the bakery." Her tongue darted out, swiping at a dab of thick cream at the corner of her mouth. "You don't know what you're missing."

Even her most casual move had an earthy sexiness. God, it had been so long since he'd kissed a woman and really enjoyed it.

Taking a quick step back, a slight frown curved his mouth. He was definitely off his game today. Instead of coming back to Port Rock he should have asked his boss to send another agent. He'd believed he could handle it, that he had everything in his life well under control. He was too damn antsy for his own good.

Pinching the bridge of his nose between thumb and forefinger, he squeezed his eyes shut for a moment. *Pull it back and put a plug in it,* he inwardly warned himself.

"Something wrong, Agent Whittaker?"

Eyes snapping open, Blake dropped his hand. "Can we get a move on, please?" His words were clipped, short and to the point. "I haven't got all day."

Gwen's smile instantly vanished. "Certainly." Mantling herself in a cloak of icy reserve, she tossed the remnants of her breakfast into a nearby trash can. "Sorry to let my stomach hold you up. I've worked two straight shifts, and I expect to be back at work in another few hours. Excuse me for needing to eat." Marching to the doors of the lobby, she pushed one open. The bell above her head tinkled merrily as she breezed outside with nary a look back.

A knot of dismay formed in the back of his throat. *Ouch.* That woman was good at giving people the cold shoulder. An expert, in fact. She'd blown him off without turning a hair.

Not that he didn't deserve it. She'd tried to be friendly and he'd practically bitten her head off. Sometimes he failed to remember keeping his distance didn't necessarily mean he had to be a rude jerk.

Taking a moment to regain his composure, Blake wiped his perspiring brow. The air around him felt heavy, stifling. *Shit.*

He sucked in a breath. "I'm an asshole." Ah, well. He was too damn set in his ways to change now.

The clerk behind the desk glanced up. "Excuse me, sir? Were you speaking to me?"

Setting into motion, Blake waved a distracted hand. "No, it's nothing. Thank you." Outside he saw Gwen Lonike was wasting no time, legging it across the parking lot at top speed. Determination propelled her every step.

He'd better catch up if he wanted a ride to the island.

Blake pushed through the double doors. The annoying little bell tinkled again, grating on his nerves. Didn't matter what Gwen might think about him. She had to put up with him for only another hour, maybe two.

It wasn't like he'd ever see her again once he pulled out of town.

Federal agents were a pain in the ass.

That was what Gwen had definitely settled on as she led the way toward the skiff moored at the end of the dock. The ride to the marina was an uncomfortable one, the silence hardly broken by her stoic passenger.

Though Agent Whittaker had looked every which way as she'd driven to the marina, he'd only answered when spoken to. With an expression set in stone and his eyes hidden by impenetrable sunglasses it was difficult to know what he was thinking or even what he might be looking at. Like the mysterious sphinx, he revealed nothing.

Dressed in a crisp black suit, white shirt, and tie, Whittaker hardly looked like he belonged anywhere near the beach. He didn't even look like he knew how to relax. Being a federal agent, he probably had ice in his veins and pissed cubes. He certainly didn't go out of his way to be friendly. The bit of animation he'd briefly displayed last night had vanished.

Maybe it was his tie. The damn thing was done up tight enough to strangle. Perhaps it was cutting off the oxygen to his brain or something.

If this is the way the boys in black operate, she thought, *my tax dollars are definitely being wasted.* Why should a large chunk of her income go to support an agency that treated citizens like they were a bother?

She cast a glance over her shoulder. Instead of walking at a normal pace, Agent Whittaker was dawdling around like an old man with a cane. Hands shoved into his pockets, he walked like his feet were glued to the ground.

Gwen blew out a breath. For someone who'd been in such a hurry to go, he sure was taking his own sweet time. What the hell was his problem anyway?

Ignoring him, she raised a hand toward the man waiting in the skiff. "Thanks for coming, Lucky." She'd known the old sea dog who ferried supplies from the mainland to the island her entire life.

Spitting a wad of chewing tobacco into the water, Lucky wiped his mouth. "Not a problem. I was heading that way." It was true. The old boat was loaded with the usual provisions Tessa ordered a couple of times a month.

Since her sister and Kenneth had returned from their misadventure in the Mediterranean, they'd stayed close to home. Gwen thought part of that might be because of their newlywed status. They'd married quietly in front of a justice of the peace, with only herself and Addison as witnesses. She imagined they were bonking like bunnies.

Gwen's stomach tightened. Oh, heavens. Though she'd never admit it out loud, she was envious that Tessa seemed to have found the perfect man. Kenneth adored her, treated her like a princess. He hadn't been a bit put off when he'd discovered Tessa was a mermaid. He'd accepted everything about her, from her moody, snotty temper to the fact that she sometimes wore a tail when she swam.

Feeling a lump begin to rise in her throat, she swallowed hard. *Wish it could happen for me . . .*

But it hadn't. And the way her life was going, it probably never would.

She shook off the depressive thought, one that occurred far too often lately. "Where's Addison?" she asked.

"She went over to the island earlier." Lucky tipped his cap toward her companion. "Who's the landlubber?" He squinted. "Don't look like he's from around here."

She stepped off the dock, boarding the skiff. "He's with the FBI," she said through her teeth, making sure Whittaker couldn't overhear. "He's got some questions about Jake."

Lucky cut a quick glance toward Whittaker. "He know about things?"

Gwen shook her head. Lucky was one of the few locals who did know about her kind. He'd kept his mouth shut for nigh on forty years. "I don't think so. I've got the feeling Jake was into something dodgy, though. Why else would the feds be poking around?"

Lucky spat again, dragging his fingers across his lips to catch a dribbling of tobacco juice. "Wouldn't put it past Jake to be in on somethin' shady. That boy always worked with his hands behind his back. All he's ever been is trouble with a capital T."

Gwen had to agree. Every time they had dealings with Jake Massey, all the archaeologist had tried to do was extort or exploit them. And she'd stupidly helped him get his foot back into the door of their lives. It was a door she should have slammed—and locked.

"That's why I wanted Tessa and Kenneth to have a heads-up the feds were sniffing around. When Kenneth bought into Jake's business, he might have gotten into something illegal."

Lucky scratched his chin. "Mighty possible." He cast a glance over Gwen's shoulder. "He don't look like he's too eager to get goin', though."

Gwen turned around, sneaking a peek at Agent Whittaker. The morning was crisp, gloriously calm. It would be a gorgeous day, but he seemed to notice nothing about it. Instead, he lingered in the middle of the dock and didn't look happy about his present location.

She drew a breath. Maybe federal agents were just natural joy killers. When they were around it was probably against the law to be happy. "We're ready anytime you are," she called.

Whittaker walked to the edge of the dock. He eyed the skiff, hardly the nicest boat on the water. *Lucky's Lady* had been in service for over twenty-five years and while her paint might be a little faded and nicked, she was the most seaworthy vessel sailing the bay.

Whittaker frowned. "You sure that thing can carry cargo and passengers?"

Gwen plopped down onto a cardboard box packed full of groceries to make room. "Of course." She patted the box. "It's perfectly safe."

Whittaker hedged. "I don't see any regulation safety gear," he noted with a frown. "Where are the life vests?"

"There's one and it's for me." Lucky cackled irreverently. "What's the matter? Can't you swim, big boy?"

The agent's jaw tightened subtly. "No," he snapped. "But I'll make damn sure to grab on to you before I go under." He smiled bitterly. "That's a promise."

Lucky guffawed and spat. "No worries." He patted the boat the way some would a pet. "My gal here isn't very pretty, but she's solid. I guarantee it."

Gwen looked up. She couldn't be sure, but she thought she saw a flicker of fear cross Whittaker's stoic expression. Hard to tell though, since his eyes were hidden behind those impenetrable sunglasses. "Really, it's safe enough."

Whittaker appeared to think it over. He finally nodded. "The sooner we get going, the sooner we can get back." He stepped onto the skiff with movements that clearly pegged him as one who'd rarely set foot on a boat in his life.

Gwen scooted over to make room. "Sit here. We'll be across before you know it."

Agent Whittaker sat. Posture absolutely rigid, his hands were clenched so tightly his knuckles showed white. "Let's go."

His attitude was clear. End of conversation.

Untying the line keeping the skiff moored to the dock, Lucky fired up his Evinrude. The little motor spluttered, then burst into a buzz saw of action, ready to go. "Hang on!" the old man called over the noise.

The skiff lunged forward, cutting out across the water.

Chapter 4

Sitting shoulder to shoulder beside Blake Whittaker, Gwen sneaked another glance. He sat stone still, unmoving. In fact, he barely breathed.

If she hadn't been sure before, she was now. There was no missing his vibe. This man clearly had no love of the water. In fact, he was terrified.

Sympathy welled up inside her. Everybody had a fear, some little something that sent a shiver down their spine. As the owner of her own little bag of insecurities, she could easily understand.

Without knowing quite why, Gwen laid a hand on his arm. She leaned closer so he could hear her over the noise of the motor. "Lucky has been taking people across these waters all his life. He hasn't lost one yet."

Fingers still locked in a clench, Whittaker shifted his body away from hers. "That's good to know."

Gwen purposely let her hand drop. He obviously didn't welcome personal contact. Still, she admired his determination. He was doing what his job required him to do, even if he didn't like it. That took a lot of guts. "I take it you aren't admiring the view."

His reply was short and sweet. "No."

Not a talky man at all.

Heavens. He was as friendly as a rattlesnake.

Her sympathy melted a bit. She was doing her best to be nice and all he could do was blow her off. "So are all agents trained to be rude sons of bitches or does it just come naturally to you?"

Like a robot going into motion, Whittaker turned his head. One hand lifted. He pushed up his sunglasses, giving her a view of his eyes. "They train us to be bastards," he answered with all seriousness. The impenetrable glasses went back down.

Then, quite unexpectedly, he grinned.

His smile caught her unaware, and her breath caught in her chest in surprise. "That's good to know," she squeaked like a nervous schoolgirl. *Oh. My. God.* The upturn of his lips made his mouth absolutely sensual.

She hadn't realized until that moment how damn good-looking he was. He had a face like granite, all sharp lines and angles: high forehead, chiseled cheekbones, strong straight jaw. He wore his black hair in a short uncombed style that helped soften the severity of his face. His suit fit him well, tailored to accentuate his muscular arms, broad chest, and washboard stomach. There wasn't a spare ounce on his lean frame.

Now that his demeanor had lost a layer of frost, he reminded Gwen of a stallion—roped and harnessed, forced to be tame. She couldn't help but think that a wild streak lurked beneath the surface of his calm, straining to break free and run loose. She could imagine how Mr. Straight-Laced Tight-Ass might be in other situations . . .

Feeling heat creep into her cheeks, Gwen quickly turned her head. While she'd never admit it out loud, she'd been reading a lot of erotic romances and wishing she was the heroine, being swept off her feet by the drop-dead gorgeous hero.

Truth be told, Gwen actually had no idea what Whittaker might be like in bed. Or any other man for that matter. Though she wouldn't admit it out loud, she'd never found a man she would dare to be that intimate with.

Yes, she'd dated, had even fooled around a little. But she'd never taken the plunge and moved any of her relationships to the next step.

She was twenty-seven years old and still a virgin.

Gwen inwardly winced. Unlike Tessa and Addison, she didn't have enough confidence in her body to strip to the buff in front of a human male. Needless to say, her boyfriends invariably got frustrated with her inhibitions and dropped her like a hot rock. And since Mers didn't age like humans, it was beginning to look like she was going to have a long, lonely life ahead.

Being the world's oldest bachelorette didn't appeal to her one bit. And just because she'd never had sex didn't mean she didn't think about it. She did. A lot.

She gave Blake Whittaker another surreptitious peek. Oh, goddess, he was pure eye candy. *If I were going to give it up, that man would be the one.* Everything about his looks appealed to her.

But there was no way in hell she'd try getting down

and dirty with a government agent. All she really wanted was for Agent Whittaker to get the hell out of town. The sooner, the better. Until that time, she doubted she'd breathe easy.

At least they were one step closer to fulfilling that objective. The ride was almost over. In another five minutes Agent's Whittaker's torture would be over.

Gwen couldn't suppress a sigh as she looked around the all-too-familiar surroundings. Even though she'd moved to the mainland to live among the human population, Little Mer continued to drag her back. The place was like a magnet. Sometimes it seemed like she'd never be able to get away.

Others of her kind had made the great escape. And they'd never come back. Nowadays very few Mer inhabited the bay. Through time their numbers had dwindled to almost nothing. It was inevitable her kind would branch out, moving onto land and joining the humans. Even members of her own family had given up and moved on, determined to fit in to a society that didn't necessarily welcome anyone who was strange or unusual.

Gwen hated being different. Being Mer. Even though she lived and worked among people, she still didn't feel she belonged. She never felt like she would. There would always be that one thing separating her from everyone else.

Killing the Evinrude, Lucky guided his boat up to the island's landing place with all the skill of an expert seaman. The skiff glided to a gentle stop. Throwing out a rope, he quickly secured the skiff to the dock. "Here we are, folks."

Gwen pushed herself off the carton. The paper towels

packed inside had made quite a comfy seat. "Thanks for the ride, Lucky."

The old man doffed his cap. "Anytime."

Whittaker also stood. During the ride over, a bit of the tension seemed to have left him. At least his hands had unclenched and his expression was a bit less sour and a little more human. "I'll need maybe an hour," he informed the skipper.

Lucky just shrugged. "I'll be around."

Stepping up onto the pier, Gwen motioned toward the house in the distance. "This way, Agent Whittaker."

He scrambled up beside her, a little bit more graceful this time. "Thank God that's over," he muttered under his breath.

"I hope you don't mind," she continued. "But I took the liberty of sending word ahead. Kenneth and Tessa aren't exactly early to rise."

Whittaker cocked a brow. "They just got married, right?"

Gwen nodded. "About three weeks ago." She thought a moment. "How did you know?"

"There's a reason the word *investigate* is in the job description," Whittaker answered behind a smirk. "It's what we do."

"Smart-ass."

He smiled slowly. "And I'd say you had a nice ass, but it would probably get me slapped."

Ah. So there was a human being under that hardcore facade he wore like a second skin.

Gwen tilted her head back to look at him. She was fairly tall herself, but he dwarfed her. The top of her head barely brushed his shoulder. He was definitely the kind of man built for sweeping a woman off her feet.

"Or sued for sexual harassment," she added drily. "And if you were trying to compliment me, you missed the mark." She offered her own smile. "By at least a mile."

Whittaker blew out a breath, then cleared his throat. "I'm attempting to apologize for being a jerk back there."

Her heart missed a beat. "*Jerk* doesn't begin to describe it," she countered.

He frowned. "Oh?"

Gwen decided to let him off the hook. At least he was trying to be civil and decent. "But it's too early in the morning to hold a grudge," she added. "So apology accepted." It helped that he presented quite a nice package to look at. She might not indulge, but that didn't mean she couldn't enjoy savoring the view.

Shoving his hands in his pockets, he rocked back on his heels. "So let me make it up to you by letting me buy you something to eat when we get back to the mainland."

She laughed. "My tax dollars at work, right?"

"Something like that." He shrugged. "Or you could think of it as my attempt to repair my terrible manners."

"So you guys really aren't trained to be bastards?"

"Only where the bad guys are concerned," he answered seriously. "You're not a bad guy, are you?"

Gwen clicked her tongue. "You'll have to use your investigative skills if you want to find out."

He nodded. And even though she couldn't see his eyes behind his sunglasses, she had the feeling he was eyeing her from head to toe.

Stepping incrementally closer, he lowered his head. The tips of his shoes didn't quite touch hers. "I could do that," he breathed in a voice that reminded her of smoky bars with shadowy corners.

Arousal leaping into blazing life, Gwen felt her knees weaken a bit. Whittaker was so close she was aware of every inch of his big body, so hard and brawny under the drape of his suit. The heat behind his murmured words brushed her cheek.

The attraction was definitely there, buzzing between them like a swarm of angry bees.

An all-too-familiar voice interrupted the moment. "Hey, you two, break it up!"

Reality crashed back in.

Clenching her teeth, Gwen took a quick step back. *Get a grip,* she thought. *Act like a grown woman instead of a desperate virgin.*

Addison's shoes clattered onto the dock. She was all noise and chatter. "What the hell?" she said by the way of a greeting. "We've been waiting since seven for the freaking feds to arrive."

Gwen grabbed her sister's arm, pulling her back. "Please, Addison, mind your mouth," she said between gritted teeth. Brash and uninhibited, the youngest Lonike sister had no sense of proper decorum. Addison said whatever was on her mind, even if it meant hurting someone's feelings. Or stepping on their toes.

Blake Whittaker straightened his tie, already perfectly positioned. The invisible shield he'd temporarily lowered clicked back into place. The human in him disappeared and the stone-cold automaton returned. "Actually there's only one fed, and I'm it."

Addison planted her hands on her hips. "Well, do you think you could get a move on? We're all tired of sitting around, twiddling our thumbs."

Whittaker pulled his mouth into a flat line. "Twiddle no more."

Gwen mentally slapped her forehead with her palm. Just when it looked like she was making a little headway, Addison's bad timing had to ruin everything. Having Whittaker in a good mood might have moved his interview with Kenneth and Tessa along a little faster.

Now he'd probably give everyone a good grilling. All she could hope was Addison wouldn't open her mouth and insert her big foot. She could practically hear the headlines blaring on the nightly news: MERMAIDS DISCOVERED IN PORT ROCK, MAINE. If anyone was going to out their kind, it would definitely be Addison.

"That little twit has to ruin everything," she muttered, following her sister and Whittaker toward the house.

As for that meal he'd offered to buy her . . .

Gwen had a feeling she wasn't getting it.

The only pictures Blake had seen of Little Mer Island had shown a lighthouse perched beside a rundown Cape Cod–style house. The lighthouse still stood in its place, keeping its unblinking watch over the open sea. The main house, however, had changed. A lot. Even from a quarter-mile distance, he could see the dwelling had morphed from simple to elaborate, tripling in size.

Blake shook his head. The intelligence report he'd received apparently wasn't the most current. He rolled his eyes. Damn. How could they not be informed about all the freaking construction? With satellite technology that could capture the image of a license plate on a car, they shouldn't have missed the massive construction activity. Hell, they could have found this with Google Earth.

He sighed. "Fucking budget cuts," he muttered under his breath. Not to mention short staffing. Since 9/11, hundreds of agents had been transferred into counter-terrorism operations, leaving dozens of positions unfilled. Even the A51 division was feeling the pain of the gutting.

"Did you say something, Agent Whittaker?" Gwen asked.

Blake shook his head. "Just admiring the construction."

"Quite a lot of it going on lately," she agreed. "Kenneth seems to have been bitten by the building bug."

Blake combed through his mental notes. He knew Kenneth Randall was loaded, the widower of Jennifer Marsham, heiress to the Marsham Investments firm in New York.

He also knew Randall had inherited quite a chunk of change after Jennifer Marsham was gunned down in a carjacking. Her grief-stricken parents had even gone so far as to accuse Randall of hiring someone to kill their daughter so he could get his hands on her money.

Their accusations were for naught. No connection was ever found between Randall and the shooter. Jennifer Marsham's death was a random occurrence, nothing more.

Whatever his story, no one could accuse Randall of greed. He'd practically rebuilt the house from the ground up. The small, cozy home had turned into a larger, cozier home. Two more cozy little cottages were being built nearby.

Addison noticed his twice-over. She pointed at one partially built home. "Mine." She grinned and pointed to the other. "And that will be Gwen's house." She winked. "For when we get married and move home with our husbands."

Blake nodded. "Nice."

Addison eyed his left hand. "You married?"

That was easy enough to answer. "Nope."

"Dating?"

No hesitation. "Nope."

"Looking?" she asked hopefully.

Blake shook his head. "Nope." Damn. She was good at prying. She'd just gotten his whole sorry relationship status in three questions. The bureau could use a sharp little cookie like her.

Truth be told, he wasn't serious about looking for a new lover. Once their biological clocks began to tick, most women wanted to put flings behind them and settle down. Blake had already had a taste of settling down and it hadn't agreed with him one bit. A little over four years ago he'd even tried shacking up with a woman.

He frowned. *What a disaster.* The only good thing to come out of that mess was his son, Trevor.

Gwen interrupted her sister's grilling. "Stop it with the third degree, already," she warned. "His life is not your business."

Addison grinned, revealing a cute little gap between her teeth. Dressed in a T-shirt and jeans, she also sported a set of wicked bad tattoos that started at her wrists and wound their way up her arms. The art was awesomely impressive. Blake didn't even want to think about the pain involved.

"Any man not wearing a wedding ring is my business," she shot back. "If he's single and over twenty-one, then he's fair game." She winked. "You know how slim the pickings are around Port Rock."

Gwen sighed toward the cottage Addison had indicated as hers. "You know I'm not moving back. Kenneth and Tessa just have this big fantasy that we'll all get married and raise our kids here." A laugh escaped her. "I have a business, on the mainland. Remember?"

"Don't know why you couldn't commute. It's only a fifteen-minute ferry trip, twenty max."

"Winter," Gwen reminded her recalcitrant sibling.

Giving half an ear to the sisters' conversation, Blake looked around the island. Some parts of it were still uncultivated, jungle wild. It was the kind of place a kid would love to run amok; climbing trees, playing on the beach, swimming in the cove. Such a wide-open space and fresh air seemed like paradise on earth, a terrific place to grow up.

Trevor would go nuts for this, he thought. When

school let out for the season, Blake would have forty-two blissful days to visit with his kid.

Blake could almost imagine bringing Trevor to Port Rock, maybe show his son where he'd spent the first half of his life. Even though he and Debra couldn't speak without shouting at each other, his four-year-old son still thought Daddy was a hero. And Blake was determined to keep it that way. The cycle of abuse and neglect he'd known as a child didn't have to continue into the next generation. Why punish his son because he felt unlovable and unworthy?

Without quite thinking about it, Blake let his gaze edge over toward Gwen. An hour ago he'd been chomping at the bit to leave town. Now he was mulling plans to bring his son to Port Rock. What was wrong with him?

Blake hated to admit it, but his heart had sped up double-time when she'd touched him. Yeah, he knew it was simply a gesture of concern. Somehow she'd sensed his discomfort and tried to calm his fear.

He shook his head. She might already have a boyfriend. Hell, she might even be in a serious relationship already. Or engaged. The one thing he did know was that her ring finger was bare.

That meant she might be open to something with him. *If I decide to pursue her,* he thought.

At this point it was all wild speculation.

He'd had these gut-level attractions before and they'd never panned out, mostly because he'd always backed off at the last moment. Once bitten, twice shy didn't begin to describe his hang-ups with women.

Then there was his job, which often entailed insane

hours and a lot of travel. Finally, he was tied up with trying to be a part of his young son's life and wrangling with his ex-girlfriend. It was a lot to take care of, and twenty-four hours just didn't cover all he needed to do.

Still, Gwen was definitely different. The simple touch of her hand had set his nerves afire. He'd had to shift away and brush her off to keep his composure. That or end up with a very prominent hard-on. She'd accepted his slight with grace.

He'd tried to make it up to her by asking her out. It wasn't much, but it was a start.

"What about a hotel on the island?" he blurted out. "You know, one of those little inn-type places?"

Blindsided by his unexpected entry into the conversation, Gwen looked at him like he'd lost every marble in his head. "Excuse me?"

Blake pointed out an acre that had caught his eye. "I was just wondering why you don't consider building on the island. With the lighthouse and access to the mainland, it seems like it would be a perfect tourist destination."

Gwen lifted her chin. "Maybe because I don't happen to have a few million dollars sitting in my checking account," she countered.

Addison jumped in. "Ken's made the offer—" she started to say.

Gwen immediately shook her head. "And I'm not asking my brother-in-law to finance my business ventures," she countered firmly. "Anything I do, I'll do it with money I've earned."

"But it's a possibility," Addison prodded.

For some insane reason, Blake nodded his agreement. "It's something I'd keep in mind. You've got a good piece of real estate. Would be a real shame to waste it."

He didn't know why he felt compelled to add his two cents. It really wasn't any of his business. It just seemed like a good idea.

Gwen Lonike was giving everyone the evil eye, looking at him and Addison like bugs she wanted to step on. She pinned her sister with a stare. "We enjoy our privacy." She coughed discreetly into her hand. "Remember."

Addison flagged a hand. "Oh, that's overrated nowadays." She threw out her arms. "How are you going to get noticed if you don't think big?"

Flashing a look of annoyance, Gwen put them both off. "I'd rather think big, but stay discreet. That gets me along in life just fine. Thank you." She jabbed a finger toward Blake. "And I'd appreciate it if you'd keep your meddling in my family's business to official business only. Whatever you've got to do, do it and go away. Please."

That said, she marched off toward the main house in a huff. For the second time that day Blake had a view of her back as she stomped away.

He had a feeling he'd be eating alone tonight.

Nibbling her bottom lip, Addison shrugged off her sister's anger. "Aw, she's just being moody today. She'll forget about it in an hour or so." She cocked her head toward the house. "Might as well come in. Everyone's waiting."

Blake nodded. Far from being put off, he found himself admiring her spunk. Gwen appeared to be unwilling to rely on anyone but herself. Her determination was appealing.

It was too fucking bad he'd probably never lay eyes on her again after today.

Guess I blew it big-time . . .

Blake had no chance to finish his thought.

Four women appeared suddenly over the edge of a nearby embankment. Dressed in some sort of scaly-looking skintight apparel, their heads had been completely shaved save for a thin strip of hair down the middle of their skulls. Stranger than their looks were the weapons they carried. Long knives were sheathed at their hips and a couple of the women carried spears.

The two who weren't armed with spears wore some kind of bejeweled adornment that looked like a snake winding from their hand to the crook of their arm. The jewels were alight, flashing with strange colors.

Addison stiffened. "Holy shit, we've got trouble."

Blake looked toward the women. They didn't look friendly and were advancing rapidly. "You know these people?"

A frown turned down Addison's lips. "I hadn't planned on meeting them, but I guess I've got no choice now. They've got their ass-kicking gear on."

Blake reached for the weapon holstered under his jacket. "Not necessarily." He stepped in front of Addison. "I'll handle it."

"You don't know what they've got," he heard Addison warn from behind. "I don't think you'll be able to stop them with just a gun. Her weapon beats yours any day of the week."

Blake's head swiveled. Nothing Addison said made sense, but he didn't care. A well-aimed bullet could stop an assailant in their tracks. And he was an expert shot.

He thumbed back the safety on his 9 mm, aimed, and got ready to squeeze the trigger. "Federal agent," he announced. "Stop there and lower your weapons."

They women didn't slow their advance. If they heard his warning, they ignored it.

One of the advancing females lifted her hand. Oddly enough Blake noted that her arm was also strangely tattooed. Just like Addison's.

At the moment he didn't make the connection.

No time to think about it either.

The jeweled object around the woman's arm pulsed, sending out a violent bolt of light.

Moments later a searing blast of heat tore through Blake's arm. The air in his lungs instantly evaporated. Fingers going numb, his gun dropped from his hand. The odor of burnt material and sizzling blood assailed his nostrils.

"Fuck!" he yelped, clamping his hand over the injured area. It felt like someone had stabbed him to the bone with a burning-hot branding iron.

A second flare whizzed within an inch of his temple. His sunglasses went flying, hitting the ground in a heap of twisted metal and melted plastic. It was so close he felt its heat and saw its blazing kaleidoscope of color. Had the blast hit the mark, his skull would have exploded like a water balloon hitting concrete.

Brain whirring frantically, Blake stared in pure shock at the advancing females. He struggled to make sense of the events as they were unfolding, but none of the pieces came together.

Pulling in a gulp of much-needed oxygen, he felt his stomach do a backflip. Acid rose from his stomach, burning the back of his throat. *What the hell's happening?*

He definitely hadn't been expecting to walk into a war zone when he'd rolled out of bed this morning. Everything around him had taken on a surreal quality, as if he'd somehow stepped from his own world into an entirely different dimension.

An extremely hostile dimension.

The women had ambushed and attacked, with no questions asked. Their only intent seemed to be to annihilate everything in sight.

A fresh volley of blasts sailed past him. He wasn't the only victim in plain sight. A man's scream of agony hit his ears, turning into a long, low moan of the mortally wounded.

Realization hit Blake. *The old man!* He started to head back toward the dock.

Grabbing a handful of his jacket, Addison pulled him backward and swung him around. "Lucky's gone!" she shouted, dragging him after her. "We need to leg it!" Her strength and speed were impressive.

Blake had no choice but to shift his ass into high gear and go with her. He didn't know what those women were armed with, but they clearly had the upper hand.

Chapter 5

Gwen was just about to lift her hand and knock on Tessa's door when Addison and Agent Whittaker came zooming up.

"Get in the house!" Addison warned, twisting the knob and flinging the door open. "We've got trouble!"

"What the—" Gwen had no time to finish her sentence. Whittaker barreled in from behind, practically shoving her under the threshold. "Move it!" he shouted.

Gwen stumbled into Addison, who tripped and hit the floor, skidding painfully on her hands and knees. This in turn scared the hell out of Tessa, who yelped and dropped the coffeepot in her hand. The pot shattered into a billion pieces. Shards of glass and boiling-hot coffee splattered everywhere.

Splashed by the hot liquid, Addison squealed and scrambled to her feet. "Ow! That fucking hurt!" Glass crunched under her tennis shoes.

Thoroughly pissed off, Tessa grabbed a roll of paper towels. "Quit clowning around, Addison!" she snapped.

"She isn't clowning." Whittaker slammed the door shut, and locked it. "I don't know what's going on, but we're being attacked."

Gwen's jaw dropped. Tessa's followed. "Attacked?" they chimed simultaneously.

Alarmed by the commotion in his kitchen, Kenneth Randall hurried in. "I thought I heard glass breaking. What happened?"

Gwen shrugged helplessly. One minute she'd been walking along. The next she'd been shoved into the middle of pandemonium. She had no clue about anything. For some reason Addison and Whittaker had all of a sudden turned into maniacs. "I don't know."

Addison supplied the answer. "That thing you said you took care of in the Mediterranean—I don't think you quite finished the job."

Recognizing the reference, Gwen felt the blood in her veins turn to ice. "Oh, my God," she started to say. "They can't be here."

Addison gave her a wild look. "They are, and they're about to play some catch up." The words barely left her mouth before a blast hit the door behind Whittaker. Flaming bits and pieces of wood flew through the kitchen. A hole about the size of a baseball appeared, edges still smoking and sizzling from the intense detonation of energy against it.

Whittaker beat at the flames chewing up his jacket. "Shit, I'm on fire!"

Another sizzling blast tore through the door. A third

followed. It was beginning to disintegrate. In another few minutes there would be nothing left.

Kenneth paled, the blood instantly draining from his face. "Everybody hit the basement," he ordered. "Now!" He grabbed for his wife, pulling her over to his side.

Nobody questioned his command.

Realizing he didn't know up from down, Gwen grabbed Whittaker's arm. "This way," she urged, dragging the confused agent in the direction Kenneth indicated.

One by one they clattered down the narrow staircase. Kenneth brought up the rear, herding them all toward the back of the basement. "Hit the safe room," he snapped.

Hand still clamped around Whittaker's arm, Gwen dragged him into a small concrete room. The final sliver of light disappeared when steel scraped against concrete.

Then everything was black. Pitch-black. The space was cold, the gloom impenetrable.

A minute later, a set of emergency lights snapped on.

Gwen blinked as the glare hit her eyes. So did everybody else.

Everyone looked around.

Addison was the first to find her voice. "I think we made it."

Kenneth stood in front of a panel, punching more buttons. More lights came on. "It's not finished, but I think we'll be okay for a while." His face took on a grim, shadowed cast.

Whittaker shook off Gwen's hand. "People usually don't have panic rooms unless they're expecting trouble." He turned an unblinking gaze toward Kenneth. "I take it those women who just tried to turn me into cinders are a part of that trouble."

Kenneth's jaw tightened. "You could say that."

Whittaker nodded. Now that the shock of the moment had passed, his features had reverted back to immobile. His expression might have been cast in lead for all the emotion he was showing. "Mind telling me why they want to kill you?"

"I hope you're prepared to stay a while," Addison piped in. "This is going to be one hell of a long story."

Gwen inwardly winced. The narrative involving Ishaldi and the opening of a tomb that was really a sea-gate-come-portal that led into another realm was almost too incredible to be believed. She'd hardly been able to comprehend the tale when she'd first heard it from beginning to end.

This is too much. Whittaker's going to think we're all nuts.

Or maybe he wouldn't.

Given the fact he'd just been ambushed, he might have more of an open mind. Either way, the situation definitely sucked.

Kenneth hedged. "Let's get settled in, first," he finally said. "Then we'll talk."

Agent Whittaker shook his head. "No time. I need to get out of here, and get those people into custody." He looked around. "Where's the communications center?"

Kenneth ruefully pointed to a section of wall where another panel was installed. Unfortunately it was just a jumble of parts and wires. "We were still in the process of putting in a two-way radio system," he explained ruefully.

"I'll handle it." Whittaker dug in his pocket and retrieved his cell. He flipped it open. "Damn."

Gwen glanced at his phone, a sleek little ultramodern number. "Let me guess. No signal."

"Right." Whittaker flipped his phone shut. "So much for the global coverage Uncle Sam has been paying for."

"Cell reception is iffy on the island," Addison said. "There are some places around here where you can't get a signal. That's why we have to rely on the old shortwave radios for communication with the mainland."

The agent pocketed his phone. "Guess that means we take care of things ourselves."

Kenneth spread his hands. "Everyone just calm down." He looked toward his wife. "Get some coffee. I think we've got some explaining to do."

Addison glanced at the ceiling over their heads. "I wonder if we've got time to drink a cup. Our visitors have got enough firepower to blast the house to bits."

Tessa gave a little start, dodging the comment clearly aimed her way. "I'll get the coffee."

Kenneth patted the walls. "It's solid concrete all around us, and its several feet thick. They shouldn't be able to get in."

Addison gave the steel door shutting them in a glum look. "Yeah, but that means we can't get out."

"That's a lot of precaution," Whittaker commented.

Kenneth's hand dropped. "We were hoping we'd never need it."

Addison eyed the small room. "Just remember the *Titanic* sank on its maiden voyage."

Her words struck Gwen as totally self-defeating. "What the hell is that supposed to mean?"

Folding her arms across her chest, Addison leaned back against one bare wall. "I think it means we're in a whole lot of trouble, for sure."

Gwen snapped, "Quit thinking."

Taking a minute to catch her breath and organize her thoughts, she looked around. When she was a kid, the basement had served as an emergency shelter during hurricane season. But it was nowhere near as elaborate as it was now. Recent renovations had turned what was a simple safe haven into an underground bunker.

Approximately thirty-three by fourteen, the bare concrete room had been outfitted as a small campsite, complete with a propane heater, microwave, fold-out table, and some chairs. A bunk bed set and adjoining bathroom with a shower completed the area. A small closet held a stash of supplies, including canned goods, bottled water, and other necessary items that were good in an emergency.

Tessa dug out some instant coffee and a gallon of drinking water. Her hands shook as she tried to take off the lid.

Kenneth stepped over to his wife. He gave her hand a reassuring squeeze. "Let me." He took over, filling the cups with water before heating them in the microwave.

Tessa gave her husband a grateful smile. "Thanks."

With a slight wince, Whittaker slipped off his charred

jacket. Deep furrows of pain had etched themselves into his forehead, yet he bore his discomfort with remarkable stoicism. "Any chance there's a first-aid kit in there somewhere?" He jabbed a finger through the hole in his jacket. "I've got a few hurts that need patching."

Noticing his injuries for the first time, Gwen gasped. "You're hurt." Shirt burned clean through, his right arm was a mass of scorched flesh.

Addison pushed herself away from the wall. "I can handle this." She headed over to the closet to dig around. "Right here." A moment later she produced her find. The familiar red cross was marked on the case. "Have a seat and I'll patch you right up."

"Gwen," Kenneth prompted as he distributed steaming cups of coffee on the table. "Set out a few more chairs, would you?"

Head still spinning, Gwen nodded. "Sure." Functioning on autopilot, she unfolded a few more chairs. Her numb fingers barely functioned. Somehow she managed to handle the task.

Whittaker took a seat and offered his injured arm to Addison, who was laying out her equipment with precision. She was rock solid. As an EMT, Addison was trained to keep her cool and her wits in an emergency situation.

"I've never seen anything like that," he remarked. "That's one hell of a weapon they've got."

Face practically encased in stone, Addison cut away his sleeve. "You're fortunate it just grazed you," she mumbled. "Too bad Lucky didn't live up to his name."

Those who hadn't been outside when the trouble began turned their gazes toward Addison and Whittaker. That included Gwen.

She frowned. "What about Lucky?"

Addison didn't look up from her work. "He didn't make it." Her tone was cold, clinical. She was speaking as a professional medic and not a personal friend of the deceased. Grief would come later, when she'd had time to decompress.

Tessa gaped at her sister in horror. "Oh, no. That can't be." She stumbled toward a chair and sat down. A fine tremor shook her body. "Are you sure?"

Addison nodded. "He took a dead-on hit. You don't survive when something like that finds you."

Kenneth frowned darkly. "Oh, man. That's bad. Just bad." His voice held a tinge of sorrow. "We didn't think it would come to this."

A raw, deep slice went straight through Gwen's heart. She'd always liked Lucky. The old man knew they were Mer and had never said a word to another living soul. He'd worked for her family almost all his life, just like his father before him.

A single tear streamed down her cheek. She hurriedly wiped it away. "He was a good man."

"Too good to die that way," Addison added. "But I won't forget what those bitches did. I'll get even. Somehow, I will."

Conversation dwindled off into silence. Nobody seemed to know what to say.

As the odd man out, Whittaker was the first to speak

again. He glanced at his injured arm. "Damn thing was like a laser. Burned right through me."

Addison applied an antiseptic wash and a layer of salve. "It's pretty clean. The injury is deep, but the heat cauterized the blood vessels, so you won't bleed to death." She wrapped his arm in a loose layer of gauze. "All in all, I'd say you're going to live."

Grunting his approval, Whittaker lifted his arm. "Still hurts like hell."

Addison dug back into her kit, offering up a generic brand of ibuprofen. "This ought to help a little."

The agent gritted his teeth against the agony. "Thanks." He popped the caplets into his mouth and swallowed. He glanced at his shirt, now missing almost an entire sleeve. "Guess I need to be grateful I still have an arm."

Tessa offered the agent a cup of hot coffee. "I'm sorry." She shot a glance toward Kenneth. "If we'd have had any idea something like this was going to happen, we would have contacted the authorities sooner."

Shoulders slumping, Kenneth stared into his coffee, trying not to make eye contact with anyone. "We weren't sure if we should say anything," he added.

Gwen hated to see the two backed into a corner. Even though Tessa and Kenneth had both wanted to go to the government with their discovery, she'd been the one to kibosh the idea. It was better to lay low, she'd said, than to lay their story out and possibly come off looking like fools. The sea-gate had been destroyed. As far as Gwen was concerned, that was the end of it.

But it isn't over, she realized. Some of the Mer who had crossed into earth's waters had obviously survived.

And now there'd be hell to pay.

Gwen turned to the agent. "It wasn't their fault." Inside, her nerves were crackling and sparking as she spoke. "I'm the one who decided we should say nothing about the incident in the Mediterranean."

Whittaker blew out a breath. "Excuse me, can somebody please explain to me what is going on?"

Tessa's hands dropped. "It's about Ishaldi." Her reply was low, almost inaudible to all ears. "We found it," she told Whittaker. Her bottom lip trembled as she spoke. "We found a lost world."

Gwen's heart slammed against her ribs, threatening to pound its way through her chest. She'd always prayed this moment would never come. Now it had. And people were going to know all about the Mer.

Goddess help us, she prayed silently.

Blake wasn't sure what was going on, but he did know one thing: These people were hiding something huge. What he'd personally witnessed outside was enough to boggle the mind. The arsenal those women had—like the one nearly blasting him into kingdom come—was unlike anything he'd ever seen in his life. A bejeweled trinket that shot beams of fire.

Something like that was out of this world.

And very dangerous. His arm was proof of that. He didn't even want to imagine what Lucky's remains might look like. Gruesome, to be sure.

Blake pulled in a breath and spread his hands. "You mentioned you'd found Ishaldi. The dossier I read equated it to some sort of vanished continent, similar to Atlantis. Am I right?"

Kenneth stepped up behind his wife. His hands settled on her shoulders, giving a squeeze of reassurance. "There's so much to tell." He shook his head as if baffled at how to continue.

"Start at the beginning," Blake urged. "I'd like to know everything, every last detail."

Kenneth Randall frowned stubbornly. "Just who are you, anyway?"

Blake tilted back his head, blowing out a breath. Here he was, locked in an underground hiding place with a wounded arm and some guy was demanding his credentials. Only people with something to hide got antsy when the feds came around.

"I'm Special Agent Blake Whittaker, Boston office." He attempted to keep his answer conversational and not confrontational. This was definitely not the time or the place to make enemies.

Kenneth's gaze continued to brew suspicion. "Got a badge to go with that introduction?"

Blake was more than happy to oblige. He pulled out his shiny gold shield and showed it around. "If you will look at that little notation right there—" He indicated a smaller line of print under his photo. "You will see I'm with the A51-ASD branch."

Everyone's face scrunched up. Of course nobody recognized his organization.

This was the part he hated explaining. "The A51-

ASD is a subdivision of the bureau that investigates strange or otherwise inexplicable phenomena."

Addison's face lit up. "You mean like the *X-Files*?" She clapped with delight. "Oh, my God, are you like the real life Fox Mulder? Does everybody call you *Spooky*?"

Blake scrubbed a hand across his face. "Uh, the sciences division doesn't quite work that way." He purposely didn't use the word *alien*. No reason for them to wonder if he'd gotten that shield out of a box of Cracker Jack. "Our cases are more based in science than in fiction. All I intended to do was ask you a few questions about your recovery efforts in the Mediterranean."

Kenneth's suspicious expression relaxed considerably. "That's it?"

Tessa's brow furrowed. "What kind of questions?"

Blake got down to business. The time for beating around the bush was over. "Scientists recorded undersea quake activity in the location your people were reportedly diving in. We understand your outfit had cameras and divers in the water at the time of the occurrence."

"You think we had something to do with the quake?" Kenneth asked carefully.

Blake shook his head. "Nothing of the sort. Look, this may be hard to understand, but ASD scientists have been monitoring an electromagnetic field in the area you were diving in. It's always been a low-level thing, something to be curious about but not concerned."

Kenneth swallowed tightly. "And now there's reason for concern?"

Having broken the ice, Blake tucked his badge away.

"That's just it. We're not sure what's going on. The force has suddenly shifted from emitting low levels of magnetic energy to a hell of a lot. It's playing havoc with electronics now. We can't get near it." He shrugged. "Radio, sonar, radars, nothing works. We thought the quake might have given whatever it is a little nudge."

Kenneth quickly put two and two together. "But you have no way to get down there now because electronics don't work?"

Blake nodded. "You got it. Since you had eyes and ears down there that day, we thought your equipment might have picked up something ours didn't before it all went haywire."

Tessa Randall glanced at him from across the table. She seemed a little calmer now, less agitated. "And that was all you were going to ask? It had nothing to do with Jake or"—choking up, she faltered for a moment—"the accident?"

Blake nodded again. "That's all we wanted to know." He lifted the cup he held, still half full of hot black coffee. Kenneth had used so much instant he was surprised the bottom hadn't melted away. "To tell you the truth, I didn't plan for it to take more than twenty minutes. Tops."

Frowning deeply, Gwen cleared her throat. "Looks like you're going to be staying a little longer than you anticipated."

Despite the pain in his arm, Blake couldn't help grinning. "Does this mean you'll be holding my room? Looks like I'm going to be late checking out."

Gwen blushed. "Of course," she mumbled, coughing

discreetly into the back of her hand. She looked every which way but at him.

Blake's stomach rumbled, reminding him that he hadn't eaten since last night. "Guess we're not getting breakfast, either."

Tessa started to stand. "I could make you something," she offered. "We've got provisions."

Blake waved her back down. "I'll think about my stomach later—after I find out what's going on here." He paused, pulling bits and pieces of the previous conversation out of his memory. "Now, back to Ishaldi. Am I correct in assuming you located some sort of ruins?"

Pulling up a chair, Kenneth sat down beside his wife. "Yeah, Jake was right. It did exist and we did locate some of the wreckage from an island that used to be in the area."

Blake nodded. "I see."

Closing her eyes, Gwen folded her arms protectively across her chest. "Oh, goddess," she mumbled through tight lips. "Here it comes."

Tessa slipped her hands around her cup, holding it tightly as if trying to draw warmth from the liquid inside. "It's hard to explain, but among the ruins we found some sort of a temple under the water. But it wasn't entirely submerged. It was whole—and something inside it was sealed. Jake—he thought it was some sort of tomb."

"And this tomb," Blake prompted. "Did you open it?"

Guilt flashing across her face, Tessa nodded. "We did."

Kenneth took up the story. "But it wasn't a tomb, it was some sort of—"

"Wormhole," Tessa filled in,

Kenneth nodded. "Yeah, some kind of a dimensional doorway."

Blake kept his face impassive. Since joining the A51, he'd heard his share of lunatic stories. He'd even encountered a few crazies wearing aluminum hats and talking into tin cans. He could tell the difference between those who were certifiably insane and those who were telling the absolute truth as they believed it.

Had a section of his arm not been fried to a crisp, Blake would have wondered what color Kool-Aid these people had been drinking. As it was, he doubted he'd hallucinated the injury. "And where did this portal lead?"

Kenneth and Tessa shared a look between them.

"To Ishaldi," Tessa said. "But it isn't all ruins. There is a city there, and another race of people."

Kenneth eyed Blake's injured arm. "And they aren't exactly friendly toward humans."

Blake's stomach rolled. "I think that's pretty clear."

Kenneth laced his fingers together and laid his hands on the table. "I just wish it didn't sound so insane coming out of my mouth," he answered, giving Blake a rueful smile. "Honest to God and I'm dying if I'm lying. There is a portal under the Mediterranean Sea and we accidentally opened it."

Digesting the information he had, Blake thought a moment. "I'm no scientist, but the opening of a wormhole would jibe with a sudden surge in electromagnetic activity," he ventured slowly.

Surprise colored Kenneth's face. "You say that like you believe us."

Blake nodded. "From what I've seen, I'm starting to." He leaned forward in his chair. "Can you tell me more about the other, um, people you encountered?"

Addison sighed and ran her hands through her short spiky hair. "They're called the *Mer*. That's short for mermaid."

"Like half fish, half human?"

Addison pointed at Tessa and then to Gwen. "Not quite, but it's what we are." She jerked a thumb over her shoulder like a hitchhiker. "Unfortunately it also describes those bitches outside."

That one caught him by surprise. "You're joking, right?"

Addison shook her head. "It's no joke and it's not very funny to us. For a long time the Mer have hovered on the brink of extinction. But we're here, the few of us that remain. And we've always wanted to learn where the Mer came from. We have always believed we had a homeland, somewhere, so we went looking for it."

Blake sobered. The entire picture still wasn't complete in his mind, but it was beginning to form a coherent image. "And that would be Ishaldi?"

Tessa took up the narrative. "Jake Massey was my fiancé at one time," she explained. "When he found out I was a Mer, he became obsessed with finding Ishaldi—it was going to be the discovery that made him a legend."

Blake thought back to the dossier. "I seem to recall Massey wasn't very highly regarded in the archaeological community."

"Everybody thought Jake was a nut," Addison put in. "Which means nobody believed him when he started jawing about the existence of an intelligent, nonhuman, sea-based species."

"Which would be the mermaids?"

"You got it." Tessa laughed shortly, a strained, unpleasant sound. "So tell me, how crazy do we all sound?"

Blake had to shake his head. "Uh, not too bad, actually. If I worked in any other division, I wouldn't have believed a word. In fact, I'd wonder what dope you were all were smoking and when the next spaceship was landing."

Addison eyed him. "Except you know better, don't you, Agent Whittaker? Care to share a little of what you've seen in your career?"

Blake shrugged. Since they were all in the jam together now, he had no reason not to be honest. "As an agent of the ASD, every bit of information I hold is strictly confidential."

Gwen brightened, peeking out from behind her sullen mantle. "Does that mean you won't tell anyone about us?" she asked hopefully.

Finishing his coffee, Blake set the empty container on the table. The painkiller had kicked in and his arm didn't ache so terribly bad. He no longer felt like someone had poured gasoline on his skin and set him afire. "Let me put it this way," he ventured after a thoughtful pause. "What you've told me today will be held in the strictest of confidence. My superiors aren't going to allow such sensitive information to be spread to the general public, if at all possible."

Gwen sagged weakly against the wall in relief. "Oh, thank the goddess."

"I'd have to agree," Addison said. "It probably isn't the best idea if we're identified as Mer, given the problem we've got going on outside."

Blake looked around the room. "If you're Mer and they're Mer, why are they trying to kill you?"

"It's me Queen Magaera wants," Tessa said.

Blake held up a hand, temporarily halting her narrative. A new name had popped up. "Now, who is she?"

A deep frown shadowed Tessa's face. "Queen Magaera rules the Mer people," she explained. "Those women who attacked us are her soldiers and they've been sent after me."

Blake ran his fingers through his hair. "Why?" A lot of information was coming his way, too much and too fast to make sense of. He'd soon need a scorecard to keep up with the players.

Tessa winced. "I accidentally rekeyed the sea-gate to accept only my resonance, my magnetic imprint, so to speak. Queen Magaera needs me to reopen it so she can bring the rest of her army into the world."

Kenneth pointed toward the ceiling. "Magaera's soldiers aren't going to go away until they kill us and recapture Tessa. In their society, people like you and me are slaves. Inferiors." He laughed shortly. "And those they don't put a yoke on, they slaughter."

Remembering the massacre of the skipper who'd ferried them across the bay, Blake felt every bit of sensation drain from his body. A cold trickle of sweat worked its way down his spine. The tension in the room was beginning to get to him.

The fact that the Mer are hostile toward humans changes the entire game plan.

Rather than merely being quarantined and suppressed, the Mer might have to be taken care of with more drastic action.

He didn't even want to think about what that might entail.

Pulling in a breath, Blake shot Kenneth a look. "So how many of these unfriendly Mer happened to follow you home?"

Chapter 6

Gwen sat on the lower bunk, back against the wall, feet dangling over the edge of the bed. Tessa sat beside her. Addison was stretched out on the top level, humming a nonsense tune.

Across the room, Kenneth and Blake Whittaker were futzing with the half-installed radio system.

"Lucky was the one who knew this stuff," Kenneth was saying. "He was supposed to come back this week and get it finished up."

Whittaker tried connecting a few wires. Sparks flew around his fingers. He jumped back. "I don't know what he's done here," he said as he examined the tip of his badly scorched finger. "But it's one huge mess."

Gwen rolled her eyes heavenward. Terrific. *Just another thing to go wrong.*

She doubted the list could get any longer. In the space of twenty little minutes not only had they been attacked by a cadre of killer bitches, they were also trapped in the basement with no way to summon help. Oh, and now a federal agent knew they were mermaids.

"This day can't get any worse," she grumbled.

Tessa reached over, squeezing her arm. "It's not so bad, Gwen, that people know we're Mer. We belong here just as much as anyone does."

Throat tightening, Gwen swallowed hard. "I've always been ashamed because we're different, the fish out of water."

"Spending your whole life hating what you are isn't any way to live, Gwyneth," Tessa murmured, using Gwen's full name. "A Mer is what you are, what you were born to be."

Feeling the burn of tears rise, Gwen quickly blinked. "I'm not like you, Tess. You've always pined for Ishaldi, imagining our great and glorious past. Not so glorious now, is it, to find you belong to a vicious, human-hating race?"

Tessa slowly shook her head. "Not all Mer are like Magaera and her council. There are others who believe humans and Mer can coexist in peace. Those are the ones we need to help. As Queen Nyala's descendants, we have a duty to try and restore the Tesch Dynasty to its rightful place."

Gwen snorted. "You're letting that queen stuff go to your head. It's hard to even believe we're descended from a royal dynasty."

"I'd believe it," Addison piped up from above. "Look at all the cool gems we have to prove it."

Tessa winced. "Had," she reminded. "The choker and orb were destroyed when I opened the sea-gate."

Addison peeked down over the edge of her bunk. "Those things are awesome," she said. "And it's too bad we don't have the other pieces. Didn't you say there was a scepter, Tessa? That went with Aunt Gail when she moved off the island?"

Tessa brushed her hands across her face. "Yeah, Grandma divided the pieces between her and Mom. According to Queen Magaera that scepter was the most powerful piece. It could supposedly give the user control over land and sea, though I'm not entirely sure how it works."

"Well, we haven't got it," Gwen said. "So it isn't going to do us any good."

Addison grinned. "But we've still got a *Ri'kah*."

Gwen felt the fine hairs on the back of her neck rise. Although it looked like nothing more than an elaborate armband fashioned of gold and semiprecious stones, the ornament was absolutely deadly when in the hands of a Mer skilled in the ways of Mercraft.

Without thinking, her hand rose to the pendant she wore around her neck, a simple unpolished quartz crystal. This was her soul-stone, a gift every newly born Mer female received at the time of her birth. But it was much more than a birthstone.

For a Mer, crystals had a magical property. Using crystals was one of the ways a Mer could tap into and enhance her own inner energies. Scientists called it psi-kinetics.

Gwen just called it a curse.

Tessa perked up. "Wait a minute. We're not as helpless as we think we are." She slid off the bed. "Ken—where's the Ri'kah?"

Her husband turned to answer. "I think I stored it with the tranq gun. Why?"

Tessa had no chance to explain. An explosion from outside hit the door.

SMASH!

The force striking the reinforced steel door heated the metal to the melting point. A large bulge appeared where the bolt struck it.

Everyone instantly understood Tessa's question.

Tessa jumped off the bunk. "That's why we need it, honey!" she shouted.

Addison rolled off the top bunk. "Shit! It didn't take them long to figure out where we are."

Whittaker eyed the damaged door. "I've got a feeling this isn't going to be pretty."

It was the understatement of the century.

Kenneth's eyes bugged. "That door is supposed to be made to withstand a freaking tornado."

"Tornado, yeah," Tessa shot back. "Bolts from a laser gun, no."

Whittaker leaped on her comment. "You wouldn't happen to have one of those?"

"Matter of fact, I do." Tessa looked to her husband. "Where is it?"

Kenneth hustled toward a panel built into one far wall. He unlocked it, pulling out some object that looked to be wrapped in felt and a small metallic case.

Tessa quickly unrolled the felt. She slipped her hand through a spiral of gold laced with crystals. Her fingers curled around the grip. A large clear-cut stone spanned her knuckles. She extended her arm. "Bring 'em on."

Whittaker moved in for a closer look. Bemusement crossed his face. "Is that all it is?" he asked, clearly expecting to see an elaborate example of alien technology. "A bracelet?"

Tessa shook her head. "Mers have the ability to pull the energy out of crystals and reconvert it into electrical voltage. Add a little heat and light and you've got a pretty damn effective laser."

"Piezoelectricity," Kenneth added. "And it packs one hell of a wallop."

Whittaker eyed the ornament. "Don't suppose you've got more than one?"

Tessa opened her mouth to answer but never had the chance to speak. A second blast rocked the door, followed by a third. The odor of metal burning and melting permeated the small chamber. The stench was horrific.

"They've still got us outgunned." The federal agent eyed the door. "And once that thing comes down, it's going to be a bloodbath. Caught in here, we're just sitting ducks."

Gwen slid off the bunk. Whittaker was right. They had literally boxed themselves in. "I'm not willing to sit here and wait for them to blast us." She eyed the damage to the wall and door. Solid steel and concrete were coming down around them.

Kenneth opened the small metallic case. "The only other thing we've got is the tranquilizer gun."

Whittaker claimed the pistol. "This is for taking down animals." A grunt slipped past his lips. "Don't you think bullets would have been a better idea?"

Kenneth shook his head. "The idea was to stop a person, not kill them."

"Considering they want to kill you, that's awfully generous," the fed shot back.

Kenneth indicated the row of ammunition. "I'll accept putting them into unconsciousness, not oblivion. When we were in Ishaldi, I had to kill a couple of those women. I didn't like it, and I won't do it again."

Whittaker quickly loaded the pistol, then pocketed a second clip. "That's admirable. Stupid, but admirable. I happen to prefer deadly force." He checked the sights. "These things usually work better when you're behind the animal, not in front of it while it's charging. Guess I'll have to make do."

Gwen's head came up. Did he just call the Mer animals? She hoped it was a slip of the tongue and not his actual feelings about an unfamiliar species.

She shivered. *They tried to kill him*, she reminded herself. *That doesn't exactly make us seem friendly.*

An idea occurred. "That's what we need to do. Get behind them." She looked to Tessa. "You said when you were in the undersea chamber that you'd teleported Kenneth and Jake down. Think we could do it again?"

Tessa snorted. "Sure, if you happen to have a wall-to-wall row of labradorite pillars in your back pocket there. It takes a hell of a lot of energy to move a human being."

Whittaker looked at the sisters. "You can teleport things?"

Another blast hit the door, hastening Tessa's explanation. "It was an accident. Alone, a Mer doesn't have enough energy to move more than small things from place to place. Even if we had the extra crystals to draw off, it might not be enough to make a complete jump to a new location. You could end up halfway through a wall or something."

Addison joined the fray. "What if we pooled our energy?" she suggested. "I've been practicing my Mercraft and I'm getting pretty good at hitting the mark."

"You could use me as a battery," Kenneth volunteered.

Tessa shook her head. "We're not using the *D'ema*. That almost killed you last time."

"What's D'ema?" Whittaker asked.

Gwen's jaw tightened. "It's the death magic. The human body carries many of the same minerals crystals do, and just like we can suck the energy out of crystals and convert it, we can also take it out of a person."

Whittaker quickly connected the dots. "You lose too many minerals and you die."

Gwen didn't blink. "Call it black magic, the deadlier side of our abilities."

Another blast hit. Instead of striking the steel door, it smacked the concrete around its frame, delivering a solid blow. A chunk the size of a Frisbee broke away and hit the floor. It shattered into tiny little pieces.

"We need a plan here, and quick," Whittaker warned. "If you can get me behind them, put me there. If I can knock a couple out while you keep them occupied from the front, it's the best chance we've got."

Although she'd always denied the fact, there was one thing Gwen knew about herself no one else on the face of this earth did. Her Mercraft was strong, stronger than she'd care to admit. Where her sisters had to concentrate to make a connection, she didn't. She needed only to flick an eyebrow to move an object. A snap of her fingers would destroy it.

While Tessa was capable enough, Addison was still the weak link. As the youngest, she was still searching for control over her abilities. Once she matured, Addison would surely surpass both her older sisters, easily and without question.

But her time hadn't come yet.

I'm going to have to do this, she thought. And it scared the living bejesus out of her. Not because she didn't know how to control it, but because she did.

When she was a small child, her mother had taken her aside and warned her to be careful with the gift brewing inside her. Gwen, her mother had told her, was different. She struggled with her identity and it tormented her. The Mer in her wanted to come out and wouldn't be denied.

It was a battle she fought every day of her life. The best she could do was keep a leash and a muzzle on the dark, black entity. For the most part, she succeeded.

But the Mer inside was always there, straining to break free.

Gwen had vowed never to use her power against anyone, but now she had no choice. It was a matter of life and death and their time was running out. She had to protect her kindred, no matter the cost. Given a few more heated blasts, that door would buckle like a plate-glass window hit by a semitruck.

A massacre was sure to follow.

A nervous sweat trickled down Gwen's spine, but she ignored the discomfort. Her nerves were already on edge. Overthink her plan now and she'd lose it.

"You and Addison pull from Ken," she ordered Tessa. "Then link to me. Pulling from you three, I should be able to get me and Whittaker out of the basement."

Tessa's brows rose in surprise. "Both of you?" she spluttered. "We could maybe transport one, but two—no way."

Gwen fixed her sister with a level stare. "Right now we really haven't got a lot of choices," she warned in a low voice that brooked no argument. "We'd better try it before they think of the same thing."

"It's risky, Gwen," Tessa warned. "Do you even know what you have in mind?"

Gwen stared directly into her sister's eyes. She refused to be intimidated or talked out of the notion simply because it was dangerous. If anyone was going to take the risk, she'd be the one to do it.

"Just trust me and do what I say."

It was the strangest thing Blake had ever seen in his life. He'd seen people panic in the face of an emergency, but he'd never seen them sit down.

He watched as Addison, Tessa, and Kenneth positioned themselves on the floor. Kenneth sat crosslegged, hands resting on his knees like some kind of guru. He blew out a nervous breath. "Oh, man. This isn't going to be easy."

Tessa knelt to his left. "Addison and I will carry as much as we can."

Addison settled down on his right side. "I'm not sure I can do this, Tess. I've never done D'ema before." She spoke in a slightly strained voice. The remarkable calm she'd shown in the face of the attack seemed to be wavering. "I've only taken energy out of crystals."

Tessa made a motion. "I'll pull the energy from Ken, then push to you. You double it and push to Gwen. After that, she's on her own."

Gwen nodded. "Just get me a boost. I'll do the rest."

"This might not work," Tessa warned.

"It'll work."

Though he wasn't sure what would happen, Blake hoped whatever they had in mind would come off without a hitch. That mention Addison had made about materializing inside of a wall didn't exactly sound appealing.

Think of it this way, came the whisper in the back of his mind. *You're actually getting to see an alien life force in action.*

It wasn't the most comforting thought he could have had. The only thing he knew—or thought he knew—about mermaids was that they had tails and swam. Some lore even had them singing songs so alluring that sailors would drive their ships aground.

He frowned. *And then they drown the crew.*

Blake glanced toward Gwen. Gone was the uncertainty and discomfort she'd earlier displayed. Like a businesswoman making a company decision, she'd taken control and was calling the shots. That alone intensified his attraction tenfold.

Looking at her, he felt his heart clutch behind his rib cage. She was brave, beautiful, and totally awesome.

Yet even as he admired her, his guts twisted. If Gwen and her sisters could really do what they claimed, the implications spoke volumes. No doubt the A51-ASD scientists would classify them as a level five, the most dangerous of aliens thus far encountered. Most aliens held in cold storage were classified as level three at most.

He frowned. And that was because they were deceased. Cadavers, even alien ones, usually didn't present too much of a problem.

Blake recoiled from the gruesome notion. He didn't want to think about what would happen to Gwen and her sisters once the sciences division pulled them into custody.

And they would.

Because it was his job to turn the Mer over.

Blake wiped a hand across his clammy brow. His tongue passed over papery lips. Shit. "Just do what you have to." The words slipped out before he could check them. This situation was going to get worse before it got better. He had no choice but to play it through to the end.

Gwen mistook his words of self-reproach for encouragement. "Everybody link up," she ordered.

Tessa put one hand on her husband's face. "Press your fingers to his temple, Addie," she instructed, showing her sister the correct touch.

Addison followed the instructions. "I'll try not to hurt you," she told Kenneth.

Kenneth drew a deep breath and closed his eyes.

"Been through this before." He winced. "Hurts like hell, but I'll survive."

Tessa held out her hand toward Gwen. "Your turn."

Addison offered hers. "Let's do this."

Gwen glanced over her shoulder to Whittaker. "Grab on to me and hold tight."

Shoving the tranq gun in the holster his service weapon had previously occupied, Blake moved up behind her and put his hands on her shoulders.

Gwen pressed back against him. "Hang on tight and don't let go," she breathed. "Focus your energy, girls. Push it out and let us have it."

At first Blake felt nothing.

Then it happened. A pressure pushing against his skin, like the beginning of a ferocious wind. The surface of his skin began to heat up, bringing with it a tight, prickling feeling. The sensation spread over his body like a layer of plastic cling wrap.

And then it started to burn.

Kenneth groaned. "Oh, God, that hurts . . ." His voice trailed off in a long, low moan of agony.

Although his instinct was to immediately push away from Gwen, Blake held on, forcing himself to tighten his grip on her body. A crazy mix of fear and anticipation coursed through him.

Gwen stiffened beneath his hold, writhing against him in discomfort. A cry broke from her lips. "Push harder, girls. I need more."

Another red-hot wave of heat rolled over Blake's body. Molten claws of energy latched onto his skin, clutching through his flesh to connect with bone. His heart thudded fast and hard, barreling painfully against his rib cage.

Blake's chest seized as he sucked in a lungful of air. He threw back his head to cry out, but there was no way his scream could pass through clenched teeth. A cold, damp sweat rose on his skin. The heat was beginning to turn to ice. He trembled under the onslaught of arctic sensations. For a moment he half expected his blood to freeze in his veins.

It was Gwen who cried out in a heroic push. Her cry echoed throughout the small room, crashing against the walls. A white-hot flash blasted out of nowhere, heading toward them at supersonic speed.

Blake barely had time to flinch and shut his eyes before the explosion hit. Every nerve in his body went haywire, his senses temporarily short-circuiting. The floor beneath his feet vanished.

Then everything went pitch-black.

The tumble through darkness was brief and abrupt.

Blake landed hard. Stumbling forward, he fell, landing on his hands and knees. He clenched his eyes shut and tried to block the dizzying vibrations flowing along every nerve ending. It didn't work. His stomach lurched, sending a wave of acid up his throat. He heaved, gagging as the taste of bitter coffee rolled past his lips.

Head spinning in all directions, Blake struggled to climb to his feet. His movements were clumsy, like those of a man who'd had way too much alcohol. He felt numb and strangely detached, as if every molecule in his being had been ripped into tiny little pieces. His veins throbbed beneath his skin.

Vision focusing, he searched for and found Gwen. She stood a few feet away. Hands pressed against her stomach, her face was dead white. Mouth open, she was gulping in great breaths of air.

Blake drew in a breath of head-clearing oxygen. The fuzziness lingering around the edges of his brain began to fade. "I never want to do that again," he gasped. His limbs still trembled like an aged and elderly man, but at least he could control them.

Gwen nodded, pressing her hands against her face. "I feel like I've just been run through a shredder."

A smile tugged at one corner of his mouth. That pretty much summed it up. He decided to stick to conventional transportation methods from now on.

Summoning his strength, Blake glanced around. "Wow." A low whistle broke from his throat. "We're outside."

Gwen's hands dropped. "I didn't mean to take us this far." They'd traveled at least five hundred feet, maybe more.

Struggling to regain his balance, Blake forced back the unpleasant feelings. Pushing his body past its endurance was part of an agent's training. Now was no time to crumble under the strain.

He reached for the tranq gun. "Better get back inside." He eyed Gwen. "You can stay here if you want."

Gritting her teeth, she shook her head. "No. Let's go get those bitches."

They hurried toward the house. The back door didn't exist anymore. Neither did a lot of the house. The entire bottom floor was in ruins, furniture overturned, walls blasted down to the bare frame. The hostile Mer had come through with the destructive efficiency of a tornado hitting ground. Nothing in their path was spared.

The sound of concrete crumbling issued up from the basement. A woman's scream of pain tore through the air.

Without considering any real plan for his actions, Blake whipped down the stairs with Gwen nipping at his heels. The basement was narrow, poorly lit.

Gun at the ready, he skidded to a halt, searching the scene. *Holy shit!* Part of the rear wall was gone, door and all.

One of the strangely dressed Mer lay amid the rubble. Her body was contorted and it took Blake a second to realize she'd literally been cut in half. Tessa had a Ri'kah and she'd used it with cold efficiency.

It hadn't been enough, though.

The safe room had been invaded.

Blake caught a glimpse inside the chaos.

Tessa struggled between two of the Mer holding her, whipping back and forth in an attempt to keep them from subduing her. Curses and threats punctuated her efforts.

Blake had to give her credit. She was doing a stellar job of giving her captors hell.

He eased a little closer.

Kenneth lay nearby. Whether he was unconscious or dead, Blake couldn't tell for sure.

Addison had the worst of it. Back against the wall, her hands were raised in a futile attempt to ward off the death strike one of the hostile Mers was preparing to deliver. At that distance there was no way her would-be assassin could miss her target. She raised her Ri'kah and prepared to deliver the fatal strike.

"Don't touch my sister, you bitch!" Gwen shrieked.

Addison's assailant whirled on her heel. She leveled her weapon, preparing to take down the new threat. She fired, unleashing a bolt of pure energy.

Blake simultaneously raised his weapon. Puny as it was, it was all he had. *Oh, fuck me!* It wasn't enough.

He stood right in the path of the oncoming discharge. No way the Mer could miss him, either. He didn't have a chance of succeeding, but he had to take it anyway.

A series of strange words flowing from her mouth, Gwen lunged forward and threw up her hands. A shimmering wall of light appeared out of nowhere. The laser-like flare struck dead-on. Blinking out of existence, it vanished with a weak fizz.

Seizing his chance, Blake fired again and again. Aimed with expert precision, the darts struck their target with a deadening *thunk-thunk* sound.

The Mer holding Addison hostage reeled, collapsing to the floor like an anchor cut from its ballasts.

Freed from the threat of being wasted, Addison launched herself toward Tessa's captors. She tackled the nearest woman, knocking her to the ground with a full-body blow. Fists flying like hammers, Addison went to town. The pummeling commenced with vicious intent.

Gwen's hands suddenly dropped, taking with it the glimmering shield of protection she'd provided. The last of her energy spent, she sagged to the ground. Weakened from giving her all, she didn't look like she had the strength to fight off a determined kitten. "I haven't got any more," she breathed, pressing a hand against her forehead. "You're on your own."

Blake cursed under his breath. "Shit." It was one-on-one now, and he clearly didn't have the advantage. His palms started to sweat, forcing him to tighten his hold on the tranq gun.

The last Mer standing snarled, an inhuman predator that wouldn't be easily subdued. The insult she hurled toward them was an unintelligible jumble to his ears. Though he couldn't understand her words, he easily picked up their meaning. She reached for the blade sheathed at her hip. The serrated edge looked wickedly sharp. Her gaze never deviated from his.

Blake had no doubts about her objective. The bitch wasn't going without a fight.

Levering a fresh clip into the tranq pistol, Blake couldn't help smiling. "Sorry, babe . . . You should know better than to bring a knife to a gunfight." His index finger squeezed the trigger. Once, twice, three times.

Every single dart halted in midair. The Mer waved them aside as if brushing away pesky flies. They dropped harmlessly to the floor around her feet.

Blake blinked stupidly. Apparently Gwen wasn't the only one with a few tricks up her sleeve.

He cursed and braced himself for the attack. The tranq gun was useless, offering no more defense than a toy cap pistol. Still, it was something in his hand and better than nothing at all.

Apprehension coursed through him. His pulse throbbed in his ears, a dull roar that muted everything except the danger looming in front of him. His assailant was an Amazon, brawny and well muscled. Years, a whole lot of years, had passed since he'd last fought hand to hand. He'd better damn well remember some moves or he'd get his ass kicked all over the place.

No doubt there.

The rogue Mer raised her wicked blade. Her lips drew back into a feral smile.

Suddenly Tessa snatched a nearby folding chair and swung it with every last ounce of strength she possessed. The flat seat of the chair connected squarely with the back of the Mer's head. A sickening crack followed the strike, which sounded much like a champion baseball player hitting a home run.

The Mer stumbled forward, striking the floor in a dead heap. Fingers losing their grip, her weapon clattered harmlessly against the concrete. She lay still and silent.

Just like that, the attack was over.

Everyone froze a few minutes, shocked by the sudden lack of frenzied action.

The silence was deafening.

Panting hard, Tessa was the first to move. The metal chair slipped from her fingers. A half-choked sob broke from her throat. Crying softly, she stumbled toward her unconscious husband. "Ken," she wailed, dropping to her knees and taking his face in her hands. Tears slipped down her cheeks. "Kenneth, babe, are you all right?"

Blake lowered the air gun. "Shit." He moistened his lips and took a steadying breath. The basement looked like a war zone, blasted and in ruins.

Addison struggled to her feet. Her clothes were ripped and covered with blood. The woman she'd attacked didn't move, not even to breathe.

Nerves going taut, Blake wondered if she was alive. He hoped not. It didn't bother him one bit if a terrorist died.

Addison wiped trembling hands across her face. "Is it over?" she asked, voice trembling as hard as her body.

Blake tossed the tranq pistol aside. "Pretty much."

"Everyone still here?" Before she'd even finished the question, Addison's eyes widened with alarm. "Gwen's down—"

Blake's heart almost stopped in his chest. Gwen's face was a pale, deathly white.

He hurried toward her, lifting her into his arms and pulling her close. He brushed his fingertips across her pale forehead, smoothing away strands of damp, clinging hair. Her flesh was ice cold.

Without opening her eyes, Gwen moaned. Her body trembled with the chill consuming her.

Blake pressed two fingers against her throat, checking her pulse. Her heartbeat was weak, almost nonexistent. "Gwen," he whispered, emotion unexpectedly tightening his throat. "It's Whittaker. I've got you, sweetheart. You'll be okay."

He held his breath, ears straining for any sound from her. *Let her be okay, please God*, he silently prayed.

Barely able to respond, Gwen cracked her lids. Her gaze was dull, laced with exhaustion. "Promise?" Her voice was little more than a weak rasp. The single word was so faint he barely heard it. Thick black lashes lowered against her bloodless cheeks. There was no spark, no animation. She was as limp as a rag doll.

Blake's inner reserve crumbled. He pulled her closer, trying to warm her body with his. He was cold to the marrow of his bones and couldn't offer much. "I promise."

Even as he uttered the words, guilt sliced through him. He wasn't supposed to care, but somehow he'd gotten sucked into a vortex of events he still couldn't even begin to comprehend. As much as he wanted to protect her, deep down inside he doubted he could keep the pledge. Though Gwen didn't know it yet, her life would never be the same once the agency found out about them.

Neither will mine, came his grim thought.

Chapter 7

The morning no longer felt crisp, bright, or promising. There was trouble on Little Mer island. Big trouble.

Jake Massey lowered his binoculars. "Shit! We've just been fucked." He shook his head. *And we didn't even get a kiss for it.*

He didn't have to be on the island to know Magaera's soldiers had botched the attempt to take Tessa hostage. They'd apparently failed, and magnificently so.

A swarm of boats and aircraft buzzed in from the mainland, some identifiable, others not so much. A small army went into motion, spreading across the landscape like the plague. A coast guard cruiser swept in from nowhere, circling the perimeter of the island like a shark looking for prey.

The thing that bothered him most was the helicopters. A couple were clearly medical craft, used to transport the critically injured. No doubt people had been wounded and needed to be airlifted to the mainland. That made sense.

But those weren't the only choppers in sight. Two larger helicopters had also landed. Painted stark black, these had no identifiable markings whatsoever. Though not military, there was no doubt in his mind who owned the aircraft.

Sweat popped up across his brow in tiny beads. He wiped them away. This wasn't how he'd imagined the morning would end. "Damn, they got there fast," he breathed. *But how?*

The question nagged like a pesky fly. What the hell were the feds doing on Little Mer Island? Their response had been too immediate to be coincidence, which meant the place must have been under active surveillance.

Are they looking for me?

Whatever the answer might be, one thing was perfectly clear. They needed to leave these waters. And quickly. No reason to tempt the authorities into coming closer. The yacht was flying a Canadian flag. Though he and Niklos had valid passports, the Mer women living aboard the boat did not.

Fury boiled up inside him, but he forced it to simmer. No time to lose his head. Blowing his temper wouldn't do any good now. They'd only had this single chance, and it was gone. It didn't matter who had messed up or why.

Standing beside him, Niklos Sarantos laughed softly. "Didn't go as smoothly as you thought it would."

Jake shot his partner a dirty look. "We've hit a little snag. Doesn't mean we're down yet."

Time to switch to the backup. Trouble was he didn't know what plan B might be. He hadn't believed Magaera's soldiers could fail in such a simple task. There was no way anyone on the island could have known they were coming. No one would have expected an ambush in broad daylight.

As it stood, the entire island was enveloped in chaos.

A flurry of movement snagged Jake's attention and he refocused his binoculars to check out the action. He couldn't miss the men whose jackets were clearly marked FBI. "I knew it," he said angrily. "The fucking feds."

Niklos also raised his specs. "Correct me if I am wrong, my friend, but it looks like they've got a couple of your queen's soldiers," he remarked coolly.

Jaw tightening, Jake's heartbeat sped up. For ten, maybe twenty seconds, he couldn't move. His body felt paralyzed by what he was witnessing. His own arrogance hadn't allowed him to consider the consequences of failure.

His gaze zeroed in on the main house. The entire building was smoking, practically in ruins.

The women Magaera had sent to retrieve Tessa weren't walking on their own two legs. They appeared to be strapped to gurneys, which were quickly being loaded into the medic choppers. The next gurney that came out carried Kenneth Randall, clearly as unconscious as the Mer who'd preceded him. Tessa ran beside the medics, trying to keep up. Another came out carrying a woman. He recognized Gwen. Addison and a man he couldn't identify followed as she was loaded onto one of the choppers.

He swallowed hard, forcing down regret. Man, too bad Gwen seemed to have gotten caught in the crossfire. He wondered how badly she and Kenneth might be wounded.

The last gurney that came out held a body in a bag.

Since he'd identified the survivors, he knew one of the Mer hadn't made it.

Jake inwardly braced himself to keep his feelings in check. He'd also seen Lucky get the blast. That was really too bad. He'd always liked the old sea dog. But Magaera had only ordered her soldiers to take Tessa alive. The rest were to be sacrificed, incidentals in the larger objective, which was to regain control over the sea-gate. If people had to die, then so be it.

"What are we going to do now?" Niklos asked. Nervous sweat beaded his upper lip. Involved in a lot of under-the-table dealings, he wasn't exactly comfortable when the law was around.

Jerking his gaze away from the chaos, Jake tapped his binoculars with the tips of his fingers. "This just upped the ante. Now that the feds are involved, there's no doubt they'll find out about Ishaldi and the Mer." That was something he hadn't planned to have happen until after he and Magaera had regained control of the sea-gate.

Tessa had just slipped between their fingers like water through a sieve.

Returning to Ishaldi was out of the question.

Jake considered the options. At this point, everyone believed he was dead. That was a blessing. He still needed the cloak being deceased offered in order to get around undetected. But there was no telling how long his new identity would serve him.

He doubted it would serve the Mer. He was certain the government wouldn't release the discovery of an inhuman species to the general public, but they'd no doubt be combing the waters around the bay and in the Mediterranean for more Mer.

The one place they wouldn't look for a sea creature was on land.

"Get us out of here before the coast guard starts sniffing around," he ordered Niklos. There was nothing he could do but take the failure and move on.

"Where are we headed?" his friend drawled. The Mer didn't really interest him as much as the lure of easy money did. He expected to be compensated handsomely for his services.

Raising a hand to shield his eyes against the glaring light of the sun, Jake considered. "Let's cruise back up toward Canada and hit Grand Manan. We can drop anchor there and take a little time to let this disaster cool. We'll be out of American waters, but close enough to cross back into the States if we need to."

Niklos gave a quick thumbs-up. "I will make it so." He shuddered. "The sooner we get out of here, the less chance we have of being boarded by the authorities. We're drifting too close as it is."

"You worry about getting us out of here," Jake said. "I'll figure out what to do next."

A grim smile wavered around Niklos's mouth. "Your queen is not going to like the news you've got to deliver."

Jake glanced toward the entry to the suites belowdecks. Magaera had retreated from the blazing morning sun to rest and recenter her strength. In her mind her soldiers could not—and would not fail.

She's in for a rude awakening.

Without waiting for an answer to his knock, Jake slipped into Queen Magaera's private quarters. He glanced around the salon, taking in the fifty-two-inch widescreen, tricked-out stereo system, not to mention the king-sized bed-and-bath combination. Her soldiers occupied two smaller rooms down the hall, bunking together in cramped quarters. He'd spent a lot of money to keep her comfortable. Though hardly a palace, the yacht provided a lot of luxury. Still, the money he'd squirreled away wasn't going to last forever. Not at this rate.

Dressed in nary a stitch of clothing, the reigning queen of the Mer sat cross-legged amid a pile of soft cushions. Her hands rested on her knees, palms up. Bronze braziers filled with a variety of small crystals were positioned around her. Her eyes were closed.

Jake had to struggle not to stare. It was almost impossible not to look at her. An involuntary shudder rippled through him. To look upon her was to look at perfection.

And he'd love to have a taste of it.

The tips of Magaera's fingers twitched. She did not open her eyes. "You dare disturb my meditations?"

Jake offered a quick and reverent bow. Magaera expected it from all her subjects. "I have news." It took every bit of nerve he possessed to keep his tone neutral.

Magaera angled her chin. "My soldiers, have they returned?"

Even though she couldn't see him, Jake shook his head.

"No, my lady. The news I bear is not what you might have expected."

Magaera opened her eyes and jerked her gaze toward his face. "What?" Her blue gaze was as intense as a sun gone nova. She seemed not to notice or care she was utterly exposed to his eyes. In her world the Mer accepted their bodies and were comfortable with nudity.

Jake's lips felt strangely numb. He'd witnessed what happened to people who had incurred her wrath. If Magaera wished to twist him into a thousand tiny little pieces, all she had to do was think about it.

Straightening his spine, he cleared his throat. "Your soldiers have failed to take Tessa."

Magaera's countenance immediately lost its tranquil composure. Her eyes narrowed into threatening slits. "Impossible!" She snorted with displeasure. "Send them to me!" The crystals surrounding her snapped and crackled, turning as dark and black as coal. Their energy was being sucked up, consumed by a hungry predator.

Jake shook his head. "I can't do that."

Reenergized, she frowned. "Why not?" Her tone was brittle with irritation.

"They have been taken hostage by the humans." He proceeded to explain the debacle as he'd witnessed it.

Anger flickered across Magaera's face. "How can that be?"

Jake forced himself not to flinch. "I don't know. But if Tessa can somehow persuade them to let her return to Ishaldi, she might attempt to rally the support of those who do not support your command of the Mer people. If she gets to the rebels, to the members who seek to restore the Tesch Dynasty to the throne—there is a chance she could seize command."

Magaera twitched her shoulders; her loose hair moved smoothly against them. She tossed it back with an impatient hand. "The Mer will never accept peace with the humans," she snapped. "We must have a care, though." Her eyes narrowed in thought. "Our position in your world is still unstable, at best. We must regain control."

Jake spread his hands. "I've been thinking on that."

Surprise brought her up cold. "Oh?"

Jake ambled a little closer to where she sat. "Back in Ishaldi you mentioned there was a piece missing from the Jewels of Atargatis."

Magaera toyed with the pendant hanging around her neck. "You speak of the scepter?"

Jake absently regarded the drained crystals. Touch them now and they'd disintegrate, nothing left of them but ash. Long ago the Mer had learned how to sustain their physical selves by feeding their bodies with energy contained within crystals. Unfortunately the practice had a devastating consequence on their world.

Ishaldi was dying.

The survival of Magaera's people was at stake. She would listen to him because she had no other choice. "Yes. Didn't you once say it was the most valuable piece?"

A frown pleated her brow, as if she questioned his motive for making the inquiry. But someone had to blink first in the showdown.

Her mask of determined indifference slipped out of place for a moment. "Yes," she finally admitted.

Jake had to keep prodding, a careful but insistent bit of maneuvering. A fast thinker, he'd always had a knack for turning things around to his benefit. "What does this piece do, exactly? Why is it so important?"

Her suspicious expression tightened. "It gives the bearer control over land and sea. With the scepter in hand, a queen becomes a goddess."

"And if you had such empowerment at hand, would you know how to use it?"

Magaera stiffened with offense. "Of course I would!" she snapped, clamping her jaw into a steely ridge. "Were it in my hand now, I would grind your people under my heel."

Jake smiled inwardly. More than Magaera's beauty, what intrigued him most about her was that she held nothing back. She had a spine of steel and would not hesitate to take down anyone who might stand in her path.

He gave her another careful nudge. "What if I told you I could put it in your hands?"

Clenching her hands into fists, Magaera's gaze sharpened. "Do not tease me with false promises," she warned. "If you know its location on this earth, tell me now."

The wheels in Jake's mind were turning a mile a minute. It was a parry and thrust, each of them determined to keep the upper hand. It helped that he had the home-world advantage. Better yet, he believed he had the craftier mind.

"I know Tessa doesn't have the piece," he admitted,

puckering his lips thoughtfully. "But I know how to find out."

Comprehension dawned across her face. "If you could indeed deliver to me the Scepter of Atargatis, I would reward you well." She arched a brow. "Very well."

Suddenly docile, Magaera rose to her feet. It was difficult not to stare as she undulated toward him, her tall, sleek body radiating female heat. The air around her stirred as she walked, shimmering with electrical sparks that she alone seemed to generate.

Standing before him, she tilted her chin up. Her hair spilled over her shoulders like liquid gold, highlighting the porcelain whiteness of her skin. Though she might have been over seven centuries in age, she showed barely any hint of her true measure of years. Her breasts were firm and round, her belly tautly ridged with muscle. Her nipples were hard little beads, surrounded by flesh that was soft, supple, and lush with promise. The shadowed cleft between her thighs enticed.

Her hand rose, palm pressing to his cheek. She regarded him from beneath a sweep of thick lashes. "I have always found you to be a most pleasing human," she murmured. "It would be fitting for a queen to have a consort, a prince worthy of standing at her side and not behind."

Jake considered her words. Though alien to his world, Magaera wasn't a stupid woman. Of the eight Mer who had accompanied her, only four remained. Her pool of guardians was effectively halved, and Tessa had been snatched out of her reach by a foe she didn't fully understand. She needed more than a human ambassador.

She needed an alliance with a strong man who shared her goal of returning the Mer to their rightful place on earth.

Raw aggressive ambition moved her.

Check.

And mate, he thought.

Despite their recent defeat, reckless exhilaration sped through his veins. This might work out even better than he'd hoped. In the back of his mind, though, he had no intention of assuming the lowly position of a mere Mer prince.

No, not by a long shot.

His mind schemed, hatching the plot that would put the power of a goddess under his control. By the time he got through with his manipulations, Jake was determined he would be a king.

Jake's mouth curved upward. *As for Magaera . . .*

It would be an insult to refuse her.

And Jake Massey wasn't exactly known for his resistance to a beautiful, naked female.

Especially one he could use.

His ego swelled even as his body heated. The tingle of desire laced with ambition burned all the way through his belly and into his groin. The bold image of two naked bodies writhing together in ecstasy filled his mind. Her moist red lips were but a breath away, easy to conquer if he so desired.

Jake molded his hand around the aching tautness of her left breast. "I am honored you have chosen me," he murmured, brushing his thumb across the tip of her erect nipple. "I will do my best to serve you well."

A tiny gasp of pleasure rolled past the Mer queen's lips. Her gaze locked with his. "Do not tell me," she urged, reaching up to thread her arms around his neck. "Show me."

Saying no more, Jake drew her forward. His hands skimmed the gleaming litheness of her body. He understood lust. Had countless times succumbed to its throes.

But the magnetic pull between the Mer queen and him was of a different caliber. Something vastly more threatening, suffocating. Something that, no matter how many times he satisfied his needs with her, it would never be enough.

An inexplicable gut feeling that they were already connected tormented him, ate away at his denial like a ravenous demon determined to have its insatiable fill. She was a beautiful woman, but no more so than the countless beauties he'd taken throughout his life. He couldn't recall ever hesitating to bed them and then leave them when circumstances shifted.

What made Magaera different? Or had *he* in some way changed?

Did it matter? It seemed they were destined to be together, and that was enough.

For now.

Jake's mouth swept forcefully, possessively over hers, his tongue delving boldly, hungrily for the sweet reward he'd so eagerly plunder.

Magaera's submission.

Chapter 8

Trapped in a brain harried by fever and a body strained by exhaustion, Gwen spent a restless night tossing and thrashing. Drifting in and out of consciousness, she was vaguely aware her body ached, throbbing from head to toe. Nausea took her over, even as a series of convulsions twisted and pulled at her limbs.

Before pain and numbness overtook her completely, a flash of absolute clarity warned that great danger was about to befall her. The sense of foreboding grew, haunting the edges of her mind with every passing hour.

Gradually, the gloom and shadows enveloping her mind receded, clarifying into figures and shapes. The world began to take on substance.

Gwen cracked open burning eyes. The first thing she knew was that she wasn't home, in her own bed. The soft hum of the unfamiliar objects positioned around her clarified as recognition drifted through her fuzzy brain.

A hospital, came her vague thought. *Why am I . . . ?*

A large void filled her mind. She couldn't remember.

She lifted a hand, intending to wipe away the crust blurring her vision. Except her hand wouldn't move. Not an inch.

Panicked by her paralysis, Gwen lifted her head off the pillow. She blinked hard, trying to focus. Her searching gaze found and focused on the soft leather strap wound around her wrist.

Her head twisted in the opposite direction. Her other hand was also similarly restrained. An IV drip had been inserted, the cannula pushed deep under her skin and taped in place. Her slim white arms were marbled and mottled with huge black bruises.

The terror of waking up and finding herself restrained surged through her.

A hot and sudden rush of tears stung at her eyes. Still unsure about what had happened to her, an anguished sob tore from her lips. "No!" She twisted against the restraints, determined to free herself.

A figure rushed forward. Strong hands clasped her shoulders, urging her to lay back. "Gwen!" A familiar voice filtered through her frenzy. "It's Addie. Settle down before you hurt yourself."

Something in Addison's calm authority grabbed on to her sanity, dragging her back from the abyss of panic. "Take a deep breath," she heard her sister say. "Just lie back and relax. It's going to be all right."

Gwen forced herself to follow Addison's command. If Addison was here, then things must be okay.

Breath rasping over dry, cracked lips, Gwen let herself go limp. For a moment she struggled to gather her wits, find the ability to speak instead of scream like a madwoman.

"Where am I?" Her voice rasped against her ears, a strangely unfamiliar croak. Nevertheless she understood the words. She sounded coherent.

Still holding her down, Addison bent close. Fear brimmed in her eyes. "You're in the hospital, Gwen." She spoke slowly and clearly. "You collapsed and then went into convulsions." A relieved smile flitted across her mouth. "For a while we thought we were going to lose you."

Trying to swallow, Gwen gagged. Her tongue felt like it had been duct taped to the roof of her mouth. "How long . . . ?" she mumbled.

Sensing her discomfort, Addison reached for the plastic carafe on a nearby bed table. She filled a small plastic cup with water, then added a straw. "You lost a whole day and a half." She guided the drink to Gwen's lips. "It's Sunday now, already past two."

Gwen sucked, grateful for the icy water strengthening her depleted system. It tasted like the nectar of the gods, cooling and strengthening her feverish body. She drank every last drop. A single worry coalesced in her mind as her thoughts clarified.

"I can't be here," she mumbled as Addison refilled the cup. "I've got to go to work."

A shadow passed across Addison's face. She pursed her lips. "It's all right." The silence hanging between them stretched on a moment too long. "Tessa's talked to Brenda and she's got it under control. She understands you might be away a while."

Gwen shook her head. "Brenda can't handle it now. She's on maternity leave, for heaven's sake. That's why I've been stretched to the max—I'm already covering for her."

Addison forced a grin, showing perfect white teeth. "She's bringing the kidlet to work with her for the interim. And she's hired a temp clerk to give you both some breathing space. She understands you need time to recover." Her easy smile belied the distress simmering beneath her calm manner.

Gwen pulled against the restraints holding her. "I'm fine, damn it. Get these things off of me and I'll be out of this bed in ten minutes." She twisted her wrists against the soft leather. "Why am I even wearing these things?"

Addison's grin vanished. "The convulsions," she reminded quietly. "The doctors were afraid you'd pull out the IV and injure yourself. It was nothing more than a security measure to keep you from harming yourself."

Gwen's brows shot up. "Harming myself?" she snapped. "You make it sound like I was trying to commit suicide or something."

Addison sighed. Pulling up a chair, she sat down. Her hand slipped into Gwen's. Her face was pale, taut. Dark circles hung beneath eyes dulled from exhaustion. "I don't want to alarm you," she began slowly. "But you went a little crazy on us. For some reason—and don't ask me to explain how—your, ah, Mercraft went haywire."

Gwen shut her eyes against the involuntary tremble shaking her to the bone. "Oh, no," she gasped. "What happened?"

Despite her question, she had a pretty good idea what

Addison's answer would entail. She was already aware her Mercraft was active when she slept.

At first she'd attributed the disturbances to her own distracted nature. Was it all that strange that glasses and car keys occasionally got lost? Her concentration was on the hotel, so she'd rationalized the misplacement of those things as stress. She'd tried getting more rest, drinking less caffeine, exercising more.

But instead of getting better, the disturbances had intensified.

And then they'd become destructive.

Through the last few months, she'd often awaken to find magazines had been ripped apart, potted plants had been tipped and mangled, and clothing shredded. Worse than that, though, was the writing that had begun to appear.

There were only two words: *I need.*

Whether written in lipstick across her bathroom mirror or scribbled by a pen dancing across paper with no hand to guide it, the message was always the same.

There was only one problem.

Gwen didn't know what she needed. It appeared her unconscious mind was trying to converse with its conscious side, but the two never could seem to make a connection. Her Mercraft had become the method of communication.

The events, which were more than a little unsettling, left her confused, frightened, and nervous. The paranormal activity had gotten really crazy after she'd broken up with her boyfriend. It was just as well. After a year of dating, Caden was eager to take their relationship to the next level. Though they'd fooled around, done a lot of heavy petting, Gwen had never been comfortable enough to move to the next stage. Even though they were practically living together, she'd always held him off, citing the need to wait until after they were married to have sex.

So Caden had done what came naturally.

He'd proposed.

And Gwen had freaked.

Then she'd said no.

And that was that. Relationship over.

Although it had been simmering in her mind to share the problem with Tessa and Addison, she'd held back. Both of her sisters wanted her to embrace her Mer side. But that was exactly what Gwen didn't want to do. So she'd kept quiet and suffered.

She could only hope no one else had.

Addison tightened her grip on Gwen's hand. Her hold was almost painful. "You, ah, well, you pushed a couple of the EMTs who were trying to help you."

Attempting to clear away the cobwebs of distracting thoughts, Gwen blinked. "I was kind of out of it," she started to say. "Maybe I just didn't realize—"

Frowning deeply, Addison cut her off. "You were unconscious, Gwen. Stone-cold unconscious. But when the techs tried to help you, they went flying." She made a flinging motion with her free hand. "And I do mean with the greatest of ease. Nobody could get near you but me and Tessa. It took all we had to calm you down and get you under control."

The silence that followed settled like a smothering cloak in the stark, white hospital room.

A wave of regret washed through Gwen's mind, covering her in a cold chill. Her instinct was to reach for her soul-stone, but her hands were still tied down. "Oh, goddess," she groaned, her words heavy with lament. Her grip on Addison's hand tightened. "Please, please tell me I didn't hurt anyone."

Addison winced but didn't pull her hand away. "They took some really hard knocks, but they'll be okay," she finally said. "I'm just hoping you'll be all right. We've got some trouble now, and you're going to have to be strong."

That didn't sound good. Not at all.

"What kind of trouble?"

Addison had no time to answer.

A man clad in a white coat stepped briskly into the room. He was spike thin with a gaunt face and a shock of white hair; his pale skin was pitted with the scars of teenage acne. A thin scraggly beard was the best he could cultivate. Chart in hand, he wore a stethoscope draped around his neck. "Oh, she's awake." He offered a smile that might have passed for pleasant had his teeth not been badly stained with tobacco. Ditto his fingers. "Good."

Addison turned. A look of disapproval flitted across her face, but she quickly squelched it. "Hi, Dr. Sterling," she greeted.

Checking his chart, Sterling pulled out a pen as he walked over to the bed. "How are you today, Gwen?" He didn't smile. He didn't look up. He kept his attention focused on his chart.

Gwen stiffened. She didn't know this man, and didn't

like him on sight. He looked like some kind of mad scientist. She almost expected him to point at her and cackle, "It's alive, it's alive!"

Although Gwen didn't care for his looks, maybe this man had the power to get those binds undone. "I'm fine, thank you very much." Her words were simply spoken, polite, and nonthreatening.

Sterling continued to scribble. "Good, good." Hooking the chart at the edge of her bed, he stepped past Addison. He performed a brief examination with an air of detached professionalism, including checking her pupils with a small flashlight, taking her pulse, and listening to her heartbeat.

As she endured his clammy touch in silence, a flush crept up Gwen's cheeks. She didn't like strange men putting their hands on her, but she had no choice.

She cleared her throat. "Everything okay?"

Sterling snapped his stethoscope off his ears, letting the instrument settle around his neck. "Seems normal from what I can tell." A chuckle escaped him. "Though I'm not sure what's normal for a mermaid."

Gwen's mouth dropped with shock. Lips trembling, her fists curled into tight knots. She unconsciously strained against the straps holding her. "A m-mermer..." The entire word refused to come out. She couldn't say it to save her life. The leather began to stiffen, blacken. No one would hold her where she didn't want to be. She'd burn these damn things away.

And then I'll leave.

Dr. Sterling's eyes bugged with alarm. "Oh, shit." He leaped back from the bed with a leap that would have done any Olympic sprinter proud. Brow furrowing with alarm, he quickly made the sign of a cross. "God in heaven . . ." he murmured.

Jumping to her feet, Addison placed her hands on Gwen's shoulders, delivering a hard, teeth-clattering shake. "Get it under control."

Straining, Gwen responded to the fear in Addison's voice. A second later it was gone. The straps held.

Hardly realizing what she'd done, Gwen collapsed against the mattress. The energy had just come, without warning or even the knowledge of her conscious mind. She'd felt threatened and it had responded by rising to her defense.

Her tongue passed across dry lips. "How do they know?"

Shoulders sagging, Addison collapsed back in her chair. "No use trying to hide it anymore." She pressed her hands against her face and rubbed her skin hard. "The Mer have come out of the closet."

Gwen's heart lurched against her breastbone. Just as it seemed her senses were recovering from the shock of her recent trauma, another blow sent her reeling.

"They?"

And then it all came rushing back.

A flood of repressed memories suddenly swamped her mind. She was dragged backward by the current of recollection, revisiting the void of thundering sounds and roiling action. She remembered her annoyance at Agent Whittaker's arrival. At the time she'd believed he had no business poking around in her family's business. Nevertheless she'd agreed to take him to Little Mer. She remembered their arrival, how he'd pissed her off with comments he had no business making. She remembered stomping off, heading toward the main house. And then . . .

All hell broke loose.

Gwen blinked, looking from face to face as if she didn't recognize them. No, no. Surely this couldn't be happening. It wasn't fair. It wasn't right.

A knot of fear leaped into her throat, threatening to strangle her. Her blood continued to pound behind her temples, and her eyes stung with unbidden tears. "I just want to go home," she whispered, as forlorn and brokenly as a lost child.

Addison shook her head as she leaned forward to deliver a hug. "We can't," she murmured. "They won't let us."

Blake Whittaker was not a happy man. In fact he was a very pissed-off man.

He wished he'd listened to his gut when he'd pulled into Port Rock. He'd known going back to his hometown hadn't been a good idea, but he'd done it anyway. All with the intention of being a good soldier and doing his job.

As if he hadn't understood what his boss had just told him, Blake repeated his question. "What the hell do you mean I'm being transferred into lockup?" The fact that two military MPs were guarding the door behind him didn't make him feel any better. Both men were well armed and ready to act at the slightest provocation. The idea of guards watching his back skeeved him out. He didn't like it one bit. He hadn't done anything wrong. And what was up with the military guards, anyway? He's have thought his people had jurisdiction on this one. Apparently he'd thought wrong.

Assistant Director Frances Fletcher adjusted the thick black frames settled across her face. "You heard me," she snapped crisply. "Your security clearance has just been elevated to all access."

Blake wasn't getting it. "What does that even mean?" he snapped. "Sounds like a bunch of bullshit to me."

Fletcher laced her fingers over the paperwork Blake had so painstakingly spent the last day and a half putting together. "It means that you're promoted." Her tone was flat and droll. "Effective immediately."

Blowing out a frustrated breath, Blake eyed the thick file Fletcher hovered over like a hawk clutching prey in its talons. He'd already been debriefed, not once or even twice, but three times. Each time he'd stuck to his story, reiterating the events as he'd personally experienced them. As incredible as it might have seemed, every word he'd recounted was true and correct to the best of his knowledge.

More incredible was that those working within the structure of the A51-ASD believed him. Absolutely and without question. After all, Special Agent Whittaker had just stumbled onto something every damn one of them hoped to find through their careers, but few rarely did.

An honest-to-God alien life form. One that was not only alive but very violently kicking up one hell of a fit.

Blake narrowed his eyes. "And just how is being confined on site a promotion?" he asked in a voice more than a little caustic. "Sounds like I'm the one who'll be in the lockup, not the, ah, hostiles who attacked us."

He preferred using that term instead of *aliens*.

Fletcher sighed and slipped off her glasses before pinching the bridge of her nose. Like him, she hadn't gotten a moment's sleep. Too much was happening too fast and the agency was scrambling to handle the crisis that had arisen on Little Mer Island. "You know the procedure, Blake." She sighed. "Any agent who makes actual alien contact is subject to be confined on site until said alien is effectively controlled. Your specific role will be to act as the main contact between the aliens and the agency as we attempt to communicate with them."

Blake couldn't stop himself from rolling his eyes. Oh, for Christ's sake. "If you want to communicate with them, just open your fucking mouth and talk," he answered tartly. "They can understand you and answer for themselves."

Fletcher's hand dropped. "It doesn't work that way, and you know it."

Damn. He tried another tactic.

"I can't put in that much time," he protested. "I get my kid this weekend. How do I tell Debra I've got to blow off my visitation for, oh, maybe years?"

Fletcher put her glasses back on. The heavy frames did her thin face no favors. "It's policy, Blake."

Blake slammed his hand down on her desk. "It's screwed!" he shot back. "Just because I work for the agency doesn't mean it should consume every hour of my life."

Fletcher inhaled a sharp breath.

One of the MPs stepped forward, ready for action.

Fletcher waved him back. "Stand down."

The guard resumed his watch.

Fletcher's gaze shifted back to Blake. At sixty-plus, she was still one tough old bird, a woman who'd fought her way up the chain of command with an intelligence and cunning most of her male colleagues couldn't even begin to match.

"You knew what you were signing up for when you agreed to uphold the policies of the sciences division," she reminded. "What we do here has a higher level of importance than even the Department of Homeland Security. Any agent working in this division can't be a weak link. You should be used to it, too. On-base confinement is a regular occurrence in the military."

Blake frowned. "I'm not in the army anymore."

"You were, Blake. And it is part of the reason why we recruited you. Because you understand the chain of command and how to follow orders. That, and your particular—ah, how shall I say it—emotional detachment."

Blake gritted his teeth. Yeah, yeah. He already knew that he had an ability to distance himself from emotional occurrences and still keep functioning. A lot of people in high-risk jobs did it every day.

He was trying to change that side of himself. Desperately. "Tell that to my son," he snapped. "I may know the rules, but Trevor doesn't. How the hell can I explain to him I won't be seeing him for God knows how long?"

Fletcher offered a conciliatory smile. "Just live with it for a while. It won't last forever. Besides, your son is only four, and you're not a part of his daily routine. He won't miss you much."

The coldhearted bitch.

It was obviously no use to try and appeal to her maternal side. "For Christ's sake, Frances. I'm fighting in court now to see more of Trevor, not less. That yahoo Debra married is bucking for a transfer to LA and if they make the move, I'll see even less of my kid than I do now."

Frances Fletcher spread out her hands helplessly. "I hear you, but my hands are tied."

If there was one thing Blake hated, it was being backed into a corner. Threatened, he would come out swinging.

He reached for the badge in his pocket. "Then I'll resign. Right now." He tossed his identification on her desk. "There. Take it. I'm through. My kid means more than the shit you're trying to pull on me."

Frances Fletcher didn't blink. "Not going to work, Blake." She shook her head. "Lose that shield and you're demoted to plain old civilian. A civilian who has information we can't allow to be released to the general public. As one who has made contact, you go into quarantine, anyway." She picked up his shield and tossed it back. "You might as well keep your rank and your paycheck. You'll be getting a raise, by the way, to compensate you for the inconvenience."

Blake reluctantly retrieved his gold shield. An emotional knot wedged in his throat. He really didn't have a choice and he knew it. "It's not enough compensation for losing Trevor," he grumbled under his breath.

Leaning forward, he placed his elbows on his knees and massaged his eyes with his fingers. He was too drained to argue points he couldn't win. As much as Fletcher's words stung, he was not deluded enough to deny them. Everything she'd pointed out was probably the truth.

After he'd made his call for aid, the agency had gone into immediate action, sweeping through the scene of the attack with a cold and calculated efficiency. Evidence was gathered, witnesses were rounded up, and a total press blackout was declared.

Blake had believed the agency would only quarantine the hostile Mer who had attacked the island. Not so. The government's grip had tightened, and they'd taken everyone on the island into custody.

Tessa and Kenneth Randall, Addison Lonike . . . and Gwen.

Their lives were no longer their own. For all intents and purposes they belonged to the alien sciences division. All freedom, rights, and liberties afforded by the Constitution of the United States no longer applied to them.

He frowned. *Apparently it doesn't apply to me either.* Life, liberty, and the pursuit of happiness had just been yanked out from beneath his feet.

"Are you going to be all right, Agent Whittaker?" Fletcher's voice was tightly controlled.

Blake finally lifted himself up with a heave. His entire body trembled with the effort. God, he was exhausted, bone tired. Nevertheless, he drew back his shoulders and called on all his inner willpower to appear calm. Inside, his stomach was churning acid.

"You guys have really backed me into a corner here," he countered angrily. "And truth be told, if this had happened before Trevor was born I probably wouldn't have blinked an eye. But things are changing for me as my son grows up. I'm beginning to realize how gratifying it is to raise a child, be there for him."

Fletcher nodded cautiously. "Go on."

Blake rubbed a hand across his face. "Trevor's still got a lot of firsts happening in his life. And I like being a part of those moments as he discovers the world around him. There will come a day when everything in Trevor's life is routine, the same old shit every day."

The older woman allowed a smile. "I have to say I missed a lot of those times with my own children."

Blake decided to lay it all on the line. "It's those times that have kept me going, Frances. Trevor reminds me I do have a purpose on this earth and that I am needed." He shook his head. "Otherwise I would probably have put a gun in my mouth and pulled the trigger a few years ago." It was true. His son kept the last of his humanity from slipping through his fingers. It wasn't much to hang on to, but it was something.

For the first time in a long time he had hope. And there was always a chance tomorrow would be better and brighter.

As his fingers drummed against her desk, Fletcher's lips pressed into a serious line. Though she didn't move so much as a brow, the wheels in her mind were turning. "I can sympathize, Blake," she finally said. "Really I can. But you're not the first person who has had to sacrifice family for work. As for your other admission, I don't think there is a man or woman working in law enforcement today who hasn't entertained those kinds of thoughts at one time or another."

In other words, he needed to get over himself.

A long silence followed as if the room were holding its breath.

Dismay tightened in Blake's chest. He might as well have been talking to a brick wall. "I see."

Fletcher's eyes took on a glacial chill. "Whether you like it or not, as an agent working in this organization, you belong to the United States government. We can keep you in custody as long as need be in the name of national security."

He tried one last compromise. "I never said I couldn't work this one," he countered. "Just don't keep me penned up like a dog, too."

The assistant director smiled thinly. "If you really want out, that bullet you spoke about may be your only recourse." She arched a well-tweezed brow. "Am I making myself clear, Agent Whittaker?"

In other words, the outfit could arrange to make him go away. And it would look like a suicide. Whether he actually pulled the trigger. Or not.

Blake leveled an unflinching gaze at his superior. Somehow he'd had a feeling this was the way events would play out.

It wasn't easy to accept. It wasn't right.

Blake stopped himself from clenching his fists. Getting mad all over again wouldn't do him any good. It would just be wasted effort and he was too damn tired to keep spinning his wheels.

"Are you finished fucking me over?" he snapped.

"There is one last thing," she added. "We'd like you to get close to the—" She checked her file. "Middle sister."

Blake supplied a name. "Her name is Gwen." He hated that the Lonike sisters were already being treated as something subhuman and lacking intelligence. The outfit regarded them as objects rather than living beings with thoughts and feelings of their own.

"Yes. Gwen. Of the three, she seems to be the most vulnerable, from what we've observed. Perhaps you could pay her some special attention."

Grasping the meaning behind her words, Blake narrowed his eyes. "Are you suggesting I should try to seduce her?"

Frances Fletcher didn't bat an eye. "If she trusts you, her sisters will be more likely to cooperate as well." She lowered her head, peering over the top edge of her thick frames. "How far you take the intimacy is your own decision."

Chapter 9

Sighing with relief, Gwen slipped on her sweater. It felt good to get out of those plain thin hospital gowns and into her own clothes.

Standing in front of the mirror, she gave herself a quick once-over. The outfit she'd chosen was simple but classy. A long-sleeved white cotton blouse and black slacks was her usual uniform when she worked. Low-heeled black flats kept the look casual and comfortable.

Satisfied her clothing was acceptable, she reached up and gave her cheeks a quick little pinch. Her skin was pale, almost dead white. A little touch of red would help her look more lively, healthier. The people who'd packed her bags hadn't included anything but the basics. She had not a single cosmetic to her name, not even a tube of lipstick. Everything going in and out of her room was tightly controlled and inspected.

A deep frown creased her mouth. She wasn't happy with the idea of strange people—government agents—

digging through her personal possessions. It made her feel violated, a person unworthy of simple respect.

She glanced toward her wrists, so recently restrained. Thank heavens those had come off. She'd hated the feel of them against her skin, reinforcing the helplessness of her present situation. Instead of treating her and her sisters like victims of a vicious attack, the government lackeys acted like they were the aggressors.

Gwen hoped they could soon straighten out such a misguided notion. She was, after all, a citizen of the United Stated, born and raised in Maine. She was educated, a business owner, and certainly a tax payer. Even though she was a Mer, surely she should be accorded all the rights and liberties of an innocent person. She didn't even have so much as a speeding ticket on her driver's license.

Gwen checked her reflection a third time. She looked like any normal person. And by wearing long sleeves she didn't have to endure the prying eyes of people who might find her outer scale pattern offensive. Even though most people took the markings for an elaborate tattoo, she didn't care to show the pattern off to the public.

She frowned at the image staring back at her. "We are *not* freaks." Somehow saying the words made her feel better. Though not much.

They still weren't allowed to go home. In fact, Gwen had no idea what would happen next. The idea of not knowing, of not being in control of her own fate, made her sick inside.

She reached for the soul-stone hanging around her neck. Thank the goddess this small pendant hadn't been confiscated from her. Though it was just a simple crystal, of no real value, for a Mer to lose her stone was comparable to being struck blind and deaf.

It was also the center of her power, the connection with the symbiote inside. Given the differences between human and Mer, it was easier to think of people as the lesser species, weaker and not as genetically advanced as the Mer. But that was wrong. Human beings had their place.

Just like the Mer should, she reminded herself. *Ishaldi is a part of this earth, too. Our origins may be different, but we share a common planet.*

That idea was the one that kept her cooperating with the people who had suddenly taken control of her life. It would do no good to throw a hissy fit. She could prove herself capable and functional through good manners and by doing what was asked of her.

Once the government realized their terrible mistake, she was sure they could all return to their normal daily lives.

At least she hoped they would.

A tear rolled down her cheek, and then a second. She knew she'd scared a lot of people when she'd gone haywire and lost control over her Mercraft. Truth be told, she had no idea how or why that had happened. Everyone was wary, tiptoeing around her like she was made of nitroglycerin. Nobody wanted to be around when she exploded again.

Swallowing hard to squelch her rising emotion, Gwen

snatched up a tissue and dabbed away her tears. If she cried, it would ruin the illusion she was desperate to create. Outside, a destination she couldn't even begin to imagine awaited her. She had no idea where she'd be going or what would be happening.

The door behind her opened.

A man clad in the familiar black suit stepped inside her room. "Miss Lonike?"

Gwen whirled on her heel, balling up the tissue in her hand. It would not do to be seen crying. She had to be strong. Showtime was near.

"Yes?" She managed to choke out the single word.

"Your sisters and brother-in-law are waiting for you." The agent attendant gave the small dressing room a quick scan to make sure all was well. "Are you ready to go?"

Gwen offered a tentative smile to show she was fine. "Yes, I am."

Time to act sane, she thought. And try not to incinerate anybody.

She followed the agent down the hall, turning into another room similar to the one she'd recently occupied. Tessa and Addison were there, as well as Kenneth. True to form, Kenneth was arguing with a medic standing behind a wheelchair.

"I'm perfectly capable of walking out of here on my own two feet." He thumped his chest. "I'm up, around, and I feel fine."

Tessa hovered close by her husband. "Maybe you shouldn't try to overdo it so soon, Ken," she warned.

Addison nodded. "Yeah," she chimed in. "You took a

brutal beating." Dressed casually in her usual jeans and T-shirt, Addison seemed not to notice or mind the stares at her arms. Her scale pattern was out there for all to see.

Kenneth eyed the wheelchair and shook his head. "I will walk," he announced. "And when I get my hands on a fucking phone, I'll be calling my attorney. It's unconscionable for your people to hold us hostage here against our will. We have done nothing wrong."

Another agent stepped into the room. The fine hairs on the back of Gwen's neck rose. She knew without looking who had come in behind her.

She turned and stared wordlessly. Her second sense was dead on. It was Blake Whittaker.

Her breath immediately caught. Her skin suddenly heated, flesh going so tight she feared it would split and fall away from her bones. Her nipples were unusually sensitive, the hard little beads pushing against her plain cotton bra.

Though she was watching everybody, in her mind's eye she saw only Whittaker. A surge of wildness rose inside her. The attraction was still there and worse than ever. Since they'd met she'd not been able to dream him, will him, or force him out of her mind.

Remembering the way his arms had slipped around her waist, the feel of his brawny body pressed against hers, her entire being ached relentlessly for more of his touch. Images of their two naked bodies locked together in passion flashed through her mind.

Her lips trembled. She pressed them together. *You haven't even known him for that long,* she reminded herself. But her body didn't seem to get the message that he was still a stranger, and what's more, off limits. Untouchable.

Gwen shifted her weight from one foot to the other. She turned her face from his sight. A bite down on her bottom lip delivered a nice bit of pain. She needed to clear her head, get her thoughts back on track. Just looking at his tall frame seemed to scorch her all the way down to the bone.

Blake Whittaker offered his hand to Kenneth. His suit was so crisp it looked like it would crack if he made any sudden moves. "Please forgive the inconvenience," he said by way of a greeting. "Right now it's merely a formality until we're able to fully examine the events that took place on Little Mer Island. As you can imagine, we have been quite taken aback to learn of the Mer, and do need time to make an assessment of these elements and the problems they present to the government."

Kenneth pulled his hand away. "Don't try to bullshit me," he snapped, staring long and hard at the agents around them. "My wife and her sisters hardly present any problems to the government. It's the Mer who attacked us who caused the trouble."

His expression blank and carefully controlled, Whittaker nodded. "I do appreciate that, Mr. Randall. Our concern right now is for the personal well-being of you and your family. You did say yourself that there may be more aggressors. If that's true, they may not be as easy to stop as those we have in custody." A grim smile touched his saturnine features. "Keeping you confined is merely a security precaution, nothing more. Once we have a full understanding of the situation we are dealing with, I am sure you will be free to go."

Whittaker's manner was calm and straightforward. Trustworthy.

For the first time since this nightmare had begun, Gwen was able to release her pent-up breath. The last few days had been too much to try and absorb. There were so many twists and turns to unravel.

She stepped forward. "Please rest assured we want to cooperate and will do everything necessary to help your agency understand the Mer." His very nearness was playing havoc with her nerves, but she forced herself to ignore it.

Whittaker turned, fixing her under his gray-blue stare. His gaze was penetrating beneath half-lidded eyes, almost intimate in their appraisal. He didn't conceal the fact he was pleased by what he saw. A smile turned up one corner of his mouth, and one eyebrow arched appreciatively. "I'm glad to hear that."

Gwen's heart raced. Although they'd spent less than a day together, there was something about him that made her blood stir. "I'm surprised to see you here," she countered.

An easy shrug rolled off his broad shoulders. "I've been assigned to accompany you to a place where the security is a little bit higher than what our facilities here can offer."

"Just where is this place, anyway?" Kenneth demanded irritably. He clearly wasn't as willing to accept Whittaker's spiel as she was.

A frown replaced Whittaker's smile. "We have a full

facility in Belmonde, Virginia. That does include an extensive marine-sciences center."

Kenneth Randall's eyes narrowed sharply. "Sounds fishy to me."

His wife immediately delivered a hard poke to the ribs. "Mind the fishy references," Tessa warned under her breath.

Wrapping one thick arm around his wife's waist, Kenneth gave her an apologetic kiss on the top of her head. "Sorry, honey. I wasn't thinking."

Gwen hid her smile behind her hand. Kenneth Randall might be a little rough around the edges and lacking a few social graces, but he was a solid and dependable man. He adored Tessa, giving her everything and denying her nothing. Her older sister had been lucky to snag him.

Tessa placed a protective hand on Kenneth's chest. "We might not want to go, but it looks like we have no choice." She looked to Whittaker. "Am I right that you're going to continue to hold us against our will?"

Whittaker spread his hands in apology. "Look, folks, if it were up to me I'd walk you to the front door and wave good-bye." His hands dropped to his sides. "Truth is, this thing has become bigger than all of us. What we consider to be a hostile species has made an attack and killed a civilian. The weapons they have access to are dangerous. I've seen that with my own eyes. We can't risk more lives—just like we can't risk a widespread panic if word of the events got out to the media."

Addison frowned. "As an EMT, I understand the idea of containment and control of anything that presents a danger to civilians," she finally allowed. "I think we should all try to accept that we're stuck and make the best of it." She looked around. "If nothing else, think of it as a little family vacation."

"A vacation under lock and key isn't my idea of fun," Kenneth grumbled.

"You won't be locked in cells," Whittaker hastened to explain. "Since a lot of employees and agents live on site, the sciences facility has its own apartment and shopping complex. Think of it as a small neighborhood."

"Surrounded by a high barbed-wire fence and armed guards, I suppose," Kenneth retorted.

Whittaker nodded. "The use of deadly force is authorized," he confirmed. "Nobody gets in."

Gwen inwardly flinched. Despite the moistness in the air, her mouth was dry. She crossed her arms protectively in front of her body. *They don't get out either, I bet.*

As a federal agent, Blake was accustomed to flying business class. Priority check-in, decent menu, good wine. He enjoyed it as one of the perks of his job and didn't abuse his expense account.

Traveling commercial was one thing, a decent way to get from point A to point B with relatively little hassle. Doing it in a private government-owned jet was an entirely different experience. There was no hassle of getting through a congested airport, no standing in line waiting for bags to be checked, no messing with trying to rent a car at the destination site.

This must be how the president travels, he mused. Every step was smooth, the well-oiled machine humming along with perfect precision. No luxury was spared. The plane was outfitted with every modern convenience that could be stuffed into its narrow frame.

Tucked in a comfy chair, Blake accepted a refill on his drink: a single malt scotch, no ice. A female agent doubling as stewardess served everyone with blank-faced efficiency.

Normally Blake didn't drink. He didn't like the idea of losing control of his senses. He was also prescient enough about himself to know he liked the taste of booze, and would swill it without restraint if he set aside his self-control. As the child of an alcoholic, he knew the damages liquor could inflict, both emotionally and physically. His mother had been an ugly drunk.

He vowed his son would never see him in such a condition. He'd sooner cut off his right arm with a hacksaw than go staggering in to pick up Trevor.

Had he not been stressed to the max, Blake would have stuck to coffee. However, the last thing he needed was more caffeine. He was already jumpier than a flea on a hot brick. And even though he'd barely slept since Friday, he'd managed to keep himself going on sheer force of will alone.

A couple of drinks would help him unwind and relax during the flight. It would also help loosen his tongue, which seemed to get tangled in knots whenever he tried to talk to Gwen Lonike.

Sipping his scotch, Blake glanced over at his seatmate. Gwen had the window side. Her head was turned to the view outside, which was nothing but a mass of clouds.

The food in front of her—steamed trout fillets in lettuce parcels with a Thai stuffing—had gone untouched. She hadn't taken a single bite. Nor had she sipped from the glass of white wine she'd requested. Whatever she might be thinking, she kept to herself. Tension compressed her lips.

Silence dragged between them.

Looking at her, Blake combed through his memory. The little bit of intelligence they'd been able to hastily gather on her didn't fill a single page. She didn't party, had no known drug or alcohol problems. Aside from her business she didn't seem to have any outside pursuits. She'd broken up with her boyfriend almost a year ago and wasn't presently seeing anyone.

All in all she should be perfectly vulnerable for an act of calculated seduction.

It looked like it would be an easy thing to do, too. Beside him sat an impressively beautiful young woman with a charming smile and a killer body. But she was also a woman who wasn't human in any sense of the word he understood.

A belated thought occurred. What if mermaids didn't mate the same way humans did?

It didn't matter. He'd been ordered to do whatever it took to get close to Gwen.

As for the notion of going to bed with her . . . He wasn't sure he'd actually go that far. A few days ago he'd been attracted enough to consider asking her out, with the vague idea he might try seeing her beyond a one-night stand. Being ordered to pursue her put a damper on the entire notion. Suddenly it wasn't play, but a whole hell of a lot of work.

He sighed. In the space of a few days his entire world had spun completely out of control.

Without turning her head, Gwen cleared her throat. "I wish you would stop staring at me," she said through tight lips. "It's making me nervous."

Unaware his perusal had become blatantly notice-able, Blake dropped his gaze. "Sorry," he mumbled into his glass. "I didn't mean to upset you."

She reached up, sliding down the cover on the win-dow. "You're not doing anything," she admitted, head settling back against her seat. "It's me. I was just think-ing how I should be home now, in my own apartment." Eyes a little puffy, her gaze was dulled with fatigue.

Flexing his fingers around his glass, Blake considered his half-empty drink. "You aren't the only one who had plans." Right now he was just as trapped as she was. If he could fling open the door and jump out, he probably would.

Crooking her brows, Gwen nodded. "I guess that's true. We all had our separate lives to lead before this got dumped on us." She glanced down at his arm. "How does it feel, by the way?"

It took Blake a moment to realize what she was ask-ing about. He reached up, touching his arm. "It's okay," he answered. "Gives me a little twinge now and again, but I'll survive."

She crossed her arms over her chest. "I'm sorry you got hurt."

He shrugged and tossed back the remnants of his drink. The scotch burned all the way down his throat, hitting his belly like a slug of lead. "It isn't the first injury I've taken in the line of duty and it probably won't be the last." He hadn't eaten much either and the booze was beginning to give him a slight buzz. Without quite knowing why, he rambled on. "I just do the job and keep my mouth shut. Don't know why, either. Overall, it's just one big hassle I could do without."

A perfect brow lifted. "I would think something like this would be a career maker for an agent working in the alien sciences division." She grimaced a little as she spoke.

Blake released a heavy breath. "Oh, please. It's been years since we've had any findings to get excited about. It's not like the world is jumping with paranormal phenomena. Truthfully, most of us sit around twiddling our thumbs until we're old enough to collect our pensions and get the hell out of government service."

"So all those claims of alien abductions and crop circles—" she started to ask.

He drummed his fingers against his armrest. "Are absolute bunk," he finished for her. "Most of them are just crazies who want attention."

A little smile crept across her sensual lips. "But you still have to check them out, I suppose."

Blake raked his hands through his hair, pushing it away from his brow. He'd allowed it to grow a little longer than normal lately, an attempt to lessen the severity of his sharp features. "Sure. It gives the government a reason to write me a paycheck and I get to feel like I'm a lot saner than the rest of the world."

"So what about when you find something, um, extraordinary?"

He shrugged. "Not sure. Haven't been through the process before. And as you can see, I'm on the same flight you are. It's a first time for both of us."

She reached for her wine, then sipped. "First time for everything I suppose."

Blake motioned for a refill. The agent wielding the liquor bottle complied. "Not a lot of firsts left in my life," he remarked, going to work on his third glass. He needed to be just a little bit drunker to loosen up. Making time with a woman was one thing. Making time with a woman he'd been ordered to seduce was quite another.

I wouldn't have made a very good gigolo. He was more than a little bit annoyed with the notion. Charming a woman who was also an alien offered a strange challenge. It definitely wasn't in any handbook he'd been given to read. Like a blind man in the dark, he'd have to feel his away along.

Oddly enough, he didn't think he'd mind the feeling part. With her full breasts, narrow waist, and gently flared hips, everything about her was perfectly proportioned. Under normal circumstances, the notion of slipping between her sheets wouldn't have been difficult.

However, circumstances definitely weren't normal. He wondered if there was a word for sex with a mermaid. And what about the tail? Oh, God. Where did they keep those things anyway?

The questions buzzed through his mind, more annoying than any insect. He supposed it was part of his job to find out.

Gwen quirked a brow. "Oh, I've got a few left, though I can strike being taken into federal custody off my list."

He sighed. "If there are more hostiles, we need to work on capturing and containing them before more lives are lost."

She traced the rim of her glass with a single finger. "As much as I don't like it, I suppose that makes sense. I still can't believe Lucky is gone. I liked that crusty old sea dog."

"Can I ask if Lucky knew about the, ah, mermaids?" The word sounded strange rolling off his tongue.

Gwen glanced up. "Sure, some people knew. I mean, know about us." She thought a moment. "Lucky, of course, and most of the members of his family. A couple of the guys Addie works with know. Since she works underwater rescue, someone's got to keep an eye out when she's under. Jake, he was engaged to Tessa for a little while. He was one of the few who actually tried to tell the world about the Mer and all it got him was bounced out of the archaeological community."

"Nobody believed him?" Observing her every change of expression, it wasn't difficult to figure out she wasn't lying.

Gwen shook her head. "Not a bit." She cocked a finger toward her temple, twirling it around. "Everyone thought he'd lost all the marbles in his head."

Blake motioned toward Tessa and Kenneth, sitting a few seats away. "I suppose Randall there knows what he married."

Gwen laughed. "Of course Kenneth knows. And in case you're wondering—and I know you are just by the look on your face—yes, humans and Mers are bio-logically compatible. There are no Mer-*men*. We have to mate with human males to reproduce, just like any woman does."

Blake eyed the couple. "They look happy enough."

Gwen looked fondly at her sister and Tessa's new husband.

"They've been married less than a month. Still in that newlywed phase where they're all kissy-faced and goggle-eyed over each other." She made a face. "Some-times it's disgusting to see two people that much in love."

Blake knew exactly what she meant. "Little jealousy simmering there?"

She sighed. "I suppose there's a bit. I can't complain, though. They're perfect for each other."

"So what about you? Any perfect man in your life?"

Her nostrils flared. "Not even close. No time really. The hotel's taking every spare minute, and most nights I'm too tired even to eat dinner. It's straight to bed. All alone."

She might have been describing his routine. Most nights he didn't even bother with bed, collapsing on the couch in front of the television. The drone kept him company. It had gotten to the point where bars were boring and the women uninteresting. He'd rather sleep. "Sounds like everybody who has a job."

She moistened her lips, a naturally glossy shade of pink. "What about you? This must be hard on you, too, having to make a sudden move."

"It's a little tough," he admitted. "I'll miss seeing my kid."

She looked surprised, then delighted. "You have children?"

Blake mentally chalked up a point. Nothing made a man more attractive to women of a certain age than children and pets. He'd have to plead the Fifth if asked how many times he'd used cute snapshots of Trevor to get in good with a woman.

It was an awful thing to do, but he had. Back then he'd had an itch to scratch. Sex satisfied the physical, chased away the loneliness for a few hours. It wasn't something he made a habit of these days, though.

Digging out his wallet, he flipped it open. "That's Trevor. He's four—almost five—now."

Something close to delight glimmered in her eyes. "He's cute."

Blake couldn't help puffing a little with pride. "Yeah, he is. And smart as a whip. He's in pre-K now and already has his letters down cold."

She pointed to a picture of Trevor with his mother. "That must be your wife. She's pretty."

Blake looked. He'd been meaning to cull that one from his collection but hadn't gotten around to making the cut. As much as he hated to admit it, the woman was Trevor's mother. He might not love her, but he had to respect her. The unintended accident between them had resulted in his son being born, and he wouldn't give his child up for the world.

Trevor was his lifeline, his touchstone to leading a seminormal life. Lose his son and he'd be totally cut adrift.

He endured the momentary discomfort, then answered. "Um, we're not together anymore." No reason to explain that not only had he not married his ex-girlfriend, but he'd moved out ten months after their son was born.

Her gaze briefly flickered over the picture again. "Sorry it didn't work out."

Blake flipped his wallet shut. "You never know someone until you live with them." He tucked it away. "We were just incompatible, you know?" He shrugged. "Debra got married a couple of years ago."

"Do you see your son often?"

He forced back a quick rise of resentment. "I see him as often as the court allows, which means from Friday at six to Saturday at six, every other week. I've got every other holiday and summer vacation, too. I'd like to have more time with him, but it looks like Debra's going to be leaving Boston soon. Doesn't look like I can stop it, either."

Gwen frowned. "That'll cut out your weekends," she murmured drily.

Blake scowled and pushed his drink away. He didn't need any more liquor. Drinking and brooding didn't mix well. "Damn right. We're fighting it out in court, but the law just isn't on the father's side."

She smiled with genuine sympathy. "I guess now isn't a good time for you to be dragged off to Virginia."

A grunt rolled past his lips. "Didn't seem to be any way to get out of it, or I wouldn't be here now," he answered flatly. His discontent with the entire matter wasn't faked.

Gwen's hand settled on his arm, giving him a little

squeeze of reassurance. Her grip was firm. The warmth emanating from her palm filtered through his sleeve. "I'm sorry." A look of quiet sympathy surfaced in her emerald eyes. "I can't imagine how hard it must be for you. I think it's admirable when a man tries to hold on to his kids. Too many are willing to walk away to avoid the hassles."

Blake was surprised. As frightened as she was, she had still managed to pull herself together and offer him reassurance. His heart lodged at the base of his throat, stealing away all the air in his lungs.

Gwen Lonike was something else.

Another tremble of response moved him.

Blake quickly shifted his gaze away from her face. It was all he could do to hold his wits together. There was no doubt in his mind that he did, indeed, want to seek comfort in her.

He just didn't want to do it as a part of his job.

Blake curled his fingers to stop himself from reaching out and touching her. Misleading her, deceiving her, would be wrong.

Shit, he thought. *I'm getting in too damn deep.*

Chapter 10

The enormity of Blake's latest assignment didn't fully begin to sink in until the plane began circling the base, preparing to land. Then it kicked in. This was real, and there was no turning back. There was no way he was going to get out of the assignment.

It bothered him more than a little that the place looked like a prison. The impression didn't bode well in his mind, either. He could almost imagine iron bars swinging shut, locking them all in.

Forever.

Virginia greeted them with a soft drizzle from a low, leaden sky. The wind pulled at their clothing, reminding everyone present that no one had packed for chilly, depressing weather. The gloomy dusk perfectly suited everyone's mood.

From long habit, Blake performed a thorough visual sweep of the place as he followed everyone off the plane.

The A51-ASD sciences center in Belmonde, Virginia, had first served the government as Lawrence Air Force

Base. Decommissioned in 1990, the on-site property to-taled over ten thousand acres. Major components of the base included an airfield, an Alert Area, and a Weapons Storage Area. It also had a large industrial area and two large hangars. Administrative, institutional, recreational, and residential areas were located at the western por-tion of the base.

The area was originally an undeveloped tract of dense forest, shallow marshes, and densely packed wild blueberry bogs, covering rolling hills with virtually no obstacles to construction. A slight plateau provided dis-tance from nearby tobacco farming areas. Sources of hard bedrock and limestone supported the construction of the runways, taxiways, and parking aprons.

Remote, the base was heavily guarded. Border and warning signs proclaimed PHOTOGRAPHY STRICTLY FOR-BIDDEN and USE OF DEADLY FORCE IS AUTHORIZED. Secu-rity agents lined the perimeter twenty-four hours a day, seven days a week.

Nobody got in or out of the facility without a top-secret clearance and proper authorization.

Blake was already aware the hostiles they'd taken into custody had been transferred to the facility a few days before. Unlike Gwen and her family, they hadn't gotten the first-class treatment. In fact, handling them had presented a whole hell of a lot of problems, which had filtered back to him in hourly reports. His Black-Berry regularly buzzed with yet another status update, to the point where he'd had to put it on vibrate instead of ring. The continual noise was starting to get on his nerves.

The last message had come in before landing. Just as soon as he settled Gwen and her family into their quarters, he was to report to the lead scientist, Dr. Hali Yadira. Dr. Yadira would be leading the team through their research of the Mer species.

As for their captive subjects—

Not only were the women totally hostile toward humans, they were utterly vicious creatures to deal with. And even though they'd been stripped of all their weapons, they still packed a hell of a wallop. Their psi-kinetic abilities went through the roof, and the only way to manage it was to keep them sedated.

In order to work with them, they'd have to be allowed to resume a fully conscious state. His latest orders had instructed him to begin pumping Gwen and her sister for information as to how the Mer could be subdued without blunting their abilities.

The corpse of the civilian and the Mer killed in the fight had been sent for autopsy. Doctors there were practically salivating to get their hands on an alien lifeform they could hack into tiny little pieces.

Though he knew it to be a necessary part of research, Blake thought it more than a little gruesome that anyone might enjoy cutting into dead bodies. The vision of a Nazi concentration camp flashed through his mind. It was easy to make the comparison, for both places worked with calculated precision to suppress and decimate anyone or anything deemed to be strange or different.

He grimaced. The Mer on the coroner's table would be coming in two pieces. Tessa Randall had practically blasted her in half with that odd bejeweled weapon she'd identified as a Ri'kah.

A cadre of black midsized sedans were lined up on the tarmac. Black-suited agents with radios and headsets hustled to collect their bags, loading them efficiently into the waiting transportation.

One agent approached, taking Whittaker aside. Portly and bald, he wheezed out his words with the effort of a man who'd long ago given up any attempt to keep himself physically fit. "Agent Whittaker," he said, offering his hand. "I'm Special Agent Dennis Thompson, director in charge of this ASD facility. Anything you need, bring it to me and it'll be taken care of."

An eerie feeling raced through Blake, hot and electric. He pulled his hand away. He couldn't help it. Thompson gave him the willies. "Thank you, sir. I'll be sure to keep that in mind."

Special Agent Thompson snatched a quick sideways glance at the small group of people accompanying Blake on the flight. His face scrunched. "My goodness, they pass well for humans," he shared under his breath.

Refusing to be intimidated, Blake tilted forward. "You don't have to talk about them like they're freaks."

Thompson's beady gaze shifted over the women. "I've never been this close to an alien," he confessed. "The few I've seen are usually in a deceased state."

Blake's jaw tightened. The man needed a few hospitality and etiquette lessons. Alien or not, the Mer deserved to be treated decently, and with a little respect. In Thompson's mind they probably all needed to be dissected or shoved into a test tube. Blake could honestly admit he didn't care for either notion.

He cocked his head to indicate their guests. "They might not have the same DNA we do, but they do have feelings."

Thompson tensed. "Ah, of course they do. My apologies. I didn't mean to be rude to those, um, people."

To make good on his apology, Thompson stepped over to introduce himself to the new arrivals. Hands were shook and greetings exchanged.

The director indicated the waiting cars with a sweep of his hand. "If you would care to go with these agents, they will get you settled in to your new quarters." He smiled benignly. "I think you will find our accommodations are quite comfortable. We're putting you in the Jefferson complex."

Agents herded Gwen and her sisters toward the waiting cars. She turned when he didn't walk along with them. "Aren't you coming, too, Agent Whittaker?" she asked.

Blake shook his head. "I've got some other matters to take care of," he explained without going into detail.

Kenneth caught their conversation. He stopped, refusing to get in the car. "What kind of matters?" he asked suspiciously.

Blake blew out a breath. Unlike the sisters, who had begun to somewhat accept the inevitably of their situation, Randall questioned or protested every move they made. No doubt the man would step in front of a speeding freight train to protect his wife or one of her sisters. He was that devoted.

Because he'd been ordered to do everything he could to gain their trust and cooperation, Blake decided not to lie. "Actually, I'm going to pay a visit to the two ladies who attacked you. They've been kept under sedation and are starting to awaken. We're in the process of arranging for them to be confined to an environment we hope they will find more suitable."

Tessa stepped up. "Is there a chance we could go, too? I thought I recognized a couple of them, but I'm not sure." She shrugged apologetically. "If they're who I think they are then I am sure Jake Massey is still alive."

Addison nodded. "I'd like to see those bitches, too," she growled under her breath.

Gwen Lonike's mouth drew down in a frown. She wrapped her arms protectively around her body. The rain was coming harder now, soaking everyone to the bone. The chill was starting to set in. "I'd rather not see them at all." She released a heavy sigh. "They've already caused so much trouble, I just want them all to go away." She shivered. "But I'll go where you do."

Blake considered. "I think that might be a good idea." Massey's body was never located, not an unusual occurrence when someone was lost out in the middle of a large body of water. Of course, with a couple of mermaids to grab on to, there was always the possibility he'd made it out just fine. Kenneth Randall had obviously survived his immersion. Why couldn't Massey?

Dennis Thompson nodded. "I don't see the harm. The hostiles will be in a controlled setting." He waved them into the waiting cars. "If you will, we'll take you to the main research facility."

Blake nodded. "Let's go." He walked toward one of the waiting black sedans. Tessa and Kenneth slid into one car, Gwen and Addison took another. Blake took a third car, pushing himself in to sit beside Thompson. The door winged shut with an ominous slam. The driver shifted into gear and they were on their way.

Thompson didn't miss a beat. "Do you really think it's wise to put them all together?" he asked.

Blake raised a brow. "Why not?"

"Because of their, ah, instabilities with their, um, paranormal reserves. I understand one of the women is particularly sensitive and hard to control. Are you sure she shouldn't be sedated as well?"

Blake couldn't suppress his frown. "Did it ever occur to you it might be a way to try and protect herself because she's scared out of her wits?" he retorted. "Whether you want to believe it or not, before this debacle occurred, these were just nice, normal people trying to live their lives. They're not some kind of green, goggle-eyed monsters just come down from outer space with ray guns blasting. Their people have lived in the waters around Maine for centuries and nobody's had a panic attack because a few mermaids are swimming in the bay."

Thompson pursed his fat lips. "Maybe you don't see this group as a threat, Agent Whittaker, but you have to consider that they have the potential to be very dangerous. That's why we had to take them all into custody even though they were not the aggressors. These Mer, as they call themselves, are an entirely different species of biped. They have abilities humans are nowhere near achieving, along with a technology we can't even begin to match. The purpose for bringing—"

Blake cut him off with a distracted wave of his hand. "Yes, I know. The purpose for containing them is to fully study the species and make a determination as to whether or not they will be allowed back into the general population."

"Right now we're having to take things as they come," Thompson reminded him. "If there are indeed more of the hostiles in the water, they will surely come ashore once they learn their compatriots have failed in their mission. As long as we have them in custody, we can protect them."

Blake rubbed tired eyes. "And as long as we have them in our custody, we can control them and make them jump through hoops like trained seals, all in the name of scientific study." Their every move would be monitored. What they eat, when they sleep, how they interact among themselves and others. It would all be meticulously recorded.

Thompson gave a single approving nod. "It's what we do, Agent Whittaker," he remarked. "You know as well as I do that sacrifices have to be made in the name of scientific advancement. The fact that we have three living hostiles gives us a lot of leeway in the testing we can execute."

Blake winced. *Execute* wasn't exactly the best choice of words in this case. "I take it you are telling me in a not so subtle way some of the tests will be quite invasive."

Thompson nodded again. "Possibly damaging." By

the tone of his voice they might have been discussing the weather.

He glanced at Thompson's face. Beside him sat the man who would help shape the final decision as to what would happen to the Mer. The idea of living test subjects in the hands of the government didn't bode well. Scientists sometimes put aside all consideration of humane treatment in their zeal to further human knowledge of the world and its inhabitants. Study was one thing. Inflicting pain whether maliciously intended or not was another thing entirely.

That's something I won't stand for. For the first time he began to consider what he'd do if the A51 was to step over the line. No living, breathing thing—alien or human—deserved to be tormented in the name of discovery.

The word *informant* filtered up from his unconscious mind.

He quickly squashed the notion. Frances Fletcher had delivered the warning that he'd be taken care of if he bucked the agency.

He'd always done his job, been a good soldier. But he was also aware he was just a pawn in the larger game. And pawns were often sacrificed in the goal to achieve victory.

A bullet could come whizzing out of nowhere, at any time. He wouldn't see it coming, and he damn sure wouldn't survive the hit. The agency had hundreds of trained professionals, any one of whom could assassinate a fellow agent without a single twinge of conscience.

Somehow he had the notion that no one who'd just entered into this top-secret compound was safe or secure. Tessa Randall and her husband, Addison and Gwen—every single one of them was walking on thin ice.

And Blake had a feeling the ice was thinnest under his own two feet. One false step and he was sure to go under.

Gwen gripped Addison's hand as their driver guided the vehicle toward one of the large hangars. Huge doors glided open at their approach, allowing the cars to drive straight through. The facility and its purpose was all too overwhelming for her to grasp at once.

"I don't like this," she whispered as the driver pulled the car to a halt.

More than a little wide-eyed, Addison squeezed her hand back. "It's awesome," she whispered back. "But scary."

The car rolled to a stop. The agent driving hopped out and reached around to open a door for them. "Ladies, this way," he invited.

Addison slid out first. Gwen followed.

The hangar that had once housed a cadre of the air force's best fighting fleet had been converted into the command post of the scientific research center. A score of security and scientific personnel went about their business with clockwork precision.

Tessa and Kenneth joined them, followed by Thompson and Whittaker. Gwen didn't exactly like the looks of the facility director. His gaze swept over her and her sisters like they'd grown tentacles or something. He was careful to keep his distance, too, letting Agent Whittaker herd them all like sheep.

"This way," Thompson snapped brusquely.

They all strode toward a security desk manned by armed guards. Heavily armed guards. Thompson bent over and spoke to his men, who quickly provided a set of badges for everyone.

Gwen pinned her visitor's badge onto her sweater. Amazingly, it had her picture on it. She wasn't sure how they'd gotten the snap so quickly and clearly, but since security cameras peered down from all angles there was no doubt in her mind their every move was being closely recorded.

She didn't fail to notice that Whittaker's badge was a little bit different. His was marked SPECIAL AGENT and ALL ACCESS. The bar code and magnetic strip on the back would open any door in the facility. Her own plastic card had no bar coding or strip on the back and simply said VISITOR and LIMITED ACCESS.

With that done, Thompson ushered them all toward a set of elevator doors. "This way, folks." He swiped his own card through a reader, and the twin doors slid open. "As you can guess, this is a high-security area. No one gets in or out without authorization."

Everyone stepped in. The elevator whooshed down with a speed that made Gwen's stomach roll.

Seconds later they all stepped into a foyer, also similarly stationed and manned by armed agents. Because it was a waiting area, institution-issued couches and chairs lined the walls. There was also a table surrounded by a few hard-backed metal chairs, a station stocked with coffee and soft drinks, along with the usual doors marked with the familiar MEN and WOMEN signs.

Thompson consulted one of the men in a flurry of whispered words. "Sorry for the delay," he announced. "We're just waiting for Dr. Yadira to join us."

Everyone waited. Minutes ticked by and fell with the weight of lead. It seemed a whole lot of trouble just to go nowhere.

Another ten minutes passed before a woman appeared, walking down the hall toward them with brisk steps. Dressed in blue scrubs and a white coat, her black hair was pulled away from her face, twisted into a tight bun. Not a single hair was out of place. Her fawn-colored eyes were bright and alert, and her skin was a rich shade of brown. A small red bindi dot centered in the middle of her forehead was her sole concession to cosmetic wear. Two assistants in scrubs and coats followed at her heels like well-trained dogs.

Thompson stepped up and made the introductions. "This is Dr. Hali Yadira, who is leading the team's research into the Mer. She is a marine biologist whose work with the Sirenia should come in handy with the research we have asked her to pursue here."

Gwen's brow wrinkled. "Wait a minute. Aren't Sirenia sea cows?"

Doctor Yadira smiled and nodded. "Not a flattering comparison, obviously. Sirenians are also referred to by the common name of sirens, deriving from the sirens of Greek mythology. This comes from an urban legend about their discovery, involving lonely sailors mistaking them for mermaids."

Tessa blanched. "Oh, my heavens! They're comparing us Mer to sea cows. I've been called a lot of things in my time, but a sea cow isn't one of them."

Kenneth reached for his wife's hand. "Take it with a grain of salt, honey. They're just uneducated about mermaids."

Yadira nodded. "You will have to forgive our ignorance. At this time we are working with the classification of *Genus Sirena* in order to clarify the distinction between the two species." She smiled. "Needless to say I am very excited about the discovery of the Mer and look forward to learning all there is to know."

Standing just behind Gwen, Whittaker shoved his hands into the pockets of his slacks and rocked back on his heels. "I'll bet you are," he muttered under his breath.

Gwen glanced toward him. By the stiffness in Whittaker's posture and the look on his face, he was displeased with the entire situation. She didn't blame him one bit. It wasn't a place she wanted to be, either.

Dr. Yadira glanced at her watch, then motioned for everyone to follow her. "We were just in the process of bringing the other Mer out from under their sedation. They should be awake momentarily." She glanced over her shoulder as she walked, moving in quick, efficient steps that wasted no time. "I don't wish to alarm you, but they are restrained for their own protection as well as that of my staff."

Thompson turned and added, "Please be assured we

are doing our best to treat them as humanely as possible," he explained, attempting to lessen the severity of his words by speaking in a neutral tone. "They have proven to be quite hostile."

Tessa nodded. "I can tell you right now they probably won't be very cooperative. In Ishaldi, which is where they come from, their society refuses to recognize humans as equals."

One of the doctors accompanying Yadira turned midstride. "I'm very interested to know more about Ishaldi and how you entered into it." He grinned ear to ear. "I've been tracking the signal strength of the magnetic emissions from the M441966 site and they've literally gone off the charts since the quake."

Thompson made a quick introduction. "This young, fresh-faced upstart is Dr. Steven Novak, formerly with NASA."

Novak nodded eagerly. "For the longest time I've suspected the anomaly to be the representation of a time or domain signal. To find out that it could be the actual entrance to a wormhole will blow all theories concerning space and time right out of the water."

Kenneth raised his brows. "So the government has actually been aware of this thing for quite a while?"

"Since before I was born, actually," Novak confirmed. "But it's always been quite muted. And we've had no way to even begin to get close to it given the instability of the seabed. It's hard to maneuver those unmanned submersibles in some of the canyon regions."

Tessa couldn't suppress her smile. "Been there, done that."

Novak's brows shot clear up his forehead. Another inch higher and they would have disappeared entirely. "Really? Tell me, is there any limitation to the depths a mermaid can descend? And how long can you stay under, if you don't mind my asking?"

Addison winked at the cute little doctor, who was about her own age. "We can stay under as long as we want and go as deep as we want." She gave him a flirty wink. "And there's nothing I like better than finding a nice, mossy rock to snooze on."

Novak was absorbing every word like the gospel. "How fascinating," he enthused.

Addison burst into amused laughter. "I'm kidding about the snoozing part."

The young doctor beamed at Addison, clearly captivated. "I'd like to find out just how far down you can go."

Addison waggled her brows. "Give me a bottle of cheap wine and a joint and you'll find out."

Their flirting was beginning to get just a little bit risqué.

Gwen gasped with embarrassment. "Addison! That's quite enough. There's no reason to be obscene in front of these people."

She shook her head. Damn, Addison was a shameless flirt. Her brashness and ability to say exactly what was on her mind often boggled her. The word *shy* was definitely not in her little sister's vocabulary.

In some ways Gwen wished she possessed the sensuality both her sisters exhibited without any inhibitions whatsoever. Both Tessa and Addison were sexually unreserved, easily accepting their bodies, including the scale pattern etched into their skin. Gwen personally couldn't stand hers, viewing it as the mark of Cain. It made her stand out, look different from the rest of the people she lived around and worked beside.

It was often a trial and inconvenience to conceal it—especially during the hot summers when everyone wore shorts and T-shirts. She supposed she looked odd in her long-sleeved blouses, buttoned to the chin and cuffed within an inch of her life. Truth be told she hadn't even put on a bathing suit since she'd started puberty. Human girls had to deal with menstrual cycles and acne. Mers had to deal with the emergence of their scale patterns and psi-kinetic abilities.

Fitting in, being normal, was all that had ever mattered to her. She didn't want to be extraordinary in the way many people longed to be. The need to be noticed, stand out in the crowd, wasn't a part of her personality. She liked being invisible, being plain old Gwen.

Plain, old Gwen, the old maid, her mind filled in. Unless she ditched her hang-ups, and quickly, she'd be the oldest virgin mermaid on the face of the earth. The idea of spending her whole life alone wasn't exactly appealing.

She snuck a glance toward Whittaker. For the first time in a long time she found herself attracted to a man. He had all the qualities she found irresistible in human males. She wondered what would have happened if that last terrible Saturday hadn't occurred. Had everything gone as expected, perhaps they would have gotten to have that dinner.

It was easy to imagine they might have hit it off, too.

Instead of showing her pictures of his little boy on a flight to Virginia, they could have bonded over steaks and red wine. And if the dinner had gone well, she could have invited him down for the weekend from Boston— kid and all. She liked children. Had even imagined having a few kids of her own someday. Whittaker's son was a cute little boy. Any daughters he helped produce would be pretty, especially with his coal black hair and eyes that reminded her of a half-clouded sky.

She sighed. With no prospects in sight, it was easy to get carried away in her fantasies.

Ignoring her sister's warning, Addison tagged the handsome young doctor with her elbow. "I'll show you my scale pattern if you show me some skin."

Dr. Novak blushed ten shades of red. "Ah, I'd like that. Um, I think." His brow wrinkled. "What's a scale pattern?"

Addison started to explain. Fortunately Dr. Yadira cut her short. "We have plenty of time to discuss those things." Her words were brisk and laced with impatience. She waved her hand, motioning for everyone to follow her through a large set of double-glass doors. "If you don't mind, I'd like to move things along."

Everyone nodded. Of course.

Pressing a single finger to her lips, Gwen shot a warning look at her younger sister, reinforcing it with a vigorous shake of her head. Oh, heavens. It was a good thing Addison wasn't the keeper of any state secrets. She'd hand them over just to make time with a cute man.

In the back of her mind she had to admit Novak was really good-looking.

Addison responded by sticking out her tongue.

Gwen rolled her eyes. Mature. Really mature.

Novak continued to grin. He was clearly taken with Addison. Had they met under any other circumstance, Gwen would have encouraged them to get together. Having a doctor in the family would be terrific.

She snuck another peek at Whittaker. Wouldn't hurt her feelings to have a special agent in the family either.

Well, she could dream, couldn't she?

She sighed. Probably not going to happen. Right now the best she could possibly hope for was that they would someday be allowed to return to their own lives.

Until then, nothing in her world would be right.

Suppressing a shiver, Gwen forced herself to concentrate on what lay ahead.

Chapter 11

The work area Yadira escorted them into was huge, sterile, and absolutely cold. The entire place seemed to be made of tile, steel, and glass, stark white with touches of silver. The filtered air held no scent. There was a lot of medical equipment, some of it familiar, other pieces not so much. By the looks of it, the place could equip any major medical facility.

The most compelling piece of equipment stood at the rear of the lab, a huge tank filled with water.

The fine hairs on the back of Gwen's neck prickled even as goose bumps raced across her skin. She absorbed its meaning in a single glance. An observation tank. One that would allow scientists to view and study the inhabitants from all angles.

The burning pressure of tears suddenly built behind her eyes. There was no doubt whatsoever in her mind that the tank was for the captive Mer.

There's no damn way they're ever going to get me

into that thing. Head spinning with a thousand different thoughts, she struggled to hang on to her composure.

Three of the Mer who had attacked the island lay on examination tables. As Thompson had warned, they were strapped in place, unable to move arms or legs. Doctors buzzed all around them, checking pulses, temperatures, and other vital signs. Several samples of blood were drawn from each.

Gwen's eyes widened. The women were totally out of it, barely semiconscious. They gazed straight ahead with dull eyes that didn't seem to comprehend a single thing. The procedures being performed on them were invasive, and they had no chance to protest.

She studied their vague expressions. As much as she didn't like them or even want to look at them, she couldn't help feeling sorry for their plight. The skin around her wrists tingled. She'd had a taste of being bound against her will and she hadn't liked it one little bit. It was humiliating to be tied down like a dog. She wouldn't wish their situation on her worst enemy.

Throat tightening, her vision wavered. *I wish they'd just leave us alone.*

At first glance their bodies appeared to be nothing but scales from head to toe. It took her a moment to realize the Mer women were clothed in some kind of form-fitting outfits, much like a spandex bodysuit. She squinted, recognizing the material as fish leather. Stranger still was the fact their heads were shaved. Only a Mohawklike strip remained. On one side of each woman's scalp was a small tattoo.

Thompson indicated that the visitors could approach the Mer. "Can you identify these women?"

Snapping out of her thoughts, Gwen forced herself to focus.

With Kenneth at her heels, Tessa stepped up to one of the semiconscious women, looking closely at her face. "I recognize this one," she announced after a minute's examination. "In Ishaldi I knew her as Doma Chiara. She is a priestess and one of Queen Magaera's soldiers."

"You're sure of her identity?" Thompson asked.

Tessa nodded. "Considering she tried to kill me and Ken, yeah, I couldn't forget her face." She looked at the Mer strapped on the next table. "Yeah, her. I know her. Her name is Raisa, and she serves as one of the queen's councilors."

"And the third woman?" Yadira prompted as one of her assistants scribbled furiously on a pad.

Tessa looked. "I don't recognize her." She frowned and shook her head. "Just another of the queen's soldiers, I suppose."

Thompson nodded. "So we can consider them as hostiles?"

Tessa took a deep breath, clearly thinking over her answer before she spoke. "Yes, I would say that would be a correct assumption. There's no doubt in my mind they would have killed everyone once they recaptured me."

To catch the doctors up on the reasons behind the attack, Blake Whittaker briefly sketched out the details he'd learned the day the Mer attacked. "They seem to want Tessa back to regain control of the sea-gate," he finished.

Listening closely, Dr. Novak stepped up. "Are you telling me that you physically commanded the sea-gate to match your psychic resonance?"

Tessa shrugged helplessly. "Really, I'm not sure what I did. In order to crack the crystalline shell that was covering the entrance, I pulled a lot of energy out of the labradorite pillars lining the chamber."

"Jake said that's what seemed to supersize her Mer-craft," Kenneth added. "She burned them out trying to get through that thing."

Everyone could practically hear the wheels in No-vak's mind turning. "Though we've never proved the existence of wormholes in space, the general theory holds that their energy is electromagnetic."

"So Massey was right when he said that's what the sea-gate is?" Whittaker asked. "An actual honest-to-god portal between two worlds."

Novak shook his head. "I'm tending to lean that way, but unless I were able to view the sea-gate for myself, I couldn't be sure. And since it's miles under the ocean and supposedly destroyed ..." He paused midsentence, switching to another track. "Do you think you could draw me some sort of picture of the temple?" he asked Tessa.

Tessa nodded. "I'm not the best artist in the world, but I could give you a rough idea."

"I didn't see the outside, but I was inside it," Kenneth added. "I could help."

Novak flashed a smile. "Excellent. If I can get some rough drawings, I can digitize them and turn them into a

3-D representation of the undersea temple and sea-gate. I'll even try replicating the destruction of the temple, to see if that will give us a clearer idea of what's happening with the phenomena right now."

Thompson clapped the young scientist on the shoulder. "Excellent idea. Get to work as soon as possible."

"I should have something ready in about a week." Novak motioned for Tessa and Kenneth to follow him. "If you will please come this way, I'll get you some paper and pencils to work with. If you need a sketch artist, I can have one flown in for you."

"That would be even better," Kenneth said. "Since I can't draw a straight line with a ruler."

The three disappeared, exiting the main lab.

Addison watched the cute young doctor disappear. "There goes the future father of my children." She sighed.

Gwen rolled her eyes. "You wish."

She turned her attention back to the bustle filling the lab. Dr. Yadira was working over one of the women Tessa had identified as Doma Chiara. Awake and aware of her surroundings, Chiara twisted violently against the restraints holding her in place.

Yadira moved to comfort and calm the rebellious Mer.

Going momentarily rigid with fear, Chiara's lips peeled away from her teeth. Then she snapped, biting, thrashing, and lunging against her restraints with every ounce of strength she possessed. Eyes narrowed with hate, a stream of angry words spewed from her mouth.

Dr. Yadira jumped back as several of the other doctors rushed in to try to calm the frantic woman.

They couldn't get near her.

Chiara settled her gaze on the nearest man. A single word tore past her lips. Some invisible force slammed against the man's chest, propelling him backward with incredible strength and speed. He struck the wall full on, sliding to the floor in an unconscious heap.

Even though Tessa had told both her and Addison about the Mer, Gwen hadn't wanted to believe a word her sister said. How could the Mer—her own people!—be such savage, hateful creatures?

A syringe was produced, filled with a clear substance. "I don't think we can get close enough," one of the doctors called.

Yadira turned to Gwen. "Is there a way to control the psi-kinetic abilities without sedation?" Her voice was laced with panic.

Another guttural sound of rage poured up from Chiara's throat.

A shiver shook Gwen. The idea of disarming a fully empowered—and enraged—Mer was something she didn't fancy taking a shot at.

Somehow she found her voice. "We need to take her soul-stone." She reached for the crystal hanging at the base of her own throat. It felt oddly cool to her touch.

"How?" Yadira called.

She thought quickly, and before she knew what she was saying, she blurted, "I'll take care of this."

Addison gaped at her in alarm. "Do you even know how to deactivate another Mer's soul-stone?" she demanded.

Gwen recalled the bits and pieces she remembered from Tessa's own account of her experience with Queen Magaera. If equal in strength, two Mer would simply neutralize each other. She had to be a little bit stronger. In any case, she didn't have a choice. Someone had to do something, and she'd stepped up to the plate. All she could hope was that her hit would be the one that won the game.

"It's my will over hers," she shot back. "Whoever is strongest will win."

Grasping the stone she wore, Gwen forced herself to focus, mentally striking out to find and latch onto Chiara's psychic vibrations. It wasn't hard to find. An aura of terrible black rage surrounded the Mer from head to foot. She had literally cloaked herself in hate, sucking in every ounce of energy her body possessed to fling it toward the despised humans.

Because she hadn't been able to reenergize herself during her captivity, there was a chink in Chiara's psychic armor. She had only a little bit of strength to give, and it wouldn't last long.

All Gwen had to do was wear her down. *I can do this.*

The rebel Mer immediately felt the connection.

Chiara struck out, sending a blinding mental blow whizzing toward Gwen.

Unable to avoid taking the hit, Gwen felt it strike her squarely between the eyes, penetrating her skull until it struck the very center of her brain. An electric wave flashed over her entire body.

A smile curled Chiara's lips. In English, she said, "You may be Mer, but you are hardly strong enough to stop one of the true-bred."

Gwen forced herself to keep standing. A wave of panic flashed through her, giving her a glimpse of the terror awaiting the loser.

Planting her feet firmly, Gwen struck back with all her might. They two women were on another plane, one not of the body, but of the mind.

The lab began to blur as swirling lines of pure energy snapped and crackled between them. Focusing through her third eye, Gwen could see that Chiara was getting tangled in the energy ropes she sent out.

The vicious Mer screamed ferociously, hurling back bolts of pure lightning at Gwen. The prospect of losing her soul-stone clearly terrified her. She was going to scratch, claw, kick, and scream to the bloody end.

The solidity beneath Gwen's feet began to thin. She felt her body quiver under the intense pressure, sliding toward the floor. A searing fire raced through her chest, exploding like a sun gone nova.

A vague thought filled her mind. *I'm losing . . .*

Out of nowhere, Addison stepped between them. Towering and in command, her soul-stone blazed at her throat. Eyes widening in disbelief, Gwen saw the stone around Doma Chiara's neck commence to glowing hotter than a live coal.

Eyes filling with horror, Chiara screeched in pain and rage, writhing against the intense flare of agony Addison had inflicted. Body flexing in an arch against the hard metal table, she collapsed into a dead heap. The soul-stone around her neck winked out, a useless dead black thing.

Ignoring the flashes of pain beating at her temples,

Gwen stumbled toward Addison. The two sisters sagged into each other's arms.

Addison gasped, fighting hard to calm her breathing. "Damn, that was one intense ride."

Remembering to breathe, Gwen sucked in a lung-ful of welcome oxygen. Her vision cleared, bringing the room around her back into focus. Everyone's eyes were round with disbelief.

After a few minutes, everyone resumed normal ac-tivity. Doctors hurried to Chiara's side, checking her vital signs. "She's still alive," one physician announced. "Though I would have sworn for a moment we lost her."

"Uh, ho," Dennis Thompson muttered. "What the hell will we do if—" He sped off without finishing the thought, exiting the laboratory without a glance back. For a fat man, he moved pretty damn fast.

Addison broke out of her hold. "Quit hugging on me, will you? I can stand up just fine." Leaning forward, she pressed her hands to her knees, taking several deep breaths. "Man, that was freaking intense."

Blake Whittaker stepped toward her. "You okay?" His look was one of sincere concern.

Waving him back, Addison nodded. "Yeah. Just give me a minute, will you?"

Whittaker obeyed with a nod. He turned to Gwen. "What about you?"

Skin alive with lingering electricity, she rubbed her hands over her arms. There was no way the people around them would have been aware of the intense psy-chic firefight they'd just engaged in with Doma Chiara. "I think I'll survive." What she didn't say was that she felt like a battery totally drained of its charge. Right now she wasn't strong enough to flick at a fly.

He returned a crooked, shaky smile. "What the hell just happened here?"

Gwen put one hand to her temple, fighting a little wave of dizziness. She couldn't tell whether it was from her recent psi-fight or because Whittaker was standing so damn close.

"Telepathic showdown," she said, forcing a weak smile. "We won. We just need to make sure we get Chiara's soul-stone."

Pulling herself back up to her full height, Addison squared her shoulders. "And I'll take care of that right now." A little unsteady on her feet, she wobbled toward the unconscious Chiara. Her fingers curled around the Mer's deadened stone. Addison snapped it off her neck with a decisive gesture. "She won't give you any more trouble now." She handed the stone over to one of the astonished doctors.

Unable to pull her gaze away from her younger sister, Gwen inhaled a breath. Although she had believed she would be able to beat Chiara, she was wrong. Had Addison not stepped in, Chiara might have come out the winner. She realized then she'd been mistaken about Addison's abilities. Of the three of them, the youngest Lonike girl might prove to be the most formidable.

Head still swimming with dizziness, Gwen let her hand drop. "If you don't mind, I think I've had enough for today. Is there somewhere I can lie down a while?"

Blake Whittaker stepped up. "Of course. If you'll come with me, I'll show you where you'll be staying."

Chapter 12

An agent greeted the group as they left the lab, guiding them toward the familiar black sedans. Tessa and Kenneth would continue on with Dr. Novak, who wanted to get started animating Tessa's sketches of the sea-gate as soon as possible. Addison had remained behind with Dr. Yadira to answer additional questions about Mers' soul-stones.

That left Blake and Gwen alone. Within minutes they were speeding through the compound toward the living facilities. A few minutes later they arrived at the entrance of a small gated community.

The guard manning the gate buzzed them through. The agent behind the wheel navigated the car onto a small cul-de-sac. A series of small duplexes sat amid beautifully manicured lawns. The area was well lit and highly secure.

Gwen leaned forward, peering out the window. "It looks normal." A note of surprise colored her tone.

Blake laughed. "Not quite what you were expecting?"

He sensed her uncertainty. She shook her head. "I'm not sure what I was expecting," she admitted. "I imagined something like barracks, you know or—" She paused midsentence.

Sensing her hesitation, Blake gave her a little prod. Part of his job was to keep her talking, earn her trust and confidence. "What?"

She waved a hand. "Nothing, really."

With her face half in shadow, Blake couldn't discern her exact expression, but her tone suggested she was surprised to see they'd be living like ordinary human beings. "Come on. You were about to say something else." He leaned back against the leather seat. "Spit it out."

Gwen nervously folded her hands in her lap. "Well, to tell you the truth I expected something more like cages or cells," she admitted quietly. "I had this terrible vision you guys were going to stick us someplace like a prison, you know. Lock us up and throw away the keys."

Blake leaned close, lowering his voice. "That's only for the ones we're going to dissect."

Gwen glanced at him. "I—I, oh . . . I hope not."

He burst out laughing. "I'm teasing."

At least he hoped he was.

She pinned him under a glare. "You're such a dog." She punched him on the shoulder. "You should be beaten, and liberally."

"Hey, take it easy there." Blake reached up, rubbing the spot she'd touched and feigning a hurt look. "You do know assaulting a federal agent is against the law." He couldn't help but enjoy the contact. It was good to see her loosen up.

Gwen leaned back, studying him from under a sweep of long thick lashes. A slight smile toyed at her lips. "So arrest me, then, wise guy."

Blake reached for the handle on the door, uncomfortable with the idea that, in a way, they already had. Shifting in his seat, he stepped out of the car. The agent behind the wheel jumped out, hurrying to open Gwen's side.

"Your luggage has already been taken to your apartment," the driver informed them. He handed over a set of key cards. "You are assigned to number three," he informed Gwen. The next card went to Whittaker. "And you, Agent Whittaker, are number four."

Whittaker accepted his key card, tucking it in the breast pocket of his shirt.

Gwen raised a surprised brow. "So you're going to be stuck here with us?"

Whittaker nodded. It had all been prearranged down to the last detail. He knew exactly what he was supposed to be doing, and why. He didn't like it, but like any good soldier, he'd do the job and do it right.

"Pretty much. I'm the agent acting as your liaison officer with the doctors who will be performing the testing on you and your sisters."

Gwen took a slight step back in alarm. "Testing?"

Whittaker hurried to placate her. "Routine stuff," he assured her. "They would like to do a complete physical, as well as do some testing on your paranormal abilities."

She frowned. "Sounds very invasive."

"You won't be forced to do anything you are uncomfortable with," he said, then added, "I'll be with you every step of the way. If you feel pressured, just let me know and I will put an immediate stop to the matter. My job is to make sure you feel secure while at this facility."

The driver set his jaw and said nothing. Of course he knew the truth.

What Blake had just told her was a total lie, but somehow he forced himself to spit it out. As it stood, the agency's scientists had three other living specimens on which to perform the more invasive—and painful—testing. As for what would happen to Gwen and her sisters, he wasn't sure. Though he'd been given a higher level of clearance, there were still limitations to the information he could access. He hoped the restrictions would ease in time. For now, he'd have to live with the fact that he didn't know what lay ahead for the Lonike girls.

Refusing to think about it, he pushed all negative thoughts out of his mind. He could keep brooding about the matter when he was supposed to be psyching himself up for seduction. Truth be told, at the moment he wasn't in the mood. Despite his attraction to Gwen Lonike, he wouldn't mind going to bed alone. In fact, he looked forward to it.

I can play the game later, he told himself. It wasn't like they weren't going to be here tomorrow. The way things were going, it looked like he was going to be spending a lot of his tomorrows in this place.

He dismissed the driver.

The agent nodded, returned to his car, and sped off. Red taillights disappeared.

Gwen slowly rubbed her palms up and down her

arms. "Thank you for telling me that." She offered a weak smile. "I can't tell you how terrified I've been of this entire thing." She shook her head. "It's like I'm caught in some sort of bizarre nightmare, and if I could only wake up, things would be all right again."

Blake's eyes followed the motion of her hands. His flagging interest perked back up. Well, maybe he could put a little effort into getting closer.

"Are you cold?"

She shook her head. "Just nervous."

"Why don't we go inside and get settled in?" Blake took her arm, an easy natural move. It was an act that could be interpreted as innocent, yet would allow him to gauge her willingness for physical contact.

Gwen immediately leaned closer, her body almost brushing his. They fell into matching steps.

Blake led her up a short flight of steps. An unlocked main entrance led into a small brightly lit foyer. There was a door to the left and one to the right.

Gwen glanced around. "Wonder where they're hiding the cameras."

Blake followed her line of vision. "Actually, there are no cameras inside the private residences. No listening devices either. Once you go through that door, you have total privacy."

She arched one well-defined brow. "That is a surprise. I'd imagined our every move would be tracked."

Blake gave her an amused smile. "We really don't need to know when you eat or go to the bathroom, or if you sleep bare-assed naked." What he didn't add was that he was the eyes and ears of the facility. Everything he saw and heard would be meticulously recorded in the daily reports he'd have to send up the ladder.

He had a feeling he'd be jotting down a lot of boring details, a whole lot of effort for nothing. Gwen and her family had lived and functioned in the human world for a long time without detection. For all intents and purposes, these Mer had passed as peaceful, law-abiding humans all their lives.

Gwen slid her card into the reader. "Well, here goes nothing." She stepped under the threshold.

Blake followed her in.

She snapped on a light and peered around. "It's bigger than I thought it would be," she murmured.

"Nicer, too," he added, giving the place a quick visual sweep.

The single suitcase agents had packed for her sat inside the door. At the time, Gwen was still confined to the hospital, semicoherent and very much a danger to herself and those around her.

All the locals knew was that there had been a terrible accident on Little Mer Island. The incident had been declared a propane-tank leak, which had done extensive damage to the main house. Lucky was reported as a casualty. Gwen, too, was reported as being severely injured.

All in all, the heavy hand of the A51 agency had managed to draw a cloak around the unpleasant event.

Yeah, there would be whispers. But those would die down in time. Lucky's body had already been examined by the coroner and released to his survivors for a very quiet closed-casket funeral. There really wasn't much left to examine. The old man had literally been blasted to bits, hence the use of a convenient propane tank. Given the extensive renovations the place had undergone it wasn't only plausible, it was possible.

Forcing his thoughts back to the present, Blake cleared his throat. "What do you think?"

Still clearly ill at ease, Gwen forced a smile. "It'll do."

Together, they explored the small apartment. The size was perfect for one, maybe two people. It was decorated in neutral shades of beige and white, a little blank but otherwise cozy. There were the usual amenities of bedroom and bathroom. The kitchenette was a bit on the small side, outfitted with miniature versions of normal appliances such as the fridge and stove. Cabinet space was limited, but hardly a problem for one person.

Gwen spread her hands out. "God, if circumstances were different this would be a great place."

Blake shrugged. "They do try and make agents living on the compound comfortable."

She offered a brief smile. "I suppose I might as well enjoy seeing where those tax dollars are spent."

"Our budget's actually been trimmed quite a bit."

She looked surprised. "Really? Couldn't tell it from what I'm looking at." She cocked a brow at the widescreen television. "I hope that thing's got cable."

"Satellite, actually. What you don't have is Internet or a phone." He shrugged again. "Sorry. Your access with the outside world does have to be limited for now. As far as everyone knows, you have been moved to a trauma facility for treatment of your wounds incurred during the accident."

Gwen nodded. She'd been given all the details. "I hate being out of touch with Brenda," she commented.

"I'm sure she can handle things just fine."

Gwen frowned. "It's not a good time for me to be away. The height of the summer season is when we do the bulk of our business. You just don't know how tough it is. Clerks and maids quit at the drop of a hat because the wages aren't the greatest. And we're in a tight economy. People aren't traveling like they used to."

Hers was the typical list of every small business owner. Too much money going out, not enough coming in.

Blake shook his head and lifted his arms in a shrug. "I think you don't give your assistant manager enough credit," he finally said. "Seems to me she's capable of handling things while you're away."

Gwen dropped onto the couch. "That's what's so frustrating. I don't know how long I'll be away."

Blake sat down beside her. "Please be assured that we're doing everything in our power to locate the rest of the Mer who came back through the sea-gate with your sister and her husband. Since I doubt very much they would know where to find you, we're beginning to believe Jake Massey must be alive. If he is, how is he getting around undetected? His passport, credit cards, phone records all show no activity since the day he vanished."

Gwen bit her lower lip as if trying to decide to speak or not. "There was a rumor going around that Jake was involved in some shady business before Kenneth bought into Recoveries, Inc. He had a partner, Niklos something or other, who was a little on the crooked side."

Blake tried to remain nonchalant. "The name of his former partner is Niklos Sarantos. I also believe they were based in Crete, which is very near the diving site where Ishaldi was found. We've gotten a few leads that he and Sarantos were involved in some artifact smuggling."

She nodded. "Yeah. That's what I thought your visit might have been about. It was my understanding that Jake used Kenneth's money to buy Sarantos out when he offered Ken a partnership."

Blake thought a moment. "That's definitely something to look into. It's possible Massey made his way back to Crete and hooked up with his old contacts. If that's so, I'm pretty sure we can catch up with him." He spoke slowly so that his words would have weight. Offer hope.

Gwen laced her fingers together, then unlaced them. Nervous energy practically snapped and crackled all around her. "That would be great if you could find him and those other bitches who are making our lives hell."

Blake reached out and caught one of her nervous hands, offering a reassuring squeeze. He had to admire her relative calm. Had their situations been reversed he doubted he would've handled the matter with as much grace. It almost pained him that his role in her life would be one of deceit. He wanted to get to know her better, not only as a mermaid, but as a woman. "We will do the best we can." He subtly tightened his hold. "I promise."

Gwen glanced down, but didn't withdraw her hand from his. "Thank you."

Blake decided to test the boundaries. "There is one good thing out of this whole mess."

She glanced up, surprise written across her face. "Oh?"

He cocked his head to one side, amusement dancing in his eyes. "Maybe I still have a shot at taking you out sometime."

She nearly lost her composure but maintained her cool. "I didn't get to say so when you asked me out the first time, but the answer is yes." A small laugh escaped her. "Though I didn't quite picture this scenario."

Blake tightened his hold. "Truth be told, I was actually hoping to get to know you better." He leaned in a little closer, taking up more of her personal space.

Gwen held her place. She let the silence linger between them for a moment. "How much better?"

Blake simply leaned forward. "This much better." His mouth brushed hers.

Gwen's body immediately quivered, telegraphing her excitement. Pressing closer, she parted her lips and allowed his tongue to seek her own.

She was interested. Definitely interested. The signals she was putting out were perfectly loud and clear.

Blake took advantage, wrapping one hand in her hair and pulling her closer. It was the longest, most delicious locking of lips he'd ever shared with a woman. Only the necessity for air pulled them apart.

"Holy shit," he said, forgetting the words he'd mentally rehearsed for such a moment. "That was . . ."

A small smile crossed Gwen's moist lips. "Terrific." She quickly covered her mouth with a hand, but the blush rising to her cheeks said everything he needed to know.

He'd really turned her on.

*   *   *

Oh, heavens!

Blake Whittaker's kiss was the best she'd ever had, hands down. Beneath his touch her skin had raised into goose bumps. The desire to feel his mouth exploring every inch of her naked skin suddenly flashed through her mind.

Too much, too fast, she warned herself.

Her life had taken a complete one-hundred-and-eighty-degree turn and nothing was normal, not her own actions or reactions. Blake Whittaker was an attractive man. It would be easy to get tangled up with him because she was feeling lonely, desperate, and confused.

Sliding away, she put a safe bit of distance between their eager bodies. Stay within touching distance and she was sure to burst into flame the next time he made contact with her.

His fine brow wrinkled at her move. "That's not the usual reaction I get after *terrific*."

Gwen forced herself to take a deep breath. The extra oxygen helped clear her fuzzy brain and slow the intense beat of her heart. "I'm just being careful," she confessed, then hurried to add, "Don't get me wrong. I'm attracted—"

"But?" Despite his coolness, his blue-gray gaze simmered.

"You're a federal agent and I'm the Mer you have in custody." She chuckled. "Isn't there some rule about fraternizing with the aliens?"

Blake turned to face her, drawing one leg up on the

sofa to make himself more comfortable. His move gave her another whiff of that sexy aftershave he wore, one that evoked the image of high snowcapped mountains and crisp cool air. The scent enticed. "Actually, I'm not sure. I don't think it's addressed in the agent's handbook they gave me," he teased.

Gwen captured his gaze again. "I've heard about instances where guards and captives get involved, you know, forming an attachment because they're confined together."

His hand reached for hers. "And you think that's what this is? I'm taking advantage of you because you can't walk away?"

Gwen shook herself loose and got up. Stay and she'd be tempted to give in. When his mouth was on hers, the very molecules in her body vibrated with energy.

The one thing she'd always promised herself was that she wouldn't make love to any man until she was sure the attraction was solid. The secret she had to share was one that could make or break a relationship, and when the time finally arose where she'd have to disrobe and reveal all, she wanted her partner to be well prepared.

Trouble was, she'd never let herself progress to the vital point of revelation. She'd always put men off pursuing the physical side of a relationship by saying they needed to wait until marriage to have sex.

That was a stalling tactic and she knew it.

Blake Whittaker already knew what she was. And he seemed to have no problem accepting it. That kiss he'd laid on her a moment ago was one hell of a whopper.

The tension in his body was strong enough to knock her down.

For the longest time she'd worn her virginity like a badge of honor. To her, it showed she was chaste, pure. Principled in her choice of a lifestyle, and a lover.

Lately, though, it had become an albatross around her neck. Instead of feeling wholesome, she felt like a frustrated, angry woman. The Mer were highly sensual creatures. It wasn't unusual or unacceptable for a Mer to have many lovers throughout her life, as her fertility would not kick in until she took a breed-mate. How could she know who the right man might be unless she dabbled her toes in the water?

Except . . .

If they were going to do this, she would have to be honest. She wondered how he'd feel about starting an affair with no expectations or attachments.

She slowly turned back to him. "I'd be lying if I said I wasn't tempted." It was true. She was tempted. More than that, she was wondering just what she'd do with herself. There was no doubt about the days being occupied. But her nights? Tessa and Kenneth were still in the honeymooners stage of marriage. They wouldn't be welcoming any company. And Addison? That girl was already making goggle eyes at Dr. Novak. No doubt the good doctor would be willing to participate in an up-close-and-personal examination.

And me?

The idea of playing solitaire or staring at the boob tube all night didn't exactly sit too well in her mind. She was used to being busy, tied up in work and worrying about the profit and loss margins of the hotel. Losing that was like having the ground yanked out from under her feet.

She didn't know what to do with herself.

He leaned back against the couch, spreading his arms across the headrest. "But?" he asked.

"I might be interested in pursuing something, ah, physical, but I'm not sure I can put anything emotional behind it."

A small pause filled the air. Gwen silently counted: one, two, three beats of her heart. She wondered why he wasn't responding, why he wasn't immediately leaping at the opportunity. This was the ideal situation for a man, right?

Whittaker leaned forward, scrubbing his hands across the five-o'clock shadow that was now a nine-o'clock one. They were both clearly tired and frustrated with their entire situation. Neither one of them wanted to be under confinement of any sort.

"So you're saying you'd like to sleep with me, as long as the only things that meet are our bodies?" His voice was flat, his tone holding a hint of disinterest. Gwen couldn't help but feel a bit surprised.

She sent him a silent plea for understanding. "Well, you have to admit some physical relief might be nice. And this isn't the best circumstance for nurturing a relationship."

He nodded. "I can understand the need for two consenting adults to relieve a little tension."

Relief filled her. He seemed to be warming to the

idea. "Exactly." She paused as a thought occurred. "But on the other hand, I would have to wonder if you were sleeping with me because you wanted me, or because of the mermaid novelty."

Whittaker eyed her from head to toe. "Based on what I'm looking at, I'd have to say I don't see a tail anywhere. I guess I'd have to go with what I see." A slight smile turned up one corner of his mouth. "And I like what I've seen so far."

She spread out her hands. "So what do you want to do?"

Whittaker pushed himself to his feet. Crossing to where she stood, he took one of her hands. "Honestly? I want to go back to the first day we met and do it all over again," he admitted slowly. "I think the right sparks were there. And I think if you give it a chance, something good might happen." His tone was courteous. Lifting her hand to his lips, he gave it a soft kiss. "But if you don't want to get involved, I'm not going to force the matter."

Unsure how to answer, Gwen forced out a smile. "Maybe you're right . . ." No reason to say anything else. The attraction they'd shared a moment ago seemed to be fizzling out right before her eyes.

Whittaker let her hand drop before he turned and re-treated toward the sliding door at the rear of the living room. Unlatching the lock, he gave her a brief glance. "It's been a long day. You should get some sleep." With that, he slipped through the opening.

Gwen sagged into a nearby chair. Her pulse beat heavily in her throat as she tried to figure out what had happened. She thought she was giving all the right signals, saying all the right words. Apparently she hadn't. Instead of sweeping her up in his arms and carrying her into the bedroom, Whittaker had beat a hasty retreat.

Disappointment welled up in her eyes. *What the hell is wrong with me?*

She'd actually been ready to offer him her most precious treasure and he'd simply suggested they sleep on it.

Sleeping definitely wasn't going to happen. She was too revved up to even think about going to bed. Especially if she had to go alone.

She glanced through the plate-glass door. From where she sat she could see it opened onto a covered patio overlooking a large oval swimming pool. An expanse of lawn ended with a thick patch of forests. Apparently they would have complete and total privacy.

Whittaker hadn't gone to his own place either. Hands shoved deeply into his pocket, he stood at the edge of the pool, contemplating its clear blue depth. Area lights positioned around the edge of the patio and within the pool itself offered an intimate and inviting illumination.

She frowned. It was no secret Blake had a fear of the water. No way he'd be stripping off and taking a dip.

But that didn't mean she couldn't.

Slipping out of the chair, Gwen reached for the button at the top of her blouse. A little smile played on her lips as she fumbled with the small pearly bead beneath her fingers.

Chapter 13

Blake couldn't figure out what the hell he'd just done. He'd either made the stupidest move a man could make, or he made the smartest. He wasn't sure.

He knew what he was supposed to be doing. He even knew how to do it. Normally he wouldn't have a problem with the idea. He wasn't an innocent, and had engaged in his share of one-night stands. And it was exactly what the agency wanted him to do.

Yet somehow the idea of bedding Gwen Lonike had taken an oddly personal turn. When she'd indicated she was open to an affair without emotional attachments, the words hit him in all the wrong ways.

Even though he knew why in the back of his mind, Blake wasn't quite ready to recognize it. There had been a time in his life when casual sex was all he believed he needed from a woman. But watching his son growing up through the years had begun to change his point of view.

Blake stared into the depths of the pool. The full

moon was reflected on the glassy surface. The clear water rippled, gently lapping at the edges.

Gwen had everything he liked in a woman, a fantastic combination of beauty and brains. He didn't want to enter into this lightly and cut off any possibility of a real relationship in the future.

But part of his assignment was to get information. He'd been ordered, in so many words, to seduce Gwen. Considering the idea, a strong tug stirred him below. No reservations there. He wouldn't mind making love to her.

What he didn't like was the idea that he'd have to deceive her.

Doubt had never bothered him before. Now it hovered at the shadowy corners of his brain like a small fanged beast, taking bite after bite out of his conscience. Misleading Gwen about his true motives, using her in any way, just felt wrong.

Such confusion and uncertainty wasn't the way he normally operated. Usually, he knew what he wanted and he went after it, with no hesitation. He knew he wanted Gwen, wanted to sleep with her. He just didn't want to have to lie to her about his motives.

He briefly toyed with the idea of contacting Frances Fletcher, telling her that he just couldn't handle it. Truth be told, she was putting him in the middle of a gray area, that of duty versus the government's need to know.

Blake's jaw tightened. He already knew he wouldn't be making that call to his superior. If he couldn't perform as expected, he'd be replaced—or worse.

Pulling a hand out of his pocket, Blake rubbed his

burning eyes. He was tired, having passed exhaustion hours ago. Right now he was powered on pure adrenaline. Without the ability to think straight, he'd make mistakes.

Maybe it was a good idea to put some distance between himself and Gwen until he managed to screw his head on straight. A good night's sleep would go a long way toward restoring his sanity. Right now it seemed to be slipping through his fingers like tiny granules of sand.

Just as he'd made up his mind to go to his own place, he heard the door sliding across its metal track, a soft, barely audible whoosh. The sound of heels clicking on the patio tile followed. He didn't have to turn around. He knew it was Gwen.

"Nice evening." Her melodic voice wafted from behind.

A series of warm prickles raced over his skin.

Damn. Now wasn't the best time to see her. Not when he had too much to sort through. Later. Later would be better.

Shaking off the heavy mantle of exhaustion, Blake squared his shoulders. He turned, determined to be friendly and agreeable. "Yeah, it is."

Gwen smiled. "Great pool they've got here."

Warm prickles turned to gooseflesh.

Blake forced himself to kill his frown. "I suppose it's nice enough if you like to swim."

Gwen smiled. "Matter of fact, I was just thinking about that." She slowly began to unbutton her blouse.

Suddenly Blake didn't feel so tired or confused after

all. His eyes widened as he watched her undo each little pearly button. Oh, man, surely she wasn't about to strip.

Yes, it definitely looked like she was.

Heat boiled beneath the surface of his skin. He grabbed his tie, loosening it a little. Its grip around his neck was getting to be too tight for comfort. "Is that right?" was all he could manage to say.

Inwardly wincing, he immediately gave himself a swift mental kick. Shit. Was that the best he could manage? Some freaking master of seduction he was. *Smooth move.*

Gwen laughed and spread her blouse open, letting it slip from her slender shoulders. "That's right." She let the plain cotton top slide from the tips of her fingers onto a nearby deck chair. Stepping out of her low-heeled pumps, she slowly unzipped her slacks and then pushed them over her hips and down the length of her endless legs. A moment later, she stood clothed only in bra and panties.

Blake's heart beat rapidly in his chest. Her lingerie was the plain, white, sensible kind, with no extra frills or ruffles. Didn't matter a bit, either. With such a smoking-hot body, Gwen Lonike didn't need anything to enhance her natural beauty. The heat in his groin was growing, threatening to take things to a more physical level. Given another few minutes to gawk and he'd definitely have something to show her. Something very hard, and eager.

"Guess that will do for a swimsuit." He struggled to push the words out over the lump in his throat.

She shook her head. "Oh, I'm not going to swim in

this." Reaching between her breasts, she undid the clasp. The plain white cups fell away, revealing the curves of two lovely breasts topped with nipples the shade of ripe cherries.

Blake's mouth went Sahara dry. Just looking at her threatened to short-circuit every cell in his body. His pulse picked up speed, doubling its rhythm. Things were about to get very uncomfortable. His clothing felt like it was shrinking down around him, instantly going two sizes too small. He couldn't mistake the signals his loins were sending to his head. He wanted her.

Bad.

Gwen continued her agonizing tease, wriggling out of her panties. She let them dangle on the tip of her index finger, giving them a sexy little spin before tossing them in the pile of discarded clothing.

And then she wore nothing. Nothing at all except that teasing little smile.

The sight was enough to make a grown man fall to his knees and beg like a dog.

Eyes drifting over her curves, Blake fought to keep control of his trembling knees when his gaze dipped below her waist. He sucked in a startled breath. She'd recently had a Brazilian wax, which exposed every last delicious inch of her mons.

More fascinating than her naked self was the pattern etched into her skin. Like her sisters, Gwen's began at her wrists, coiling up her arms, around her shoulders and down her back and abdomen. A sexy swirl around her hips continued all the way down to her ankles.

She took a deep breath. "I've never been fully undressed in front of anyone before," she confessed in a breathy voice. "You're the first human to see me like this."

Pulling his wits together, Blake fought to find his voice. "I—I'm honored," he stammered before a smile crept onto his lips. "And delighted."

A little blush crept into her cheeks. The flash of white teeth revealed two cute dimples hovering at the corners of her mouth. "There's also something else I want to show you."

With a delicate step that lent her hips a sexy swaying motion, she walked toward the swimming pool. Coming to its edge, she paused briefly. Then she took a deep breath and dived. She cut through the water cleanly, barely adding a ripple to the surface.

Though he held no desire to go in after her, Blake stepped closer to the edge. The pool was lit, giving him an excellent view of her naked body as she swam beneath the surface. Without coming up for air, she made a few graceful glides and turns.

And then it happened.

Like a rose blossoming into its full bloom, a series of bright sparks raced across her skin, grabbing and twisting her legs together. A long, graceful tail unfurled, shimmering with iridescent color. It happened so fast he almost couldn't process the change.

Surfacing, Gwen swam to the edge of the pool. Settling her elbows on the tiled surface, she propped her chin on one damp palm. "Come on in," she invited. "The pool's heated."

Shaking his head, Blake took a step back. Desire fled

before the uneasy sensation spread through him like a deadening disease.

Wishing for a good numbing shot of whiskey, he licked dry lips. There was nothing he'd love more than to strip off and dive in, pulling her slippery naked form against his own eager body. But it wasn't going to happen, except in his imagination.

He gritted his teeth. "I can't swim," he said.

Her attention settled on his face, intense and focused. She was watching his every move, gauging his every reaction, physical and otherwise. "Not even the shallow end?" she asked.

A tremor rippled through him. Instead of feeling big and bad when he contemplated the pool, he felt small and weak and absolutely terrified. "Nope. If it's water and it's above my ankles, I don't go into it."

Disappointment tugged at the corners of her mouth. "Is there a reason why?" She'd clearly had other plans.

Tension tightened Blake's shoulders. Like Gwen, he had his own dirty little secrets to hide. Wiping a hand across his brow, he hedged. "There is, but now isn't the time or place to swap childhood tales."

Eyeing him from head to foot, she cocked her head. "So what happened? Did some nasty little brat push you in and hold you under?"

Involuntarily, he took another step back. "Something like that," he mumbled, more than a little taken aback by her perceptive words.

She nodded. "I sensed that in you when Lucky took us across the bay. It must have been terrifying."

Blake shook his head to clear it of past fears and

phantoms. "It was a long time ago, and best forgotten." He paused a beat, giving himself time to recover his composure. "Besides, I'm enjoying looking at you."

Drawing a breath, she met his gaze. A smile twitched at her lips. "Well, this is me. Wearing my tail." Lifting the tip out of the water, she wriggled the unwieldy appendage, giving a flash of pretty blues and pinks etched with black. "Are you freaked-out yet?"

Exhaling the breath he'd forgotten he was holding, Blake immediately dropped onto his haunches. Whatever exhaustion he'd felt a few minutes ago had definitely vanished. He was totally and utterly snared in the magic of a mermaid.

"Freaked-out?" he repeated. "My God, no. It's gorgeous. You're gorgeous."

Biting her lower lip, she peeked out from beneath lashes at least an inch long. "You don't think I'm an abomination against nature?" she asked quietly.

He cleared his throat. "Hell, no. I think it's amazing you can do what you do. It just proves there are still wonderful things in this world yet to be discovered."

Gwen's smile vanished. "Yeah, *things*." She pushed away from the edge, bobbing in the depth. "That's all people see us as. Things to look at, the way you'd look at an animal in a zoo."

He lifted his hands in protest. "That's not the same at all."

She flicked her head in a defiant gesture. "Sure it is. Admit it. In the back of your mind you think we're some kind of mutants. Now that you've got us here, all you want to do is poke and prod us, study us under micro-scopes to find out what makes us different."

Blake shook his head. "That's just part of science," he countered, using logic to support his argument. "Part of the process of discovery."

Though he didn't say it out loud, he did have to agree with her. If the general public actually knew about mermaids, what would they want to do? Put them in a tank so they could look at them the way they did any-thing else that was strange or unusual. But that was an inborn part of human nature. People had the desire to look at, admire, and yes, even study things they didn't understand.

But caging a lion in a zoo or a dolphin in a tank was an acceptable practice. Those were animals, seemingly without the ability to think or rationalize about their state of captivity. The Mer were creatures with an in-telligence comparable to that of humans. But they also possessed abilities many people would find alien, and therefore frightening.

Frowning, Gwen pouted. "What if we don't want to be discovered?"

He shrugged. "I don't guess you've got any say in the matter."

Swimming to the steps leading out of the pool, Gwen shifted. Rivulets of water ran off her skin as she left the depths behind. "What if I don't want to be exposed?" she asked in a plaintive voice. "What if I want to be hu-man, just like everybody else?"

Blake slowly walked around the pool, giving the edge

a wide berth. He didn't stop until he was within touching distance. Intimate touching distance. Her hair, soaking wet, clung to the curves of her face like a second skin. He reached out, brushing a few damp locks off her forehead and cheeks. "Don't settle for ordinary," he told her. "There's already too damn much of that going around. Be what you really are, Gwen. Be extraordinary. Hiding who you are, what you really are, is no way to go through life."

Gwen's gaze locked with his. Her compelling green eyes glimmered with the rise of tears. "Will anyone accept what I really am?" she asked softly.

Blake's gaze locked with hers. Standing so close to her caused a fluttering sensation deep in his stomach, not to mention the delicious throbbing of need in his loins.

Pulse shifting into a higher gear, he stepped a little closer. His heart rate soared as he slowly reached out to trace her moist, full lips with the tip of his finger. "I'm someone who does."

She shut her eyes, soaking up his caress. The sound of her breathing was a sexy, seductive rhythm in his ears. "Really?" she murmured against his fingertip.

Unable to stop himself, Blake reached for her slender hips. Pulling her warm wet body closer, his mouth grazed hers.

At first Gwen held back, shutting him out. To entice her to open up, Blake slid his tongue along the seam of her lips. She relented a bit, granting him access. Instead of sweeping in and conquering, he dipped into her with a slow, light move.

Hands rising to his chest, Gwen curled her fingers into his shirt. The momentum built as she pulled him closer. Her hips pressed against his, bringing them together in a way that said all the necessary parts and angles would fit just fine.

Blake had to force himself to come up for air. As far as he was concerned, he could stand there and kiss her all night. Except that his body had other ideas, more urgent and pressing.

He wanted her.

Now.

Bending, he swept an arm under her knees, lifting her with hardly any effort at all.

Gwen locked her arms around his neck as he carried her back into her apartment. Barely a minute later she found herself lying across a bed made up with a pretty quilted comforter. A plump pillow rested beneath her head.

She stretched out, feeling sexy and sensuous.

Blake's gaze romanced every inch. "God, you're beautiful." He didn't waste any time shedding his clothes. Struggling to get his shirt and tie off, he carelessly tossed them aside. Kicking off his shoes, he unzipped his slacks, pushing them down over narrow hips. He wore those body-hugging boxer briefs, which perfectly displayed the rock-hard slabs of his abdomen and long, muscular legs. The tight briefs also prominently outlined an erection she couldn't possibly ignore.

Gwen smiled. If this is what it felt like to let herself go

and enjoy her sexuality with a human male, she was glad she'd opened her mind to the possibility. And there was no doubt she affected him on the physical level.

As for herself, the attraction she felt for him was powerful, and real.

Without taking his gaze off her, Blake placed his hands on the waistband of his briefs. "Are you sure you want to do this?" There was no doubt on his side. Desire flared in the depths of his eyes.

She let silence pass between them a moment before answering. "Yes, I do. Very much." If she wanted to change her mind, now was the time. But she didn't. She wanted—no, needed—this night to happen. It had been entirely too long in coming.

Blake quickly discarded his briefs. Naked, he stretched out beside her. The eager swell of his erection pressed against her thigh as he drew her into his arms. His gaze took on a new smoldering intensity as he stroked a hand down her cheek. "Me too."

Acutely aware of the feel of his heated flesh pressing against hers, she realized her hand was a few inches away from his pulsing erection. Somehow it felt right lying here beside him, both of them naked and exposed in every way. It was a relief to shed her inhibitions and simply enjoy the moment.

Without really thinking about what she was doing, Gwen let her fingers trace a path from the plum-ripe crown, down the length of him. Her exploring hand cupped and marveled over the heat emanating from his engorged flesh.

She heard Blake suck in his breath. A low, almost inaudible groan drew her gaze up to his face. "Damn," he gritted, body trembling from the intimate contact. "Keep that up and I won't last long at all." His voice was taut, as ragged as his respiration.

A tingle burned all the way down her spine. Though she'd fooled around at various times with past boyfriends, she'd never stripped down to the skin and gotten in bed with a naked man. Her experience was limited to exploration without actual nudity or penetration. She had a feeling she was in for a treat.

"Don't lose it," she countered breathlessly. "I want all of you."

Blake stroked her hip. "We're going to have to take it slow." He moaned softly as her hand made another leisurely trek. "Really slow."

"I can handle slow." She nipped his lower lip with her teeth.

Blake shuddered. "And I'm about to show you everything I've been fantasizing about doing to you."

Threading his fingers through her damp hair, he brought her face within an inch of his. Their kiss started out slow, but didn't remain that way. Desire had built between them since they'd first met, and need was too urgent to contain.

Sensation took over.

Hand slipping down to the curve of her hip, Blake's grip tightened. His chest felt like a rock wall. The solid ridge below his waist grew harder, its pulse more insistent.

As their lips parted, Gwen exhaled the breath she hadn't been aware she was holding. "I can't believe this is happening."

Blake traced his fingers over her skin, following the thick lines of her scale pattern. Her fingers grazed his chest, ruffling through the thick patch of hair growing there. A lot of the men she saw on the beach were shaved down to bare skin. She liked that he kept things natural. He had a real man's body.

Trailing his fingers down her side, his hand graced her left nipple. The little nub hardened, igniting a whirlwind of sensations deep inside her core. He rolled the tip between thumb and forefinger, gently tugging.

A soft moan slipped from Gwen's lips. Her heart beat rapidly against her rib cage. "That feels so good," she gasped.

"It's about to feel better."

Lowering his head, Blake drew the quivering peak into his mouth. His tongue painted the tip, circle after damp circle. A soft moan slipped over her lips. To her surprise, her nipple tingled under the roughness of his tongue. Her lower body arched against his, a silent plea for more. Her body quivered with pent-up tension.

Responding to her sounds of delight, Blake flicked and teased each nipple in its turn. At the same time he brushed the flat of his palm down her belly as he sought the softness between her thighs.

Gwen momentarily stiffened.

He sensed her hesitation. His hand froze. "Should I stop?"

She quickly shook her head. "I haven't been with

anyone in a long time," she explained, hedging around the truth. "I might be a little, um, tight."

Blake relaxed and resumed his exploration. "Tight is good." He pressed a kiss to the tip of one tented nipple. "Relax."

He slowly eased two fingers inside her slick depth. "You like that?" he whispered in a sultry tone.

Back arching, her hips lifted to join the tempo of his hand. "Mmmm . . . yes." Hovering like a hummingbird in flight, all she could do was feel.

He grinned. "Then you'll love this."

Blake slipped lower, adding the soft pressure of his mouth. His fingers moved in and out as his talented tongue worked at her most sensitive flesh.

Gwen's hips jerked upward, the beginning of a grinding, rocking motion that was sweeter than it was hurried, more paced than it was furious. With every gliding thrust, Blake's fingers delved farther into her depth. The friction was almost too much to take.

Tremors engulfed her, minute shivers that gradually became frantic convulsions. The agony was so prolonged, so exquisite that Gwen wanted to cry out for harder, faster thrusts.

Just as she was about to climax, Blake slowed the pace.

The moment slipped through her fingers, taking pleasure with it. "Damn," she moaned.

Blake laughed low in the back of his throat. "Take it easy. Give me a minute and I'll make it feel even better."

Reaching over the edge of the bed, he snagged his discarded slacks and fished out his wallet. Opening it, he produced a foil-wrapped packet. Blake tore open the foil with his teeth. "Being prepared doesn't hurt anyone." He extracted the rubber and rolled it down the length of his shaft with a practiced hand.

He stretched out over her, supporting his weight on his outstretched arms. His hips sank between her thighs.

Gwen's hands slipped over his shoulders, down his back. She knew he was letting her get used to his weight, his length and size. "I want you, Gwen," he whispered. There was a slight hesitation. "But only if you want me."

She pulled him closer. "I want you, too," she murmured against his lips.

Unable to restrain himself another minute, Blake thrust into her. Gwen arched with pleasure and agony, unleashing a startled cry into the air. Her nails dug into his flesh. She bit her lip, fighting the urge to moan.

Between them they began a sweet rhythm that steadily grew more frenzied and eager. Her initial pain faded into something far different, something delicious. Heat leaped and flickered inside her, burning all her nerves to cinders.

Gwen's trembling hands instinctively slid lower, cupping his firm ass. "More." Her gasped sobs of pleasure mingled with his own rasping breath.

Rocking up against him, she allowed him even fuller and deeper access. With every plunge of his hips, Blake went farther inside her. The crescendo of climax came without warning, sweeping both of them away.

Body shuddering with release, Blake growled a rough sound in the curve of her neck. His hips slammed into hers a final time, triggering her release.

Tossed through one shimmering wave of ecstasy after another, Gwen writhed beneath his weight. She cried out with wonder, glorifying in complete and total fulfillment.

Even after their bodies collapsed, the pressure of his weight continued to send tiny little spirals of sensation whirling through her core.

Gwen wrapped her arms around his waist. She doubted she would ever breathe normally again. "I don't want this night to ever end," she murmured into his ear.

Shifting his weight, Blake rode on his elbows and stared down at her face. A grin parted his lips. "Oh, trust me," he said impishly. "I'm just getting started."

Gwen tightened her grip. "Oh, trust me," she countered with more than a little delight. "That's the best thing I've heard since this entire mess began."

Chapter 14

Blake awoke to the sunshine filtering in through the blinds covering the windows. Brow wrinkling in confusion, he glanced around the unfamiliar surroundings. It took him more than a few seconds to remember where he was.

And who he was with.

He glanced over to the other side of the bed. Gwen lay curled in a ball, her arms wrapped securely around a pillow. Strands of red hair were spread out around her head like a fiery halo. Eyes closed in sleep, her breath winnowed softly through her lips.

It had been years since he'd woken up with another person in his bed. He'd gotten so used to living and sleeping alone that getting up with someone else lying beside him was almost scary. Living alone meant he didn't have to worry if he left the toilet seat up or a pile of newspapers scattered across the couch. An avowed grouch, he didn't even want to hear the sounds of another human being's voice before he'd had at least two cups of coffee when he first woke up.

Glancing at Gwen, Blake felt his throat tighten. Damn. She looked so gorgeous lying there. *You are one hell of a lucky man.*

He blinked. Now where had that idea come from?

He wasn't quite sure. But one thing was for certain. Every move of his muscles reminded him about last night's vigorous exertions.

He had to admit he felt good. Great sex, good sleep, waking up beside a beautiful woman. What more could a man ask for?

Rolling over onto his side, Blake had to resist the urge to reach out and touch her. Exhausted in the aftermath, he didn't even remember falling asleep. Blurry images wafted across his mind's eye, entertaining him with glimpses of their recent lovemaking. They'd gone after each other like two teenagers, barely taking the time to breathe before attacking each other again. Gwen had been insatiable, begging, urging, pleading for more. He'd delivered until every last reserve of his strength had been depleted. He'd done his best to be a generous and giving lover, making sure her wants and needs were well satisfied.

Francis Fletcher had better have a medal tucked away with his name on it. He'd gone over and above the call of duty and service to his country.

Trouble is, last night didn't feel like work. It felt like pleasure. It felt personal. Somehow his needs as a man had gotten between his duty as an agent. Heart beating faster, he suddenly felt nauseous. His skin felt all prickly, his mouth as dry as cotton.

He should have gotten up and gone home last night. Waking up in bed with Gwen had only sealed the deal. He wanted to wake up with her beside him every day.

Somehow it just felt right.

Not that he could let anyone know. If his superiors felt he'd become compromised in any way, they'd pull him off the assignment in a heartbeat. That would mean being separated from Gwen.

He'd have to tread carefully. The line between exploiting the Mer and protecting them was a very thin one, indeed. Technically he was supposed to be on the side of the government. Morally, though, he wasn't so sure. Did the government have the right to invade the lives and suppress the rights of those society would view as strange—or alien?

Someone had to watch out for the Mer.

And he'd be the man who took the job. Whether he wanted it or not, the responsibility had dropped in his lap.

He reached out, laying a gentle hand against Gwen's bare arm. *If anyone harms her or her family . . .*

There would be hell to pay.

His touch woke Gwen.

Groaning, she pushed away the pillow and rolled onto her back. Seeing him, her eyes widened in surprise. She yelped and pulled the sheet up around her nude body, but the effort was too little, too late.

Blake grinned. " 'Morning," he greeted. "I can tell by the look on your face that you weren't expecting see me here."

A heated blush rose to Gwen's cheeks. "Honestly, I wasn't."

Blake eased himself over beside her. The mattress dipped under the shifting of his weight. "I hope you aren't regretting it." His head dipped and he brushed his lips over one of her bare shoulders.

"No." She shook her head. "I'm not." She lifted her chin in an almost defiant manner. "I wanted it to happen."

Something in Blake's heart twisted. It. She'd used the word it to describe their lovemaking. She hadn't said she wanted him, or that she'd enjoyed having sex with him. She'd simply said she wanted *it* to happen.

His gaze met hers, zeroing in on her face. "It did happen and it was pretty damn good."

Gwen bit down on her lower lip.

He caught the subtle move. "Something wrong?"

She shook her head. "I'm just a little stiff, and sore." Pulling the sheets closer to her nude body, she started to slip off the bed. A gasp broke from her lips when she stood up. "Oh, no!"

Blake's gaze tracked hers. A small pool of blood stained the place where she'd slept.

Face scarlet with mortification, Gwen reached out to tug the fitted sheet off the mattress. Blake barely had time to stand up before it was whipped out from under him. "Oh, I can't believe this is happening," she muttered, balling the soiled linen before pressing it protectively against her stomach.

Blake shrugged. He knew the facts of life. A woman couldn't help her menstrual cycle. It was a normal, natural thing. An accident. It also gave him another clue into Mers. Their bodies seemed to be exactly the same as any human female.

"Take it easy. We can flip the mattress. It's just an accident."

"I didn't know that would happen," Gwen hurried to explain. "I mean, I did, but I didn't, you know. It—it's my first time . . ." Her words of embarrassment trailed off into silence.

Blake's head nearly did a one-eighty swivel. "Wait a minute." He held up his hands, making a time-out motion. "What do you mean it's your first time?"

She looked at him plaintively. Tears of frustration welled around the edges of her eyes. A long minute stretched into two. "It's my first time ever having sex," she admitted, voice strained from the awkwardness of her confession.

Blake's brows shot up as he realized the implications. Very aware that he stood stark-ass naked in front of the woman he'd just deflowered, he quickly reached for his underwear and slacks. Stepping into his clothes, he zipped and buttoned with haste. It felt wiser to be covered up for this conversation.

"Now, let's talk," he said, seeking clarification. "This can't be right. Are you saying you're a virgin?"

Refusing to let a single tear fall, Gwen blinked hard. "I was last night." She sagged into a nearby chair.

Blake shook his head. "I see." That was definitely one thing he would never have expected to find: a twenty-seven-year-old virgin. In a society that had sex shoved in its face twenty-four hours a day, seven days a week, it was a rarity. Especially for a woman of Gwen's age.

She'd chosen him to be her first. It was then Blake knew what had happened between them was more than the satisfaction of a physical itch. Their bodies had fit together so perfectly, almost as if they'd been made for each other.

"I hope you're not upset with me." She closed her eyes, rubbing her face. "I should have told you."

As she spoke, the mirror over the bureau cracked. Like a windshield struck with a pebble, a tiny hairline fracture began to form in the thick glass.

Blake's gaze flew to the mirror. His self-protective instincts kicked into gear. He knew she could tear him to pieces with a thought. *Oh, damn . . .* Not good. His head turned back to Gwen.

She leaned forward, planting her head against her knees. "It wasn't supposed to happen this way." The moan issuing up from her was low and mournful.

Eyes widening, Blake watched the single crack grow larger. He could hear the glass breaking apart. The cracks multiplied, branching out in a spider's web, snaking with unnerving speed.

The one thing Blake had noticed about Gwen was that she seemed to have a hair trigger when it came to unleashing her psi-kinetic energies.

Forcing himself to stay calm, he walked over to where Gwen sat. She was still hunched over in her self-protective shell.

Kneeling in front of her chair, he reached out and took her by the shoulders. Holding her in a gentle, yet strong grip, he forced her to sit up. It was the same hold he'd used dozens of times before. He usually used it on a four-year-old boy throwing a temper tantrum.

Grabbing on to her felt like taking hold of a hot wire fence. The blood pulsing beneath her veins thrummed with power. The tips of his fingers tingled as he held her. In a few seconds, her body heat seemed to fall to a low simmer. "It's okay." He forced his voice to remain steady. "It's no big deal."

"I feel so stupid." Tears rising all over again, she wavered. "I tried to tell you last night. You know . . . when I said it was the first time I'd ever showed anybody my tail."

Blake slipped his fingers under her chin, caressing the hard line of her jaw. "I have to admit I was so busy looking at you that it totally flew over my head." That was pretty true. At the time, a semitruck could have run over him and he wouldn't have noticed. He was too enchanted by the lady in the water.

A smile tugged at her lips. "I've never met a man who I thought could accept me—the real me. Even though I look human, there's always the Mer hovering in the background, waiting to emerge. It's hard to find someone you can share it with."

He suddenly got a glimpse of Gwen's inner demons. Beneath the facade of confidence and control was a woman struggling to accept herself and her place in the world. It was a burden all people carried at one time or another. Everyone had their trials as well as triumphs. Hers was heavier than most because of her complicated heritage. It would be hard to find a man who would love her—tail and all.

Emotion took over. His grip loosened around her arms and he rubbed her shoulder gently. "I'm honored you chose me to be your first." As he said the words, he knew he meant them.

She sniffed. "Damn it, I hate to cry." A wavering smile crossed her lips. "This wasn't quite the way I'd imagined this would happen. I had something a little more romantic in mind and not—" She squinched up her face. "Ugh. A big mess." Her trembling body gave him comfort. The attraction was not one-sided at all.

He raised an amused brow. "Trust me when I tell you I'm used to dealing with women's issues." He laughed. "I've got a kid, remember? This is nothing compared to diapers and food flung all over the house."

Gwen relaxed enough to laugh. "If nothing else, I guess it will be a night I'll always remember."

Blake cupped her hands in his. "I'll remember it, too," he admitted. "You're definitely not a woman I could ever forget."

"In a good way, I hope," she added.

Relieved to have the crisis under control, he nodded. "Always in a good way."

She sighed. "Guess I should take a shower."

That remark got his attention. Anticipation kicked his heart into a faster rhythm. "Maybe I could join you," he hinted, hoping she'd say yes. "Then we could get that meal that's been delayed a little too long."

I can't believe it happened.

Mind half in a daze, Gwen made her way toward the next-door unit. Tessa and Kenneth had one apartment, Addison the other. She needed to talk to her sisters, and soon.

Gwen threw a look over her shoulder, half expecting to see an agent shadowing her as she made the brief trip between the duplexes. To her surprise, no one seemed to be watching. At least not anyone she could see. By all outward appearances the identical duplexes with their precise landscaping looked like any middle-class neighborhood early in the morning. Only the high barbed-wire fencing looming in the distance shattered the illusion.

She made her way up the stairs and into the foyer separating the apartments. Since her apartment didn't have a morsel of food, Blake had offered to go to the commissary and grab a few supplies. Though he could have called and had the food delivered, it seemed that he needed a time-out as much as she did.

A slow smile pulled at her mouth. Heat mingled with memory, fusing into something warm and fuzzy in the center of her stomach. They'd made love in the shower, and it was even better. She knew it was crazy, the way they'd come together, but she didn't regret it.

I'm a virgin no more, she thought, punching at the buzzer of apartment number 1.

When no one answered, Gwen hit the buzzer again. "Come on," she murmured. "I need someone to talk to." Neither one of her sisters was up with the sun. The last few days had been exhausting and tense for everyone concerned. She'd be surprised if anyone rose before noon.

Still . . .

She punched the buzzer a third time, holding it down. "Please get up, damn it."

One minute passed, and then another.

The door finally cracked open. Tessa's sleepy face appeared. "What the hell?" she groused. "It's way too damn early to be bothering us."

Gwen held a finger to her lips. "I need to talk to you."

Tessa yawned. "Can't it wait until later? I was up all night listening to Ken rant and rave about our rights."

She shook her head. "I've got something important to tell you."

Pulling her robe tighter around her body, Tessa ran a hand through her tangled hair. "Unless you've talked that agent of yours into letting us go home, you haven't got anything I want to hear."

"He's not my agent," Gwen started to say, then stopped herself. Well, maybe he was. Her insides were practically bursting to share the news. "I think I did something stupid."

Tessa gave her a grouchy glare. "What?"

Biting her bottom lip, Gwen blurted, "I had sex with Whittaker last night."

Her sister's sleepy eyes immediately snapped open. "No way."

Gwen nodded. "We did."

Flinging the door wide, Tessa dragged her inside the apartment. It was decorated in the same bland neutral colors as her own. "I want to know everything," her sister demanded, heading toward the kitchen to start a pot of coffee. A caffeine kick was the first thing Tessa needed to get going in the morning. Finding the cupboards bare, she pounded a fist against the counter. "Why the hell isn't there any coffee?" she complained. "Don't they know we need food, too?"

Gwen slid onto a nearby stool facing the counter. Her muscles ached, but in a pleasant way. Aside from a little soreness, she felt pretty good. Better than good, actually. "Blake's gone to get us some breakfast," she said. "But that's beside the point. What do you think?"

"About you having sex with the man who's spying on us?" Tessa retorted. "What the hell were you thinking, Gwen?" Her older sister's words hit like a sledgehammer to the gut.

Gwen's bubble of giddiness slowly began to deflate as the cold hard reality of their situation set in. She winced. Talk about having one's brain take a vacation. "I made a mistake, didn't I?"

Tessa leaned across the counter, tapping her temple with her index finger. "In case you haven't figured it out yet, we're being held here for more than our own safety. The government wants to know all about Mers, and they've not only got us locked up, they've got their beady little eyes trained right on us. Don't you think it's kind of funny they'd put an agent right next door to you? Sounds like he got more than an eyeful of you last night."

Elation fizzling, Gwen laced her hands together. She suddenly felt stupid, an absolute fool. "I guess you're right. What better way to get to know a mermaid than to sleep with one?"

Her sister propped a hand on her chin. She drummed impatient fingers against the countertop. "So did you tell him all our Mer secrets, like we're cranky bitches without our coffee in the morning?"

Gwen shook her head. "I, uh, actually gave him something a little more personal than that," she confessed.

Tessa pinned her under an assessing stare. "Oh?"

Gwen felt her throat tighten with embarrassment. Her heart raced along with her pulse. It was always less painful when the bandage was pulled off fast. She decided to plunge right in and confess. A thousand words tangled inside her, so she spit them all out in a rush. "Last night was the first time I've ever made love to a man."

Tessa stared, speechless. "That's not possible," she finally spluttered. "You've been with men before. I've seen you give the eye to every hot hunk in a tight pair of jeans. And you and Caden were practically living together."

Gwen blinked, suddenly wishing this were a dream and not real life. "I like men," she admitted. "But I've never been with one. I mean, yeah, Caden and I fooled around a little, but I always put him off." Feeling her throat thicken, she paused to swallow. "I never could bring myself to, you know, take off all of my clothes."

Her sister held out her arm, showing a bit of the design etched into her skin. "Because of your scale pattern?"

She nodded. "That, and I never could get around to telling him I'm a mermaid. There never seemed to be a right time to roll out the tail."

Tessa looked at her oddly. "Maybe because you've never wanted to admit you're a Mer."

A sinking sensation rolled through Gwen's gut. As hard as she'd tried to fit into the human world, it was like pounding a square peg into a round hole. In trying to deny her Mer side, she'd practically stifled her life. Instead of living, she was existing, a prisoner in a cage of her own design.

And she hated it.

In a way it was a relief that people knew. She didn't have to hide it or pretend anymore. She could be herself.

"No," she said. "I'm not as brave as you and Addison are about it. I've always thought I could get through life without having to tell anyone."

Tessa's knowing gaze met hers. Her expression softened. "But, Gwen, that would mean being alone your entire life. As much as we sometimes think we don't, Mers need human males. They are our mates, the father of our children. Without them, we have no future."

A shiver ripped through her hard enough to make her body quiver. "I know," she said, desperately trying to make her brain function. "I always meant to tell him, but I never could make myself say the words. I was so afraid he'd look at me like I was a—"

"Freak," Tessa finished for her. "We're all afraid of that moment when we have to open ourselves up to other people. Do you think it was easy for me to tell Jake? Or Kenneth?"

Gwen couldn't help cracking a smile. The way Tessa told it, Kenneth had caught her quite by surprise when she was wearing her tail. "As I recall, you weren't exactly thrilled when Kenneth came back to the island looking for you. Hadn't you just about decided you'd had enough of human men?"

Tessa smiled. "Yeah, I was just about finished with men when Ken came along."

Gwen stared at her older sister. "Then you have to understand why I held off so long," she said simply. "I was afraid no one would accept me."

Careful to keep her expression neutral, Tessa asked, "So you made love with Agent Whittaker because he knows you're a Mer?"

Gwen felt sweet agony roll inside her as memories of the previous night began to reemerge in her mind. Instead of responding to Whittaker as an agent with a job to do, she was drawn to him because she found him attractive. There were no barriers between them, no more reasons to lie because he already knew what she was. She didn't have to explain her scale pattern or wait with bated breath as he absorbed the details of her origins. He'd simply treated her as a woman he found attractive.

Gathering her frazzled nerves, she nodded. "Even though it probably wasn't the smartest thing to do, I let him seduce me. Or maybe I seduced him. It just happened."

"Did he know you were a virgin?"

Self-conscious, Gwen felt her scalp prickle with embarrassment. "No. Not until afterward."

Tessa gave her sister a look. "Addison and I always assumed you were doing just fine. You always seemed to have a handle on things."

Gwen shook her head. How do you tell someone, the people you love, that you're falling apart inside? "I didn't want to be a burden. You already had a lot on your hands. Breaking up with Jake, trying to hang on to the island . . . for a while there it seemed like everything was on the verge of falling apart."

Tessa's expression softened. "Your problems aren't a burden, Gwen. We're sisters. Sticking together and supporting each other is what we do. I know you've spent your whole life wanting to fit in. In a way I think we all do. But it shouldn't come at the cost of our identities as Mer. What are we supposed to do? Shore up and die because we don't belong in this world?"

Propping her chin on her hand, Gwen sighed. "I wish I could fully accept being a Mer."

Tessa lifted a hand, stifling a yawn. "This is the only life you've got, kiddo. Might as well make the best of it." She broke into a mischievous smile. "So was it good?"

Gwen felt heat rise to her cheeks. The question brought a reluctant grin. "It was great." She cleared her throat. "All three times."

Tessa's brows rose. "Wow." She fanned herself with a hand. "That man's got staying power."

"A lot of it," Gwen added drily.

They didn't have a chance to exchange more of the dirty details.

Kenneth ambled into the living room. Dressed in a pair of pajama bottoms and a plain white T-shirt, he stretched and yawned as he made his way through unfamiliar territory. "Who's got staying power?" he asked with a sleepy grin.

"There's no coffee," Tessa announced. "And we weren't talking about you."

Kenneth made a face. "What the hell are we supposed to do about that?" he demanded.

"Agent Whittaker's gone to fetch breakfast," Gwen offered helpfully. "He's bringing coffee and something to eat." It felt odd referring to the man she'd just slept with in such a formal manner.

"Serves the fucker right to be errand boy," Kenneth griped. "After all the damn trouble he's caused us, he should be shining my damn shoes, too."

Tessa shot her husband a warning look. "Settle down, Ken. You're talking about Gwen's new boyfriend."

Kenneth looked from woman to woman. "Get out," he started to say.

Pulse pounding like a jackhammer, Gwen felt hot blood rush to her cheeks. Now that the fantasy had faded with the night, she was faced with some cold hard realities.

With a groan she let her head drop into her hands. "He's not my boyfriend," she said, peeking up between her fingers. "I just slept with him. Uh, last night."

Kenneth's brows soared. He stared at her, his expression incredulous. "What? Why would you do that?" Suspicion crept across his features. "He didn't take advantage of you, did he?"

Gwen let her hands drop. Right now she felt like a two-year-old who'd been caught stealing cookies before supper. "No, I think it was the other way around," she admitted, giving a little wince. "I kind of showed him my tail, and things went from there."

The ringing doorbell interrupted further conversation.

Grateful for the interruption, Gwen slid off the barstool. "That should be food," she announced, and hurried toward the door. Her hand trembled, fingers fumbling with the knob.

Blake Whittaker's big frame filled the threshold. He carried two plastic sacks that looked overstuffed with goodies. "Delivery," he announced. "Hope this is the right place."

The sight of him caught her short. Heart leaping to her throat, her breath stalled in her lungs as she remembered how he'd looked undressed, his magnificent chest covered with a dark thatch of matted hair. The ripple of muscles beneath his taut flesh. She'd seen a lot of men in her life, had admired them. But Blake Whittaker had the power to take her breath away. He was all male. As much as she might have wanted to, she couldn't deny the attraction. It was as strong as ever.

She silently gave herself a swift mental kick. *What have I gotten myself into?*

Swallowing hard, she stepped back. "Sure is."

Blake Whittaker breezed past her, carrying the groceries to the counter. "Sorry you woke up to an empty fridge, folks," he said, pulling out a big can of coffee, followed by a small bag of sugar and half-and-half. "I just grabbed the basics from the BX. Later you can go for your own supplies."

Tessa snatched the coffee and popped the lid. She took a deep sniff of the aroma of pure Colombian coffee. "I needed this," she said, adding a few heaping spoonfuls into the coffeemaker before pouring in the water.

Kenneth crossed his arms, a suspicious look playing across his face. With his hair sticking up at all angles, he looked like an angry rooster. "Well, aren't you just Johnny on the spot? I suppose we're going to be seeing a lot of your face around here."

Dressed in one of his immaculately pressed suits, Blake Whittaker dodged the lethal frown. "Yes, you will." His shoulders rolled in a casual shrug. "Guess you'd better get used to it," he said.

Kenneth cut the agent a sharp look. "I know part of your job is to spy on us." He smiled, but it was a cold, hard smile. "That's a given. But I'd like to know where it's written in your job description about having sex with my sister-in-law."

Gwen gasped, feeling the contact of his words like the blast of a mortar. A ripple of uneasiness spread through her. "Really, Kenneth, I don't think that's any of your business."

Whittaker refused to take the bait. "Anything you want to know, you can ask Gwen," was all he said. "I won't discuss it."

Kenneth barely spared Whittaker a glance before homing in on her. "If he's taking advantage of you to get to us, Gwen, it is my business." He pointed a finger toward the agent. "I don't care what you think your job is, Whittaker. If you hurt her, you'll answer to me."

Seeing the anger in her brother-in-law's face, another ripple of uneasiness went through Gwen. His reaction shouldn't have startled her. She should have known she'd be dragging her family into the mix when she'd taken Blake into her bed.

I've made a mistake, came her panicked thought. There was only one way to make things right.

Stay as far away from Blake Whittaker as possible.

Chapter 15

Later that day, Gwen barely gave Blake a second glance as she slid into the seat on the passenger's side. Since his little dustup with Kenneth, she'd given him the cold shoulder, replying only when spoken to and staying close to her family.

Walking around to the driver's side of the car, he couldn't blame her. While he'd been ordered to get close to her, seduce her, he hadn't planned for the dirty deed to happen just last night. He'd planned to take a little time, work his way into her confidence. Instead he'd steamrolled in and taken her straight to bed.

Oh, yeah. He'd also taken her virginity.

Casanova you are not, he thought as he pulled the door shut and snapped the seat belt into place. After enduring a very uncomfortable breakfast, the day's agenda had been revealed with a call from Director Thompson. They were on their way across the compound where the hostile Mer were being held in quarantine. Now that the women had been disarmed, his superiors wanted to question them. Any answers they offered might help speed the hunt for the remaining fugitives.

Blake glanced toward Gwen. He'd deliberately maneuvered the travel arrangements so that they could have a few minutes alone to talk.

Hands neatly folded in her lap, Gwen stared out the window. It looked like he was going to be ignored for the rest of the day.

He sighed, turning the key and starting the engine. Pulling away from the curb, he guided the big sedan toward the facilities housing the hostile Mer.

Maybe it would just be better to say nothing. Pretend it hadn't happened. Although he knew what Frances Fletcher expected, he'd found the idea of seduction to pry out information distasteful. When he wrote up his report later today, it would not include the fact that he'd slept with Gwen. That was none of the government's business. What had happened between them wasn't anything that would bring the country to its knees if revealed. They'd made love and it was a private matter. Period.

Somehow he had to make Gwen understand that his desire hadn't been faked. He'd reacted with all the instincts of a man excited by the idea of having a woman he craved.

He cleared his throat, preparing to speak. "I'd like to clear up a few things about last night."

Gwen gave a slight shake of her head. "Let's not talk about it," she said, keeping her voice low and neutral. "As far as I'm concerned, it never happened."

Blake's grip tightened on the steering wheel. "Because you feel I took advantage of you?"

A long silence lingered between them.

Gwen finally shook her head. "No, I don't think you took advantage." She inhaled a deep breath and her breasts rose beneath the soft peach fabric of her blouse, kicking off all kinds of erotic images in his mind. "I was willing. I wanted it to happen. But I should have thought about the consequences. It's like Kenneth said. Everything you see and hear, you're going to write down. Nothing that happens between us will be private."

Fighting to keep his head clear, Blake nodded. "To an extent, that's true. I do work for the government."

Gwen said nothing, just looked at him impassively with her beautiful, long-lashed green eyes.

"So you're going to give me the silent treatment from now on?" he inquired.

Folding her arms across her chest, she stared at him. She was beautiful, even when suspicious, and the only thing he wanted to do was pull her close and kiss her crazy. "I'm waiting for you to whip out your recorder so you can capture the conversation."

Blake immediately put his foot on the brake. The car slammed to a halt. "Let's cut the bullshit, shall we? I slept with you last night because I wanted to. Not because I was ordered to."

It was a lie. But it also wasn't. Even though Frances Fletcher had tacitly suggested that he get close to Gwen, she'd also told him that it would be his own decision as to how far he pursued the matter.

The tension surrounding her eased. "Really?" she finally asked.

Blake nodded. "The spies in movies might tumble into bed with the pretty woman to find out all her secrets, but that's not the way I work," he said. "There's a certain place where I draw the line. My body isn't for sale." What had happened between them wasn't anything he'd let be exploited. Gwen deserved better than that.

So did he.

She seemed to be mulling his words and she wasn't smiling.

"That's nice of you to tell me and I thank you for your honesty. Last night was good—"

His brows rose. "Only good?"

Her green eyes sparked, showing a bit of the animation that had attracted him to begin with. "More like magical," she admitted and a flush began to creep into her face.

Blake nodded. He didn't dare to smile even though that was what he felt like doing. "Magical's good."

Gwen blushed. Really blushed. A rosy glow suffused her high cheekbones with wonderful color. "It was everything I imagined my first time would be like." She made a quick face. "Well, except the, you know, accident."

"I wish I had known."

Anxiety creased her smooth forehead. "If you had, would you have gone ahead?"

"You want the whole truth?"

Biting her bottom lip, she nodded. "Yes. I do."

Her question had put him between a rock and a hard place, but now wasn't the time to begin lying to cover his own ass. An attraction had simmered between them from the beginning. It was one he wanted to follow through on despite the bizarre circumstances that had brought them together.

But if she was going to trust him, really trust him, he'd have to tell her the absolute truth. That way he could still satisfy the requirements of his job without betraying her trust. It would be a delicate balancing act to manage, but with a little finesse and luck he could pull it off.

Blake reached for her hand. Her flesh felt warm and firm underneath his palm. The connection between them was so strong he could practically feel the sparks. Her body heat seemed to enter straight into his veins, spreading like molten lava. "Had I known, I would have done things a lot differently," he admitted.

Gwen didn't look as if she liked the sound of that, but she nodded. She swallowed hard and moistened her lips. "Oh?"

Blake reached up, stroking a strand of hair away from her face. "I would have tried to make it more special, you know? Been a little more gentle with you."

Anxiety creased Gwen's smooth forehead. For a brief moment her fingers tightened around his. "It was good." She gave him an apologetic look before gently slipping her hand out of his. "But I don't think it's anything that should happen again. As much as we might want it, we're really on different sides of the fence. I've got to protect myself." She pulled a deep breath. "And I've got to protect my family."

He nodded. "I understand."

Gwen's throat worked briefly. "Thanks." She turned her head toward the window, cutting him out of her view. "Guess we should go."

There. Just like that she'd cut him off. He was trying to be cool; however, a part of him was fuming at her reaction. But in a way it was almost a relief. He wouldn't have to lie to his superiors when he reported no progress. He could do so with a clear conscience. It was easier to do the job when his loyalty wasn't divided.

Blake shifted the car back into gear. "Don't want the others to think we got lost."

It took them a few minutes to catch up with the rest of the group, partly due to the fact he was unfamiliar with the massive compound. The building housing prisoners was low and nondescript, marked only a by a sign with DETENTION stenciled across its face.

Tessa, Kenneth, and Addison all waited in the main foyer with accompanying agents. All three shot Blake a suspicious look as they hurried to catch up, but said nothing. Putting Gwen between them, the sisters made sure Blake couldn't get anywhere near her.

They're going to cut me off at the pass, he told himself. In a way he didn't like the thought of that. He'd enjoyed his time with Gwen last night, and would like to spend more time with her. Not necessarily in bed, either.

Kenneth looked around sharply, his eyes questioning. "Explain to me what we're supposed to be doing," he demanded again as they followed an agent down a long narrow passage.

"We'd like for Tessa to talk to the Mer women, see if

they have any information that can help us find the rest of the fugitives."

"That makes sense," he grunted.

Blake resisted a smile. "We'd like to think so."

The agent in front led them into a large area outfitted with a two-way mirror in the wall. Through the mirror, everyone could see a table and a couple of chairs sitting inside an adjoining room. For the moment it was empty.

Dennis Thompson ambled up to them. "They aren't being very cooperative."

"I doubt you'd get anything out of them since they hate humans," Tessa commented.

Thompson blanched. "Yes, we've figured out we're not anyone they want to deal with. We're doing our best to accommodate them with reasonable comfort, but they've refused all food offered. I'm afraid they're on a hunger strike of some kind."

"What have you offered them?" Addison asked.

Thompson shrugged. "We've tried a variety of normal foods, along with fruits, vegetables, and even seafood. Both raw and uncooked."

Tessa shook her head. "They don't eat with their mouths," she informed the director. "In their world, they've moved beyond physical needs. They draw the energy they need to feed their bodies from crystals. In a sense it makes them immortal."

Thompson's eyes widened. "Is that even possible?"

Tessa nodded. "Unfortunately it is. But it comes at a price. Their search to lengthen their life spans meant they had to drain the life out of Ishaldi."

Thompson offered a crooked smile. By the look on his face, the newly discovered species was turning out to be a lot more complicated than he'd bargained on. "Amazing. So if we give them stones—crystals—they will be able to feed themselves?"

"Yes. And since they have no soul-stones, they can't manifest the energy they draw in outside their own bodies."

Thompson's eyes gravitated to the simple pendant hanging around Tessa's neck. "But you can?"

All three of the Lonike sister raised their hands toward their necklaces. "Yes," Tessa answered.

Addison narrowed her eyes. "And the only reason we haven't blasted your asses to pieces is because we're peaceful Mer."

Gwen elbowed her younger sister in the side. "Addison, please. That's not the way it works." She directed a beaming smile toward the director. "We don't blast anyone with our Mercraft. To use the D'ema is strictly forbidden."

Blake shifted uncomfortably in his place. He dimly recalled hearing this word the day they'd been attacked on Little Mer. *Death magic*, he remembered Tessa explaining. As if in response, his injured arm gave him a little reminder twinge. He'd had a firsthand glimpse of what the Mer could do with those crystals, and he didn't want to be on the receiving end a second time.

Director Thompson had the good sense not to hit the panic button. "I'm taking you at your word that you'll be on your best behavior," he told the women. His gaze narrowed, sharpened. "At this time we want our relationship with the Mer people to remain friendly and peaceful."

Giving Addison a surreptitious pinch, Gwen stepped up to take the lead. "And we're absolutely committed to prove that we are not a threat—not now or in future times. Whatever you need us to do, we're willing."

Kenneth stepped up and interrupted her. "To a point," he said, wrapping one protective arm around his wife's slender waist. "My wife and her sisters may be willing to cooperate, but keep in mind there are limits. And I'm certainly not bending over and spreading my ass cheeks so you guys can look up my butt."

Director Thompson frowned at him. "I'll certainly keep that in mind."

"You do that," Kenneth snapped back. "I seem to recall the constitution saying something about life, liberty, and the pursuit of happiness."

Gwen mentally held her breath. If things kept going the way they were, human-Mer relations would soon deteriorate to the point of no return. Thanks to Queen Magaera's soldiers, her entire species was skating on thin ice. Their invasion of Little Mer had been committed with hostile intent. They'd come prepared to kill anyone who stood in their way of recovering Tessa. Had things gone their way that day, Lucky might not have been the only casualty. There was no doubt in her mind everyone around Tessa would have faced immediate extermination.

Thompson gave him a sour smile. "As long as it doesn't interfere with national security," he reminded, "you're in the clear."

"We're not a threat," Gwen reiterated.

Addison glanced toward the two-way mirror. "They're bringing one in," she announced.

Gwen tried not to wince as one of the Mer women who'd attacked them was led into the room. Gone was the tight-fitting fish-leather suit, replaced now with a plain green jumpsuit with PRISONER stenciled across the front in large yellow lettering. Hands in cuffs, the woman was barefoot. Despite her captivity, a look of hate mingling with defiance lingered in her narrow eyes.

Gwen clenched a hand at her side in an attempt to keep herself calm. An unsettling thought wiggled through her brain. *That could be one of us.* The few days she'd spent in restraints were enough for her. She never wanted to be that helpless again.

"This is the one you identified as Doma Chiara, correct?" Thompson asked.

Clearly shocked by the change in the woman, Tessa nodded. "That's what I knew her by, in Ishaldi."

"If you don't mind, we'd like you to attempt to communicate with her," Blake Whittaker said. "Anything you could get her to say might be helpful."

Tessa nodded. "I understand."

One of the agents opened a door leading into the interrogation room. "If you'll come this way."

Tessa slipped out of Kenneth's embrace. "Stay here, babe," she said.

Gwen stepped up. "I'm coming with you," she said, speaking in a voice far stronger than how she felt inside.

Blake gave his superior a look. "Okay?"

Thompson waved them on. "She's restrained. I think we have her under control."

Nodding, Whittaker escorted them into the small chamber.

Doma Chiara eyed them with a combination of suspicion and hostility.

Gwen forced herself not to flinch, staring back at this creature that was, for all intents and purposes, totally alien from herself. Despite the fact that Chiara was handcuffed, she still didn't trust the woman.

Tessa took a seat opposite Chiara and the agent guarding the prisoner. Blake Whittaker stood at the end of the table. That left Gwen to hover behind Tessa.

Chiara's eyes narrowed in recognition at Gwen, clearly remembering the psychic fight they'd had a few days ago. A low growl of disgust broke from her throat.

Tessa glanced to Whittaker. "What do I say?"

Whittaker thought a moment. "Ask her if she feels she is being well treated?"

Tessa relayed the question.

No answer.

"Try speaking to her in our language," Gwen prompted. "She doesn't have a soul-stone to help her read the psychic vibrations, and her grasp of English probably isn't that solid yet."

Tessa nodded. "Good point." She asked the question again, this time speaking in the Mer tongue.

The words sounded odd to Gwen's ears, probably because it had been so long since she's heard it spoken. When they were smaller, their mother had often communicated in the lyrical language. The girls had picked up bits and pieces, enough that they could talk amongst themselves as long as the conversation remained simple.

To her surprise, she heard Chiara give an answer.

"They starve us," the Mer said.

Tessa translated the brief answer for the humans in the room.

Whittaker nodded his understanding. "Tell her that we will make every effort to provide what she requires to sustain her body. Ask her if she's able to eat normal food."

Tessa spoke to Chiara again. Her dexterity with the Mer tongue was slow and a little clumsy, but she was able to make herself understood.

Chiara made a face. "To eat with the mouth is for the lessers. We have moved beyond the physical."

The two women had a brief conversation. Gwen followed as well as she could, picking up on the fact that Chiara would rather starve than belittle herself by eating like a human.

She leaned toward Blake, relaying the information. Tessa was trying to talk some sense into the woman, but Chiara refused to listen. The Mer had stated she would rather die than accept anything touched by human hands.

Blake rolled his eyes. "God, why do they have to be so dense?"

Gwen bristled. "She's not stupid. It's simply the belief she was raised with. In her mind humans are a lesser species and she will treat them as such, even though she's the one in chains."

"Can't she see how much easier it would go for her if only she'd cooperate?" he groused.

Gwen shrugged her shoulders. "Try telling her that."

"Well, before she starves herself to death, ask her if Massey is still alive."

Tessa asked the question.

The obstinate woman lifted her chin. "He wisely serves my queen," she answered in haughty but perfect English. "One day you will all bow before my lady and tremble as she walks among you."

Blake's brows shot up. "Ah, so you do understand us."

Chiara bared her teeth. "Of course. Yours is a simple language."

He shrugged. "Guess that means I can speak for myself."

Chiara turned her head. "Perhaps I shall not listen to you, lesser." She was a woman obviously used to wielding her disdain like a blade to cut lower beings to their knees.

Blake shoved his hands in his pockets. "Perhaps you should. My people seek to make contact with your queen and we'd like to be able to do so peacefully, without further causalities. If you could help us do that, we would be willing to provide the sustenance you need to sustain yourself."

Doma Chiara's lips rolled back in another feral snarl. "I refuse to betray my queen," she spat.

Blake tipped back his head, blowing out a frustrated breath. "Listen, it's time for some straight talk," he said, speaking slowly but precisely. "Right now the Mer are considered an enemy of my people. If we have to go after your queen, hunt her down, then there's going to be trouble. Maybe more trouble than she's prepared to handle." He paused. "Do you understand what I'm saying?"

A grim smile touched Chiara's saturnine features. "As a soldier I understand the ways of war, its losses and gains," she answered, imitating his precise manner. "You are saying she should surrender because our kind are presently outnumbered."

"It wouldn't have to be a surrender, per se," he said. "Perhaps more of a diplomatic meeting. Something that would allow us to assess the needs of her people now that they are emerging from Ishaldi."

Chiara stared at him long and hard. By the look on her face she wasn't a woman who would tolerate beating around the bush. "The waters of earth were ours a long time before humans learned to build the fragile shells that would carry them from land to land," she said coldly. "The waters belong to the Mer, and my queen will accept nothing less."

"The world has changed a lot since the Mer were a power to be reckoned with," Blake reminded her. "Your kind is welcome again, but only if they come in peace. Anything less will be unacceptable."

Chiara stared at him through an icy veil, her gaze so cold and hard that Gwen felt a corresponding chill penetrate all the way to her bones. This person, her kinswoman, was a creature of destruction from beginning to end. There was no mercy in her, no empathy for the human race.

Gwen curled her arms around her body to chase away the uneasy feelings that suddenly sprang to the forefront of her mind. *She would just as soon kill us all as to look at us,* she thought.

"My queen's ambitions and justifications are her own," Chiara countered, spitting the words at him in a blaze of fury. "Once she recovers that which has been stolen, all of humankind will lay prostrate at her feet."

Tessa suddenly paled. "The scepter," she gasped. "Are they going after it?"

Distracted by Tessa's words, Blake turned his attention away from the uncooperative prisoner. A puzzled look crept across his usually neutral expression. "The scepter? The one you said was with your aunt?"

He never got an answer.

Before anyone could make a move, Chiara launched herself out of the chair like a big predatory cat. Flying across the table, she charged at Whittaker, ramming her head and shoulders into his midsection. He barely had time to bring his pistol up before he was knocked off his feet.

Two flailing bodies hit the floor simultaneously. A stray shot zinged through the room, striking the agent who'd been guarding Chiara. The man fell like a stone, dead before he hit the floor.

Straddling Whittaker, Chiara pressed the chain of her cuffs against his neck, effectively throttling him. A savage's scream erupted from her throat. She was strong, angry, and determined to kill as many humans as possible.

Unable to get an aim on his assailant, Whittaker

tossed his weapon out of her reach. It skidded across the floor.

Tessa scrambled toward it. "I've got it," she shouted.

But she never had time to pull the trigger.

Gwen was faster. Terror swept through her with such power that she couldn't draw a breath.

Realizing she had only seconds before Blake lost consciousness, she threw her hands out toward Chiara. Energy snapped through her like thunderbolts, shocking her body with the electricity flooding through her veins. Heart racing with her pulse, she focused outward, driving a discharge of pure white-hot energy straight toward her target. A scream matching the force of her blast echoed inside her head.

Caught by the explosion, Chiara went flying. Her screech of agony ripped through the air seconds before she struck the wall full force. Skull slamming against the concrete, her body slid to the floor. She lay unmoving, a crumpled heap of flesh and bone.

Realizing what she'd done, Gwen felt shock rippling through her. Eyes big as saucers, Tessa just stood, slack-jawed and pale. Whittaker's weapon dangled from one limp hand. "Geez, Gwen ..." was all she said.

It had taken place within seconds.

There was a thunderous boom as the door rammed open, filling the room with a wave of agents. Somehow Kenneth broke through the mass, heading toward his wife. "What the hell happened?"

The gun slipped from Tessa's fingers as she sagged against her husband. "She just went crazy," she tried to explain.

Heart raging in her temples, Gwen swallowed back the dizzying nausea threatening to overtake her. She heard herself breathing hard. Fear gouged a jagged path through her chest when she realized Blake was still down.

Pulling her wits together, she hurried toward him. He lay sprawled on the floor like a fallen bull. A couple of agents were helping him sit up. "You going to live, Whittaker?" one of them asked.

Blake raised a shaking hand to his neck. The imprint of Chiara's handcuffs was etched into his bruised skin. "Yeah, I'll make it." He waved the hovering men away. "Give me some air."

Gwen's hands shook uncontrollably as she dropped to her knees. She stared at him, feeling the words she wanted to say tangle in her throat. Somehow she managed to say something. "Are you all right?"

Recognizing her voice, he gave her a weak smile. "I think I just had my ass kicked by a woman," he answered in a croaky voice. He looked sheepish for a moment.

Feeling relief solidify, she closed her eyes. For one dreadful moment she'd feared Chiara would succeed in her attempt to murder him. "It happened so fast nobody had time to think."

Jaw taut with tension, he shot her a look. "You did."

Gwen frowned. She'd been acting purely on instinct and the desire to protect Whittaker. Apparently he'd worked his way a little deeper under her skin than she wanted to admit. She blinked back the beginning of tears, but a few dampened her lashes anyway. Now was a silly time to get emotional, but she couldn't seem to help herself. Just thinking how close she'd come to losing him made her pulse speed up.

This is crazy, she warned herself. *I'm not in love with him.* The thought shook her so profoundly she couldn't think straight.

She choked down the lump in her throat. "Don't remind me, please."

Whitaker rubbed his bruised neck again. He had a sheen of sweat on his skin even though the room was positively chilly. Taking a deep breath, he glanced toward the dead agent. "Shit, I didn't even see her coming."

"She's a soldier in Magaera's army," Tessa said from behind them. "Her only function is to fight and die."

He rubbed his hands against his pale face. "I wouldn't doubt it." His gaze searched for and found the unconscious woman. "Is she still alive?"

One of the agents knelt beside the downed prisoner. "I think so."

Director Thompson surveyed the unconscious woman. "Get a stretcher and page Dr. Yadira immediately. Once she's stable, I want the hostiles contained in solitary. They are to have no contact with one another, and are to remain sedated at all times."

Gwen let out a breath that wasn't quite steady. She wondered if she'd be the next to go into a cell. She braced herself for surrender when Thompson headed her way.

"That's a very interesting ability you have there, young lady," he said.

Gwen forced her gaze to meet his. "It's all a part of our Mercraft," she admitted. "I don't use it very often."

Thompson arched a brow. "I think we'd like to do a few tests on that," he said in a conversational tone. "Do you think you'd mind participating?"

She stared at him, trying to keep her thoughts straight. Gathering her frazzled nerves and the remnants of her composure, she said, "Are you asking me, or are you telling me?"

Thompson cocked his head, staring at her through narrow eyes. "Let's just say we'd like to see a little more of what the Mer can do."

Gwen felt her stomach tighten into hard knots. Somehow she didn't think that was going to be a very good idea.

Chapter 16

Grand Manan Island
Three days later

Grand Manan Island was the perfect place for a
fugitive to hide. In keeping with the intense privacy pursued by the people who visited and lived
there, nobody asked strangers many questions at all. It
wasn't difficult for a newcomer to get around in relaxed
anonymity.

Money, of course, paved the way.

In order to get away from Queen Magaera's stifling
presence, Jake had sent her shopping with Niklos and
a handful of cash. Since they'd become lovers, the Mer
queen had become like an albatross around his neck,
continually demanding attention and action. She'd
made a leech of herself, locking on and sucking him dry.
He hardly had a moment to himself.

The demanding bitch. Queen Magaera didn't like the
restrictions and regulations of the human world, limi-

tations that also applied to queens as well as common people.

It had taken a lot of time and talking to placate her. As it stood she had no place in this realm, and wouldn't, unless they regained the last valuable piece forged by Atargatis for her people.

Did such a thing even exist?

If so, they had to find it. Had to have it.

But where the hell was the freaking thing?

Having been engaged to Tessa Lonike, Jake had learned bits and pieces about her family through the years he'd known them. Lonike was their father's name, he himself carrying a heritage that included the local Native Americans as well as the Scotch-Irish roots that gave him—and his three daughters—their flaming red hair.

Jolesa Lonike, Tessa's mother, was more of a mystery. Jake had no idea what her maiden name might have been before her marriage, nor did he know anything about her except she had a sister named Gail. According to Tessa, this was the sister who took the scepter before departing Little Mer.

So where had Gail gone? And what had become of the vital missing piece?

Snapping his fingers at a nearby waitress, Jake pointed at his empty cup. "Another, please." He spoke the words with a light French accent.

The girl nodded and scurried off. A few minutes later she delivered a fresh cup of steaming hot espresso.

Jake thanked her and paid her, tipping well. He'd tied up her table for hours, but he needed the connection the café offered to the outside world. The best thing to do when in search of information was to turn to the Internet.

Having snatched Niklos's laptop, he was presently in the middle of a search. The Internet offered a variety of ways to find people, if you were willing to pay the price. Using a disposable Visa card that he'd purchased with cash, he'd spent the last few days running down the Lonike family history.

Frustratingly, there was almost nothing to be found. He'd located a bit about Tessa's father, David, but drew a blank wall at their mother. Like the Lonike sisters, he suspected their mother and her sister had been privately educated to keep them out of the public school system. Both Gwen and Addison had gone on to attend the local community college, which he suspected their mother might have done.

Searching through the alumni records, he finally landed on Jolesa Davis. That at least gave him a last name to begin tracking.

The next place to head was those sites that allowed people to track their family heritage online. Lots of people tended to log into sites like it and begin entering their information in the hopes of finding lost loved ones or missing pieces of their past. As far as he knew, Gail had rejected life on Little Mer Island and integrated with humans on the mainland. There had to be a trail for Gail Davis. True, there might be a billion women with a similar name, but somewhere online a connection had to be lurking that would connect the dots to which Gail Davis was the sister of Jolesa Lonike.

It took three days and almost a thousand dollars to narrow down the possibilities.

A smile crossed Jake's face as his fingers whipped across the keyboard, logging into a popular genealogy site. Whenever names and dates started to fall together, the system would prompt the user to other entries from public records or other relevant members by adding twigs to the genealogy tree one could build online.

Yep. There were some twigs to follow.

He moused over an icon and clicked. There was a Gail Davis who had a sister named Jolesa Lonike.

And then he frowned. His fingers tapped out a few inquiries.

Damn.

Gail Davis was listed as deceased. The Social Security Death Index Record gave the location as Florida and the year as 2009. Her passing had been fairly recent, less than two years ago.

He frowned. Not good. Not good at all.

Jake leaned back. His shoulders were knotted with tension from being hunched over the computer day after day. He had to admit being a fugitive wasn't sitting well with him.

For one, he didn't like the anonymity it imposed on him. As Jean Luc, he was a nobody, just another Canadian with a bad accent who spent too many leisure days sailing around.

As Jake Massey he was an archaeologist, explorer, and adventurer. Didn't matter that his reputation was shot to shit for his theories that an "intelligent nonhuman species," existed concurrently and alongside Homo sapiens. He thought he'd laid out his case well enough.

The university elders didn't agree. They'd pulled his sea grants and rejected his tenure by saying he did not meet department requirements. It was all a bunch of bull and politics. He wasn't the first professor to be bounced for introducing theories that fell outside the accepted box of religion, creationism, and general science.

He had no chance of redeeming his reputation until he produced solid evidence. He had such evidence at his disposal now.

But showing up with Magaera for an appearance on the evening news just wasn't what he wanted to do. He didn't want to introduce the Mer as an oddity, nor did he want to be caught in the circus the media would inevitably create to feed the nonstop monster that was cable news.

He reached for the small white cup sitting at his elbow, sipping at its contents. He grimaced. Yuck. It had gone cold.

He signaled the waitress again. "Another, please."

Walking over, she rolled her eyes. "That is your fifth," she complained. "Why do you order it and then waste it?"

Jake smiled, surreptitiously giving her the once-over. The little brunette was young, cute, and buxom. Just the kind of college coed he liked to sit down and spend an afternoon with, impressing her with his vast font of knowledge before making the move that would inevitably end with his hand up her skirt, inching beneath her panties.

Fishing more bills out of his wallet, he pushed them her way. "Maybe I just like looking at you," he teased. "Keep them coming and I will make it worth your time."

His gaze lingered on her breasts as he spoke. He rarely looked into a woman's eyes. He wasn't interested in her brains or her thoughts about anything. Her body and what lay between her legs was all the interest he had in the female sex.

Nothing like objectifying a woman.

The girl blushed. "I'll bring you a fresh one, on the house." She tucked the money between her ample breasts.

Jake smiled. "*Merci, mademoiselle*."

The waitress giggled and hurried off.

Jake watched her from behind as she flounced across the café. Maybe he'd make some time for her before he left the island.

Until then . . .

He tapped his fingers on the laminated tabletop. What to do about Queen Magaera. Honestly, she was worth nothing unless she had power. And she had no power without the scepter. Showing her off as a sideshow oddity simply wasn't acceptable. More than money, more than power, the one thing he wanted was the sole thing that had always eluded him.

Respect.

As an ambassador of a powerful Mer queen, he'd have that. In spades. Otherwise he'd just be reduced to the level of managing a freak act, like those sleazy agents who pimped people with inexplicable medical deformities like the Elephant Man.

A shiver trekked down his spine. No. Definitely not.

Sighing, he continued digging into Gail Davis's life. Two hours later he had a marriage certificate, this time filed in Mimosa Springs, Florida. Gail Davis, at the ripe old age of twenty-four, had married James "Jimmy" Newsome, listed as twenty-nine years of age.

"Hmm," he muttered. "Small-town Maine girl ends up landing in Florida, another state almost completely surrounded by water." Striking out on her own would have been hard enough without the Mer stigma attached.

Following the leads he'd found, Jake typed out a few more inquiries.

Ah, look here. Birth records.

Approximately nine months after their marriage, in 1988, Jimmy and Gail had been blessed with twin daughters. Kendra and Sandra. How cute. The names were almost too precious. No doubt they dressed the girls in identical outfits and paraded around in one of those strollers made for two babies.

It was enough to make him puke.

Nevertheless, the thrill of discovery went all the way to his toes. "Hello, girls," he whispered and chuckled.

A few curious heads swiveled his way, wondering what the joke was.

But Jake wasn't sharing. He was all wrapped up in his own little world, scheming and dreaming about how to make life better for himself. In this world there were the "haves" and the "have nots." Having had a taste of both, he was determined to put himself back in the former category as soon as possible. He couldn't dump Jean Luc fast enough and get back to being his old self, name and all.

He needed personal information. Present location and addresses. Switching the direction of his search, he logged into a social networking site popular with college-aged kids, Connect Friends. His old page was still there.

In less than thirty seconds, he'd pulled up the page for Kendra Davis. Her page was loaded with tons of personal information, along with a cadre of photos of her with her twin, Sandra, and various friends. The girls were typical sun-kissed Florida blondes, pretty and pert. They were also oh, so unwise about the real world and the predators lurking in it.

Shit. It was too easy, like sticking a foot in front of a blind man to trip him up. Young people had no qualms whatsoever about throwing their personal information up on the Internet for anyone to find—and use—against them.

Kendra Davis, he now knew, was a senior at Strayer University. She'd majored in graphic art and design, and was looking forward to her forthcoming graduation. She had a boyfriend, a nice-looking dude named Kevin, and a little mongrel dog named Peetems.

Aw. They were the perfect all-American couple, clean-cut young Democrats. Just one look at their smiling faces and you knew the future would be better and brighter.

Switching programs, Jake logged into Google Earth.

He loved the fact they could make the trip to Florida without leaving the water. Thanks to 9/11, entering and leaving the United States was a nightmare because of heightened security.

Jake absently drummed his fingers on the tabletop. He would most likely have to come ashore under the cover of darkness, literally sneaking into the country.

No, it wasn't the best plan, but it was the only one that made sense. They needed the elusive artifact, and that meant making contact with one of Gail's children. He hoped like hell one of the girls knew where it had ended up. Otherwise the entire endeavor would be one huge waste of time.

If there was one thing Jake Massey hated, it was spinning his wheels. He wanted things done—his way, the right way and as soon as possible. Nothing else would satisfy.

A pair of female arms wrapping around his shoulders interrupted his solitude. A scent akin to damp musty linen permeated his nostrils. "My consort," a familiar female voice whispered in his ear. "This thing you call shopping is a delight. The bounty of your world is endless." She laughed a sound that grated on his nerves. "And the lessers . . . they are so eager to serve."

Jake frowned. If there was one thing he hated, it was a clingy woman. Magaera made it clear to anyone who cared to look that he belonged to her.

The waitress who'd spent the afternoon hustling his coffee shot him a dirty look. Any chance he'd had to make time with her vanished like a puff of smoke in the wind.

Jake's mood, which had been great a minute before, deflated faster than a punctured balloon. No stray nooky tonight. And that was a shame, too. He liked variety, and a lot of it. The idea of monogamy had never been hard-wired into his genetic structure.

Of course, right now he had to appease the Mer queen. She was still his best ticket to bigger and better things, and if he could exploit her and bed her, then all the better.

"They always are," he grated through gritted teeth. *When you're flashing a wad of cash.* It cost money, a lot of money, to keep a Mer queen in the luxury she was accustomed to. The 1.9 million he'd stashed away was slowly dwindling down into the red zone. At this rate he'd soon be completely broke.

Niklos glanced over his shoulder at the screen. "Any luck?" The look in his eyes pleaded for a break. His demotion from formidable smuggler to squiring a Mer queen around town wasn't exactly sitting well with the Greek at all.

It didn't help that none of the other Mer females would give him the time of day. With his swarthy skin and black hair, Niklos did not appeal to any of the women as a potential mate. They found him inferior. Common.

Jake would have to agree. But he'd never say it to his partner's face, as it was better not to insult the man at this point. Niklos still had his uses.

Shutting the lid on the borrowed laptop, Jake glanced up at his partner. "I think our luck is about to take a turn for the better."

They were one step closer to the scepter.

But he didn't want to say anything to Magaera. Not yet.

Not until he was sure he could lay his hands on it.

And Jake Massey was silently betting ten to one he could do just that.

Queen Magaera wasn't a stupid woman. Even if she didn't have the abilities as an empath at her disposal, she would have had to be deaf and blind to miss Jake Massey's manipulations.

As it was, she knew exactly the type of man she had on her hands. He was manipulative, a liar, and a user. Which, in Ishaldi and in the human world, made him the perfect consort. A scheming queen needed someone who would protect her in every way, even as he spun the webs of his own devious schemes.

So far Jake had handled the job admirably. He wanted power, hungered for it the way a slave struggled against his chains and felt starved for freedom.

Though many centuries had passed since the human and Mer realms had met and merged, it had taken her very little time to adjust to the new sights and sounds around her. Nothing had changed much. Ships still crossed the seas, trade and commerce was strong, and even a stable money system appeared to be in place. Civilizations might rise and fall, languages might change, but underneath it all the baser emotions of conniving, greed, and one-upmanship were still the way the world operated.

Jake was a conniver. And he was greedy. He envisioned himself as due to reap the rewards the world had to offer.

But he didn't know what true power was.

The archaeologist believed he wanted the respect of his peers, the recognition that he alone held the key to a lost world.

Magaera knew better. She wanted neither respect nor recognition.

She wanted *power*. The ability to make the ground tremble beneath men's feet, to crack the skies above with a single command. She wanted humans to come to their knees, acknowledge her as the reincarnation of Atargatis.

But having the ambitions of a living goddess was one thing. Actually attaining the power quite another. Nothing would happen without direct action. As much as she hated having her hands practically tied together, she still had one advantage.

Jake knew how to get things done. He knew the ways of his world and how to manipulate circumstances to his advantage. Rather than thinking of him as a hindrance, she'd begun to think of him as a useful, but ultimately disposable, pawn.

That last surviving piece was the most important of all. Jake knew how to find it. Once she had the valuable artifact in her hand, she wouldn't need the feckless human to do the talking for her. She'd be able to communicate in a way that would force mankind to sit up and take notice of the Mer.

And so I will sit back, she counseled herself. *And have patience.*

As for Jake . . .

In the interim, he could serve her wants and satisfy her needs. His own ambition would be his downfall. She'd have no qualms about executing her consort when she no longer found him useful.

Humans, after all, were expendable.

Chapter 17

Blake winced as the coroner's assistants uncovered the body of the hostile female killed on Little Mer Island. This was definitely a part of the investigation he would have preferred to skip. He did not like being caught unaware and didn't relish the fact he hadn't been briefed beforehand. He had no desire to watch people digging around in someone's carcass, be it human or alien.

Carefully preserved, the Mer's remains had been thoroughly dissected by doctors seeking to learn more about a mermaid's internal anatomy. Not that there was much they could find out. The woman had taken a direct blast to the abdomen. Curling, blackened flesh peeled away from the remaining bits and pieces.

Blake's stomach rolled, sending a wave of acid up the back of his throat. He swallowed hard. He wished he hadn't had a second ham, cheese, and egg biscuit and an extra cup of coffee. Even though the initial shock had passed, he had a feeling it wouldn't be in his stomach much longer. At least he had a sheet of glass separating him from the examination room. He doubted he could have taken the odor.

Dennis Thompson stood beside him. The look on his face said he'd rather be elsewhere, too. "Going to be a long day," he muttered.

Blake nodded. "We've only been here four days and it feels like a century." Aside from placing a few quick phone calls to Trevor, he hadn't been able to give his son any quality time.

It also didn't help that Debra was still whining about the move to California. She was pulling every dirty trick, including refusing to delay their next court appearance until after he could shake free from his current assignment. It was true his lawyer would still be showing up. But it didn't bode well that a father fighting for more visitations would have to miss a court appearance. It was entirely possible the judge would rule in her favor.

And that would hit him. Hard.

And then there was the other side, the fact that his work had gotten him tangled up with Gwen Lonike. Though they had agreed their first night together would also be their last, he couldn't stop thinking about her. Especially the way she'd jumped to his defense when he was attacked. Even though it had meant totally exposing herself and a Mer's abilities, she hadn't hesitated to help him. He need only look into her eyes to know she had feelings for him.

Feelings he refused to take advantage of.

He'd already decided against letting the agency know he'd slept with her. And no matter how hard Fletcher might push for a closer relationship, she'd just have to be disappointed when he reported complete and total failure. He'd just shrug and say he wasn't any sort of Casanova. As for Gwen ...

He closed his eyes, easily calling to mind the more provocative images of their single sultry encounter. She'd set his senses reeling with waves of carnal delight as her lips had blazed a path from the curve of his chin to the silk-encased tautness of his shaft. Her mouth closing over him had brought the heat to a boil. Desire and grasping hands had brought them together, her limbs coaxed wide by his eagerness to enjoy the pleasure of her sex. Raking his fingers through the fiery mass of her hair, he'd slammed his weight into hers.

And heaven had followed.

Blake had to admit he was totally gone on her. Caught like a fly in her honeyed web, he found himself thinking about her, constantly and continually. He wanted to be with her, and not just when they were making love. They got along just as well out of bed, and the hours they'd spent together had given him an intimate glimpse of her life. Finally free to really share herself with someone who wouldn't judge her for being different, Gwen was beginning to open up. His glimpse into the Mer world was fascinating.

It was, unfortunately, something he couldn't enjoy. A frown pulled his lips into a downward arc. The gaze reflected back at him in the glass was shadowed with guilt. Though they'd agreed to keep things nonsexual, deceiving Gwen about his true feelings felt wrong.

He wanted more, damn it. Exclusivity. One on one.

To follow the road and see where it would lead. Without lies. Without deceit. And without the government poking an intrusive nose into their personal life.

"Goddamn it." The oath slipped out under his breath. Both he and Gwen were prisoners of someone else's agenda and he didn't like it one little bit. He was being manipulated just like she was. The nooses were tightening around their necks, too. The light at the end of the tunnel no longer looked like a way to freedom. It looked like an oncoming freight train, one that would smash them both flat.

The devastation could never be undone, either.

Dennis Thompson mistook his utterance for something else entirely. "Damn disgusting." He rubbed a hand over his face. "These doctors look happier than a kid in a candy store with a twenty-dollar bill."

Blake had to force himself to put his personal thoughts aside. Tucking away his memories of Gwen for later review, he slipped on his mask of cold indifference. Don't think. Don't feel. Just do. He'd always been good at following orders. It was best to continue doing so until he could figure a way out of this mess.

Face obscured behind a surgical mask, Dr. Yadira poked through the woman's open torso, using a pair of forceps to move vital parts around for better viewing. "I see the remnants of the alien organ, what they call the symbiote," she reported. "But there's too much damage for any sort of extraction. It's shriveled into nothing."

Thompson hit a buzzer so he could be heard in the lab. "Any way to extract DNA from it?"

Yadira shook her head. "We've tried. The few strands we've extracted had been incomplete, most likely because of the decay of the body. The samples we've obtained from the live specimens have been promising, though. From what we can determine, the Mer DNA carries an additional gene sequence we can neither replicate nor explain at this point."

Blake pressed his lips together. He didn't like the term *live specimens* one bit. The scientists still considered the Mer to be little more than lab rats. "Why do you need that thing anyway?"

Thompson let his hand drop. "We're hoping this is something we can eventually replicate in all humans." His eyes briefly widened and flared with something akin to glee. "Everything they can do seems to be centered around that particular organ. We know they are able to breed with humans just fine, though we don't understand the process that allows them to only engender female offspring. Something during the gestation period seems to kill off male sexual chromosomes and imprint female Mer ones."

Blake kept his expression neutral. "Looks like you've been studying my reports."

Thompson shrugged. "You've gotten her to talk, and that's excellent." He shook his head. "We're still trying to get a bead on that scepter, whatever it may be." He rolled his eyes. "If such a thing actually exists."

"You might want to take what they say a little more seriously," Blake warned. "So far we still don't know exactly what we're dealing with here. As primitive as it might look to our eyes, their technology far surpasses our own. Crystal-powered lasers is something we can't even begin to touch on."

Pondering his words a moment, Thompson puckered his lips thoughtfully. "That's why it's your job to keep pumping them," he said. "We need to know everything about this species. What they are, what dangers they present and—most important—how to contain their threat."

A spike of guilt cut right through Blake's conscience. He hated pushing Gwen and her sisters for more details to add to his paperwork. But the girls had been very forthcoming, answering his questions as honestly as possible.

He wished he could simply date the woman instead of spy on her.

Blake forced himself to offer a nonchalant shrug. "Just doing my job."

Thompson chuckled obscenely and gave him a slap on the back. "Now, if you could only get her into bed, Whittaker. You really need to work harder on your seduction techniques."

It took every ounce of self-restraint Blake possessed not to slug the nasty little bastard right then and there.

Blake cleared his throat. "She's shown no interest in me, sir," he countered, speaking in a cold, clipped manner. The asshole was beginning to wiggle under his skin like a maggot. "I can hardly force myself on her."

Thompson didn't seem the slightest bit offended. "Just keep trying to work your way into her panties." He scratched one of his two chins. "We're just getting started on these things."

Things.

Blake's gaze narrowed on Thompson. "They are not *things*," he snapped. "They are intelligent beings, able to think and feel and react just the way humans do."

Thompson's own wall of indifference didn't budge one bit. "I hope you're not taking your involvement with these things too personally, Agent Whittaker. First and foremost, the Mer have been classified as aliens, albeit indigenous to Earth. Beyond that, they are not human. And we are aware they are dangerous and can turn on people at any moment."

It didn't take much to drag up the incident Thompson was referring to. "What Gwen did when I was attacked was just her reaction to a moment of stress. If she hadn't helped, I probably wouldn't be here now."

No need to mention that his lack of preparation and clumsy reflexes had gotten a fellow agent killed. They'd badly underestimated the hostile Mers. Even without their soul-stones, these women were well trained in hand-to-hand combat. They were also prepared to sacrifice their lives to serve their monarch.

They were damn lucky Queen Magaera and Jake Massey hadn't managed to lay hands on Tessa. He could only imagine what it would be like to have thousands of Mer soldiers streaming into the Mediterranean Sea.

That knowledge in turn presented another dilemma. Now that they knew Tessa controlled the sea-gate, it wouldn't be safe to let her go. Lifetime captivity seemed to loom in everyone's future, hardly a pleasant thought at all.

"And that is why we have them in quarantine and

under observation," Thompson reminded. "We have to know what we're dealing with on all levels."

Blake couldn't resist rolling his eyes. "Oh, come on," he scoffed. "Their kind has been here as long as humans have. Maybe even longer. More people die in car accidents than from rogue mermaid attacks."

"That we know of," Thompson added seriously. "Who knows how many unreported incidents are out there? There has to be a reason they went into hiding."

It was getting harder and harder for Blake to keep cold indifference in place. Arguing with Thompson was aggravating. And it was giving him a headache. Not to mention an intense desire to slam the asshole's head into the wall. Many times, and with much force.

"Maybe because they were driven to extinction," he retorted.

Thompson drew himself up to his full height, which wasn't much at all. "That is not the story we've gotten so far," he countered. "According to the facts as I have them, the sea-gate was closed because of tensions between the two races. Tensions, which I will remind you, still exist to this very day."

Blake reached for calm, but it lay just beyond the tips of his fingers. Tension formed painful hard knots in his shoulders. "I will grant you the Mer of Ishaldi are hostile. But Gwen and her sisters definitely are not. They're on our side."

Planting his hands in his pockets, Thompson rocked back on his heels. "The sisters may have been born on our side and may have adapted to our human ways, but others of their kind do not seem to be as domesticated."

Beneath his heavy brows his eyes became twin pools of steel. "That is, if my understanding of the story is correct. I did get my information from the report you filed, which Tessa Lonike verified with an addendum in her own words." His gaze narrowed, threatening slits of displeasure. "If it isn't, you'd damn well better have some corrections on my desk. ASAP."

Blake gave in and nodded. As much as he didn't like it, Thompson was his direct superior. He had to answer to the man. Getting emotional wouldn't do any good. If nothing else, he must maintain the facade of distant professionalism if he wanted to be kept in the loop.

"Just don't be so hard on the girls. They're doing the best they can to cooperate. All they want is to go home and go back to their lives."

Thompson smirked. "They'll have to dream on. The chance of that happening is a million to one. Whether they like it or not, the Mer are now the property of the U.S. government."

Their conversation was interrupted when two more attendants rolled in another body stretched out on a gurney. One of the hostile Mers was strapped to its cold metal surface. The gurney holding the corpse was removed, and hers rolled into its place. Stripped bare from head to foot, heavy straps restrained her at wrist and ankles. Her head lolled weakly from side to side.

Blake absorbed most of it in a single glance. The fine hairs on the back of his neck prickled with attention. The woman was still very much alive. So why was she in a room designed for autopsy?

The foreboding he felt intensified with every passing

second. *Surely they aren't going to try it.* He stopped that notion dead in its tracks. "What the hell's going on?" he demanded.

"They are going to attempt to retrieve samples from a more viable source," Thompson answered simply.

Blake didn't even want to think about it. "There's one problem with that idea," he protested. "She's still alive."

"Don't be such a pussy. She did try to kill you. Turnabout is fair play." Thompson waved a hand. "She will be euthanized in the most painless way possible." His reply was coarse and direct.

"Why do they have to kill her to get it?" he demanded. "Why can't they take samples by performing a live surgery?"

Dennis Thompson didn't bat an eye. "The doctors have decided they want a cadaver fully intact to explore before they go trying live surgery on one of those things." He glanced toward the unlucky mermaid. "You know this is the way science works, Whittaker. We wouldn't be where we are today if someone wasn't willing to do the dirty work."

Blake could hardly believe his ears. Dirty work was one thing. He'd performed a lot of it himself, as a ranger and a sniper in the army. He knew what dirty work and double dealing was all about. But murder, plain and simple, was a whole other ballgame. One he didn't want to be associated with. This went above and beyond the call of duty to any government.

Blake continued to stare at Thompson, all the while feeling rage and hatred rising within. "I don't think death is painless."

Thompson leaned closer, giving Blake a whiff of his tacky aftershave. "This isn't the first time we've done this," he said under his breath. "The Mer aren't the first alien life-forms we've encountered and they won't be the last." He shrugged. "You know the old saying. There are more things in heaven and earth than are dreamt of in men's philosophies."

Blake brushed him off. "I'm aware it goes something like that." His voice was pure ice.

He didn't think he wanted to know what else the agency had hidden away in its endless vaults. He had a feeling he wouldn't like what he'd find if he were to take a look. The moral and spiritual ramifications were already causing him more problems than he cared to admit.

Blake forced himself to turn away from the viewing pane. He wasn't going to watch this shit. No way. Jesus H. Christ. This wasn't science. It was torture, little more than government-sanctioned slaughter.

And it was wrong.

An image of Gwen stretched out naked and helpless flashed through his mind.

It'll come down to her, a prescient voice whispered in his ear. *One by one, they'll all go under the scalpel.*

Tests. Tests. And more tests.

The damn testing was starting to get on Gwen's nerves. She'd been run through the wringer until she was ready to scream.

At the moment, she sat in a simple white room, windowless and no exit except for a single door. The isolation was necessary, they'd explained, because they wanted to measure her cognitive psychic abilities without interruption or outside influences.

Good enough.

The room was outfitted with a simple folding card table and two metal chairs. Not much of a distraction there. The doctor running the experiment, who'd been introduced as Von Drak, was a middle-aged man, balding with a pot belly. He spoke in a thick Austrian accent. Every time he opened his mouth, all she could see in her mind's eye was an aging, fat, bald Terminator.

She inwardly winced. *Sorry, Arnold.*

Dr. Von Drak worked a series of cards, some with letters, some with simple pictures. A yellow notepad and pen sat nearby ready to record his findings. The idea was he would envision the image on the card in his own mind, and then Gwen would supposedly pluck it from his brain.

"Are you ready?" he asked.

Gwen nodded. "Sure. Fire away."

Von Drak held up the first card. His forehead wrinkled with intense concentration. "Can you tell me what I am looking at?" he asked in all seriousness.

Gwen leaned forward, planting her elbows on the table and lacing her fingers together. She wrinkled her own brow with what she hoped was a display of appropriate intensity. "Yes," she answered. "It is a number three."

Von Drak's eyes lit up. "Correct." He placed the card to one side and drew another. "And this one?"

Gwen concentrated harder. "It is a cat."

"Excellent," the doctor exclaimed. "You are most perceptive." He drew a third card. "And this?" he asked after a minute had ticked by.

Gwen paused. Really, this was too damn easy. "It's a star," she finally answered.

Von Drak scribbled some notes in an almost indecipherable handwriting. They went through the rest of the stack in about ten minutes.

"All cards identified correctly," he announced at the end of the test. "Amazing."

Hands still laced in front of her body, Gwen blew out a breath. "Not so amazing." Freeing a hand, she pointed toward his glasses. "The cards are reflected in your lenses. I can see everything you look at, backward but perfectly clear."

Von Drak groaned in disappointment. "How stupid of me," he muttered.

Gwen bit down on her tongue to keep from saying anything that would reveal her own ideas about the entire matter. She was tired of having her time wasted with such trivial shit.

So what if the Mer could pick up on people's feelings or draw a little energy out of a stone? Did it really matter much? In her mind, no. In their minds, however, they'd gotten hold of something more valuable than raw plutonium.

"Sorry," she offered. "It was too easy."

Von Drak laughed. "I suppose it was. Tell me if you will, though, how psychic are the Mer?"

Gwen shrugged. More damn questions. "Not very."

She hoped the sooner she answered the sooner she could get out of here. Except for brief glimpses of Tessa and Addison, she'd been almost totally isolated from her sisters during the testing. The girls were being kept far apart. It didn't take a rocket scientist to guess why, either.

Because we're more powerful when we are together.

It was true they had time in the evenings to catch up with one another, but those meetings were more than a little awkward. Nobody wanted Whittaker around and nobody wanted to answer his questions anymore.

For the sake of her family, Gwen did her best to dodge him, putting as much distance between them as possible. She didn't want to be around him, or alone with him at all. Mostly because she feared she'd give in to the temptation to have him again.

Damn it! Even though they'd spent just a single night together, she wanted him more than ever.

When she was alone, she let her mind drift back to that night. Reliving his every word, every gesture, every touch. The way his big hands had teased her body through flashes of heat. The way his lips had traced the curve of her neck and breasts. The way his hips had moved against hers as he conquered the very core of her womanhood.

Memories of Blake tightened the muscles across her belly and thighs, producing an indescribable surge of pleasure deep inside her body. Her heartbeat quickened, sending a hot throb of blood through her. Even the tips of her toes tingled.

It was easy to picture the only time she'd seen him,

naked and stretched across her bed. She'd been stunned by the way he'd looked at her, his brooding gaze drinking her in even as a smile of satisfaction turned up one corner of his sensual mouth.

By the goddess above. She'd loved being with him. Loved being taken by him. For the first time in a long time, she wasn't plagued by her Mercraft running amok as she slept. Her mind was too preoccupied spinning sensual fantasies around Blake. He'd been exactly what she needed.

And she wanted more.

She swallowed tightly. As much as she hated to admit it, it was difficult to keep her heart out of the equation. She'd met the perfect man.

And I can't have him, her wicked brain cells reminded. *The man I've waited all my life for.*

Of course it was his job that separated them. Technically, he was one of *them.* An agent of the government holding them against their will. Yes, she knew the spiel. That it was for their own preservation while authorities hunted for Jake Massey and the rest of the rogue Mer.

There was one small problem.

She didn't feel very safe.

With so many thoughts and concerns pressing in from a thousand different sides, Gwen felt exhausted. Physically and mentally tired. An ache was beginning to build behind her temples, warning of the headache to come.

Dr. Von Drak interrupted her thoughts. "Well, since the results of this test have been nullified, do you mind if we move on to something else?"

Gwen sighed. "Must we?"

His grin was self-effacing. "Hopefully this next challenge will be a bit more difficult for you." Pushing away from the table, he indicated that she should follow. "Come this way, please."

Gwen followed him down a short hall and into another room. This one was a little more elaborately outfitted. It looked like a firing range. Two more doctors worked with Addison, who was sliding the Ri'kah off her wrist.

Seeing her sister, Addison grinned. "Hey, you missed some hellacious shooting." Laying the weapon down, she pointed to a series of mannequins. The plastic replicas of humans were blasted and blackened, hardly recognizable.

Gwen gasped as she surveyed the carnage. "What the hell did you do?"

Addison extended the thumb and forefingers of both hands, imitating guns cocked and ready to fire. "They're testing our psi-abilities. Man, mine's really starting to come out. The more I practice with that thing, the better I get."

Her answer was precisely what Gwen didn't want to hear.

She looked at Von Drak. Remembering what she'd done to Chiara, she felt cold hands clamp around her spine. "You can count me out. I will not use my Mercraft again in any way that is destructive."

Addison squinched up her face. "Ah, come on. It's fun to show off."

Of course Addison would go into it whole hog and damn the consequences.

Gwen rounded on her sister. Closing her fingers around Addison's arm, she dragged her to one side. Fury, wordless and totally incoherent, welled deep in her throat. "I don't know what you think is going on," she snapped. "But we're not here to show off and make a spectacle of ourselves. This is serious business, Addie. Right now their entire perception of the Mer is based on violence and the damage we can do to humans. I don't know about you, but this isn't the sort of attention I've ever wanted. I want to go home."

Addison immediately jerked her arm away. "I want to go home, too," she yelled back. "That's why I'm trying to cooperate, show them everything. If they know all we can do, they won't be afraid." Offering a little smile of apology, she shrugged helplessly. "Right?"

Gwen studied her sister's adamantly squared shoulders and fiery eyes. She refused to be cowed, or intimidated. Unlike her, Addison was willing to embrace her inner Mer, revel in the power and abilities being a mermaid offered. She wished she could accept them as easily and without reservation.

"I know you're doing what you think is right—" she started to say.

Addison cut her short. "Don't you ever get tired of hating yourself, Gwen?" she asked. "Being afraid of being different is no way to live. We are what we are. It's time you accept what you can't change. You're a Mer. Get over it."

The people in the room cringed, waiting for the inevitable explosion.

It never came.

Swallowing hard, Gwen let her hand drop. "You're right," she admitted slowly, in a voice laced with resignation and defeat. "I can pretend all day long I'm human, but deep down inside I'm still a Mer. I can't change it, can't stop being what I am."

Addison reached out, giving her arm a little squeeze of reassurance. "It's not so bad here, Gwen. We could actually start over if we had to." She paused a moment, then continued. "I'm starting to feel like I fit in. You know?"

"Well, I don't!" Gwen snapped back. "And I never will."

Dr. Von Drak cleared his throat. "If you don't feel up to further testing today, perhaps it should be put off for another time."

Setting her personal ruminations aside for later examination, Gwen glanced at the remnants of the mannequins Addison had destroyed. Her gaze sidled over to the Ri'kah confiscated from the hostile Mer. Tessa's had also been taken into custody, giving researchers two good examples of ancient Mer technology.

Her jaw clenched automatically at the thought of using it against anyone. Her gaze slid toward the people in the room. The humans. Throwing her craft against Chiara to defend Blake was one thing. But using it against a human . . .

Her heart rate bumped up a notch. *What if I had to defend myself against them?*

Would she be able to do it?

Sucking in an anxious breath, she made a quick decision. It was time to stop being intimidated by what others might think about her. She'd spent twenty-seven years jumping at her own shadow. Enough was enough.

Gwen swore under her breath. *I won't be afraid anymore.*

Drawing back her shoulders like a soldier about to march off into combat, her attention shifted back toward the waiting scientists. "Put out some fresh targets and get ready to step back." She flashed a smile toward Addison. "I'm about to show this kid how to do it right."

Chapter 18

An hour later, Gwen slid the Ri'kah off her arm. Although she'd intended to give a display of guns ablazing, the most she'd managed to extract from the thing was a few weak sizzles and pops. She simply could not make the weapon work the way Addison and Tessa could.

She frowned at the uncooperative weapon. "Why won't you work for me?"

Addison pressed a soothing hand to her shoulder. "It's not important," she stressed. "You just haven't worked with it the way Tessa and I have. It's always been a hands-off thing for you, I know. You can't just expect to pick it up at random and use it perfectly. It took me forever to master it."

Jowls sagging, Dr. Von Drak looked downright disappointed. "So you are not familiar with this item?"

Letting her hand drop, Gwen shook her head. "Really, I'm not." She winced. "My talent seems to lie more on the kinetic side."

A familiar voice interrupted the conversation. "Damn." A low whistle followed. "Don't use that thing on me."

Gwen turned around.

Her breath caught in her throat. The moment her gaze fully settled on Blake, she experienced a small frisson of shock that shot all the way to her toes.

Whoa, he looked good. Impossibly tall, broad shouldered, yet with a wiry leanness that suggested he could move as fast as a puma on the prowl. There was almost an animal maleness about him that seemed to add an edge of danger to his look.

She dipped back her head to look into his beautiful eyes. His irises weren't just blue-gray, they were the color of the early-morning dawn, just as the sun began to peek over the edge of the horizon to break night's lock on the world.

I wish we were alone. The thought swept through her mind and she felt her cheeks flush.

"Don't worry," she reassured him. "I'm not the fighting kind."

Blake caught her blush. "That's not my experience," he teased. His smile grew wider and his unabashed stare ranged over her in a more than impersonal manner.

Gwen's blush grew hotter and she could barely meet his eyes with her own. Even though she wasn't human, she was still a woman of flesh, blood, and bone. A woman who was finding it hard to keep head and heart separated.

I think I'm in love with him.

She froze at the thought, her mind whirling in panic. Did she really mean that? A desperate need to keep her feelings guarded and impersonal forced her to maintain a calm demeanor.

Snapping out of her reverie, Gwen gave him a care-free smile. "We were just finishing up here."

Blake nodded. "I think I've seen enough today," he said, addressing the scientists in a curt tone. His manner was more than a little strained, tense. "I'd like to take these ladies home."

Dr. Von Drak waved his fat little hands. "Of course. It's been a long, tiring day for all of us."

Blake nodded again, polite but firm. "Good." He looked toward Addison and Gwen. "Are you girls ready to go?"

Gwen quickly nodded. "I think I've had enough." She brushed damp strands of hair off her forehead. Her arm felt more than a little weak. She was absolutely worn down to the bone.

"I'm tossing in the towel, too," Addison announced. "And I'm starving." She poked one of the doctors. "You do know you have to feed us or we die," she groused.

"We'll get some food in you as soon as possible," Blake said as everyone walked down long corridors that were becoming way too familiar. The usual black sedan waited to whisk them back to their living quarters.

Gwen slid into the backseat beside Addison. She let out a sigh of relief. "I'm glad that's over."

Whittaker muttered under his breath, "Amen." Instead of getting in beside her, he chose the front passenger's seat. *Why would he do that?* she thought. He had openly flirted with her at the lab, but now she couldn't fail to notice his desire seemed to have cooled off.

Addison gave her arm a light punch. "What are you thinking about?"

Gwen absently shook her head. "Nothing much."

Addison's gaze softened. "Don't worry about the Ri'kah thing. At least your kinetic abilities are worlds beyond what Tessa and I can do."

Gwen nodded absentmindedly. Not really wanting to talk, she stared out the window. The weather had been rotten these last few days, matching her mood perfectly. At least the rain had settled down, reduced to a light mist that made the damp air sticky. As the gloomy remnants of day began to descend into an even gloomier evening, clouds sank low to the ground, creating a purplish luminescent fog. It blanketed the land, giving the impression the A51 compound and its people were wrapped in a layer of gauze—a beautiful, if eerie, sight that perfectly suited her mood.

She didn't like this place, not one bit. If she had her druthers, she'd just walk into the fog and disappear forever.

A few minutes later the sedan rolled to a stop in front of their assigned duplexes.

Addison got out. "You want to come over to Tessa's place?" she asked. "We're pulling out the Monopoly board."

Stepping out beside her, Gwen shook her head. "I'm not in the mood for games."

Addison shrugged. "Okay, be that way." She flounced off without a second look.

Gwen sighed. Silence. It pulsed in her ears, throbbed in her temples. She felt sucked dry, emptied out, weak. The rain kicked up into a hard drizzle. She didn't move.

Whittaker opened his own door. "You okay?"

Already soaked to the skin and feeling a little feverish, she shrugged. "I guess so."

Hand on her arm, Whittaker hurried her toward the entrance of the duplex they shared. "Better get out of this rain before you catch a chill." Since Kenneth had warned him off, he'd kept a polite distance. Never saying or doing anything that would hint he had put any thought into their single night together.

Fishing out her key card, she glanced toward him. "Would you like to come in?"

He shook his head. "Thanks for the invite, but no. I'm behind on my reports."

Disappointment stung, but she masked the feeling. He was respecting her need for distance. No reason to lead him on by playing coy. "I would hate to think about what you've said about me in them."

Blake reached for his own key card. "All I can say is it's classified."

She allowed a smile. "All that top-secret agent stuff, I suppose."

He cocked his head. "Something like that."

She couldn't help lingering one more minute. If only she had the nerve to say what she really felt . . . "You know where I'll be if you want me."

Blake nodded and offered a brief, impersonal smile. "I know where you're at." Opening the door to his own place, he disappeared inside and shut the door.

Gwen stepped into her own place. The apartment was silent, stark, and empty. She turned on the lights and then the television. She hated the silence. Like a tomb, it creeped her out. For a moment she considered heading over to the neighboring duplex, spending a little time with the family she'd neglected.

No. If she couldn't see Blake, she'd rather be alone. Misery would be her company tonight.

Feeling the chill all the way to her bones, she decided a long hot shower would be just what she needed to help her relax. In her bedroom, she kicked off her shoes and shimmied out of her clothes, all the while thinking about Blake.

If this is love, it's miserable, came her vague thought. The upside-down feeling was tearing her apart inside.

Sighing, Gwen padded barefoot toward the bathroom. Twenty minutes later the chill was gone, replaced by calming warmth. Throwing on a sweat suit, she combed out her hair and arranged the damp curls into a messy chignon.

Needing to relax, she claimed a chilled bottle of wine from the fridge. It wasn't her favorite, but it would do.

Bottle and glass in hand, she drifted into the living room. She began to arrange a quiet haven, turning off the television and lighting a few candles. The musky scent of sandalwood filled the air as the flames licked their way down the wicks.

Sinking onto the couch, Gwen poured herself a glass

of wine. She drank it down in a single gulp, poured a second and drank it, too. She hadn't had anything to eat since breakfast and the alcohol went straight to her head. She was hungry, but couldn't eat. Maybe later. She just couldn't face another sandwich or single-serve microwave meal.

Closing her eyes, she plumped up a throw pillow and stretched out on the couch. Of course, she thought about Blake.

A little smile played around the corners of her mouth. She realized just how much she looked forward to his company.

The ringing of the doorbell jolted her out of her reverie.

Addison didn't wait for her to answer. Pushing the door open, she stuck her head inside. "Tessa says to stop moping all by yourself and come for pizza." She paused a moment, then added, "Saying 'no' is not an option."

Releasing a sigh, Gwen reluctantly sat up. She had to admit that it was better than being alone.

"Sure." She reached for the wine. "I'll bring the booze."

Closing the door to his apartment, Blake leaned back against it. Even though he'd wanted to be with Gwen, the day's events had drained him completely dry.

Closing his eyes, he wiped a hand across his damp face. Damn, what the agency was doing to the hostile Mers was wrong, dead wrong. Instead of treating them like coherent, thinking beings, the A51 gave them less respect and dignity than a common dog. The cruelty had to be stopped. But how?

I'd have to blow the whistle.

The very idea made the hackles on the back of Blake's neck rise. A barrage of impressions and images circled through his already cluttered brain.

Do that and he wouldn't have a job. Do that and his career would be toast. Do that and he'd be betraying the oath he'd sworn to protect his country against all threats, foreign and domestic.

But did that oath also cover the Mer?

A larger notion loomed. Did that oath cover torture?

Needless to say, his orders were clear. And, of course, he could hardly question the intelligence of his superiors. That would be too dangerous to attempt. A man probing for answers instead of following orders was immediately a suspect, especially when seeking the answers wasn't his job in the first place.

In the chain of command, he was many more rungs toward the bottom than he was toward the top. Right now, his only choice was to obey his supervisors.

"Mine is not to question why," he muttered under his breath.

At least that was what he tried to tell himself.

Too bad it wasn't working.

Breathing deeply, he quickly rubbed his sore temples with the tips of his fingers. The moral implications of dealing with alien life forms was getting muddier, not clearer. With each day that passed, scientists were getting more and more intrusive with their experiments and procedures. All in the name of science, discovery, adding to man's knowledge of the world around him.

It all made sense, sounded logical.

And it was nothing he felt good about being involved with. The lies and deceptions, small and insidious, were beginning to gnaw on his soul. A piece here, a piece there. Pretty soon he'd be eaten down to the bone. He didn't like the feeling. Or the guilt.

This has got to end soon. I can't take much more. The low rumble of thunder punctuated his thought with an ominous finality that raised chilly bumps on his skin.

Leaving the door behind, he walked into the living room.

He shot a glance at the wall clock. Six thirty. Somehow he'd frittered away a half hour without even realizing it. He should sit down and catch up on his paperwork.

A quick glance at his desk and the laptop waiting there told him that was exactly what he didn't want to do.

Gritting his teeth, he tried to distract his mind. It might help if he got something to eat. He couldn't remember the last morsel he'd put into his mouth. The entire day had left him feeling numb and drained. Definitely brain-dead.

He drifted into the small kitchenette. It was barely big enough to turn around in. He checked the fridge. It was almost empty. The idea of food wasn't very appealing anyway.

He needed a walk, a chance to clear his head and think things through. He had looked at all the angles before he made any irrevocable decisions. Whatever course of action he chose wouldn't affect just him. It could possibly bring down the veil of secrecy surrounding the entire A51 and its covert explorations into alien life forms.

He flung open the door and stalked outside.

The covered porch offered a sanctuary from the rain. He cut across the lawn and was about to hit the pavement when he noticed the cheery glow emanating through the living room window of the apartment Tessa and Kenneth shared, which was cracked open a bit. There was movement inside, noise. The sounds of a family interacting with each other.

Feeling a bit like a Peeping Tom, he walked over to look inside. The four of them—Kenneth, Tessa, Addison, and Gwen—sat around the dining room table. Pizza boxes from the commissary were scattered around. A hot game of Monopoly was taking place.

He had to admire them. They were doing their best to maintain a sense of normalcy. Every one of them had shown grace under pressure. Even Kenneth, as prickly a pain in the ass as he was, was doing his best to cooperate. They seemed determined to prove that the Mer, far from being extraordinary creatures, were perfectly normal. Boring, even.

Not that there was any way he'd ever think of Gwen as ordinary. She was special. A keeper. No doubt about it.

He often thought about what it might have been like if they'd actually gotten to have the date he'd asked her out on.

If only. . . .

He started to back away from the window. *I should leave them alone, let them have a night's peace.*

Addison glanced up. Her sharp eyes narrowed. "Hey, we've got company." She pointed toward the window. "Someone let him in."

Kenneth left his seat, heading toward the door. A moment later he came outside. "What the hell are you standing in the rain for, Whittaker?"

Feeling like an absolute fool, Blake shrugged. "Just standing," he mumbled, having no good reason at all.

Kenneth frowned. "Looking in the window isn't a very good way to spy on us."

Blake shook his head. He hadn't been spying. He'd been admiring the close-knit family and wishing he had something like it himself. Suddenly his life felt empty. Worthless. It was true he had Trevor. But a kid deserved a mom and a dad, living together under one roof. As much as he hated it, Debra was right. The move to California would be the best thing for Trevor and the family she was trying to build.

Maybe it was time to let his kid go.

That would leave him all alone, but there was nothing he could do about it. He'd just have to suck it up and endure. This was the life he had chosen. He was a G-man, whether he liked it or not.

"I was just taking a little walk to stretch my legs," he lied. "I was thinking maybe I'd hit the commissary for something to eat."

To his surprise, Kenneth Randall jerked a thumb over his shoulder. "We've got pizza," he offered. "And beer. And if you can handle having your ass kicked, there are some moguls in the making waiting to take all your cash."

Blake perked up, shaking off the dull chill of the night. It was the best offer he'd had in a long time. "I could surely use a beer," he admitted. "Maybe even two." It would also give him a chance to spend a little time with Gwen. That thought alone cheered him immensely.

Kenneth clapped him on the shoulder. "It'll be easier to spy on us if you're on the inside"

Blake nodded. "Yeah. I suppose it will. But don't remind me I was whipped by a woman, please." So far Gwen had pulled his ass out of the fire twice.

Kenneth scrubbed a hand over his jaw. "Sorry. Guess you've figured out those Mer can be fierce when they're riled."

Curiosity nudged. "So what's it like, being married to one?"

Kenneth cut him a hard look. "Are you asking me as a spy, or as a man?"

Blake tried to laugh but didn't quite manage. "Dunno. Maybe a little of both."

"I'll just say that's something you'd have to find out for yourself." He paused, then added, "I know you and Gwen had your moment. I probably shouldn't say this, but I know it meant something to her, despite the brave face she's putting up."

"I wasn't using her," Blake hastened to say. "I never would—"

"For her sake I'm glad to hear you say that," Kenneth said, cutting him off a bit awkwardly. Blake could tell feelings weren't Kenneth's strong suit as well. "For what it's worth, if the circumstances were different I think you two would have been good together."

Blake would have smiled if his nerves hadn't been so frazzled. "Thanks."

The rain started to fall a little harder, pelting them with hard fat drops. Light scratched at the gray belly of the sky.

"We'd better get inside before we're soaked," Kenneth urged.

Following Kenneth into the apartment, Blake peeled off his rain-soaked jacket. "I hope you don't mind me joining you."

The women all waved and smiled their welcome. "Of course not," Tessa said, bustling around to find an extra chair. "Sit down and join us."

Feeling more than a little out of place, Blake took the chair, which Tessa had made sure to place far from Gwen's. She might welcome him to her table, but she wasn't giving him easy access to her sister. He couldn't say he blamed her one little bit. They most likely thought he was a total heel. Hell, he felt like one and probably deserved every dirty look they threw his way.

He sneaked a peek across the table at Gwen as he sat. Sitting in a faded gray sweat suit, her hair was freshly washed and pinned up. Without a lick of makeup, her skin was flawless, as fragile as porcelain.

"You look good," he said, attempting to keep his tone casual. Inside his heart was racing a mile a minute.

Gwen's hand self-consciously rose, brushing a few stray curls away from her face. "Thanks. You look drenched." Her eyes met his and within their depths he saw the memories of the night they'd made love. She hadn't forgotten.

Neither had he.

Frustration coursed through him. The memories of her were seared into his brain like a brand. Blake shoved them away. He couldn't have her, damn it. She'd been clear about that. Thinking about her was a stupid, futile exercise.

"Rain tends to do that to you." Realizing his body had suddenly turned icy, he shivered. "I suppose I could use a cup of coffee more than I could use a beer."

"I can put on a pot," Tessa offered.

"That would be great. Thanks." He looked at the game pieces scattered across the table. "Sorry to interrupt your game."

Addison shrugged. "It wasn't a very good one. Ken's been sulking since he went bankrupt."

Reclaiming his place and reaching for his beer, Kenneth took a hearty drink. "I wasn't sulking," he said, curling his lip. "I was working on my getaway plan. Being stuck in this place is driving me stir-crazy."

Blake's inner antennae swiveled. He knew what the sisters were capable of doing when they pooled their Mercraft. It would be possible for one of the girls to teleport themselves outside the compound, no problem. He realized the only thing really keeping the women put was their own good graces. Any one of the Lonike sisters had the capability to turn lethal in the blink of an eye.

We still don't really know what we're dealing with, he thought.

"I don't think that's such a good idea," he ventured.

Kenneth frowned. "Of course you wouldn't, Whittaker. You're one of *them*."

Blake shook his head. "That's true. But I'm still looking at it from the point of view that you're safer here than outside on your own." He raised a hand to his neck, still mottled with fading yellow bruises. "I don't know about you, but I wouldn't want to run into any of those Ishaldi mermaids in a dark alley. They're vicious and they're out for blood."

Tessa delivered a steaming cup of coffee. "He's right, Ken. We weren't prepared to defend ourselves against them and they kicked our tails all over the place."

Addison reached for her wine. "That won't happen a second time," she muttered after taking a sip from her glass. "I've been practicing my Mercraft and I'm really getting the hang of it. I think I could hold my own."

Gwen's eyes narrowed. "That's precisely what I don't want to do. I don't want humans to think we're all vile, violent creatures who go around blasting each other to bits."

Addison shrugged. "Why not? Humans do it all the time."

Gwen sighed. "You would think we could reach a point in evolution where violence wouldn't be necessary."

Tessa looked up. "Isn't that something we all wish for?"

"Well, the world doesn't work that way," Kenneth said. "It's always going to be an eye for an eye and a tooth for a tooth."

Skipping the sweetener, Blake added milk to take the bitter edge off his brew. "That's enough to make me want to skip the coffee and go straight to the whiskey." He lifted the steaming mug to his face, closing his eyes and inhaling the rich aroma.

Kenneth killed the rest of his beer and crushed the can. "You a drinking man, Whittaker?" he asked.

Blake sipped his coffee. Damn, it was strong enough to eat through steel. He recognized the fact that Randall was prying, trying to get a little information out of him. He didn't blame the man. "I drank a little before my son was born," he admitted. "It was getting to be a problem, so I did some time in AA."

"So it's under control?" Kenneth asked.

Gwen shot a sharp look toward her brother-in law. "Really, Kenneth. There's no need to pry."

Kenneth laughed. "Ah, come on Gwen. It's all in good fun. He knows everything about us. We should know something about him. Kind of a fair exchange of information."

"You did sleep with him," Addison added bluntly. "Wouldn't you like to know something about the man you bumped uglies with?"

Gwen instantly turned ten shades of red. "Oh, God," she murmured. "You people are too much."

Blake shook his head. "It's okay," he said. "My life's pretty cut and dried. I grew up in Port Rock and joined the army after I graduated."

"So you're a local?" Tessa asked.

Blake shrugged. "Somewhat. I haven't been around there for almost sixteen years."

"Any particular reason you left?" Kenneth asked.

Blake felt his stomach curdle around the coffee he'd

consumed. What had began as a pleasant evening was beginning to take a turn for the worst. He never talked about his mother, had never told another living soul what she'd done to him.

But his mother's ghost refused to stay buried. No matter how hard he tried, he'd always found it impossible to put Loretta Whittaker to rest. His mind was plagued with horrors of the past and the sorrow that both his innocence and trust had been taken from him at such an early age.

Remembering how the water had closed over his head time and time again, he felt a chill creep down his spine. His heart slammed heavily against his rib cage; he suddenly had difficulty breathing. It was as if a giant's hand had gripped his body and was closing, tighter . . . tighter . . .

Drunk and filled with hate, his mother was not particularly concerned about the psychic wounds she'd inflicted on her young son. She'd beaten and belittled him until she'd made Blake fear and mistrust women.

Jaw tightening, he fought the squeeze of icy fingers around his heart. Long, sharp nails dug deep, and— damn, it hurt! He had hated being a child, hated the feeling of helplessness.

As a boy, he'd learned to keep out of his mother's sight as much as possible. The less Loretta saw of him when she was drinking, the better.

"I don't have any brothers or sisters. I'm an only child." He'd often thanked God he didn't have a sibling. He couldn't stand the idea of someone even smaller and weaker being put through hell, too.

Regaining her composure, Gwen gave him a little smile. "Oh? So you were the single spoiled brat, eh?" She reached for her own glass of wine, taking a tiny sip of the rosy liquid.

Blake shook his head. "Oh, my mother thought I was a brat, all right. And she knocked the hell out of me every chance she got." There. He'd said it. Might as well give everyone a shock. It hurt to say, but he accepted the reality.

Gwen glanced up sharply. "You don't sound like you're joking."

Blake didn't want to look anyone in the eye. He stared into his half-empty coffee cup instead. "My mother abused me," he said quietly. "In short, she hit me. A lot."

Silence. Dead silence. Who wanted to hear things like that?

He glanced up. Everyone's faces were taut. No one spoke.

Good way to scare people off, he thought. *Tell them your dirty little secrets.*

Gwen finally cleared her throat. "I'd suspected something," she said. "I've felt the tension boiling under your skin at certain times." She cocked her head. "It's always there, but it's worse when you're near water."

Blake's stomach coiled into tight knots. Now that he had started talking, he couldn't seem to stop. "When she was pissed, really pissed at me, my mother would fill the bathtub with cold water. She'd hold me under until I'd nearly pass out, then pull me back up again. The harder I struggled, the longer she kept me down." Even though his pulse was pounding like a jackhammer, he spoke in a clinical matter-of-fact way, relating the events the way he'd recount unpleasant facts to a superior. It helped distance him from the trauma. If he didn't get emotional, it didn't hurt as much.

"By the goddess," Tessa murmured. "That must have been horrible for you."

Blake raised his chin a notch. "I survived." Refusing to cringe, he kept going. The poison he'd held bottled up inside his soul was finally coming out. "But I never trusted women. It's why things didn't work out between me and Debra. I was always afraid she'd get emotional and hurt Trevor to get even with me."

"The way your mother got even with you?" Addison asked.

Lifting a hand, Blake pressed his thumb and forefinger against his eyes, rubbing hard at his burning lids. "Yeah. My dad wasn't any kind of a champ, and neither were the bastards she took up with after he left. I can't tell you how many stepfathers I cycled through."

He shook his head, making a mental count. There were at least eight, maybe more. Sometimes his mother married them, sometimes she just shacked up. Loretta Whittaker had the magic touch when it came to picking scummy losers. They'd drink and beat her. She'd drink and beat Blake.

Yeah, the neighbors often heard the ruckus and called the police. The cops would take one look at his staggering, bloodied mother and her equally battered kid and haul the current doped-up son of a bitch off to jail. Yet no one ever bothered to ask Blake just who exactly was doing the hitting.

Always, men were the baddies, the ones who swung a fist or a belt. His mother was good at playing the victim, too. She knew how to manipulate the system so she'd come off looking like the innocent, injured party. By the time he'd gotten old enough to evade his mother's murderous rages, he'd learned one lesson, and learned it well.

Look out for yourself, because no one else will.

Once he'd left Port Rock, he left for good. Even when he'd been informed of her slide into illness, he'd refused to go back. A few months later he'd gotten word she'd died, a victim of the cancer riddling her uterus. He didn't claim her body, and the county had done what it did with most indigents. She'd gotten a cheap cremation and a scattering over the bay by some morgue assistant.

Blake hoped she liked the water better than he did.

He couldn't say he'd ever loved his mother. Nor could he claim he missed her now that her time on earth had ended. The only thing he'd felt after her passing was numb relief. Her grief in this life was over.

He realized then he hadn't really been living himself. Just existing, marking the days off, one after the other. Having Trevor had helped bring a little joy back into his life. But even his happiness over Trevor's birth was tainted by the fears he harbored deep in his heart. Perhaps if he'd simply opened up to Debra and shared his feelings instead of continually stifling them, things might have worked out between them.

Gwen gave him a sympathetic look. "I can't imagine how hard it was for you," she said, watching him closely. Was she looking for signs of deception? He wasn't sure.

Blake wished she was closer, just so he could reach out and touch her. Desire rose. He wanted to get her alone, just so he could tell her their one night together had meant everything to him. But he had to stay silent. She was the one who'd backed off. He had to respect her wishes, no matter how much it hurt.

He drew a quick breath, silently willing away the un-welcome emotions swamping him. "It's over and done with." Having finished the coffee, he put the cup aside. "In case you're all wondering, I've never told anyone. I lied through every psych test I ever took. They always thought I was the perfect soldier because I didn't freak out under pressure."

Her head cocked subtly. "Must be tough always hold-ing people at arm's length." Despite the distance sepa-rating them, there was a definite connection. He could feel it. Really feel it.

Gathering the remnants of his composure, Blake glanced up. He couldn't look at the faces around him without feeling a particular funny twist in his heart. In-stead of placating him or trying to offer their interpre-tations, they had simply listened to him talk. He hadn't intended to spill his guts like a kid in the counselor's office, but now that he had, he felt better. The millstone around his neck seemed to fall away. For the first time in his life he'd been totally honest about his past.

Why he'd felt compelled to share . . . Well, he wasn't sure. Maybe it was because he wanted to forge a more personal connection with Gwen, as if by opening up he could show her he was more than a bastard with a badge.

He genuinely felt these were people who cared, people who would accept him at face value if only he'd be honest. Even though he'd only known Gwen and her family a short time, he liked them. They were such a close-knit group. Even Kenneth Randall, a human, had managed to fit in just fine.

It was something Blake wanted for himself. Badly.

But how could he be honest and build a relationship with Gwen when his job demanded he practice deceit?

You're playing with fire, he warned himself. *And you're going to get burned.*

Chapter 19

Located just outside Fort Lauderdale, Mimosa Springs, Florida, was a planned community, a location desired by the upper-middle-class because of family-friendly orientation.

Kendra Newsome and her boyfriend resided at the Sherwood Forest apartment complex, a distinctive blend of timeless Spanish architectural design and impeccably maintained tropical landscaping. Its close proximity to all of South Florida's major metropolitan areas made the location perfect for a young couple.

Parking his rental car, a nice sporty Lexus, in the visitor's area, Jake wound his way around a swimming pool with a heated whirlpool spa, a basketball court, an exercise facility, and a tennis court. Apartment number 12 was on the second floor.

Pausing a moment to check his reflection in a window, he adjusted his blazer. He'd made sure to dress well: crisp slacks, white shirt, fitted jacket, no tie, along with a five-hundred-dollar pair of Italian leather boots polished to a high sheen. Though shorter and darker, he'd kept his hair at a flattering chin length. He didn't like the gray tinted contacts, but since they matched his new passport he wore them anyway.

He looked good. Respectable. Trustworthy.

Confident he could pull off his plan, he rang the door-bell.

A few minutes later the door opened just a crack. A chain spanned the two-inch space. Even though Mimosa Springs had one of the lowest crime rates in the nation, it was better to be safe than sorry when living in a large city.

Half of a pretty girl's face appeared. A dog yapped loudly in the background. "Yes?" she asked. By the tone of her voice, she clearly hadn't been expecting company.

Jake flashed his best movie-star smile. "My name is Jean Luc D'Marquis." He gave her his false name though he'd dispensed with the phony French accent. "I understand your name is Kendra Newsome."

The single eye staring through the crack narrowed. "That's right. What would you want with me?"

Jake widened his smile. "I'm here because of your mother, Gail Davis Newsome."

A frown. "My mother passed away two years ago."

He nodded. "Yes, I am aware of that. But did you know your mother had a sister, Jolesa Davis?"

"Yes, I think that's right," she answered from behind the impenetrable shield of her door. "I never met her, though, if you're looking for her." The dog's incessant yipping almost drowned out her reply.

Patience, he counseled himself. *Take it slow and ease in.*

"I know where she is, actually," Jake said, wishing the damn dog would shut up. The barking was beginning to get on his nerves, big-time. "And she has daughters who have been looking for their aunt—and any possible children she might have had."

Kendra Newsome turned, attempting to quiet her dog. "Peetems, hush. You'll get us kicked out of here." He was thankful that the canine minded his mistress. She turned back to the door. "Are you like that guy on television, who finds missing family members?"

Jake nodded. To back up his say-so, he presented a business card. Recoveries, Inc., had become Family Recovery. All it took was a quick trip to a do-it-yourself print shop. Thirty minutes later he had a small stack of cards in hand. The phone numbers were fakes, but he doubted she'd call them. It was so easy to fool someone.

Not that he intended to be deceptive. He'd honestly give her all the information she needed to locate Tessa and her sisters if that was what she wanted. In return he hoped he'd get the information he needed to locate the missing pieces of the puzzle.

"Exactly."

The door closed. The chain latch slid off.

"Please come in," she invited a moment later. "I'm dying to hear what you have to tell me."

Jake smiled to himself. Yep. He'd hooked and reeled her in. People always trusted the guy on television. She'd tell him everything. No doubt about it now. The best way to get someone to trust you was to prove you had their best interests at heart.

He stepped into an apartment designed to maximize the wide-open living area. A gourmet kitchen with an open serving bar added an extra touch of luxury.

Kendra Newsome indicated a chair. "Please, have a seat Mr.—" She blanked on his name.

"D'Marquis," Jake filled in politely.

"Is that French?"

"I'm Canadian actually," he replied, giving her necessary but vague details. Along with his passport, he also had an enhanced Canadian driver's license. The secure documents denoted both identity and Canadian citizenship and were acceptable documents for entry into the United States by land or sea.

She pinned his card onto a bulletin board covered with the usual notes and photos people collected. "Can I offer you something? Coffee? Tea?"

Jake smiled again. "Thank you. Coffee would be terrific."

"Great. I can handle that." Flicking a smile his way, Kendra Newsome headed toward her neat little kitchen, which sported a nice gourmet coffee machine.

Jake sat down. The dog, a medium-sized cross between a terrier and a poodle, hit his lap at top speed. Less than a minute later his clothes were coated with kinky hair. Tongue lolling and dripping saliva, the dog sat in a happy stupor.

Like all pet owners who were oblivious to their pet's bad behavior, Kendra Newsome laughed it off. "You'll have to excuse Peetems. He loves everyone."

Jake gritted his teeth. "So I see." He resisted the urge to push the dog away. If he had his druthers, the only thing it would get would be a swift boot to the ass. He tolerated it instead. Once he'd pumped the necessary information out of Kendra, he could go along his merry way.

"So how long have you been working in genealogy?" she inquired across the open countertop.

Jake had already mentally prepared his answers. The simpler he kept the facts, the better it would be. "I've worked in archaeology about sixteen years." It was easy and convincing to say because it was true. "But recently I've turned my attention toward helping families locate lost members. You're actually my first case."

Toting two cups of perfectly brewed cappuccino, Kendra joined him in the living room. "I have to say I'm very excited to know I have cousins." She handed over a cup. "I've always felt there were more of us out there."

Glad to exchange the mutt for the coffee, Jake cut his gaze toward Kendra's neck. The stone he expected to see hanging there was missing.

She doesn't know.

Instead of nurturing the symbiote inside her daughters, Gail Newsome had chosen not to tell them. Over time it had probably died, leaving them mere humans. That was a shame, too. Gail's daughters probably had no idea of their true heritage.

Pity. He liked the Mer race.

Jake sipped his coffee. The brew had a slight mocha flavor and was delicious. "Do you have any idea why your mother might have cut ties with her family?" he asked.

Kendra sat down. Peetems jumped up beside his mistress, curling up on a couple of throw pillows. At least the mangy beast was somewhat well behaved. "Honestly, I'm not really sure," she answered. "I think there was some sort of family quarrel, over property or money."

"That's a common reason for family rifts," Jake opined as though he really knew what he was talking about. It sounded like something logical to say.

She seemed to agree. "Mom sometimes mentioned her mother had cheated her in favor of her sister. Beyond that, she wouldn't say much more. As far as I know, they never spoke again after she left home. That was in Maine, I think, but I'm not clear on all the details. My mother was very secretive about her past."

My goodness. The girl was going to be a fountain of information. The gods were truly smiling on him today.

"The records I uncovered indicated that your mother passed away in 2009. I couldn't find a cause of death, however."

Smile vanishing, Kendra Newsome stared into her cup. She shook her head. "It wasn't pleasant," she finally said, releasing a deep sigh. "In fact, all we've wanted to do is just forget."

Jake immediately sensed her tension and knew he'd stumbled onto something important. He leaned forward in his chair. "I'm sorry to bring back bad memories. I'm also sorry to say her sister Jolesa is also deceased." Give a piece of information to get a piece. It was a fair trade and one he didn't mind talking about. It wasn't like it was his own mother.

Kendra nodded. "I see." A pause. "How did she pass away?"

Jake dug back through what he knew about Tessa's past. "She and her husband—David, I believe his name was—were killed in a car accident about fifteen years ago."

She gasped. "That's terrible. Her children must have been quite young."

Jake sipped more of his frothy cappuccino. "They were."

Curious blue eyes met his. "How many cousins do I have?"

Jake parceled out the information. "Three. Tessa is the oldest. She's thirty now. Then there's Gwen. She's about twenty-seven. The youngest is Addison. She's just a couple of years older than you."

Kendra put aside her forgotten beverage. "Wow. Just wow. It's so great to know all this. It felt so strange to think Sandra and I were the only two left from Mom's side of the family."

Jake put on his coyote's grin. The meeting was going so much better than he could ever have imagined. "Well, the good news is you're not. You have three cousins who very much want to meet you—if you're willing, of course."

Kendra's face lit up. "Of course I am! Sandra is, too. I want to know everything about Mom's people."

"The girls have wanted to know everything about their aunt, too," he said, carefully maneuvering the conversation back toward the person he held the most interest in. "They will be disappointed—that they missed the chance to meet her."

Kendra suddenly crumbled. Eyes going teary, she plucked at a nearby Kleenex box. "That was tough." She dabbed at her red-rimmed eyes.

Peetems raised his head, looking at his mistress through quizzical eyes. Recognizing her distress, he moved closer, laying his head on her lap. The animal was clearly devoted.

Jake subtly probed. "I take it her death was unexpected."

Kendra stroked the dog's head with an absent hand. "Yeah, it was." A pause, followed by a quick rush of words. "Mom chose to end her own life."

Oh, dear. That was something he hadn't expected. In all the death records he'd found, including the obituary, a cause of death wasn't revealed. Now he knew why. Obits rarely mentioned suicide as a cause of death. "Was she ill?" he ventured, attempting to keep his voice neutral.

Kendra frowned deeply. Minutes ticked by before she finally answered. "I am sorry to say it, but my mother was schizophrenic. It was a struggle for her to control what she called 'the beast inside.'" A single tear rolled down her cheek. She quickly swiped it away. "I'm afraid it got the better of her."

Despite his detachment from the matter, Jake felt his stomach roll over. *A Mer out of water,* he thought. Like her niece Gwen, he suspected Gail had also attempted to suppress her true nature. It must have been a battle she couldn't win.

He gave her a few minutes to regain her composure. Mention of her mother obviously opened a deep psychological wound for Kendra. "I'm very sorry for your loss."

Stifling her tears, Kendra pulled her shoulders back. "It was a relief, actually."

"Oh? How so?"

A blush of embarrassment stained her cheeks. "Mother's black spells would just put your nerves on end," she explained. "Literally, she would drive you crazy with her imaginary world of queens and mermaids and all sorts of crazy nonsense about the sea."

Putting on his best clinical face, Jake nodded. "I see."

He shifted in his chair, leaning forward to encourage intimacy. "You mentioned earlier your mother might have felt cheated over some money or property."

Kendra nodded. "Yes, that's true."

He had to jump in with both feet and hope he hit solid ground. "There are some family heirlooms your mother inherited. Tessa has expressed an interest in regaining some of those pieces."

Kendra's hand drifted toward her dog. She gave the hound a reassuring scratch behind the ears. "Heirlooms?" she repeated. "Such as?"

She didn't seem disturbed, so he pressed on. "Your grandmother split some pieces of the family jewelry between Jolesa and Gail," he explained. "Your mother inherited the larger and most valuable piece."

The girl blanked. Nothing computed in her mind. "She did?"

Jake held his breath. Here was the moment he'd

anticipated for days. "Yes. It might have been a rather large piece, such as a scepter."

She thought a moment. "No, I don't think Mom ever had anything like a scepter. Isn't that something like a king or queen would have?"

Hope dimmed. *Damn.* Disappointment balled in his chest, heavy and leaden. He imagined the unseen thing slipping through his fingers. Queen Magaera would not be pleased. "Something like it." He kept his answer vague.

"She did have this really gaudy trident." She rolled her eyes. "My God, it was the ugliest thing."

Jake's heart damn near stalled. "Trident?"

Kendra absently shredded the used Kleenex she held. "Yeah, my father donated it to the Mimosa Springs Museum of Art after Mom died." Balling up the mess she'd made, she offered a smile. "Sandra's boyfriend, Damien, is an artist and he created a life-sized bronze of Poseidon for the museum's Mythical Forces display. Dad decided to let him have the piece to complete his sculpture." She waved a dismissive hand. "It wasn't like it was valuable or anything. Just a lot of junky fake stones. Ugly thing, really."

Jake felt his blood pressure drop. His mind was working a mile a minute to process the information.

The scepter was on display. In a museum. For all the public to see.

Jake sucked in an excited breath. *Holy shit!* He'd just hit the mother lode.

Nevertheless he deliberately forced himself to keep a neutral expression. No reason to let the cat out of the proverbial bag. "Neither you or your sister wanted it?" he asked, keeping his voice bland.

Kendra pressed her lips together. "Frankly, no. The damn thing was part of Mom's craziness and we didn't want it around after she died."

Jake lifted a brow. "Part of her craziness?"

Kendra Newsome let out a long-suffering sigh. Now that she'd started talking, she seemed eager to keep going. "She claimed the thing belonged to some mythical goddess who had given her people command over land and sea. It was sad, really. Her delusional state only got worse as the years passed."

"Uh-huh."

By this time Jake wasn't listening. Her words had become little more than a drone in his ears. No, his mind was on the scepter, the valuable, coveted piece he'd traveled halfway around the world to lay his hands on.

There was only one problem.

How the hell were they supposed to lay hands on a scepter that was part of a public display?

The Mimosa Springs Museum was a place of pride and enjoyment for all citizens and visitors of the community. The goal of the museum was to create a stimulating environment reflecting the city's diversity and character through pieces put together by local artists. Though not always consistent, many of the displays had an eccentric charm.

In typical Florida fashion, the museum had the look of an overdone mausoleum; the grounds were lush and perfectly kept and the inside, done in muted grays and whites, had a hushed atmosphere of cold reverence. The paintings and statuary on display ranged from the absurd to the avant-garde.

Jake had spent two days scoping out the museum and how best to breach its security system. He'd decided a full-on assault in broad daylight would be the most successful and striking way to make a statement. He didn't anticipate any trouble for the simple plan he'd devised.

The museum's staff was small. Attendants were on site to guide visitors through the displays or point the way toward the restrooms or gift shop. Aside from simple black velvet ropes strung around at random, there was no obstacle between the public and the pieces on display. A few security guards milled through the browsing people, looking thoroughly bored and totally uninterested in their staid surroundings.

It was into this quiet refuge from the blazing Florida sun that Queen Magaera and her attendants marched, clad in full battle regalia and weapons at the ready.

Many people turned and watched with interest as the Mer swept across the granite floors. The museum often hosted performance-art pieces, and most simply assumed this display was one of them.

Jake himself followed closely at Queen Magaera's heels, smiling and waving to onlookers. *Yes!* He loved to be the center of attention. He'd decided it was time for the Mer to make a showy entrance—announcing to the world they were here and ready to reclaim their place in the human world.

The Mythical Forces exhibit was one of the most popular, given the city's proximity to the sea. Although most expected something in the tradition of classical sculpture when thinking of Poseidon—perched on a ledge with a sea-nymph simpering at his feet—what the artist presented was another thing entirely. The thing—and it was just that—looked like a heap of tin cans arranged into vaguely human shapes.

Jake frowned in disapproval when he saw it. *Oh. My. God.* It was a travesty to call the display art. The trident looked tacky perched against the bronze heap. No wonder the family had pawned it off on the public. The next-best place for this hot mess would be a garbage dump.

As he'd been told, the final piece belonging to the collection of Atargatis was indeed a three-pronged trident—an elaborate staff of pure gold set with a slew of precious jewels. He thought it ironic a relic dating back thousands of years should be mistaken for nothing more than faux rocks and plain worthless metal.

Magaera's eyes widened with recognition. "By the goddess." A smile curled the corners of her mouth. "I never thought I would see it in my lifetime. It is blasphemy to see it abused by such careless hands."

Jake couldn't help smirking. "It's just like I promised you," he reminded her. "I told you I'd recover it for you."

Magaera glanced toward him. "You have indeed proven yourself, my consort. And for it, you shall be well rewarded." She marched toward the stone god, intending to claim her prize.

A surprised attendant rushed over. "Excuse me, miss!" she called out. "You can't touch that."

Hand moving to the dagger strapped at her side, one

of Magaera's guards immediately cut the woman off. "You may not approach Her Majesty," she growled. Her orders from her queen were clear. She was to take out any unexpected obstacles that came into their path.

Nobody would get near Magaera and survive.

The woman stepped back, confused. "Nobody told me we were supposed to have a show today," she stammered.

By now more than a few curious people had begun to gather. A few clapped, encouraging the performance to continue.

One of the guards, as huge as a pro linebacker and looking just as menacing, came running up. "What's going on here?" he demanded.

Jake snorted a chuckle. "I'd suggest you all step back and let the lady have her treasure."

The guard reached for the nearest Mer's arm. "I think it's best if you all leave the building right now."

It was the biggest mistake he would ever make.

And his last.

The Mer soldier lunged, grabbing his left wrist. She twisted his body around and took him to his knees in one clean, easy motion. Dagger simultaneously unsheathed, she dragged the sharp edge of the blade cleanly across the man's throat.

The guard's limp body pitched facedown onto the cold stone floor. A faintly guttural sound escaped him, the last he'd make. A great pool of blood fanned out around his head and shoulders.

At first there was silence. Dead, awed silence.

And then it dawned on the onlookers. This was no act. It was absolutely real.

The crowd freaked, scattering in all directions, a mass of hysteria and panic.

Jake's vision wavered, but he forced himself to hold steady amid the carnage. *I'm not the one doing the killing,* he reminded himself. In his mind, his hands were unsullied by the taint of cold-blooded murder.

Braving the stampeding crowd, another security guard ran into the fray. The poor man wasn't armed with anything more than a walkie-talkie and pepper spray.

Armed with the deadly Ri'kah, another of Magaera's soldiers raised her arm. A quick burst from her weapon heated the air. The laserlike blast struck the man dead-on. He dropped in his tracks, dead before he struck the floor. His chest was an empty hole, his heart and lungs instantly fried to a crisp.

Heart pounding like a jackhammer, Jake gagged as the smell of burning flesh permeated the air around them. He clenched his teeth against the rise of nausea.

Silent minutes ticked by. The horrified bystanders had disappeared, leaving them standing amid the chaos. The distant wail of sirens sounded in the far distance.

He surveyed the damage. Though unpleasant, a display of force was necessary to show the Mer were capable of defending themselves. As for those who died, they'd have to be written off as collateral damages. "I believe you've proven your point," he commented drily.

Brows drawing together, Magaera's icy blue gaze glittered. "They are humans," she snapped through a glare. "Their lives have no meaning."

Jake was aware of her eyes blazing. Aware of her rigid posture. Aware of the hostility emanating from her in waves of blistering heat.

He looked into Magaera's eyes, which held no sign of remorse or regret. She was a true queen, proud and fierce in her determination to lead her people. Nothing would stand in the way of her merciless ambition to reclaim a place for the Mer in the human world.

"There's no turning back now," he warned. "This will mean war."

Lips set in a hard line, Magaera gave the dead bodies a twitchy stare. As a queen, she had never been accountable to fear, suffering, regret, nor compassion. She embraced honor on her own terms. Wielded justice according the laws she had written.

"So be it. If more come, then more will die." Stepping up to the statue, she triumphantly reclaimed the last surviving piece Atargatis had fashioned for the queen who ruled Ishaldi. She lifted it above her head in triumph.

Placing their hands across their chests, the Mer soldiers dropped to one knee in reverence. "At long last, we have our soul back."

Magaera smiled, baring her perfect teeth. "And the human world shall bow to my will." She brought the trident down, striking its tip against the stone beneath their feet. "Behold the power of the goddess!" She began a low crooning, a chant rising and falling with a strange rhythmic cadence.

Jake's eyes widened as the trident instantly came to

life, its bejeweled length lighting up like a Christmas tree at midnight. The entire length of it glowed, becoming nearly transparent in Magaera's hand. Jagged flickers of sparking colors moved along it. A pulse of sheer power emanated from it, lighting the walls and floors with an effervescent intensity.

"Our people shall rise again from the waters that have consumed us."

The electric tension surrounding them grew and throbbed. Lightning flared above their heads. The stone around them began to crack.

Jake clenched his teeth as thunder seemed to snap the air apart around them. It was akin to the force Tessa had summoned when she'd destroyed the undersea chamber surrounding the sea-gate. Except it was much more powerful and potent.

His gaze shifted to an eerie mist swirling with dizzying speed and growing wider and wider until it seemed to enclose the museum. The mist pulsed with life, changing from bluish-white to green, then gray before going to bluish-white again within mere seconds.

Jake's heart slammed against his chest, and then seemed to rise and lodge in his throat. His blood turned to ice, while his skin felt afire. Vibrations emanating from the mist penetrated all the way to his bones, a force potent enough to rip him apart down to the last cell.

Queen Magaera swept around him and stepped into the vortex she'd created. The mist snaked around her as if to draw her in. But still she lingered, watching him, her chest rising and falling on heaving breaths. It was at that moment Jake understood her, completely and without question. Her cruelties were necessary to protect her people. She would do whatever it took.

He had no idea what would happen next, and wasn't sure he was ready for it.

Not that he had any choice.

In the blink of an eye the mist swept in around him. Everything suddenly vanished under a dizzying sweep of pure white light.

And the security cameras rolled on ...

Chapter 20

The Monopoly game was in full swing. Kenneth was in mogul mode, having snatched up Boardwalk and Park Place in his attempt to own the priciest real estate on the board.

Blake had bought up several railroads and utilities. Addison hadn't passed GO enough to accumulate any money and had gone broke. To keep things honest, Tessa was the banker. Blake had accused her of embezzling to help her husband build his fortune.

Gwen was playing modestly, having claimed Connecticut, Vermont, and Oriental avenues. She'd put hotels on every piece of property she owned, naturally.

"You are so going to owe me some money," she crowed when a roll of the dice landed Kenneth on her most luxurious property.

Kenneth handed over the faux cash. "You'll come around to Park Place soon enough." He winked at Tessa and slipped a wad of colored money her way. "Sell me a couple of houses, baby. I want that sister of yours to pay through the nose on her next visit my way."

Tessa laughed. "You two are going to break each other." She handed over two small plastic game pieces.

Kenneth put his houses in place. "Now, that's living the good life," he teased.

Tessa sighed and reached for her glass of wine. "I just wish we could get back to our own lives." She winced. "I don't even want to think about what the house must look like."

Kenneth patted her arm. "It'll be okay, honey. We can rebuild. I never liked that kitchen anyway. Too small. And we can get back to enlarging the nursery, too. I'm thinking it might need to hold more than one crib."

Tessa beamed. "I'm not even pregnant yet."

Kenneth waggled his brows in a most lecherous way. "You will be."

Stretched out on the nearby sofa stuffing her mouth with chips and dip, Addison paused long enough to roll her eyes. "If I hear any more from you two lovebirds, I'm going to puke. Really, we don't need that much information."

Hiding a smile behind her own hand, Gwen glanced at Blake. He seemed to be enjoying himself. So far he'd taken all the teasing from her family with relatively good humor. He didn't even flinch when Addison nicknamed him "the family fed," and ribbed him unmercifully about spying on innocent mermaids.

The teasing was good-natured and everyone seemed to enjoy the brief moment of normalcy in their otherwise upside-down lives.

He'd fit in.

Everything would be perfect if only they could all go home. Almost two weeks had passed since their confinement began, and investigators seemed no closer to locating hide nor hair of the Mediterranean fugitives. After the attack on Little Mer Island, nothing more had been found of Jake Massey or Magaera.

There were no doubts about them being out there. Who else could have masterminded the attempt to get Tessa back but Jake and his cohort queen?

Gwen reached for her own glass, taking a sip of the rich red wine. She'd had more than a few glasses and was thoroughly relaxed.

She sneaked another little peek toward Blake. Though she probably shouldn't, she'd been letting herself imagine what life might be like after they left the protective custody of the A51 compound. Blake lived in Boston, she in Port Rock, Maine. The distance wasn't too terrible. Maybe there'd be a chance they could go on seeing each other once this entire nightmare came to an end.

At least she hoped they would.

Without knowing quite how or why, she'd handed the man her heart. He was her first lover, and the only man she believed she'd ever want. They'd only made love a single night, but she wanted more. A lot more.

A darker thought crept into her mind. She still had no idea how he might feel about her.

If he felt anything at all.

Since she'd nipped things in the bud, he'd kept his dealings with her respectful. And chaste. He hadn't so much as tried to kiss her.

She sighed and sipped. *All I can do is enjoy it while it lasts.*

It would be her last happy thought of the night.

Blake's cell rang. Everyone froze at the sound that had become unfamiliar in their lives.

Cursing under his breath, Blake held off rolling the dice to answer. "Whittaker," he snapped. Going silent, he listened. A moment later his face paled. His lips thinned.

Gwen immediately picked up on the change in his demeanor.

Heart lurching in her chest, she stiffened. She had a feeling something terrible had happened.

The one-sided conversation couldn't come to an end fast enough. Whatever information was being exchanged, it clearly wasn't good.

Blake finally flipped his phone shut. "I have some good news and some bad news," he announced after a minute's pause.

Tessa seemed to know right away who it concerned. "It's Jake, isn't it?"

Blake nodded. "Yeah, it is. Looks like he and Queen Magaera have finally come out of hiding."

Addison bounded off the sofa. "That's great your guys have caught up with them."

Gwen smiled weakly. "Does that mean we can go home now?"

Blanking his face of all emotion, Blake shook his head. "I'm afraid not. It seems Massey and the Mer from Ishaldi invaded a museum in Mimosa Springs, Florida, to steal an item on display there. Two security guards were killed, cut down in cold blood."

Gwen's heart immediately dropped to her toes. She watched Blake's face as he spoke. He showed remarkable poise under pressure. If the news had upset him, he wasn't showing it. It occurred to her that he had to be tempered of steel to work in such a top-secret division.

"But they're in custody now, right?" she asked hopefully.

Blake delivered his answer with another discouraging shake of his head. "No, they're not. In fact, we don't know where they are."

"How could they get away?" Kenneth demanded. "Didn't someone call the freaking cops?"

Blake threw up his hands in confusion. "They vanished."

"How?" was the next question flung at him.

Blake tried to explain the events as they'd been conveyed to him. "I'm not clear on all the details just yet—everything's on red alert right now and we're scrambling to contain the scene."

Tessa leaned forward on the table, burying her face in her hands. "Damn it. I'll bet Jake's found the scepter. It was the last piece missing—and the most important. Somehow that bastard tracked it down."

"He's good, damn good," Addison agreed.

"Whatever it is, it seems to be a potent weapon they've got at their disposal," Blake continued. "Security cameras filmed the entire incident. At least we can get a look at what we're dealing with."

"So what happens next?" Kenneth wanted to know.

The answer arrived as a knock on the door. Without

waiting, a cadre of heavily armed agents invaded the apartment.

Addison groaned as two agents headed her way with handcuffs drawn. "Don't tell me we're being arrested for what someone else did?" she cracked in a caustic tone.

Blake's impenetrable mask slipped a moment. A look of consternation crossed his face, as if he couldn't compute the answers he had to deliver. "I'm sorry," he said slowly. "Because more civilians have died, the Mer are now considered alien terrorists with the intent to kill."

Kenneth refused his cuffing, wriggling between two agents. "By whose fucking say-so?"

"The A51 is invoking the Antiterrorism and Effective Death Penalty Act," Blake answered. "A significant event usually involves people being killed or wounded by foreign invaders. The Mer have just been reclassified as enemy aliens."

"Which means?" Kenneth retorted.

"You're all being taken into custody and remanded to solitary confinement until the government decides what to do with the Mer."

Kenneth made a lunge toward Whittaker. "Why the hell didn't you tell us?" he demanded angrily. "Did you think we were going to pelt your people with little plastic hotels?"

Blake held up his hands. "I still have a job to do," he explained quietly. "And I didn't want things to get out of hand. Just keep your cool and it'll be all right."

"Fuck you, Whittaker," Kenneth snapped back. "You've done nothing but exploit my family."

An electric flash of anger rose in the back of Gwen's mind. For a full minute she stared straight ahead, hardly able to comprehend the bizarre turn the seemingly normal evening had taken. For some insane reason she'd begun to trust Blake. Had considered opening up enough to let him know how she really felt.

Thank the goddess she'd had the sense to keep her mouth shut. Kenneth was right. Blake had done nothing but exploit their trust. Every move he made was done to serve his job. She suspected everything he'd told them was a lie, simply to prey on their sympathies so he could worm his way in.

Nothing more.

Keenly aware of the blood throbbing through her veins, she felt her composure crumble when she settled her gaze on him. *We were so stupid!*

Her anger swiftly morphed into fury, boiling and rising to the surface. If she let the beast loose, nothing would be able to stop her . . .

Blake must have sensed the impulse building inside her. His gaze locked with hers. He gave a subtle shake of his head.

Please don't, his silent plea said.

Though she didn't like it, Gwen picked up on his signal. Strike out now and it would only reaffirm the fact the Mer could be dangerous adversaries.

Shaking from exertion, she fought to harness the beast inside. The sound of her heart thumping against her chest seemed inordinately loud. The unspent burst of energy bounced off the walls of her skull. A headache began to build at her temples. Perspiration broke out on her skin and her clothes, her clothes clinging uncomfortably to her body.

Cuffs in hand, one of the nameless agents stepped up to her. "If you would, please."

Clenching her fingers into fists, Gwen offered her wrists. "This isn't necessary." She fought to control the agitation in her voice, and failed. The cold metal bit into her skin. She refused to let her mind linger on the sensation.

"We're not like the other Mer," Addison put in.

Tessa frowned at the cuffs circling her wrists. "We've done everything we can to cooperate."

Though cuffed himself, Kenneth wasn't finished complaining. "And all you're doing is treating my wife and her sisters like they are part of some huge terrorist organization. They may be labeled as aliens, but I'm a goddamned citizen and I am more than aware I've got rights—rights that you people have trampled all over."

"Nobody here is listening," one of the nameless agents advised him drily. "We can make this easy or we can make it hard." He shrugged. "Your choice."

Blake Whittaker stepped in. "You will treat these people with due respect until they prove they deserve otherwise." He arched a brow toward Kenneth. "In turn, I am sure they will continue to cooperate with us as we attempt to sort through this grievous mess."

Kenneth failed to take the hint. "I want a goddamned attorney," he groused, then added, "And I've got enough money to sue the pants off the federal government. It's wrong to treat my wife and her sisters like criminals."

Tessa shushed her husband. "Take it easy, Ken." She offered a small smile of reassurance. "You're human and you'll get out of here."

"I won't leave without you girls," he insisted.

Apprehension tightened Gwen's throat. Somehow she had a feeling they'd never get out of this place alive.

The ride across the compound was short and sweet. And silent. No one dared to speak.

Rounded up like fugitives, they were all taken to a new facility, one they'd never seen before. Heavily guarded, the place looked cold and foreboding.

An elevator whisked them to corridors deep underground. And then they were all split up. Tessa and Kenneth were hustled off in one direction, Addison another.

That left Gwen by herself. Alone and very afraid.

Guided down a long corridor, each step toward the final destination felt like doom in her heart. She tried to switch off her mind, but that was impossible. The freeze coming off the agents attending her felt like walking across the North Pole naked.

Separated from her sisters, Gwen was taken into a room by herself. There she was stripped of her cuffs and clothing and given a quick spray down with some sort of antiseptic wash. The liquid smelled like wintergreen and burned like rubbing alcohol.

They're afraid of us, came the vague thought. Funny, she felt just the opposite. She was afraid of them. An image of herself stretched out on an autopsy table flashed across her mind's eye.

One of the female agents handed her a one-piece jumpsuit. "Put this on," she instructed.

Gwen's numb fingers barely functioned to allow her to dress herself. Her hands, she noted with no amusement, were trembling. The jumpsuit was stiff and starchy, and it rubbed uncomfortably against her skin. At least she'd been allowed to keep her own underwear. That was a small blessing.

Somehow she managed to get through the humiliating experience. It was too damn bad her self-respect was in tatters. Disciplining her fear was important at this stage. Lose control now and she'd crumble into a million tiny pieces. She'd just have to suck it up and deal.

Turning her mind away from her present predicament, Gwen wondered how long it would take for Brenda to figure out she probably wasn't coming back to work. No doubt her absence would soon segue into an unfortunate death. It would be easy enough for the government to fabricate her passing. She wondered if she'd get an obituary in the local paper.

She shivered. Her legs threatened to buckle under her weight. Somehow she managed to keep standing. *Don't let them get to you,* she counseled herself. She closed her eyes and rubbed her lids with the heels of her hands. When she was ready to look at the agents again, it was with a measure of dignity.

The cell she was led to was stark white, all steel and concrete. Harsh lights from above glared down, lighting every angle. There was nowhere to hide. Aside from a bunk bolted into the wall, there was only a metal toilet and small sink.

Under full guard, Gwen was made to stand in the center of the cell. Swaying a little on unsteady feet, she clenched her fists with frustration. This was ridiculous! She'd only used her Mercraft to defend Blake.

I shouldn't have saved his sorry ass, came the dark thought.

A moment later, Dr. Novak arrived. Face dead pale, he carried a small electronic device. His eyes flicked her a rueful look. "I've got to put this on," he said by way of an apology. "Will you please sit on the bunk and give me your ankle?"

Gwen sat, then tugged up one leg of her jumpsuit. She had the odd feeling Novak was ashamed of what he had to do.

Her jaw muscles tightened. "Is that what I think it is?"

Dr. Novak glanced up. "Not quite," he mumbled through tight lips. "It's a monitoring device, but not the kind anyone would want to wear."

She barely registered his answer. Unbidden chills crept up her spine when she felt the circle of cold metal bite into her skin. "What kind is it?"

Novak refused to glance up as he fixed the device around her ankle. A slight flush of red mottled the skin of his neck. "It's an SCSD, a Secure Continuous Shock Device."

Her brows shot up. "Shock device?"

Dirty deed completed, Dr. Novak climbed back to his feet. "It's a security precaution to control your psi-abilities. Should you show signs of aggression, this little gadget will deliver a high-voltage shock to your system."

Her astonishment was huge, but quickly absorbed. "Like a stun gun?" she asked, still not quite believing the nightmarish turn the evening had taken. One minute they'd all been sitting around sipping wine and playing a game. The next, they'd been thrust into a hell composed of iron bars, concrete walls, and instruments that bordered on torturous.

Dr. Novak laid a hand on her shoulder and bent close. "Don't make them use it," he warned under his breath. "These things are powerful enough to knock you unconscious."

Her neck and shoulders knotted with tension. "You've got to be kidding me."

Novak shook his head. "Unfortunately, I'm not." He frowned, clearly unhappy with his involvement.

Gwen looked into his face, searching his eyes. "You don't really believe that me or my sisters would do anything to hurt anyone, do you?"

She need not have asked the question at all. By the way he was looking at her, she knew without a doubt that he'd seen the damning videotape Blake had told them about not a half hour ago. She couldn't imagine the impression it had made upon his mind. He no longer trusted any Mer, even those he knew.

Ruffling a hand through his hair, Novak sighed. "I'm just doing what I'm ordered to." He turned and left. Gwen was all alone.

She didn't relish being locked in a small cell all by herself. Surely they'd allow her some kind of entertainment. Books, maybe. Perhaps a small radio. If there was one thing that grated on her nerves, it was silence. She couldn't stand it. It's why she always had the television playing in the background.

Lifting her foot onto the bunk, she tugged the cuff down to cover the hateful thing. It vibrated against her skin, sending out a subtle threat. One wrong move and it would bite her.

Terrible danger.

Her thoughts went temporarily ballistic. She thought of killing. Right now. Just blast the bastards. Every last one of them. The Mer had the right to protect themselves against danger.

She clenched her hands, forcing the balls of her fists into her lap. Tamping down the anger and hurt took all the willpower she could muster. Only the goddess knew what would happen to her kind now.

Blake sat in Dennis Thompson's office, watching the scenes of carnage in the museum unfold. Dismay twisting with disbelief tightened his chest.

Had he not already had an encounter with the Mer himself, he could have thought the incident too incredible to be believed. It turned his stomach to see two men killed, viciously and without being given a chance to defend themselves.

Remote in hand, Thompson flipped off the television. "You're lucky you survived their attack on the island." He snorted. "Those poor bastards didn't have a chance. Never knew what they were up against."

Blake glanced up at his superior. "Neither did I," he said, thinking about the blast he'd taken. The wound had healed, leaving a nice scar behind as a memento. He barely noticed it since he had a collage of others to show from his time in the service. Had it not given him a twinge now and again he would have already forgotten it. "And I wouldn't have gotten out alive without Gwen and her sisters helping me."

"It wasn't like they had a choice," Thompson returned with evident sarcasm. "Their own asses were on the line."

Thompson's words irritated him. Blake despised him all over again. Since their initial meeting he'd done all he could to make a wide berth around the fat little man. He hadn't liked him on sight and couldn't wait until he could leave the A51 compound behind.

It won't be anytime soon, came his dejected thought.

"But you're treating them like they were the ones who attacked," he retorted. "Throwing them in solitary and treating them like war criminals, Dennis, that's cold. Is it really necessary?" He was hoping he could beg for a little clemency on behalf of the Lonike sisters. After all, they hadn't been involved in the butchery. Their only crime so far, if you could even call it that, was being born Mer.

Thompson nodded. "I'm just following established protocol. Right now we're on lockdown where the Mer are concerned."

"I know all that," Blake snapped irritably. "All Mer have been declared enemy aliens. But Gwen and her sisters don't belong behind bars. They've helped us since day one."

"They're still Mer," Thompson countered. "And they have the capabilities to turn on us anytime they want. They're still an enemy we don't know how to fight. Even though it seems primitive, their technology is leaps and bounds ahead of ours."

"There's still so much we need to know," Blake reminded. "And they're the only ones who can help us."

The A51 director offered a sycophantic smile that played more than a small part in cementing Blake's dislike of the man. "Which is why I am following contain-and-quarantine procedures."

Blake refused to twitch an eyebrow. Even though it was difficult, he forced himself to remain detached. The idea of Gwen, locked in a cell and wired to be shocked like an animal if she showed the slightest sign of aggression, was enough to send him through the roof. It was just another subtle way the A51 sought to strip the Mer of their dignity.

"For how long?" he wanted to know.

Face grim, Thompson shrugged. "Until I get an extermination order," he replied coldly. His answer compelled immediate attention.

"Wait a minute—are you telling me they're going to be put down?"

Taking a seat behind his desk, Thompson spread his hands. "For now, no." His hairless brow creased. "But you know as well as I do we can't have knowledge of these things spreading among the general population. Think of the backlash, the panic." He waggled an index finger like a teacher scolding an errant pupil. "The number one objective of the A51 is to find Massey and this Mer queen he's helping to infiltrate our world. And we've got to do it without alarming the public. That won't be easy."

Devyn Quinn

It was a very tricky tightrope for officials to walk.

Fortunately the bystanders in the museum had scattered before witnessing anything truly damning. For now the press and public were being told it was the statement of a radical group of domestic terrorists whose motive and identity were yet to be identified.

Blake braced himself against saying too much, or revealing his true feelings. "I can see where that makes sense." But in truth, his blood was running cold.

Leaning forward, Thompson locked his hands over his desk. "We're putting together a covert taskforce to handle the mission of recovering Massey and his Mer cohorts." He pointed toward Blake. "I can already tell you that you're going be tapped to lead it."

Blake's eyebrows rose. For a moment he couldn't breathe.

"Me?" He felt his pulse quicken at the base of his throat. It was the last thing he wanted to do.

Thompson pressed his lips into a serious line. "Of course. You have experience with engaging the Mer in warfare. You know their capabilities. Your background as an army ranger doesn't hurt either." He paused a moment, tapping at a few letters on a nearby keyboard and consulting the resulting information displayed on the screen. "You were a sniper, a very damn good one from what it says here."

It was true, but the idea of hunting the Mer with the intention to completely eradicate them from the face of the earth was another matter entirely. Especially since they were the people of the woman he was growing to love.

He sighed, feeling the exertions of the last few weeks come crashing down on his head. There was no chance he'd sleep tonight. He had too damn much to grapple with.

First and foremost was Gwen's imprisonment.

His heart rose up into his throat and he blinked against the dryness in his eyes.

God. He would do anything to have her back, safe in his arms. But what could one man do against the agency?

"Something wrong, Agent Whittaker?" Thompson's gaze probed, searching for signs of weakness, a chink in the soldier's armor.

Blake mustered the willpower to keep his wits in check. "I understand what you are saying about the dangers the Mer present. I've seen them in action. Not once, but twice. And I do believe Queen Magaera presents a threat that needs to be contained." His palms started to sweat. He forced himself to keep still instead of wiping them across his legs. "But to judge all Mer to be alike would be like saying all Germans were Nazis."

Thompson waved a hand. "We're not throwing them all together because they are a part of the same species. But until they have a leader who is willing to open diplomatic channels and negotiate peacefully with humans, we have no other choice but to treat them all as hostiles."

Blake's mind was working a mile a minute. "Gwen's family was a part of the Mer monarchy," he reminded Thompson. "It was a relative of theirs, a Queen Nyala, who chose to seal the sea-gate and end the hostilities brewing between human and Mer. Restoring one of her descendants to the throne of Ishaldi would make sense. We know from what Tessa has told us not all Mer are sympathetic to Queen Magaera's rule. Ishaldi and its people could one day become an ally and not an enemy."

Thompson sighed heavily. "I've read the reports and know this just as well as you do. But at this point it's all uncharted territory. Do we even want to help an alien species reestablish itself in our world? That in itself would be a political nightmare."

Blake studied the stubborn features of his superior. "I would think we would want to help any free-thinking, intelligent species survive and thrive," he countered. "At least I thought that was the policy of those we elected to govern our country."

The two men exchanged hostile glances.

Thompson broke the eye-lock by leaning back in his chair and lacing his fingers together. For a moment he studied Blake carefully. "I understand you've probably grown fond of these Mer because you have a personal connection with Gwen Lonike," he said, switching the direction of their conversation back around to Blake. "But that part of your assignment is terminated as of today. Any emotional ties you developed for her need to be cut. ASAP. And it is an order I expect you to follow."

Blake shifted impatiently in his seat. He absently rubbed a throbbing vein at one temple. It took every bit of self-restraint he possessed to keep from leaping across that desk and putting his hands around Thompson's neck. He believed he could strangle the shit out of the man and smile as he did it.

"My personal feelings have no bearing on this matter," he replied, making sure his tone was appropriately chilled. "All I am saying is the A51 should consider utilizing the Mer we have on our side to help take Massey and Queen Magaera down." He jabbed a finger in the air to make his point. "They have a lot more knowledge than we do. And they are better equipped to defend themselves against an enemy they understand."

Having allowed Blake to make his argument, Thompson exhaled slowly. "It would make sense," he allowed.

"Then do it."

Thompson lifted his arms in a gesture of helplessness. "My hands are tied, and you know it. I don't make the decisions, Whittaker. Like you, I just follow orders."

He rubbed burning eyes. He could go round and round with Thompson for hours and it would just be a colossal waste of time and breath. It also wouldn't change anything for Gwen or her sisters. It looked like they'd be confined to solitary until the A51 decided to dispose of them.

Blake knew there was only one way he could play the cards he'd been dealt. If he played things smart, he could manipulate the circumstances to his advantage. Instead of beating his head against the wall, he had to find another way around it.

Keep cool and keep focused, he reminded himself.

"So when is this taskforce due to deploy?" he asked.

Refusing to join the squad would be worse than cutting his throat. He'd simply be bounced to the outer edges and ignored. He might as well take whatever power he could grab and use it to help Gwen.

Gaze sparking, Thompson leaned forward. "As soon

as you say yes to the job and start assembling your squad. You'll have access to our best agents and the sciences team. Just tell me who you want."

Blake pushed his seat back. "I'll get started right away."

Thompson gave a single approving nod. "Don't blow it, Whittaker," he warned.

Blake answered with a curt nod. He couldn't suppress the little smile that drew the corner of his mouth into an upward arc. *Blow it?* Oh, he was going to do more than that. He knew exactly what his next step was going to be.

And why.

He was going to take the A51 down from the inside and watch it burn.

When he walked out of here tonight, Gwen and her sisters were going with him.

Blake didn't know how he was going to make that happen.

He just knew he would.

Chapter 21

As far as travel went, teleporting from point A to point B was a terrific way to take a trip. It was fast and efficient. Unfortunately it also had side effects, particularly if you were a human unaccustomed to having your feet swept out from under you without notice.

Having the world around him disappear one minute and reappear the next sent Jake's senses spinning into overdrive. All at once, the atmosphere around him was not so peaceful or calm.

The air around him shifted, and for an instant he had the queer sense of passing through space and time. Spectral voices warned him to run. He clamped his hands over his ears as the force swept him away, and locked his teeth against an outcry. The energy surrounding him reeked of death and decay. It lashed against him, intermittently at different angles, as if manipulating him in a specific direction. If he tried to resist moving with its flow, the force grew colder and colder until he found it unbearable. It warmed when he complied.

Every molecule in his body was disassembled and reassembled, a process happening with such speed that the human mind could barely comprehend the switch in locations. The human body, however, registered the change. And it didn't feel good.

Jake panted for a long moment, then gulped in air as he fought for control. The stillness surrounding him became a heavy, suffocating cloak, so weighty it took all his willpower not to sink to his knees. He gulped to keep the contents of his stomach from rising into his throat. Pressing a hand to his gut, he fought to focus his eyes.

What he saw chilled him to the bone.

The ruins of an undersea metropolis stretched out in front of him. Like a carcass stripped to the bone, only relics of the city remained, skeletal and plundered by the war of an age remembered only as a myth. The recent quake had torn jagged crevasses along the seabed, making navigation treacherous.

He swallowed and clenched his teeth, then shook his head hard to clear his mind. Could he really believe his eyes? He wasn't sure. It all *looked* real, but was it?

His gaze roamed the rock walls and discolored mortar in his immediate line of view. Crumbling temples constructed in a vaguely Grecian style were surrounded by quake-torn pathways that had once been paved with polygonal stones. But nothing was new, bright or gleaming. Everything was crusted with the degradations and decorations the sea inevitably imposed on its land-loving visitors.

Hardly able to believe his eyes, Jake blinked to clear his blurry vision. He couldn't be sure, but it seemed like water should surround the fallen objects. Except there was none. Every last drop seemed to have dried up, as if sucked away by a giant vacuum.

Jake's gaze dropped to examine the ground beneath his feet. The soles of his shoes crunched against the silt-laden sea floor. *How is this possible?*

Seeming to appear out of nowhere, Magaera advanced. The last four of her remaining soldiers followed on her heels, obediently awaiting her next command.

Dizziness receded enough to allow him to think. "Where the hell are we?"

The Mer queen clutched the precious trident in a death grip. Her profile revealed wide eyes and pale, taut skin. "This was once the isle above the water that marked the entrance to our great city." She glanced around, taking in the devastation. As unwelcoming as the remnants were, this was the only place on earth she knew or felt safe. "The elements have all but erased it from the face of this planet."

Vague images filtered through his sluggish mind. He last recalled catching a glimpse of the ruins after Tessa had destroyed the temple guarding the sea-gate. Magaera herself had granted him the Mer's precious breath of life, allowing him to survive the cold depths of the sea.

His brow wrinkled. "Where did the water go?"

Queen Magaera smiled and pointed above her head. "The hand of the goddess shields us."

Jake tipped his head back. Majestic in height and breadth, a ceiling of shimmering water quivered above their heads, as if some giant invisible glass dome had been lowered into the water.

"Holy shit," he murmured. "That's incredible."

For the first time he heard a low, almost undetectable humming. It was just beyond the level of sound, but it was definitely there. *Some sort of sonic vibrations,* his mind filled in.

The one thing he'd learned about Mercraft was most of it was grounded in science. How such a primitive people had harnessed and manipulated such forces to bend to their will was still beyond him. Perhaps he was wrong and the Mer weren't entirely indigenous to planet Earth. Who knew how many interdimensional wormholes might riddle the planet and where they might lead?

Their present location reminded him of a giant terrarium, and the relics inside it were part of the display.

Magaera smirked. "To see is to believe."

The pieces were starting to come together, however slowly. "Then it is the Jewels of Atargatis that makes all this possible?"

Magaera's eyes narrowed and a half smile appeared on her lips. "The orb and choker gave us control of the sea-gate." She lifted the trident. "The scepter allows control over the elements above and below the water."

Jake moistened his dry lips with the tip of his tongue. "The real estate is great," he deadpanned. "But it's not much to look at." The remnants of the temple guarding the sea-gate were among the ruins. The monolithic stones were tilted at odd angles. Only the single rear wall had survived the devastation of the quake Tessa had summoned. A mass of color and light, the sea-gate itself swirled, a blind, unblinking eye that would never close.

Giving him a tolerant half smile, Magaera said, "Behold the power of Atargatis." Slamming the heel of the trident against the ground, she chanted, "I charge thee to obey all commands named by me. At my word, so let it be!" Her intuitive knowledge of the mystical force she wielded was driven by the deft sureness and skill gleaned from centuries spent studying the ancient knowledge.

Thunder rumbled loudly above their heads. Triple-pronged lightning descended from nowhere, striking the seabed with an electrifying jolt. A ball of light flashed out around the scepter in her hand.

Magaera continued, issuing her commands in a clarion voice, her arms held out at her sides and her face tilted to the scepter's caressing glow. "The powers of wind, earth, water, and fire . . . join with the goddess and grant me my desire. From the north, the south, the east, and the west . . . I call upon all forces to come at my behest. Rebuild, renew, and reclaim this place in the name of she who gave us life."

Thunder rumbled more ominously above them. Static electricity crackled, producing brushlike discharges in the air around them.

The ground beneath his feet began to shift, a great section of the earth peeling away from the bottom of the sea. Several miles wide and just as long, the newly forming landmass rose upward, breaking through the protective barrier of the shield. Tons of water fell away and they were suddenly under a clear blue sky. Gradually, the rumbling quieted. In the space of seconds an island had appeared, where before there had been nothing but mile after mile of water.

But it was far from over.

The scepter commenced to vibrate with a whining intensity. Then it screeched, and the deafening sound increased tenfold until the illumination emanating from the crystals exploded, stretching out into tentacles of multicolored light.

From all directions, Jake felt energy feeding into the atmosphere, causing it to expand. He scooted back several feet, stopping alongside a crumbling pillar as the luminous whirlwind drifted all around him.

The tendrils of light circled throughout the ruins. As the light brushed the crusted marble and pitted stone, a strange glowing vapor materialized, wiping away the decay of centuries within seconds.

Jake was awestruck by the vision, and dazzled by the sheer force of power Queen Magaera had unleashed. As the illumination and mist dissipated, his eyes widened. The restoration was complete.

As though taking a step through a rip in the fabric of time, the haven of Ishaldi stretched out around them. A series of temples and other buildings were surrounded by wide, perfectly paved pathways, green enclosed gardens, and tall, elaborately wrought fountains. Decorative statues and other ornamental items were perched among banks of flowering shrubs.

They stood in silence for some minutes, before anyone dared to interrupt the majesty of the moment.

"My God," Jake breathed. "It's like Eden."

Scepter in hand, Queen Magaera dispassionately surveyed the world her people had been a part from for almost two thousand years. She moved to a rocky outcropping that overlooked the nearby shore. Below, the sea crashed into the newly formed impediment, relentless and insistent.

"There was a time when this great metropolis teemed with life," she said, more to herself than anyone listening. "Our world is dying, but this one—" She made a wide gesture with her arm. "Given its resources, we can rebuild Ishaldi, make it even stronger."

Jake trailed her toward the edge. Instead of thinking like a human, he had to think like a Mer. Had to be cold, hard, and impassive toward the lesser species, the humans. Nothing less would suit Queen Magaera's megalomaniacal visions.

He made an imperative gesture. "We still need Tessa to gain control of the sea-gate," he reminded her.

Queen Magaera spared him a brief glance. Her facial muscles were stiff, betraying no emotion. "I will have her soon enough." A self-satisfied smile parted her lips. "There's no place she can hide now on the face of this earth."

Chapter 22

The barred door slid shut, lock clanging into place with a curious finality. She was alone.

Silence. The beating of her heart. Her thoughts were her own, images stealing through the dark corridors of her brain, distant voices calling in whispers, each vying for attention.

Gwen had poked at every nook and cranny of her cell, searching for a way out.

There wasn't one.

She wondered how her sisters were doing, if they felt just as afraid and panicked as she did.

She tried to think of something comforting. Blake. Right behind her sisters, she wanted him to be all right.

She sat and leaned back against the wall. Her eyelids lowered. She felt a blur floating in front of her vision.

Her eyes snapped back open. She didn't want to go to sleep. Not now.

But her exhausted body had other ideas.

She was on the verge of drifting off into a doze when

heavy footsteps hurrying down the hall broke into her thoughts.

She had no idea how many hours she'd sat there. At least two, maybe more.

The cell door slid open.

Blake stepped into her cell. He nodded to the woman accompanying him. "Thank you, Agent Doyle," he said briskly.

Doyle nodded. "Of course. Anything else I can do for you, sir?"

Blake raised a single brow. "If we could have a moment's privacy, I would appreciate it."

Agent Doyle glanced toward Gwen, then back toward Blake. She wavered a moment, then finally shook her head. "I'm not sure that's a wise idea, sir."

Blake's face turned to stone. "If you won't allow it as a courtesy, then I will make it an order," he spat with a grimace of displeasure.

Doyle snapped to attention. "Of course. Let me know when you're ready to go." She quickly stepped out of the cell, shutting the door behind her.

Gwen watched the brief exchange with some curiosity. She'd never seen Blake throw his weight around or give a single order. As he'd explained it, he was simply assigned to act as a liaison between the Mer and the compound's scientists. If he had any rank, he'd never pulled it before.

There was something different about him, though, a subtle change in his bearing. He was standing ramrod straight and had spoken to the female agent with a brisk, snappy voice. It was a tone that said people had better listen up. He clearly wasn't taking any bullshit from anyone. She liked it.

Gwen tried to smile. "I don't guess you've come to tell me we're going to get out of here." Her voice quavered ever so slightly.

Frowning, Blake shook his head. "I'm sorry."

She shrugged. "So?"

Irritation twisted his features. "The compound is on total lockdown," he informed her. "No one gets in. Or out."

She glanced around the small cell. "I think I've figured out that much."

He tried to explain. "When people get scared they lash out in the wrong ways. I'm afraid government and intelligence don't go together."

The last ember of hope burning in her heart faded. Damn. "That's something I've suspected for a long time." With an unexpected move, Blake crossed the brief distance separating them. Gathering her up in his arms, he pressed his lips to her forehead. "You know I couldn't stay away."

She recoiled. "Please, don't touch me."

Blake pulled back, giving a hollow-eyed, grim frown. "You don't trust me."

Gwen's nostrils flared. "No. Every time I think I trust you, something worse happens."

"I've done everything I can," he started to say in his own defense.

Gwen shook her head in regret. She desperately wanted to believe him, but felt he'd always give his allegiance to the government he served. "It's not enough," she countered angrily. "The road to hell is paved with good intentions."

He gazed back at her in consternation, as if the future had suddenly turned into a black hole. "You're angry," he said. "I understand."

"Anger doesn't begin to describe how I feel right now, Blake."

Lifting her leg, she showed him her ankle. "Look here." She stared straight into his eyes. "If they think we're going to get aggressive, they can shock us."

Blake swore as he examined the hateful device. Anger stormed his expressive face. "This is a travesty." It was clearly an obstacle he hadn't been expecting. "You don't deserve to be treated like an animal."

Stomach churning, Gwen tugged her cuff back down. "They don't see us as human."

Blake rose to his feet. "They're wrong."

She shrugged. "Nothing you can do to change their minds."

Blake shook his head, bringing a tumble of hair onto his pale forehead. He flicked the strands to move them out of his eyes as walked to the cell door. "Yeah. Well, we'll see." He rapped a fist against the metal. "Agent Doyle, could you come in here, please?"

The cell door immediately slid open. Doyle slipped under the threshold. "Yes, sir?" she inquired, with no small suggestions of annoyance.

Blake nodded toward Gwen. "Take that goddamned thing off her leg." His teeth were clenched so tightly with anger that he could barely get the words out.

Doyle wavered. "I'm sorry, sir," she said after a moment's hesitation. "We're under strict orders to make sure she is confined and controlled at all times."

Blake didn't hesitate. He gave the recalcitrant agent another glare. "Maybe this will help change your mind." His voice had the sound of metal scraping stone. Hand snaking under his jacket, he slid his weapon out of its holster.

Doyle made a quick lunge for the security panel embedded near the door.

Blake smoothly caught her arm and slammed her back against the wall. He pointed his weapon directly at her head. "Don't move, don't scream, or it'll be the last thing you ever do."

Hardly able to believe her eyes, Gwen immediately froze in her place. It looked like the man had just lost every marble in his head. Surely he didn't really believe he could break her out of a high-security facility all by himself. "What are you d-doing?"

Blake snagged Doyle's weapon, disarming her. Pulling her away from the wall, he shoved her toward Gwen. "We've got less than ten minutes before they figure out something's gone wrong and cut off my access." He pulled his startled colleague away from the wall, shoving her toward Gwen. "Get that thing off her ankle," he ordered.

Doyle stumbled, dropping to her knees. "It'll never work," she spat. "This place is already on lockdown."

Blake gave her a little prod. "That's why we're going to need a little Mercraft."

Gwen shook off her lethargy. Blake was going to give

her the chance to run. It was totally insane, maybe even a suicidal choice.

She decided to take it.

She stuck out her ankle. "Let's go," she urged.

Doyle unlocked the device. "It's done."

Gwen gave Blake a hard look. "No going back now."

"Not likely." Snagging Doyle's cuffs off her utility belt, Blake tossed them toward Gwen. "Put those on, but make sure you can get your wrists out."

Gwen slid the cuffs on, locking them loosely. "What are we going to do?"

Blake yanked Agent Doyle to her feet. "We're going to take a little walk to the other side of the guard's station." He turned to Gwen. "When we reach it, can you give them enough of a blast to knock them out?"

Gwen nodded. "I think so." At least she hoped she could.

Doyle dug in her heels. "You won't make me a part of this."

Blake prodded her with the barrel of his gun. "I'll use it if I have to," he warned. "And at this point I don't think I've got anything to lose."

They hustled out into the corridor.

An elevator stood a few strides beyond the door of the cell. Security cameras recorded activity from every angle.

Everything seemed to move with glacial slowness as the metal doors clanged shut.

Gwen flexed her fingers, readying herself for the confrontation. She wished she had a few big crystals to power up on. Since she didn't, she'd have to make do with her soul-stone and her own inner energies.

The doors slid open.

Doyle saw her chance, bolting ahead of them with lightning speed. "Whittaker's turned!" she screamed at the agents manning the monitors. "They're trying to escape!"

The startled men jumped to their feet, reaching for their weapons.

In a split second, Gwen tossed off the cuffs to free her hands. Without even stopping to think about what she was doing, she threw up her hands, sending out a blaze of energy that sizzled all the way up her fingers.

Zapped by an invisible force, the men went flying backward. Hitting the wall behind them, the two half-conscious agents slid to the floor like sacks full of potatoes.

The effort of sending out so much energy so fast nearly made her knees buckle. She struggled to stay on her feet.

In her dazed state, it seemed others were passing her by, a wild mass of lights and voices. She vaguely realized it was Whittaker tussling with Agent Doyle.

Grabbing Doyle's right wrist, Blake twisted it with the intent of taking her to the floor in a hammerlock.

Trained in hand-to-hand combat herself, Doyle pivoted. Her left hand swung out with the intent of delivering a forward punch.

Blake blocked the blow coming toward his face. He was equally skilled, and much bigger and stronger than Doyle.

"Sorry I have to do this," he panted, smacking the hapless agent upside the head with the butt of his gun.

Breath whooshing past her lips, Doyle dropped. She lay, unmoving.

Heart pounding like a jackhammer, Gwen looked at the downed agents. They lay stretched on their backs, eyes closed. By the goddess, they looked so fragile.

"Did I . . . ?" The rest of her question stuck in her suddenly dry throat.

Blake quickly checked their vital stats. "They're still breathing," he panted, fishing their weapons and badges out of their pockets. "You did good." He tucked the extra guns in the waistband of his slacks. "Let's go get your sisters. We've got only a few more minutes before all hell breaks loose."

Chapter 23

It was going to be touch and go as they bolted toward the exit of the prisoners' station. Driven by sheer determination, Blake waved for everyone to follow him. He'd taken them out the back ways, intending to lead them toward a part of the parking area hidden behind the north wing of the building.

Now that the breach had been detected, agents were beginning to swarm the area. Outside, two security agents ran toward them with guns drawn. A burst of bullets riddled the air around their bodies. Clearly the agents had their instructions: Shoot to kill.

Blake raised his own weapon, returning their volley with a few shots of his own. He wasn't intending to do more than wound, aiming for legs and vulnerable kneecaps. One agent fell, and then another.

He pulled the trigger again. It clicked uselessly. Damn. Out of ammo. He tossed his service weapon aside and reached for one of the guns he'd stolen.

Addison Lonike eyed his puny stash. "That all you got?" she demanded.

Blake shot a glance her way. "Can't say I really thought this thing through," he admitted as they skidded around a corner only to be greeted by another fast burst of gunfire.

Kenneth gave him a look. "Shit, toss me one of those and I'll help you out."

Blake eyed him. "You know how to use one of these?"

Tessa peeked around the corner. A single shot caused her to pull back. "Geez, I could sure use my Ri'kah about now," she grumbled. "Nice of you guys to take everything away from us."

Pressed against the wall, Gwen reached for the pendant hanging around her neck. "We're not totally without resources."

Addison nodded. "We can throw up a shield."

Blake gauged the distance to the parking lot. When he'd rolled up to the facility, he'd had only the vaguest plan in mind. He wasn't even sure he'd have the nerve to go through with the idea of busting out of the complex.

One look at Gwen's face had made the decision for him. Right now they were running on a wing and a prayer. There was no way he could walk out of that cell and leave her behind. It just wasn't going to happen.

Another burst of gunfire filled the air around them. Clouds looming overhead had sank to the ground after dusk, wrapping everything in a fine, misty cloak. The cold drizzle chilled.

Blake clenched his teeth. To get to the vehicle, they'd

have to break from cover and make a dash across open pavement.

He ducked back behind cover. The dampness on his brow wasn't just from the rain. His underarms were hot and wet. He hoped he hadn't just led these people to their own executions.

"We're going to have to make a run for it." He glanced from face to face. "It looks like they've pretty much got us surrounded. Now would be the time to surrender."

Reaching for Tessa's hand, Kenneth was the first to shake his head. "I'm not going back in that fucking cell and neither is my wife."

Tessa nodded her concurrence. "We've fought our way out of worse places than this."

Addison squared her shoulders. "I'm good to go."

Blake looked to Gwen. He wondered if there would ever be a time when he could hold her in his arms again.

He hoped so.

His gaze locked with hers. "You in?"

Pale faced, she nodded. A glimmer of hope lit her sparkling green eyes. "I have been from the beginning," she reminded him through a wry smile.

He nodded. "Good." In for a penny, in for a pound.

Another burst of gunfire interrupted the lull. A couple of bullets whizzed past Blake's head, close enough to split the air by his left ear. He winced. Another inch and his brains would be splattered all over.

Blake eyed one of the dark sedans, then Kenneth. "Ready to run?"

Gwen stepped up. "If we pull together, we can shield you and Ken."

Blake didn't relish the idea of letting a few women shield him. Not that he had any choice. "You sure you can do it?"

Tessa nodded. "We can do this."

"Piece of cake," Addison chimed in.

The sisters linked hands.

"Let's go," Tessa said.

Breath catching in his throat, Blake silently prayed the sisters could handle it. If it didn't work, they were finished.

From out of nowhere, darkness swept around him, cocooning him in an airless void.

At first Blake wasn't sure what surrounded him. It was a blur of light, rapidly shifting shape and brightening as it settled into place. He could no longer see the parking lot, or even the ground beneath his own feet. The manifestation of pure glimmering light dominated his vision.

The sisters stood in the heart of the luminance.

Gwen smiled. "Follow us."

Terrified by the inexplicable illumination, agents responded with a barrage of shots. The bullets simply bounced harmlessly off the light.

Without quite knowing how his feet were carrying his weight, Blake scuttled toward the vehicle. Relief gripped him as he slid behind the wheel.

Kenneth barreled in beside him as the three women took the backseat. They collapsed in a heap, almost totally drained. "Drive," he shouted. "Put the pedal to the metal."

"Hurry," Tessa urged, her voice sounding strained to

the max. "We can't hold them off much longer." As if to second her words, a bullet pinged the windshield. It cracked, but didn't break.

Blake glanced over his shoulder. A vein pulsed at Gwen's left temple. She winced as if in pain.

"You okay?"

Lifting a hand toward her head, she stopped short of making contact. "Drive," she mumbled, eyes going half-mast.

No doubt about it. The sisters were fading.

He had to get them out of here.

Now.

Shoving the key in the ignition, Blake stomped down on the clutch and shifted into drive. The vehicle shot forward, clipping the bumper of a neighboring car as he sped out of the parking lot and hit the asphalt.

A cadre of agents claimed their own vehicles, taking off behind him. The escape was turning into a high-speed chase. It wouldn't last long unless he could get them off the compound.

Not really sure what he'd do next, he turned a sharp corner and headed toward the runways.

Blake tried to come up with a plan. His heart was pounding so fiercely he could barely think. Fingers clutching the wheel in a death grip, he quickly combed through his memories to bring up everything he'd learned about the compound since his arrival. The A51 facility was less than two miles from the beach. All he had to do was get Tessa and her sisters to the water and they'd be okay.

Easier said than done.

Panic tightened his chest when a couple of cars zoomed in ahead of him, intending to cut him off.

Kenneth's mouth worked but no words came out.

"Look out!" Addison screeched at the last second.

Cursing under his breath, Blake twisted the wheel hard. The sedan made a sharp right, barely missing the other two vehicles.

More cars moved in behind them, speeding perilously close.

Blake considered his options—they were rapidly going from slim to none. However, pulling over and surrendering wasn't an option at this point. Not only had he thrown his entire career away with this one impulsive act, he was probably looking at a very long stretch behind bars.

If they let me live, came the grim thought.

Damn it all to hell.

As if to second his thought, thunder boomed, its crashing bass symphony shaking the ground. Lightning cracked and clawed the sky with electric fingers. The rain was making for slippery, treacherous driving. The runway would be coming to an end at any moment. At the end lay a long stretch of nothing . . .

Blake made a quick decision. Whipping the car around, he headed straight for the hot-wire chain-link fence surrounding the A51 compound. Anyone trying to climb the thing would get one hell of a shock.

However, a car going through it at over one hundred miles an hour had a much better chance of success.

Even though he was strapped in, Kenneth threw his hands against the dashboard and braced for impact. "Holy shit!"

"Do it," Gwen urged from behind.

"Anything to get us out of here," Addison chimed in.

Without taking a moment to second-guess himself, Blake floored the accelerator. His mind vaguely processed that this might be a bad idea.

No time to think about it.

Speeding ahead full throttle, the sedan crashed through the fence like a sledgehammer hitting concrete. Metal screeched against metal. Sparks flew all around.

The sedan hit a low embankment, skidding on damp, muddy ground. For one heart-stopping moment he feared the mud would get the best of the spinning tires.

"Everyone okay?" he called.

"Yeah," a chorus of voices answered.

The roar of vehicles closing in from behind warned him he wasn't the only one who was going to risk the treacherous terrain. Three vehicles—two black unmarked cars and an SUV—sped through the hole he'd left in the fence. A chopper closed in from overhead.

Blake's heart rate climbed dramatically. Somehow he managed to spin free of the boggy marsh, regaining his traction. A stretch of rain-soaked asphalt appeared in his headlights. He steered onto it, glad to be back on solid road. In less than a mile, there would be a sharp curve and the highway would run parallel to the beach.

His plan had to work. They were running out of time and there was still a chance the pursuing agents could cut them off before he could get Gwen and her sisters to the water.

Close. They were so close.

Seconds ticked with the length of hours as the car ate up the highway. The rain pelted the windshield harder.

One of the drivers pursuing them tried a daring maneuver, speeding ahead and zipping in front of them in an attempt to cut them off. Seeing the chance to take him off the road, the chopper's pilot swooped in low. Its landing gear scraped the roof.

Blake hit the brakes to keep from slamming head-on into the obstacle. The sedan hydroplaned across the slick two-lane highway, sending them into a long skid.

Blake's heart leaped into his throat. He fought the impulse to jerk the wheel and slam on the brakes, which would have sent the car rolling. The engine ground, a sound of tearing metal that made his hair stand on end. A bank of red lights flashed on across the dashboard.

The car came to an abrupt and immediate halt.

The other cars pursuing ground to a halt. Several agents jumped out, guns raised. A stray bullet zinged off the bumper.

"Shit." He cranked the key and prayed.

The engine roared back to life. Thank God the car was American made. Designed for high speeds and performance, this model could take a beating and keep on going.

"We need a little diversion," he called toward the backseat.

Gwen answered, "I've got it." Pressing her hands against the window, she sent out a quick burst of psi-energy. One of the advancing men toppled, slapped to the ground by an invisible rush of blistering heat.

Addison offered a high five. "Good going."

Shifting into second, Blake mashed the accelerator. Laying down burning rubber, the sedan took off like a bat out of hell.

The chase resumed.

Blake shot a worried look toward the fuel gauge. The needle hovered toward empty. Oh, terrific. It would be a crying shame to get this close to freedom only to run out of gas.

He silently cursed himself for his lack of preparation. *Stupid!* What he'd done hadn't only been impulsive, it had been totally unplanned. These people were trusting him to keep them safe, and he was flying by the seat of his pants.

His foot pressed the accelerator. When in doubt, go faster. He had to take it all the way, even if it led nowhere. At this point nobody was in the mood to turn back and surrender.

If they went out in a blaze of glory, so be it.

Kenneth was the first to spot the distant shoreline. "There's the beach."

Blake cranked his head to the left. Over the edge of a precipitous drop, he caught a glimpse of white sand. In the distance a shimmering mist danced atop the choppy water, lending it an elusive and unreal quality.

There was no place to pull over.

The only way to reach the water was to go over the edge. The incline was steep and rocky, but they just might make it.

The sedan crashed over boulders and gravel alike, tires crunching against the rocky unstable terrain. The halt was sudden and abrupt. He'd driven the car straight onto the beach. The heavy vehicle sank to the bumper, pulled under by the damp sand.

Everybody abandoned the car, making toward the nearby shoreline. The women splashed into the water.

"Come on!" Addison shouted at her sisters. "We haven't got much time." She stopped, shimmying out of the prisoner's jumpsuit like a snake shedding its skin. A second later she dived, disappearing beneath the waves.

Tasting the strong bite of salt on his lips, Blake stopped at the edge. The wind was sharp and strong, fierce enough to push him another step toward the water.

But he could go no farther. Even if he had wanted to, he couldn't force himself into the churning sea. As his weight sank into the sand and the cold water closed around his ankles, he knew it was the end of the line for him. He'd have to stay behind.

Kenneth waded into the water, almost to his knees. "Damn, I hate doing this." He came to a sudden stop.

Tessa reached out for her husband's hand, trying to pull him in with her. "Aren't you coming?"

Kenneth shook his head and jerked a thumb toward Blake. "I can't let Whittaker take the heat alone."

Tessa's gaze sought her husband's. "You can't stay."

Kenneth laid his hands on her shoulders. "They won't do anything to me," he insisted. "I'm human. Besides, when you hit land again, you'll be calling our attorney. He'll handle it from there."

She looked skeptical. "Are you sure?"

Kenneth nodded. "I am." Pulling Tessa close, he gave her a final quick kiss. "The sooner you get your tail moving, the sooner you'll be safe. Just remember Magaera's still out there somewhere."

"It's a big ocean. She won't find us anytime soon." Tessa reluctantly turned. A splash followed her departure. Shifting beneath the surface, a brief glimmer surrounded her body as she shifted into her mermaid form. And then she was gone, heading out toward the deeper waters of the Atlantic.

Only Gwen remained, lingering in the depths.

Blake cast a glance over his shoulder, gaze searching the top of the ravine he'd driven into. In another few minutes their pursuers would figure out what he'd done. And like bloodhounds on the scent, they would follow.

Blake waved an arm at her. "Go." The wind tore the words from his lips, carrying them away into the stormy night.

To his surprise, Gwen abandoned the water. Her wet clothes clung to her body like a second skin. The pendant hanging around her neck glowed softly, lighting her features with an otherworldly illumination. A nymph belonging to the sea, she looked mythical and magical.

Blake's heart lurched in his chest. God, even soaking wet she was utterly gorgeous. A painful knot formed in the core of his heart. It was going to hurt to send her away, but it was for the best. In the water, the Lonike sisters would be safe, out of harm's reach.

Blake's breath rushed in and out between clenched

teeth. Every second wasted was another their pursuers drew closer. In another few minutes the net would close around them.

A powerful shudder gripped his body. "You should go."

Closing the distance separating them, Gwen reached out for him. "Come with us," she urged, taking his hand. She tried to pull him farther into the water. "I can take you under. You'll be able to breathe beneath the water." She offered a reassuring squeeze and a smile. "I promise you'll be safe."

The image of icy water closing over his head, filling his mouth and nostrils, cut through Blake's mind. Bad, dark memories rose up, crippling his courage. Like a sparrow with a broken wing, he'd never fly again.

Sometimes the weak have to be left behind.

He gulped, fighting back the rise of panic in his gut. "I can't." He shook his head. Fear intensified in his head, growing in volumes until he was sure his skull would crack open. "I just can't." It was sheer agony, wanting to follow her and knowing he couldn't.

Moving an intimate step closer, Gwen wrapped her arms around his neck and leaned in to him. The contact between them was pure electricity. Her gaze lifted to his. "I don't want to go without you." Her voice reached inside his chest and clutched his heart.

Blake was all too conscious of the soft, feminine body pressed against his. His skin tingled as if ants were running beneath it. His blood simmered. Emotions he'd fought to put aside came flooding back, and he didn't have the strength to deny them.

Tears glimmered in her eyes. A breeze ruffled the damp strands of her hair.

A choked sound came from him. "You have to," he whispered achingly. "I'm going to have to let you go."

A shiver passed through her. "What's going to happen to you?"

Blake stroked a few clinging strands of hair away from her face. Just touching her stirred wild sensations in his chest. The emotions flying between them clouded his reason. "I don't know." Nothing good, that was for sure.

Gwen tilted her head back, offering her mouth. "It doesn't have to be good-bye," she murmured.

Blake wasn't sure what to expect when he took possession of her mouth, drawing her into a passionate kiss. For a few precious moments, the outside world around them was forgotten. He desperately wished he could follow her beneath the choppy waves, but a lifetime of fear couldn't be erased overnight.

Suddenly, the sound of the chopper closing in from overhead shattered the spell of their kiss.

Faster, they needed to move faster. *Time's running out*, he warned himself.

He ended the kiss, then took three paces back. She'd become his love, and his life.

But he had to say good-bye, even if it destroyed him.

"You have to go!" he urged, his breaths coming in short, hoarse spurts.

Gwen nodded as the helicopter made another threatening pass over their heads. A spotlight came on, pinning them under its luminous glow.

"Don't move!" an anonymous voice ordered from

above. Sirens screamed, moving closer and closer. The screech of tires on the highway behind them warned of their impending capture. Car doors slammed and armed men began to climb down the side of the steep ravine. The staccato of gunfire filled the air around them. They were clearly aiming for the Mer.

Blake ducked. He expected to feel heat tearing through his skin at any moment. "Get out of here," he yelled. "Now!"

Gwen's mouth opened to protest, then closed again. What could she say? Nothing.

Backing away, she hurried toward the water.

And then she was gone, diving beneath the waves.

Watching her disappear, Blake knew he'd done the right thing. Relief washed through him. The women had gotten away.

Weapons drawn, a multitude of agents rushed up from behind. "Freeze, asshole," one of them shouted with a little too much enthusiasm.

The two men exchanged a glance.

Kenneth just shrugged. "Those Mer will get you every time."

"Tell me about it," Blake muttered under his breath.

The entire shore buzzed with activity. The noise level tripled as more backup arrived. The sounds barely registered in Blake's mind. He'd danced. Now it was time to pay the piper.

His hand rose, and he swiped his thumb along his lips. Gwen's sweet taste still lingered. A curious sensation passed through him, something akin to a warm breeze caressing him from within.

The frenzied agents rushed closer, yelling a barrage of commands.

He raised his hands to show he was unarmed. The twirling lights of the sirens danced with the mist, throwing choppy shadows to and fro. Everything looked unreal, strangely disjointed. "We're not going anywhere," he called out.

Following his lead, Kenneth Randall nodded and raised his own hands. His silent signal was clear. They were in this together.

Expelling a gush of air from his nostrils, Blake stared out over the restless sea. The chase had ended. He knew the agency had ways of dealing with those who stepped outside the boundaries. Frances Fletcher's not so subtle warning filtered back into his mind.

A block of ice formed around his heart. Tension coiled in the pit of his stomach. This new vision temporarily overtook his senses, bringing with it a rush of unbidden images. It was entirely possible a stray bullet might somehow work its way into the back of his skull.

He closed his eyes and waited for the inevitable. The distinct sound of waves crashed against rock outcroppings. The damp chill permeating the night air clung to his skin, a heavy wet cloak. He drew a deep breath, taking in the salt of the sea. Oddly enough, he felt no fear. Only relief.

Two agents rushed forward, shoving him to the ground and twisting his arms up behind his back. A streak of white-hot pain swept up his arms. "Be still, you bastard!" one of the men snarled in an ugly tone.

They handcuffed his wrists, but he hardly felt the unforgiving metal biting into his skin. The air continued to vibrate with the thundering roar and crash of the sea.

Blake let his body go limp. He no longer had the strength or ability to resist. Now that the real danger had passed, he no longer cared what happened to him.

All that mattered was that Gwen and her sisters were safe.

Chapter 24

Washington, DC
One month later

Gwen sat stiff and uncomfortable in an ornate room, surrounded by dark-suited agents. Tessa and Kenneth sat on her left, Addison to her right. Everyone was stone-faced in the hushed atmosphere.

The silence around them was deafening, and oppressive.

She shifted in her seat. Her navy blazer and blouse felt unusually tight around her shoulders. She reached up, subtly undoing one of the buttons closing her collar around her neck. Ah, thank goodness, she could breathe a little better now.

She drew in a quick breath in an attempt to still the butterflies harrying her stomach. As much as she'd dreaded the notion, testifying before a closed congressional committee hadn't been as terrible as she'd imagined. Through these last nerve-racking weeks, Kenneth, Tessa, and Addison had appeared before the panel.

Her mind slipped back to the day they'd escaped from the A51 facility. After spending a week in the water—the longest she'd ever worn her tail—all three girls had come ashore in New Jersey, three sopping-wet fugitives on the run. Getting to a phone, Tessa had made a collect call to Kenneth's attorneys, setting the wheels in motion toward gaining his freedom, as well as beginning the negotiations that would grant them asylum.

Gwen sighed. The process had not been pleasant or easy. But it had been necessary. Once Tessa had opened the sea-gate, she'd unwittingly let the genie out of the bottle. Unfortunately it was one that hated humans.

We'll have to prove we belong.

And right now Gwen felt she belonged nowhere. To no one.

A strange pang of emptiness filled her.

She glanced at the agents guarding the room. Blake Whittaker wasn't among their number, though she had heard from Kenneth that he'd been in court, testifying on their behalf. For a brief time she'd had his love. And now? Nothing.

Forcing herself to put Blake out of her mind, she mentally reviewed her recent testimony. Going before the committee, she'd tried to speak intelligently, clearly, and precisely. Now was no time to let emotion get the better of her actions. There was a lot riding on the outcome of this hearing. Their freedom, their very lives, were on the line.

Much to her relief, the men and women listening to her speak hadn't treated her like a freak. But she wasn't entirely happy with the outcome. Instead of showing a willingness to embrace the Mer people and begin building diplomatic ties with the newly discovered race, those in government felt it was wiser to suppress knowledge of her kind from the general public.

Still, those in the know now had a conundrum on their hands. As legally born citizens of the United States, the Lonike girls technically had all the rights afforded to any citizen, regardless of race or origins.

After a round of legal wrangling followed by hard negotiations by their attorneys, a compromise had been settled on that everyone involved could agree to.

Reclassified as "resident aliens," the three of them—Gwen, Tessa, and Addison—would be allowed to resume their lives among the human population. But with one caveat: They must continue to squelch all Mer-related activities, as well as subject themselves to regular observation by the government and its scientists. The best news of all was the horrible experimentation on her kind had been completely halted.

Gwen grimaced. It wasn't over yet, though. Not by a long shot. Danger still loomed as long as Queen Magaera and Jake Massey continued to wreak their havoc. Both were considered fugitives, armed and dangerous, and very much enemies of the state. Part of their monitoring would include security, as Tessa's safety was still very much in question. She was, after all, the key to the sea-gate.

The government felt confident enough in its own tactical abilities to handle the threat Magaera posed. After all, it wasn't the first terrorist attack the American people had weathered, and it probably wouldn't be the last.

Plans were currently in motion for the newly formed Undersea Search and Exploration Taskforce. If found and taken alive, Magaera would be imprisoned, joining Raisa and Chiara in permanent lockup. What the powers that be intended to do about the sea-gate and the Mer still inhabiting Ishaldi was a question yet to be answered.

Nibbling her lower lip, Gwen frowned. *All this trouble for nothing,* she thought. Once again her kind would be shoved into the shadows. It wasn't the best solution, but it was workable. Nobody wanted to ignite a widespread public panic, which could trigger an unpleasant backlash against her species.

Addison touched her arm, scattering her dark thoughts. "Everything okay?"

Gwen forced a smile. "I'm fine. Just a little tired." So much had happened in such a short span of time. Her head still spun from all the details. For better or worse though, their lives would never be the same again.

Addison gave her a reassuring squeeze. "It's been tough for all of us," she whispered back. "Hard to believe it's almost over."

Lowering her head, Gwen briefly pressed her lips together. "At least we'll be going home soon," she allowed, trying to sound positive. Her words sounded hollow to her own ears.

Addison frowned. "I'd hoped for more, but I guess it just isn't going to happen."

"Maybe it's for the best." Truth be told, Gwen didn't think she was ready to face total public exposure. But instead of finding comfort in putting back on her cloak of obscurity, she felt strangely empty. On a private, intimate level, she'd taken a few vital steps toward self-acceptance. She had to admit she'd liked the feeling. A lot.

She wanted to continue exploring those wonderful new feelings. She just didn't want to do it alone.

Not that she seemed to have any choice in the matter.

Addison cocked her head toward the nearby humans. "They just aren't ready for us. Not now, but someday, I hope. We still scare them on so many levels."

Gwen reached up, fingering the little crystal pendant. Though the power still simmered beneath her skin, it no longer hassled her the way it used to. She had better control, more command.

Thanks to Blake Whittaker.

Drawing in a breath to cool the surge of heat rushing through her veins, she closed her eyes. She hoped to see him again. Just one more time. As much as she wanted to, she couldn't pretend that he hadn't affected her.

She'd fallen deeply in love with him.

Blake had touched her, not just physically but emotionally. She'd trusted him enough to reveal her true self.

Tail and all.

A sudden commotion of sound and movement filtered through her ears. Addison poked her violently. "Oh, my God," she whispered under her breath. "There he is."

Gwen opened her eyes in time to see Blake Whittaker escorted into the room by federal agents. A man she assumed was his attorney followed closely on his heels. Both men were careful to keep their expressions neutral.

Gwen almost jumped out of her skin at the sight of him. Oh, heavens! He looked terrific. An electric jolt went through her when he turned around and smiled her way. She hadn't seen him since their parting on the beach.

Her gaze drank in his tall, solid body. He looked handsome in a charcoal gray suit, no tie. Every inch of him was cool and reserved. He'd let his hair grow, and a thick wavy mass framed his clean-shaven face.

Her throat tightened. He looked good. Damn good.

She remembered everything about him, too. She missed the feel of his hard frame under her exploring hands, his deep kisses, the way his hips rocked into hers when they made love. But more important, this was the man who had risked everything to save her and her sisters. She would never forget it.

Their eyes met across the hushed chamber briefly. His lips curved in the faintest of smiles.

Pulse bumping up a notch, Gwen nodded at him. She cut a glance back at the agents positioned by the doors. She was aware Blake had charges of treason leveled against him based on the way he'd chosen to resign his position within the top-secret organization.

But Blake had fought back by shining a light on the torture inflicted on the rogue Mer behind closed doors. When the pursuit of knowledge bordered on torture, it was wrong. He'd been strong enough to stand up and expose the practices of the A51. But his attempt to do the right thing might come with a hefty price tag.

Gwen steeled herself against the idea he might be looking at a very long prison sentence. In one reckless moment he'd thrown his entire career, his life, away to help her. She couldn't help but feel for him, knowing it would break his heart to lose contact with his son, Trevor.

Blake broke away from his attorney and strode across the endless chamber.

Kenneth Randall rose to his feet, offering a hand. "Well?" he asked, as anxious as Gwen to know the outcome of Blake's fate.

Giving her brother-in-law's hand a quick shake, Blake finally allowed the briefest of smiles. "It's over. All charges have been dropped."

Kenneth clapped Blake on one shoulder. "That's excellent." He shot a quick thumbs-up toward the attorney he'd hired to defend Blake.

Blake demurred. "Thanks for taking care of my legal costs," he added quietly. "There was no way I could have covered it myself."

Kenneth shrugged off his thanks. "Glad to do it."

"I will repay you," he added. "Though I've been bounced from the outfit, I did get a full pension in return for my silence." He shrugged. "I've been told it would be a good idea to move on, if you know what I mean."

Kenneth nodded. "I hear you." They'd all gotten similar warnings, loud and clear. Keep a low profile, and the Mercraft under wraps.

Just like that, it was over.

Gwen propelled herself to her feet. Just looking at him—so near yet so out of reach—sent tiny little shivers rippling over her skin.

"If you'll all excuse me," she mumbled. "I think I could use a breath of air." She hurried toward an antechamber leading to the restrooms. She needed to get away. Fast.

She didn't glance back, instead concentrating on putting one foot ahead of the other. Glance over her shoulder now and she'd fall down for sure.

A flurry of steps hurried to catch up. A hand caught her arm.

Recognizing the familiar touch, Gwen came to a halt. Heat instantly spread through her veins. Pivoting on one heel, she looked up.

Hand falling away, Blake stared down at her. Closer now, his eyes revealed his true feelings. His gaze simmered with untapped desire. "Gwen," he murmured. "How have you been?" By the look in his eyes, he still wanted her.

Gwen's heart leaped into her throat. Feeling like an awkward virgin all over again, she barely had time to collect her senses.

Folding her arms across her chest, she drew in a breath to steady herself. "I'm good," she replied politely, acutely aware all eyes were on them.

He smiled. "You look good, really great."

She couldn't return the compliment without gushing like a lovesick fool. She searched for something intelligent to ask him. A neutral subject finally popped into her head. "How's Trevor?"

Blake at once frowned at the question before releasing a long sigh. "As much as I hate to say it, he'll be moving to California." A forced shrug rolled off his shoulders. He was trying to act casual, but the subject clearly bothered him.

She could tell by the look on his face that the loss stung him deeply. If there was one person she knew Blake loved absolutely and without reservations, it was his son.

"So you're going to be moving, too, I imagine, to be closer to Trevor?"

Blake's gaze darkened. "No," he answered tersely. "I know I've got some issues to work out, but I can't keep letting them hold my son back from having a normal life. Debra's a good mom, and she married a responsible man. I'll see Trevor when I can, you know. Summers, holidays, and anytime I want to fly down and spend a few weekends with him. But for now I've got to let him go."

She nodded politely. "That's a good step in the right direction."

A hesitant smile turned his lips. "I also didn't want to move because I've got some unfinished business here . . . with you."

The directness of his reply threw her completely off balance. A minute stretched into two as he drew her aside, away from prying eyes and listening ears.

Blake shifted uncomfortably. "I wanted to apologize to you again." His words came out in a sudden gush tinged with remorse. "And if you'll give me another chance, I'd like to take it."

Gwen's heart missed a beat, then kicked into over-drive. "I'd like to," she said slowly. "But I can't leave Port Rock. My whole life's there. As much as I hate to say it, that's where I'll always be."

He responded with a lazy grin. "I'm not asking you to leave," he said. "I'm willing to go wherever you are."

She was shocked. Knowing how much he hated the town, his words stunned her. "Really? You would move back to Maine, for me?"

His gaze delved into hers, looking straight into her soul. "Absolutely."

"What about—" she started to ask, but got no further.

Blake pressed a finger to her lips. "The past is gone, Gwen. I've got to start living for the future. I'm willing to go the extra mile and do whatever it takes to make you a part of it."

Oh, my. She had no chance to reply. His mouth covered hers, warm and oh, so possessive.

A few dazzling, dizzying seconds ticked away.

Coming up for air, Gwen looked at him. She swayed on legs threatening to collapse beneath her weight. "I don't know," she returned. "Do you think you can handle being with a so-called alien species?"

Blake drew her even closer. "I've got it on good authority you mermaids can be slippery." He gave her a quick wink. "But I'm going to hold on tight. I'm not letting you go a second time."

Gwen flexed her fingers around the rippling muscles of his arms, soaking in the strength and solidity he presented. A fresh surge of desire burned away the last lingering remnants of her doubt.

Blake Whittaker was a man of his word. If he said it, he meant it.

A discreet cough behind them made no impression. "Ahem, guys," Addison prompted. "You two lovebirds are blocking the way to the restrooms."

Pulling Gwen out of the way, Blake laughed drily. "Sorry. We had other things on our minds."

Addison breezed past. "Obviously," she muttered under her breath. Nevertheless she made a quick thumbs-up gesture before disappearing into the ladies' room.

Gwen chuckled. "It looks like my little sister has given us her official seal of approval."

Blake eyed her. "Think Tessa and Kenneth will support her endorsement?"

Gwen tipped back her head, happy just to look at him. "Guess you're going to have to stick around to find out." As she spoke, hope surged through her, bringing with it a renewal of strength and spirit. She'd never experienced such happiness, love, or pride before in her entire life. It was as if the dark clouds hanging over her head had finally cleared out, and days of sunshine and laughter beckoned.

She wasn't sure what the future might hold, but one thing was certain. With Blake at her side, she'd be able to face the obstacles life threw her way.

Come hell or high water.

Read on for a peek at the next book from
Devyn Quinn
in the thrilling Dark Tides series,

Siren's Desire

Coming from Signet Eclipse
in February 2012.

This doesn't look promising, Addison Lonike thought as the twenty-seven-foot Boston Whaler headed toward the orange life raft bobbing on top of the choppy waters. Now that summer was coming to a close, people were attempting to squeeze a few more precious days of sailing out of the season.

Her heart sank as she performed a quick head count. When the distress signal had come in to harbor patrol, the pilot of the crippled yacht had radioed that four people were aboard. "I see only two survivors," she called as Sidney Rawlings guided their rescue boat around the raft, attempting to use the larger vessel as a break wall to give the smaller dinghy a little relief from the gusty wind and pummeling water. As far as pilots went, Sidney was one of the best. If anyone could handle navigation in a dangerous situation, he was the man. A few seconds later the raft scraped the side.

"We got 'em!" she called as she threw out a line to

secure the smaller craft. Joined by a second crewman, she worked to bring the survivors on board.

Two sopping-wet people collapsed on deck, a man and a teenaged girl. Both were blue from the cold and shivering. Addison quickly snuggled them both in thermal heat wraps.

"My w-wife," the man stuttered frantically, "and m-my s-son are still in the boat."

Paramedic Jim Witkowsky quickly scanned the water. "I don't see anything," he called over the lashing zephyr. "What happened?"

The man shook his head in confusion. "I don't know. We were cruising along just fine, heading toward the mainland. Then there was some—" He shook his head in confusion.

"Some sort of explosion," the teen filled in, blabbing a mile a minute. "From the engine room, I think. There was a lot of smoke and fire."

The kid's father broke back in. "I sent a distress signal that we were going under. I—I managed to get the life raft out and inflated, but the cruiser started sinking." Face contorting with pain, he shrugged helplessly. "It just went over on one side."

The boat wasn't what concerned Addison. The fact that two people were still in the water did. Unless they had life vests, there was little to no chance of survival. "You said your wife and son were still aboard," she broke in.

Still half in shock and suffering the effects of hypothermia, the man nodded. "Brenda and Sheldon. They were below deck, in the galley fixing lunch. Barbra wwas with me. I'd been giving her lessons on piloting the boat."

The girl's face scrunched up as the realization set in. "They never had a chance," she said, sagging to the deck. A tear slid down her pale cheek, and then another. "There was a big hole in the hull and it just went under."

Addison winced. *Damn it.* The rescue effort had just turned into a recovery mission. If there was one thing she hated, it was fishing dead bodies out of the water. The mayday call had come in roughly half an hour ago. Though they'd headed out within minutes, the exact location of the wreck had been unknown, preventing them from reaching the area sooner. The chances of locating more survivors had just gone from slim to none.

"It must have went down fast, and straight to the bottom," Witkowsky continued. "There's no way. . . ."

Jaw tightening, Addison elbowed her crew mate. The last thing you wanted to say in front of the family was that there was no hope. But Witkowsky was a newbie, and still had to learn the finer points of empathy when in an emergency situation.

"There's always a chance," she cut in smoothly. "Last year a woman survived underwater, in an air pocket of a sunken boat, for more than twenty-four hours."

The girl looked up at her, desperation written across her young face. "Is there any way to get down to them?" she asked hopefully. Even as she spoke, her gaze found and fixed on the diving equipment the rescue vessel carried.

Witkowsky shook his head. "We should probably

wait for backup from the coast guard before we proceed with any diving."

Addison wasn't listening. Her mind had already been made up. The girl couldn't be older than thirteen, fourteen at the most. Having lost her own parents at an early age, Addison knew what it felt like to suddenly have family members ripped away far too prematurely. There was no way she'd let the chance pass without attempting to do all she could to change the course of an already tragic day.

Stripping out of her EMT's uniform, she began to put on her diving gear. Every minute that ticked away was another one lost. Though she usually didn't bother with a wet suit, today she'd awoken with a nagging feeling she should be prepared to go into the water. She was already putting hers on when the distress signal came in. *Call it a little Mer-tuition,* she thought as she put on the heavy oxygen tank and mask.

"Tell Sidney to hold it steady," she called.

The pilot was already one step ahead. "I've got it here," Sidney yelled back, throttling the engines down into idle.

Addison gave him the diver's signal for all systems go. "I shouldn't be long, Sid."

Sidney nodded. "Will do. I've radioed the coast guard that we've made contact and are commencing with recovery efforts. We've got the go ahead if we think we can handle it."

Witkowsky speared them both with a look of pure disbelief. "Sending a single diver down into an unknown situation definitely isn't a good idea. There needs to be at least two in the water in case something goes wrong."

Addison tossed him a nod. She already knew what Witkowsky didn't, that the sea was a mermaid's natural environment. She was actually safer in the water than out of it. Nevertheless, it always took an event like this to break in a new member of the team. A freshly minted paramedic, Jim had less than two weeks with harbor patrol under his belt.

"It's your first time out with the team, so I'll cut you some slack for your disbelief in my diving capabilities."

"Lonike is our most experienced diver," Sidney cut in. "And since she's the captain of this vessel, she outranks both of us. Going into the water is her call." He paused a moment, then added. "If she can't handle it, no one can."

Witkowsky shook his head. "Fine. But I want my protest logged."

"Your concern is duly noted." Addison hated to pull rank, but when lives were on the line, she'd do whatever it took to do her job. The chief had wanted to gauge how well Witkowsky performed under her authority before letting him in on her true identity. The guys she worked with had to be trusted to watch her back when she went into the water. "When we return to the mainland, we'll sit down with Chief Simms and have a little talk."

Witkowsky pulled a sour face. "You bet we will."

Addison ignored him. She didn't have the time or inclination to quibble. Recent events concerning her kind had made it necessary to keep a very low profile. Now that the Mer had begun to emerge from Ishaldi, the powers that be weren't exactly welcoming to the newly revealed species. Mers were still viewed as aliens, and treated as such. One of the conditions for release from the government's A51-ASD complex was that she and her two sisters must keep a low profile among the civilian population. They would be allowed to resume their lives in Port Rock—as long as they lived and acted like regular people.

But that was proving to be difficult. As much as she tried to mimic landlubbers, she just wasn't human.

Heading down the side boarding ladder, she eased into the water. Although she'd learned years ago to dive the human way, she found all the heavy equipment annoying. Disappearing beneath the waves, she stopped when she was about fifty feet below the surface, deep enough under the water where no one could see her.

Without hesitating, she ripped off the mask and mouthpiece. Giving the unnecessary items a quick wink, she quickly worked a little Mercraft. A little flare surrounded the items and then they were gone. The heavy tank across her back soon followed.

Freed of a few less things to carry, Addison stretched out and made a slow roll through the water. The change from her human form to that of a Mer occurred in the blink of an eye. One moment she had two legs. The next moment a spark of bright colors raced like wildfire across her skin. Her wet suit melted away, leaving her completely naked. The lower half of her body had also changed, becoming a beautiful multicolored tail. It had taken less than thirty seconds for the metamorphosis to complete itself. She was, again, a creature who belonged and thrived in the cerulean blue waters of the deep sea.

Addison nodded with satisfaction. All those hours she'd spent practicing her magic had finally paid off. With just a thought and a little push of energy from the crystal she always wore around her neck, she could make small objects appear and disappear at will. Her elder sister Tessa had taught her that trick. Although it had taken much trial and embarrassing error, she'd finally gotten the hang of the spell. She had no clue where it all went, but when she wanted it again, all she had to do was think about it and everything would return.

Free to swim unencumbered, Addison dove toward the bottom. Though the day was clear and warm, the waters were cold and murky, strangely devoid of fish and other sea life. It was as if the creatures sensed something had gone terribly wrong and had abandoned the area.

Minutes later, the wreckage of the yacht loomed into view. The craft had turned almost completely upside down as it had sunk.

Putting her tail in motion, Addison swam toward the crippled vessel. As the girl has stated, there was indeed a gaping hole in the hull. A thin stream of gasoline and oil eddied up from the exposed engines. The sight saddened her. A family outing had turned tragic in the blink of an eye. No doubt the coast guard would salvage the yacht to determine the cause of the accident.

Why the vessel had sunk wasn't her concern. She needed to locate the remaining passengers. Even though it had been foolhardy, she'd practically promised the girl a miracle. She intended to deliver one, if at all possible.

And with a Mer in the water, anything's possible, she reminded herself.

Reaching the interior of the cabin wasn't going to be easy. A diver wearing full gear would find it almost impossible to wriggle beneath the yacht and into the interior of the cabin. It was a tight fit for a mermaid, but Addison somehow managed to squeeze through.

Amazingly the galley's emergency lights were still functioning, lending an eerie illumination to the swamped interior. The body of a woman floated nearby.

Addison swam through the narrow space, checking the woman's pulse. Nothing. She was cold, motionless. One look at her empty expression and gaping mouth told her the spark of life had been snuffed out.

But the child . . .

Addison looked around. It took a few moments for her sharp gaze to pick out the little boy floating among the debris of cushions from a nearby bunk. With soft blond curls fanned out around his head, he looked like a doll abandoned after a day's play.

Her heart squeezed painfully. Oh, no. He couldn't be more than five or six. She reached out, laying the tips of her fingers at the pulse point of the boy's throat. *Please, oh, please,* she thought, stilling her own breath and striking out with her sixth sense. The spark of life was there, but rapidly fading. Deep inside she felt his desperate struggle, sensed his lungs burning with the need to drag in a precious breath of air.

Giving thanks to the goddess that the child still had a chance to survive, Addison pressed her mouth over lips that were cold and unmoving. As an empath she had the ability to generate energy within her own body, and then remanifest it in physical kinetic form. The soul-stone around her neck began to glow softly as she filtered living electricity from her body into the youngster's motionless figure.

Seconds later the child's eyes fluttered. He coughed, gasped for air. The lungs in his chest expanded, filtering out sea water and taking in pure oxygen. He was awake, but only on a peripheral level.

Relief whirred along her nerve endings. *You'll be all right,* she mentally telegraphed. Under the enchantment of a mermaid's kiss, the boy was capable of comprehending her silent words. The spell was only temporary and would last until his lungs again drew oxygen above the level of the water. He would have no memory of her in her Mer form.

Smiling with relief, Addison gathered the little boy into her arms. It took a bit of creative maneuvering to get back through the narrow passage and away from the sunken wreck. Guiding the child toward the surface, she quite forgot that she'd doffed her diving gear.

Seconds later their heads popped above the water. Bobbing with the waves, Addison swam toward the rescue boat. She saw Jim Witkowsky lean over the edge, pointing her way. "There she is," he called. "And she's not alone."

Catching hold of the ladder, Addison hefted half her body out of the water before lifting the limp child toward Witkowsky's waiting hands.

The man and his daughter stumbled toward the semiconscious boy even as Witkowsky began resuscitation efforts. "Sheldon!" the man cried from behind the paramedic. "Come on, son. Breathe."

A moment later the child heaved out a stream of bile mixed with water. A splutter, followed by a healthy wail, rolled past his blue-tinged lips. And then he was breathing, above water and on his own.

Witkowsky gave a quick thumbs-up. "I think he's gonna make it."

The man gathered the boy into his arms. "Thank God," he murmured against the wet hair pasted to the child's forehead. "He's alive."

But not everyone's eyes were on the rescue efforts taking place. Even as she clung to the ladder watching events on board unfold, Addison had the uneasy feeling that she was being watched. She looked up to see the girl's gaze fixed upon her. A look half of horror mingling with fascination colored the teen's expressive features.

Addison winced, giving herself a quick mental slap. She'd just made the worst blunder a Mer could make: letting humans see her in her true form.

The teen raised a hand and pointed her way. "D-Daddy, something's not right," the girl exclaimed in a shaky voice. "That lady has a tail!"

Everyone looked. And gaped.

"Holy shit," Witkowsky exclaimed, eyeing her exposed breasts and slender hips.

For a few beats, Addison couldn't think to react. The tension throbbed between them for a minute or so. It didn't take a mind reader to know what everyone on board was thinking.

Sidney Rawlings gave his errant crewman a slap upside the head. "Stop staring. You're being rude."

Regaining self-control, Addison belatedly pressed an arm over her bare beasts as she slid back into the water. "Shit," she grated under her breath. Talk about having one's stupid hanging out. Even though her elaborate scale pattern afforded a bit of modest cover, above the waist she was still as naked as a jaybird.

During those gut-wrenching minutes when she'd been underwater, her only concern had been to save the boy's life. Eager to get him to the surface, she hadn't given a second thought to making sure she came up in the same equipment she'd gone down in.

It really was a mega screwup.

ABOUT THE AUTHOR

Devyn Quinn resides in New Mexico with her cats, seven ferrets, and shih tzu, Tess. She is the author of twelve novels. Visit www.devynquinn.com.